Tobias parted the cut in her dress, ripping it slightly wider to get at the injury...

When he pressed the cotton to her skin, the muscles in her stomach clenched reflexively, and he heard a soft gasp whisper between her lips. His gaze shot immediately to her face, and he found himself staring into eyes the color of an African violet and just as soft. Framed by her inky lashes, they held him riveted with her calmly curious expression.

"I'm sorry," she said, her voice low and husky and tumbling from between lips so sweet and red he thought they ought to come with a warning label, "but I don't think we've met before. Who exactly are you?"

"A sexy, engaging world spiced with humor that draws you in, never lets you go, and will leave you begging for more!"

—Cheyenne McCray, national bestselling author

SHE'S NO
FAERIE PRINCESS

Christine Warren

St. Martin's Paperbacks

This is a work of fiction. All of the characters, organizations and events portrayed in this novel are either products of the author's imagination or are used fictitiously.

SHE'S NO FAERIE PRINCESS

Copyright © 2006 by Christine Warren.
Excerpt from *The Demon You Know* copyright © 2006 by Christine Warren.

For information address St. Martin's Press, 175 Fifth Avenue, New York, NY 10010.

ISBN: 0-312-34776-6
EAN: 978-0312-34776-5

Printed in the United States of America

St. Martin's Paperbacks edition / November 2006

St. Martin's Paperbacks are published by St. Martin's Press, 175 Fifth Avenue, New York, NY 10010.

10 9 8 7 6

For J, K, and S. Again. Because they love me
even when I don't speak to them for weeks at a time.

SHE'S NO
FAERIE PRINCESS

CHAPTER 1

"She's three hundred and thirty-seven years old. That's a bit late to be running away from home."

"She aren't running away from home. She just taking a vacations."

"It looks a lot like running."

"And how does you know what running look like, you big pansy? You is too old to get faster than a hobbles!"

"Shush!" The hiss in Fiona's voice got her companions' attention, and they fell into a tense, bristling silence. "Silent" or "sniping" described how Babbage and Squick spent nearly all their time together, but at the moment, Fiona had other things to worry about. She couldn't afford a distraction. "I told the both of you that if you wanted to come see me off, you were going to have to be quiet. If you can't manage that, I can always send you back to the palace."

The pixie and the imp exchanged fulminating glares, one from the spot where he fluttered beside Fiona's head, the other from his perch on her shoulder. She ignored them both, concentrating on making sure they weren't being followed as she picked a path through the dense, cool forest north of the Summer Palace. Normally, no one would have cared that she'd gone and certainly no one would have stopped her, but as she had recently realized, very few things these days were "normal" at the Seelie Court.

"Your Highness," the pixie broke in again, his tone clearly disapproving, "I really think it would be better—"

She fixed him with a sweetly dangerous smile. "Babbage, my dear friend, if you don't shut up in the next five seconds, I might just change my mind and take you with me."

The resulting silence lent a genuine curve to her smile. She could hear Squick chortling beside her ear, but she ignored him. She'd learned long ago not to encourage the imp. Or any imp. It only gave them ideas.

The pixie continued to flutter beside her head and cast disapproving glares in her direction, but disapproval didn't bother Fiona. She'd grown far too used to it over the years. Babbage, on the other hand, lived in mortal fear of Queen Mab's disapproval, which was why the threat of bringing him along to the human world had shut him up in such a hurry. Fiona's aunt had decreed this particular vacation destination off-limits to her people ages ago, and Babbage had never been one to disobey a direct order. Unlike Fiona.

Turning away from examining the trail behind her for followers, Fiona started forward again, her violet eyes scanning the forest on either side of the trail for any sign of pursuit. All remained eerily quiet. For about fifteen seconds.

"Personally, I thinks a little vacation are a fine idea, Princess," Squick piped up, and Fiona didn't have to glance over at his perch on her shoulder to know he'd be grinning tauntingly at Babbage as he spoke. "Things has been getting real . . . complicated at court. A nice refreshing tour of boring human land are just whats we needs for lifting our spirits."

Fiona shot him a sideways glance. "Who said anything about we?"

The imp looked shocked. "But Missy Fiona! You has to take us with you! Who will protects you if I's not there? The human land cans be a hideous, dangerous places."

"I think I can handle it, Squick. It can't be any more dangerous than court is becoming."

She grimaced at the truth of her own words. For someone who had grown up at court, as she had, a certain amount of danger was to be expected. There were always intrigues and deceptions to deal with, enemies to avoid and loyalties to question, but these days, the perils of politics had grown unexpected teeth. Ones that had just yesterday attempted to clamp down on Fiona's unwitting head.

Her mouth firmed into a line of displeasure as she recalled the experience of being cornered in a remote alcove by a particularly ambitious courtier. The entire population of Faerie knew the queen was planning on naming her heir from among one of her two dozen or so nieces and nephews before the next Passing Moon, and apparently the odds on Fiona were high enough to make her an attractive target of would-be consorts. No one seemed to believe her protestations that she had no interest in ascending to the Seelie throne. It had taken a snapped temper and a knee to the groin to get the message across well enough to make her escape, but it had taken significantly less to convince Fiona it was time to take a nice, long, remote vacation.

Too bad her chosen spot was on the banned-travel list.

Ever since an incident a few years ago when the queen's nephew had been spotted by several humans as he gallivanted around New York, Her Majesty had gotten a lot tougher about enforcing the ban on travel between Faerie and the human world. Most people tried to stay away from upsetting Mab.

There hadn't been much chance that anything would come of the sightings, considering most humans had stopped believing in the existence of the Fae—Faeries, as they called them—many human centuries ago, but Mab did not like to be thwarted.

Fiona didn't see how anyone could consider a quick little vacation to the human world as "thwarting," though. After all, it wasn't like your average human would be expecting to see a Fae walking among them, and with a little glamour—the smallest form of Fae magic—she could make sure all they did see when they looked at her would be a perfectly normal human woman.

Even without magic, her basic appearance didn't give her away. She was human shaped, with one head, two arms, two legs, and the requisite number of eyes and noses and such, and at five feet, four inches, tall she fell easily in the acceptable height range for a human female. Her black hair might be a bit long, since she wore it to her hips as most Fae did, but it's not like it hissed or anything. And if her skin was paler than the average human, well, she could always say she was afraid of skin cancer. The Fae were immune to it, but she'd read that it was a big concern for mortals. The real need for the glamour came from the subtle, luminous bits of magic that nature had woven into her being. The glow that made her skin look more like moonlight than peaches and cream. The bright glitter of starshine in her pure violet eyes. Those were the things that might give her away, but humans, in her experience, were not that tough to fool.

And while the world full of mortals went about its business in blissful ignorance, she'd be able to do some shopping and take in a few concerts. She'd done it before with no problems. She didn't foresee any this time, either.

"I'm telling you, I have a bad feeling about this," Babbage grumbled, apparently unable to bear the living silence of the forest clearing a moment longer. He'd lasted longer than Fiona had expected. Pixies were not well-known for their taciturn natures. "If you step through that gate, you'll be sorry."

"You is always feeling bad," Squick grumbled. "That ain't nothing new."

"The only reason why I would be sorry would be if the queen found out," Fiona said. "And the only way my aunt could possibly find out something like that would be if you told her. Which you're not going to do. Are you, Babbage?"

The pixie remained stubbornly silent. For once in his life.

Fiona's hand darted out, pinching his gossamer tunic between her thumb and forefinger and hauling him right up to her face. "Are you, Babbage?"

He glanced from her to the gate on the other side of the clearing and back again. His wings drooped at the edges. "No, Princess Fiona. I will not tell the queen of your rash and ill-advised excursion into forbidden territory."

"I've asked you not to call me 'Princess,' " she said, and released him with a flick of her fingers.

From her shoulder, Squick stuck his tongue out at the pixie.

Babbage flew back a couple of feet and gave a wounded sniff. "You *are* a princess."

"Sure, along with ten of my female cousins, and that's not counting the other cousins who happen to be princes."

She peered around the trunk of an old oak tree and scanned the break in the thick vegetation for any signs of movement. Just because she wouldn't let the fear of getting caught stop her from going through the gate didn't mean she wasn't going to try to avoid it.

"None of them had parents who died and left their care directly in the hands of the queen."

"Babbage, do you *want* me to take you with me?"

"You can takes me!" Squick shouted, jumping up and down excitedly.

The renewed threat shut the pixie up, but the damage had already been done. He'd reminded her of something she spent a great deal of her time trying to forget, and now she'd spend at least the rest of the day with it hanging over her head. Pesky pixie pest.

Fiona knew that ignoring the truth wasn't going to make it go away, but that didn't keep her from trying. On a daily basis. She despised court life, whether it was at her aunt's Seelie Court or at the Unseelie that was ruled by Mab's former husband and Fiona's still officially uncle, Dionnu. The idea of taking the throne when the peace between the two courts had been uneasy at best for most of her lifetime made her break out in hives. And that was exactly the reason that she needed to take a vacation. She didn't have the patience or the deviousness required to be a successful leader of the Fae, and she had no intention of developing either. Her parents might both have been sidhe—the noble race of Faerie—but she swore that sometimes she wished they'd been goblins or trolls or pixies or sprites or even a dryad and a satyr. Any type of Fae under the sun or moon would have been fine with her, so long as it wasn't a member of either high court. Sometimes, she reflected, life as a Faerie princess pretty much sucked.

Thinking about it only steeled Fiona's resolve to screw the rules and seize the opportunity for her much-needed vacation. In the human world, she'd be able to blend in for a little while, to be a nobody. She wouldn't stand out, and with most of her magic drained from her by the unfamiliar surroundings, she wouldn't have been able to make much in the way of waves if she tried. It sounded perfect.

She took one last careful look around, set Squick down on the ground beside her, and shouldered her small travel bag. Grinning, she flicked the imp and the pixie a jaunty wave.

"Take care, little friends," she called, hurrying toward the shimmering Faerie gate and into the simple, predictable world of the humans.

Tobias Walker hadn't gotten laid in at least three months. He knew very well that this hardly qualified as an emergency, but he did consider it symptomatic of a larger issue. Not only had he not had sex in all that time—which was not inconsequential for a bachelor werewolf in his prime—but he also hadn't gone on a date, gotten an uninterrupted night of sleep, watched an entire ball game, or taken a day off. Considering all that, was it any wonder that his mood edged toward cranky as he stalked through his 3:00 A.M. park patrol?

Technically, this wasn't even his patrol, a fact that only contributed to his case of the grumps. As beta of the Silverback Clan—second in command after the alpha pack leader—Walker had been put in charge of the Lupine-led policing of Manhattan. That meant he got to assign shifts and theoretically give himself one off now and then. Tonight should have been his night to get a decadent five hours of sleep after a double shift on his regular beat through Central Park. Unfortunately, the packmate who had been assigned up here in Inwood Hill Park had come down with a raging case of pregnancy, and her mate had refused to let her out of the house.

Walker could sympathize with the sentiment; his own Lupine instincts would have driven him to react the same way if he'd had a mate. Something attached to the Lupine Y chromosome turned them into raging Neanderthals where the safety of their mates was concerned, but Walker was still single. He also still had an entire city to patrol and a security force already stretched thin to cover it.

He growled and stuffed his hands into his pockets as he stalked through the park, his sharp gaze constantly sweeping the surroundings for anything unusual.

You'd think by now he'd be used to the whole overwhelming thing. It had been like this for nearly six months, ever since the Council of Others and its equivalents from around the world had entered into secret negotiations with the humans. The delicate nature of the talks necessitated an atmosphere of peace, no matter how tense, if the two sides were going to reach an agreement that didn't lead to bloodshed on either side. And when you were negotiating with vampires, shape-shifters, Others, and human politicians, Walker reflected, bloodshed was always a possibility, no matter how hard he and his pack worked to prevent it.

These negotiations would alter the course of the future, for both the Others, who had finally taken their first step out of hiding, and the humans, who now needed to acknowledge that so many of the things they believed to be safely fictional actually did walk among them. It meant asking the humans to discard centuries of fear and superstition to allow what many of them considered to be monsters to enjoy the same rights and legal protections as anyone else. So in contrast, beefing up Other security to be sure no one got out of line and did anything to frighten the humans into another Inquisition seemed like a wise course of action.

The Council had put the Silverback Clan in charge of making sure that the Others kept themselves in line and did nothing to frighten the humans into breaking off the talks. Since Walker was pack beta and his day job happened to be as head of security at the largest private club for Others in this half of the world, it fell to him to coordinate that security force. Which was why he was currently on his third patrol in twenty-four hours instead of facedown in his mattress.

Heading north at the fork in his path, Walker considered all the changes he and his kind had faced over the past months. No one had really been prepared. Sure, Others had been debating about the Unveiling on and off for most of the last century, but that had been a theoretical sort of thing, an "imagine if " approach to the future. It hadn't prevented the shock of learning a few months ago that a radical sect called the Light of Truth had gathered enough evidence to take the decision out of their hands and reveal their existence to the humans whether they were ready or not.

That news had convinced the Council of Others that the time had come to take the first steps in claiming an open place in the world around them, hence the secret negotiations. Even the most optimistic members of the Council knew better than to break the news to the human public without first gaining some assurances from their governments that the rights of the nonhumans would be preserved. Optimistic did not equal foolish.

For their part, the Others were prepared to make certain none of their kind did anything stupid, like attack a human. Or even be seen within ten feet of one who happened to be dead, injured, or mildly inconvenienced. The last thing they needed was for the humans to abandon the bargaining table. Walker figured he was currently doing his best, and the best of at least three other people to boot.

Thankfully, things were staying pretty quiet—quiet enough that twenty-four-hour patrols probably weren't strictly necessary, but you just never knew when that one problem you wanted to avoid would rear its ugly head.

Or scream bloody murder.

Before a sharp feminine cry had even faded from an "eek" to an echo, Walker had whipped around, pinpointed the source of the sound, and launched himself toward it, sprinting through the trees in a blur of speed and swear words.

CHAPTER 2

Fiona stepped out of the other side of the gate and into an inky blackness, sighing in irritation. Darn it, one of these days she was going to have to get a handle on those stupid time changes. She stepped forward into the dark, muttering to herself, and promptly tripped over something immovable laid directly in her path. It might help her vacation relaxation plan if she didn't go stumbling around blindly and walking into things like an idiot. She paused for a moment to let her eyes adjust from the bright daylight of Faerie to the dimness of a Manhattan night, or at least one in the depths of the city's wildest park.

It only took a few seconds before she could see almost as well as she could have in the middle of a sunny afternoon. Hitching her bag higher onto her shoulder, she scanned the area around her and stepped over the fat tree root in front of her bare feet. She headed toward the park entrance, confident she knew where she was going. This was the same gate she'd used on her other trips to the human world, so at least things looked familiar. And she knew exactly where she wanted to go—straight into the East Village to see if any of her favorite bands were playing. Some frenetic music in an overcrowded human club sounded like the perfect way to spend her evening. She couldn't think of much else that would be as drastically different from a night at the Fae courts.

At this time of night, her path through the woods appeared deserted, but Fiona didn't plan to jeopardize her vacation by taking chances. She made a subtle gesture with her hand and stirred up a little of the magic inside her to cast a small glamour. She had planned ahead and brought a small reserve of magic with her from Faerie in case of emergency. She could have spared her reserves and tried to gather up some of the scarce fragments of Fae magic that managed to linger in the human world, but such scraps were few and far between here, and what magic did exist in this world was almost completely inaccessible to her. No one had ever really explained why that was—why the Fae couldn't tap into the magic inherent to the human world and why the rare mortal witch who had visited Faerie over the last couple of millennia had found it equally impossible to harness the magic of that world. Something in the molecular fabric of the two worlds made their forces incompatible. Like oil and water, Fiona and the magic of the mortal world didn't mix, but she didn't expect to use much magic during her trip. That had been one of the reasons she'd opted to come here. She could afford to tap into what she'd brought with her.

The little shimmer that accompanied the spell barely registered in the darkness, but it made a significant impact on her appearance. The long fall of her jet-black hair turned into a close, shaggy crop of electric blue, moussed on its ends and tipped in shocks of bright fuchsia. Her pale, cream white skin took on a golden cast from a liberal sprinkling of freckles on every inch of visible skin, and her new outfit left a lot of skin visible. In place of the gown she had been wearing were a couple of casually layered and strategically torn tank tops in black and blue. Below them, she wore a pleated plaid skirt in a tartan Scotland had never intended and a length that was guaranteed to make any man she met take a much closer look. Her legs were covered in lacy black thigh-high stockings that ended just about where her hem began and disappeared at the other end into heavy black boots that laced halfway up her calves.

Grinning, Fiona added a swagger to her stride. She was in Manhattan. Now she would fit right in.

She let the twigs snap under her feet as she practically skipped down the path in anticipation of the amusement awaiting her. Once she got to the park's entrance, she could hop a subway to 9th Street and see what she could see. Maybe CBGB would have a good show. Or there were always Manitoba's as an alternative, or Mona's if she changed her mind and decided to go for Guinness and songs that reminded her more of home. Somehow she didn't think that would be happening.

Ooh! And maybe she'd try that little noodle house she'd spotted near Washington Square last time, just to see if they still made that *pad mi ga ti* dish. . . .

Nearly tasting the coconut milk and hot chilies, Fiona sent a pebble skittering down the path. She watched as it bounced off the cloven hoof of a very large, very black, very fiery-eyed, and very not-nice-looking creature with curling horns and waves of heat rolling off its hulking frame.

That was about when she screamed.

Right after that was about when she ran.

Her heart leaped into her throat and her stomach sank into her boots as shock and fear and confusion took over, sending her sprinting for safety.

Sweet stars above, that's a demon!

Her mind raced along with her feet across the forest floor. She veered off the path and darted around trees, cursing as she heard the muffled thunder of the creature's footfalls echoing close behind hers. Not only was that a demon, but it was now chasing her over the uneven terrain.

She knew it was a demon even though she'd never seen one before. In fact, she couldn't think of a single soul who had. The creatures had been banished from the human world and then from Faerie ages ago at the end of the Fae–Demon Wars. They were supposed to be bound to their own world, the Below, not lurking in the middle of Manhattan to prey on any Fae who happened to travel by.

Apparently, no one had bothered to mention that to this fellow.

She could feel its hot, fetid breath at her back and poured on a fresh burst of speed. She had no idea what could be going on or where the beast could have come from, but she didn't intend to slow down long enough to ask. She didn't intend to slow down at all. She may not have met a demon before, but she knew enough to realize she didn't want to meet this one. Everything she knew came from the stories of her people, and her people weren't exactly the biggest fans of those who walked Below. A few centuries of violent conflict could do that to a relationship.

Casting a frantic glance around, Fiona looked for an

escape route or a hiding place or a weapon or a miracle. She wasn't picky, so long as it kept her alive past the next five minutes. If she could just get back to the gate, she might be able to dart back through and lose her pursuer. The meager store of magic she'd brought with her from home would never be enough to cast any sort of effective defensive spell and she obviously couldn't gather up any mortal magic, but in Faerie she'd be able to tap into the magic of the land if the demon managed to break through the wards and follow her there. Considering her current options seemed to boil down to that or getting her heart ripped out of her chest, it might be worth a try.

Tucking her head down, she lengthened her stride to its limit and called up her last reserves of speed. Praying her luck and her ankles would hold, Fiona ran flat-out straight for the trunk of a huge old pine tree and darted suddenly to the side, digging in her heels, spinning on a dime, and heading on an angled path back the way she'd come. The demon snarled something that she was glad not to understand. Just the sounds struck her as foul and corrupted, and she shuddered even as she ran.

She heard a horrible roar and a rending and glanced back over her shoulder just long enough to see the creature grab onto the same pine she'd spun around seconds before to stop its forward momentum. It worked, but the tree didn't survive. Its roots tore free with a painful snap, and the demon tossed it aside like a stick of kindling to crash to the forest floor.

Fiona did not take this as a good sign.

Hauling in a ragged breath, she decided the small reserve of magic she'd brought with her might just have to do. If the demon got much closer, she wouldn't have any choice but to throw whatever power she had into a spell and hope it would be enough. She just hoped it wouldn't come to that, because a spell that strong might drain too much power from her and leave her completely and totally vulnerable.

She gathered her legs beneath her to leap atop the first of several boulders gathered together in a wide outcropping at the edge of a small clearing in the trees. She needed to get to safer ground, and failing that, she needed to get to ground the demon wasn't on.

Behind her, she heard it roar as it reached out with one grotesquely elongated arm, its claws catching around her ankle and stabbing through the heavy leather of her boots to scratch the delicate skin beneath. She cried out reflexively and grabbed onto the stone with both hands. The cruel grip on her leg made her teeth clench against the urge to whimper. She felt the first real welling of fear when the demon began to pull, reeling her in with the slow deliberation of a fisherman with a bite on his line. Her grip on the rock began to slip, and the tips of her fingers scraped raw as her body slid backward over the rough surface. Wriggling desperately, she twisted her hips to get a better angle with her free leg and sent her booted foot slamming into the beast's skull just between its malevolently glowing eyes.

The demon roared again and stumbled back a handful of steps, but its grip never wavered. It dragged her with it, shaking its great horned head to clear it. Fiona found herself dangling upside down above a carpet of stone and pine needles, gazing directly at the monster's oddly misshapen legs. It took her a minute to realize that they weren't misshapen, just jointed backward like a goat's. She almost expected them to be covered in fur, but instead the skin looked like tightly woven plates of matte black scales. Instead of feet, it had cloven hooves and Fiona found herself idly wondering if it had a tattoo of a Baphomet pentacle on the back of its skull.

Her arms waved in a search for purchase and balance, grabbing desperately. Her hands felt only air, and her heart nearly stopped when something slammed into the demon from behind. The great beast reeled, thrown off balance in a way her single forceful kick hadn't managed. The creature launched her hard toward the tree line, wobbling on its feet as Fiona felt her spine slam against the base of a stately elm.

That's gonna leave a mark.

Blinking, she pushed herself up on her elbows and peered through her momentary double vision to see where the demon had moved to. It wasn't like she could get up and run at the moment, but it never hurt to know which direction the death blow would be coming from. She hated to be caught unprepared. Instead of getting a clear view of the demon that had attacked her, Fiona found herself staring at the back of a very unfamiliar figure. This one might not have looked all that big in comparison to the demon, but even the half-dazed Fae could tell he was enormous. Standing close to seven and a half feet tall, he put himself directly between Fiona and the beast and set off a low warning growl that made something finally click in her mind. The newcomer was Lupine. A werewolf.

He stood in his were form—half man, half wolf— huge and hulking with muscle but somehow still sleek compared to the demon. That monster had the thick, bulging musculature of a troll and the long, skeletal skull of a bull, topped off with two curling horns that grew backward from just above its sunken, banked-ember eyes. In contrast, the werewolf looked lithe and graceful. His muscular form rippled with power, but on him it looked right and natural under a thick, healthy pelt of silver-gray fur.

She couldn't see the werewolf's face, but she finally got a clear look at the demon, and the clearing was small enough that she could smell the filth of it, like coal and decay and the choking stench of burnt flesh. It crouched facing her and the Lupine, its too-long arms brushing the ground, dark shining nails combing through the forest debris.

The two powerful figures eyed each other for several tense minutes, neither making a move forward. Each subtle alteration in the position of one evoked a mirror image in the other. Then the demon shifted its soulless gaze from the Lupine back to Fiona, and the werewolf's warning growl turned into a vicious snarl.

Just that quickly, the battle began. The first attack was a blur, a lightning-speed crash of black and gray, dull, scaly skin against thick fur. She almost expected the ground beneath her to shake with the violence of the impact. Both figures shook and twisted and grappled and roared in primitive fury. Hoof and claw dug into the mess of earth, stone, and organic litter that covered the ground, seeking purchase. Claws slashed across scales and fur. Fangs glinted, and muscles bulged and shifted. Fiona's eyes widened as the Lupine seemed to briefly hold his own against the impossibly powerful demon.

Even as the thought crossed her mind, the demon lowered its massive bovine head and rammed its horns directly into the werewolf's stomach. Fiona heard a loud whoosh as the impact drove the air from his lungs. His clawed hands raked furrows in the creature's flesh even as he went airborne, landing at the opposite side of the clearing from Fiona at the base of another tree.

She winced in sympathy at the dull thud of his landing, but she had no time to wonder how he was feeling. The minute the demon shook him off, it turned back toward her, perfectly clear in its focus on her as the preferred target. Which made no sense. Everything she knew about demons told her they were indiscriminately murderous. They didn't care about the identity of their victims unless someone told them to. Normally, they would just attack whatever stood more clearly in their paths. So why was this one so intent on ripping out her heart when she assumed the werewolf had a perfectly good heart of his own?

Something here didn't add up.

Fiona pressed her back against the tree trunk and kept the demon clearly in her sights. It looked like the cavalry that had ridden to her rescue might be having some problems of its own. She'd never been much for sitting around wringing her hands and waiting for help—yet another reason that she made such a lousy princess. Unlike her aunt the queen, who liked to send her knights into the fray to deal with any problems, Fiona preferred to handle everything on her own. That way there was no one around to tell her what she was doing wrong.

The demon stepped slowly forward on its crouching, satyric hind legs, spewing puffs of yellowed, noxious-smelling smoke from its nostrils. Holding her breath against the stench and her own unease, Fiona levered herself into a sitting position and took a deep breath. She raised her hands before her as if to ward off the monster while she grabbed a thin thread of the magic left inside her and pulled hard.

It yanked free of her in a flash of bright blue energy and swirled into a small, powerfully glowing tornado of magical energy. The demon uttered something in a guttural snarl of pain and rage and stumbled a few steps away. Squinting against the glare in her hands, Fiona watched it stumble backward, right into the force of the Lupine's renewed attack. Between the light and the noise and the violent clash, she felt like she'd gotten caught up in a lightning storm. She could only hope the demon did, too.

At least it seemed to hate the disc of bright blue light she had conjured up. Its reflexes seemed slower this time, and it appeared to have trouble tracking the werewolf's movements. It didn't see its opponent duck beneath a clumsy blow and dive toward its hind legs, claws flashing. With two quick slashes, the Lupine sliced through the tendons at the backs of the monster's legs, sending it crashing to the ground and bellowing in rage.

Quickly, instinctively, Fiona jumped up from her tree, light balanced between her fingertips, and raced forward. She stopped a few steps short of the felled demon, took aim, and sent the swirl of light flying toward the creature's gaping mouth as if the light were a Frisbee and the demon were an overeager border collie.

She should have stopped a few steps shorter. As the magic missile made impact, the demon lashed out with one arm and caught her across the lower torso with the tip of one glistening claw. It sliced through her clothing as if she wore cobwebs, and she gasped at the fiery pain of her skin parting unnaturally, leaving a crimson line in her pale flesh.

Dazed, she looked down at her injury with wide, confused eyes. The pain registered along with the ticklish trickle of blood across her stomach, but she stayed on her feet, unmoving. She couldn't even raise a hand to cover the wound. Weakness crept over her, making her sway where she stood. Her little magic trick had taken more out of her than she had planned.

In the background, she thought she heard a roar that sounded more like an angry werewolf than an attacking demon. She wanted to ask if he was all right, but she couldn't form the words. She just stood there and tried not to fall on her face even as the demon began to stir and struggle to right itself. The roar came again, louder this time, and then the Earth tilted on its axis as Fiona's legs collapsed beneath her and sent her sinking into darkness.

CHAPTER 3

Walker wanted to grab the woman and shake her for being so stupid as to rush up to the demon like that. Then he wanted to thank her for distracting the demon with that spell of hers. And finally, he wanted to get a better look at what he remembered as being a truly fine backside, this time without the distraction of a rampaging demon to dull his pleasure. But at the moment, he had other things to do. Like getting them both the hell out of Dodge before the demon learned how to run with severed Achilles tendons.

Walker scooped her unconscious figure up in his arms and sprinted for home. The demon reacted about as positively to that as Walker had expected, but thankfully, the injuries slowed it to a point where the combination of werewolf speed and the thick tree cover foiled its pursuit. That didn't mean Walker slowed down any.

He ran a good two miles before he felt safe in slowing to a brisk, ground-eating trot.

Through it all, the woman in his arms remained limp and still. He wasn't sure if she was asleep or unconscious, but either way, she was so out of it that he contemplated setting her down for a minute so he could shift back to human form before they left the park. The general rule for Lupines stated they shouldn't walk in were form anywhere they might be seen by humans. Wolf form could be written off easily enough as the appearance of an especially large and long-legged dog, but there was nothing in the human world that could account for a seven- or eight-foot creature covered in fur with the posture of a man and the facial features of White Fang. The human mind was only so elastic.

In this case, Walker weighed his options and decided that if he stuck to the alleys on the trip back to his apartment and didn't get too close to any streetlights, he'd be better off going as he was. If he shifted back to human, he might not risk psychically scarring a wandering human observer, but he did risk spending the night in a cell with a public-indecency citation hanging over his head. Given the way his night had been going so far, he didn't have time to go to jail.

He reached the borders of the park and scanned the street from the cover of the last few trees. He didn't see much movement, which did occasionally happen even in New York, and at three-something in the morning the streets of the metropolis were about as deserted as he could ever hope to see them. It was now or never.

Taking a deep breath and immediately regretting it because of the crack the demon had left in his ribs, Walker bowed his head, clutched the woman tighter against his chest, and dived into the shadows. His long strides ate up the ground between the park and his neighborhood. At a dead run, a werewolf could move faster than a sprinting racehorse and might even give a cheetah a thing or two to think about. Luckily, Walker could maintain his speed for distances closer to those of the equine than the feline, because it was a good couple of miles to his apartment.

He made it without incident, ducking into the alley behind his street and breaking his speed, slowing to a walk for the last hundred yards to his building. It took him a second to catch his breath, but both he and the woman had made it in one piece. And, he hoped, without being seen.

Hitching the unconscious woman higher against his chest, Walker scanned the area before he rounded the corner, balancing her carefully in one arm while he paused outside his apartment door to retrieve his spare key. He kept it hidden for just this sort of emergency. In his line of work he never did know when he'd be coming home without pockets. The fact that his door was set down half a flight of stairs as a basement entrance made those times easier, too, by offering a bit of concealment from the odd passerby.

He let them inside and kicked the door shut behind them. Though the entrance to his apartment looked like it led to a basement, he actually occupied two floors of the narrow old building, and he used the bottom floor as a workroom and Spartan home gym. His living space was upstairs. He carried his guest up and directly to the sofa, depositing her on the soft cushions before he straightened and shifted back to his human form.

He felt the sting and then the easing as his genes reformed his body, knitting together the crack in his ribs, sealing the scratches he'd gotten wrestling around the forest. When the change was complete, his shoulders rolled in instinctive adjustment.

The woman never moved, and he frowned down at her, crouching beside the sofa to examine her limp form. He'd felt the steady beat of her heart and the rhythmic rise and fall of her breathing as he'd carried her home, so he knew perfectly well she wasn't dead. And that was what had him frowning. No human woman or witch should have survived the demon attack, which meant she must not be human. He knew from her scent that she wasn't Lupine or any other sort of shifter, for that matter. There was nothing earthy about her, nothing animal. She smelled too pure for that, and the fact that he could smell her at all meant she wasn't a vampire. Her skin felt too warm and smooth and elastic to belong to any other nonliving life-form, and she looked too much like a human for him to identify her origins by sight.

He didn't like that his sense of smell had failed him here. One good sniff ought to give him all the information he needed to place her species, but instead it only gave him a raging erection. He didn't know what the hell was the matter with him. Sure, just like any other male in existence, a good brush with death tended to bring out the horny in him, but this felt like more than that. He didn't just want sex; he wanted sex with her, with this woman— or whatever she was—and he wanted it now. In fact, he seemed to want it more with every breath full of her scent that he inadvertently inhaled. He struggled to block the tantalizing aroma from his mind and pushed to his feet. If he didn't get control of himself, she would end up getting a hell of an awakening. Maybe from the inside out.

Gritting his teeth and taking slow, shallow breaths through his mouth, Walker braced himself against his uncontrollable arousal and forced himself to take stock of her wounds. Starting at her feet seemed safest, and the ragged puncture marks in the leather of her high boots looked pretty nasty. He dealt efficiently with her laces and tugged the boots off, setting them aside under the coffee table. Without the heavy covering, her feet looked tiny and fragile beneath their veil of sheer black stockings, which were dotted with blood around her left ankle. The demon's claws hadn't bitten deeply, thanks to the leather, but the punctures would need a thorough cleaning.

His gaze moved up the length of her slim, graceful legs, which did totally inappropriate things to his libido, but they appeared to be free of further injury. The only other wound he could see was a slash across her stomach, and that was the injury that worried him. Carefully, he reached out to lift aside the hems of her skimpy tank tops, one eye on her face to be sure she hadn't woken up. Her eyelashes didn't even flutter, and her expression remained tranquil. Walker wished he could say the same for himself, but one good look at the ragged gash in her pale, freckled skin had him cursing a blue streak and gritting his teeth against the urge to howl in anger.

The cut bled sluggishly, much less than he would have expected, but it looked nasty all the same, with jagged edges darkened to black by the poison on the demon's claws. Jaw clenching, he dropped her hem and headed straight for the first-aid supplies in his bathroom. On the way back, he paused in the bedroom to grab a pair of jeans and ease himself into them. No reason to scare her to death by having her wake up eye to eye with the part of him most anxious to make her acquaintance.

He stepped back into the living room with his hands full of disinfectant and bandages, and he froze. The blue-haired punk he'd left on his sofa had been replaced by a dark-haired goddess with skin like whipped cream and a torn and tattered gown of a fabric so light, if it hadn't been for the pale lilac color, he couldn't have sworn it even existed. The clothes she had been wearing had disappeared, and she slept on as if nothing had happened. Now he had proof she wasn't quite human. A witch, maybe? That would explain her human appearance, since technically witches were humans who just happened to have evolved the ability to use magic, and a spell fading would explain the change in her appearance. At least, he thought it would. He wasn't all that up on the rules of magic.

And none of the rules he had heard before explained why the very scent of her made him want to strip her naked and introduce himself to her womb, up close and personal.

Forcing his mind off his crotch, he returned to the sofa and knelt on the floor at her side. Her wounds took precedence over his curiosity at the moment. Until he did find out who and what she was, he'd be better off treating her injuries than speculating about the effect she had on him. When she woke up, he'd get his answers.

Still, he was frowning as he poured disinfectant liberally onto a sterile pad. He parted the cut in her dress, ripping it slightly wider to get at the injury. When he pressed the cotton to her skin, the muscles in her stomach clenched reflexively, and he heard a soft gasp whisper between her lips. His gaze shot immediately to her face, but her expression remained relaxed and tempting in sleep. Reluctantly, he looked back at his task, only to see that the wound in her abdomen appeared to be a lot less serious than he'd thought, now that he'd cleared the dried blood and dirt away. In fact, it almost looked as if it had begun healing even before he'd washed it.

Oh, this wasn't good.

Swallowing a curse, Walker leaned back from his unconscious guest and took a really good look at her. One that had his stomach sinking into his toenails. He took in the moonlight-pale, velvet-smooth skin, the miraculously healing wounds, the magically transformed appearance, and saw that his bad day had just gotten a hell of a lot worse.

"Aw, shit."

Muttering to himself and whatever god currently watched and laughed at his predicament, Walker took a deep, bracing breath, eased his hands into the tumbled mass of the unconscious woman's raven black hair, and lifted it gently away from the delicate shell of her ear. An ear that swept gracefully up from small, unadorned lobes to a distinct and elegant point.

Fae.

The woman currently passed out on his sofa, bleeding from an unexpected and determined demon attack, was Fae. As in full-blooded, non-Changeling, born-and-bred-beyond-the-gates-in-Faerie Fae. And high sidhe from the look of her. This wasn't a sprite but one of the aristocratic race. So what the hell was she doing in his living room?

Okay, he had carried her there, but that wasn't the point. The Fae weren't even supposed to be in this world. Their ruler, Queen Mab, had made that long-standing custom a law after some kind of incident a few years ago, but the end result was that Walker could count on one hand the number of Fae he'd met in all of his thirty-five years. This one made number three. *Not* his lucky number.

Pushing to his feet, Walker shoved a hand through

his already-rumpled hair and began to pace across the quiet room. He didn't need a Lupine sense of smell to know this whole thing reeked of trouble, and he wasn't just talking about the demon stench. He already had enough on his plate trying to keep the Others in the area from inadvertently starting a war with the humans. The last thing he needed was the Fae and demons putting in an appearance and throwing everything into chaos.

Walker bit back a curse and looked over at the sofa, directly into a pair of sleepy, darkly lashed eyes the color of African violets. It felt like taking a stone giant's fist straight to his gut. Even the demon hadn't packed this kind of punch. Asleep, the Fae woman had been beautiful. Awake, she stole the breath from his lungs and the brains from his head. All he had left was the blood in his veins, and that was sure as hell easy enough to prove, considering it had all rushed right to his groin the minute she opened her eyes.

While he stood there, blinking like an idiot and probably drooling like one, his guest raised her arms over her head and arched her body in a lazy, feline stretch that left him cross-eyed and half-delirious. Then she collapsed back into the cushions and her full lips curved in a sensual smile.

"Hi." Her sleep-husky voice had the same effect on his dick as the average Lupine female in heat waving her tail in his face, only magnified exponentially. He probably had zipper marks running up and down his shaft. "My name is Fiona. Who are you?"

Walker groaned and rubbed his hand over his eyes, quickly discovering that the image of Fiona stretching had been burned indelibly into his retinas.

"Shit. I'm screwed."

CHAPTER 4

FIONA FELT HER LIPS twitch, but she figured it might be considered rude to laugh at someone who had saved her life. "Ah, all right. Do you have a nickname?"

The werewolf scowled down at her. "Tobias Walker. But I think the more important question, lady, is what in the hell are you doing here?"

Pursing her lips, Fiona swung herself into a sitting position and winced when the movement pulled at the slash in her belly. The wound had begun to heal, but with as much magic as she had expended, she guessed it would be a couple of days at least before she did any dancing. Which was a shame. The idea of performing one of the seductive, erotic, hip-grinding dances of Faerie for her erstwhile rescuer held a definite appeal. And judging by the current fit of said rescuer's jeans, she thought he might turn out to be an appreciative audience.

"Lady," he growled, jerking her attention off his pants and back to his face. "You want to answer my question?"

"Not particularly."

She bent her head to examine the wound on her belly, so she couldn't see his face, but she could definitely hear his biting curses.

"Do it anyway."

Fiona looked up, saw the edge of a ruthlessly controlled temper looming, and sighed. She'd been raised around her aunt's warrior guardsmen and knew a dominant man in a snit when she saw one. In her experience, it was always better to humor them. "I'm taking a vacation."

He opened his mouth, looking for all the world as if he planned to huff and puff and blow her house down, then snapped his jaw shut in confusion. "A *vacation*? What? Was the Fae Riviera overbooked?"

She blinked innocently up at him. "No, but I just hate getting all that sand stuck in my hair."

"Oh, right. I see." He glared at her, the sarcasm dripping off his tongue. "I'm sure that as soon as she hears your reasoning, Queen Mab will personally drape you in a lei and sing you a chorus of 'Bon Voyage.'"

This time it was Fiona's turn to pull up short. She eyed the Lupine warily and offered a soothing smile. "Really, Tobias. Let's not be childish. There's no reason to bring Aunt Mab into this—"

"*Aunt Mab?!*"

Fiona watched with fascinated horror as the top of the werewolf's head seemed to lift off and hover atop a molten-lava eruption of furious disbelief. Maybe she shouldn't have mentioned the family connection? But of course, he'd latched onto it with the ferocity of a pit bull and was shaking it for all it was worth. Which, in Fiona's book, wasn't a whole hell of a lot.

"Queen Mab, High Lady of the Sidhe, Queen of the Summer Court of Faerie, Mistress of the Living Forest, and Empress of Earth and Water, is your bloody fricking *aunt*?"

Now seemed like a good time for Fiona to stand up. And take a few steps back. And maybe make sure she was standing somewhere far away from corners and close to an obvious escape route.

"Um, a little."

"A little? She's a little your aunt. So I suppose she'll only make my life a little miserable when she finds out you're here. That's just fabulous."

"Don't you think you're overreacting just a tad?" she laughed, not really amused. "Mab can be a little bit . . . temperamental, I grant you, but she's not entirely unreasonable. She's not going to get all bent out of shape with you just because I took a little trip."

Walker crossed his arms over his chest and pinned her with his stare. "So then you got permission to visit before you crossed through the gate from Faerie that no one on either side is ever supposed to use except in direst emergency?"

Fiona made a face. "Not exactly."

"Then what the hell makes you think Mab isn't going to pitch a royal Fae fit?" he snapped, stalking toward her until she could have sworn the force of his irritation blew her hair back like a hurricane wind. "You broke the goddamned law, and not only that, but you picked the worst possible time in history to dump your pretty little troublemaking ass into my lap, sweetheart. I've got enough to worry about without trying to prevent an interdimensional incident with the Summer Sidhe!"

Fiona's curiosity leapfrogged over the protestation of innocence she had been about to make. Rumor had it, there was a sprite somewhere back in the branches of her family tree, and it was moments like this that lent credence to the story. Eyes glinting, her need to know everything hurled her right into the provocative part of his diatribe. "How is this the 'worst possible time in history'? Is something going on?"

Walker teetered back on his heels, his expression slowly shifting from anger to confusion. It looked like he'd just hit a brick wall after accelerating to full speed. "What?"

"What's going on at this particular moment that makes the timing of my vacation so bad?" she asked, ignoring the bark in his tone. "There must be something major going on. You seem stressed out. Is there something I can do? Anything I can help with?"

"You've got to be kidding me."

"Well, there's no need to sound so astonished. Just because I'm Fae doesn't mean I can't be useful. Not everyone who grows up at court is a dilettante. Just tell me what the problem is, and I'll be happy to lend a hand."

The werewolf stifled another curse that had Fiona wondering about the extent of that particular portion of his vocabulary. It seemed quite amazingly comprehensive.

"The only way you can help me," he grumbled, abruptly backing up a few steps and resuming his earlier pacing, "is by doing whatever it is you do to magic yourself something to wear that looks less like it came out of a Victoria's Secret catalog. Then you can follow me back to the Faerie gate you came in through and get the hell home before anyone important realizes you were ever here."

Fiona blinked and raised an eyebrow. "That was a little harsh. Is that what passes for manners in the mortal world lately? No wonder we have so many jokes about the irony of mortal civilization where I come from."

His head snapped around, and he scowled at her through fiercely narrowed eyes. "Now is not a good time for you to lecture me, sweetheart."

The predatory glow in those wolfish eyes caught Fiona by surprise and sent a shiver of awareness skittering down her spine. All at once her senses seemed to register the power of his muscled body, the breadth of his lightly furred and distractingly bare chest. The heat that radiated off him in waves along with something subtler, deeper, and infinitely more unnerving. Typically, Fiona reacted to the warning of her instincts not with a strategic retreat, but with a slightly suicidal tug to the tail of the beast.

"Oh? What time would work better for you?" she asked, opening her eyes wide and guilelessly, even as her subconscious streak of self-preservation had her backing up another step or two. Or four. "I'd be happy to take a look at my calendar and work you in—"

By the time she heard his warning growl, it was already too late. In the time it took for her synapses to fire, the werewolf had leaped across the distance separating them and slammed bodily into her, sending her careening into the wall five feet behind her. She hit the drywall with a thud and a hiss, the air in her lungs whooshing out and into the mouth of the beast.

She would have felt a lot better if she could have thought of him as beastly, if she could have mustered up something like outrage or indignation or even some judicious fear. But no. Instead, all she felt was a wave of intense dizziness and a weakening of every muscle in her body as it melted against his. Her lips put up no resistance as he forced them apart with his own and surged inside like a conquering chieftain. His tongue claimed her mouth with bold strokes, marking the sweet territory as his. His teeth nipped sharply at her lips, before soothing the brief pain with suckling kisses.

Moaning, she sank into him, letting her knees collapse. He didn't seem to need any help keeping her upright. He had her pinned against the wall like a canvas, held in place with the weight of his body. It worked for her, leaving her free to do nothing but savor the surprising, intriguing, intoxicating flavor of him.

He tasted of rich, dark coffee, thick and heavy with sugar. Traces of spice and forest filled her senses and made her tremble as she dissolved in pleasure. Her hands slid up the cool surface of the wall and tangled in his hair, curling into fists and holding him tight against her lips. He didn't seem inclined to go anywhere else, but at this point, Fiona didn't want to take chances. She wanted to devour him. Or let him devour her. Either option would work so long as he never, ever stopped kissing her.

A low rumble, half growl, half purr, vibrated between them as he leaned more heavily into her, into the kiss, nestling his hips into the cradle of hers, pushing against the flimsy barrier of her gossamer gown until she felt the rough scrape of denim against the center of her need.

She moaned and wriggled against him, wanting to magic the barriers of cloth away, but she had used up her magic in the demon attack, and stars knew when she'd be able to get a refill. Probably not until she got back home.

Even as the thought brushed through the edges of her consciousness, Fiona became aware of the passion between them, shifting, changing, becoming something more. Sheer, teasing tendrils of magic began to form from the energy of their mutual desire. The tendrils swirled and danced in the pit of her stomach, then spilled out, finding the wound in her flesh and smoothing over it. The magic knit skin and muscle back together, found foul, oily molecules of poison, and wrapped around them, insulating and separating them from her bloodstream and dissolving them into individual atoms that could be benignly flushed from her system.

The healing magic filled Fiona with a rush of warmth and energy, replenishing her depleted stores of magic until her wish became a reality and the barriers of clothing between her and her werewolf disappeared, leaving him pressed hot and hard and naked between her thighs. She moaned and clutched him tighter, canting her hips invitingly, seeking to draw him inside her body, into the hot, moist depths that ached with emptiness only he could assuage.

Unfortunately, the brush of molten heat against the crown of his shaft seemed to snap him into some hideously noble sort of sense. He tore his lips from hers and grabbed her wrists, jerking her hands from his hair and setting her bodily away from him. Far enough that her blindly seeking hips couldn't reach his and squirm their way past his guard.

He swore violently and stood glaring at her with eyes that burned with heat and frustration and a distinct sense of unease. Holding her at arm's length, he struggled to regain his breath even as she struggled to free herself and press against him once more.

"Just what the fuck do you think you're doing?" he

demanded. His voice was so harsh, so low, and so animal that he sounded more like wolf than man. It took a few seconds for Fiona's overheated brain to translate the question and even longer for her to understand what he meant. For some reason he seemed to be upset by the fire leaping between them.

Frowning, Fiona tested his grip on her wrists and found it just as steely as ever.

"I wasn't thinking," she said, impatient and uncomprehending. "I was too busy tasting you. But I don't know what you have to be so upset about. I mean, it's not as if—"

"Sweetheart, I almost fucked you up against a wall, and I've known you for all of seventy-two minutes, sixty-three of which you spent unconscious! You bet your ass I'm upset!"

Fiona felt her frown deepen. "But why? Is there something wrong with the wall?" She craned her head to look at the pale-cream-colored surface behind her. "It seems perfectly functional to me."

Walker made an odd choking sound. "That's *not* the point. Jesus, this is crazy. It's completely impossible."

Fiona let her gaze drop pointedly to his erection and felt her eyes widen. My, but he looked . . . enthusiastic. And impressive. Borderline challenging.

"It looks very happily possible to me. Probable, even, if you'd stop yelling for a few minutes and just let me get a little bit closer—"

She slid a bare foot up his muscular leg to hook behind his hip and urge him toward her. For one delicious moment, she thought she saw his eyes start to glaze over and his body begin to sway nearer, but then he caught himself, jerking back as if electrocuted and shifting farther out of reach.

"Would you stop that?"

If she hadn't known the man in front of her to be a predator, Fiona might have called the look in his eyes just then hunted, especially once he glanced down at himself and really noticed that the reason he probably felt like she touched him through the fabric of his clothes was because he no longer wore any. But to be fair, neither did she.

His head snapped up, and his expression hardened. "Put them back."

Fiona didn't pretend to misunderstand. Instead, she sighed. "I can't."

"What do you mean, you can't? I'm not the one around here who does magic, lady, and I'd sure as hell remember it if I'd undressed you, so I think it's a pretty safe bet that you're the one to blame."

"Accusations are so not constructive—"

"Put them back," he repeated, in a tone she bet made all the female werewolves swoon. "Now."

"I told you, I can't." Since her gorgeous but grouchy companion had seen fit to kill the mood, Fiona gave up and leaned against the wall, which was not nearly as much fun as it would have been if he'd been pressing her up against it with that yummy body of his. The thought helped her muster up a respectable scowl of her own. "I don't have the magic. I'm drained."

Seeing the Lupine's confusion and not in the mood to be accused of lying, which she felt sure would be his next step, Fiona explained. "Fae magic is different from the magic you have here. It's an entirely different system, almost like another language, and the only language I speak is Fae. I might be able to puzzle out some of the important words if I concentrate really hard, but that would take more energy than I'd be likely to gather. Which means that if I want to use magic while I'm in this world, I need to use magical energy I brought with me from Faerie."

"Then do that. Use what stuff you brought with you."

"Like I just told you," she said, glaring, "I'm drained. I used up all the magic I brought when I was trying to keep from being eaten by a demon with a serious case of the munchies. I don't have anything left. That's why you're seeing what I really look like, instead of the glamour I had on when I got here. When I used the last of my magic, I couldn't even keep that simple a spell cast."

His expression reflected his skepticism. "If you can't do any magic, where the hell did our clothes go in the first place?"

Fiona shifted uncomfortably. Somehow, she didn't see Walker being all that comfortable with the idea that she'd basically fed off the energy created by their intimate encounter. It was one of the inherent talents of the sidhe branch of the Fae that sex fueled their magic, and while that failed to even raise eyebrows in Faerie, it occasionally proved a bit disturbing to inhabitants of the human world, Other or not. With that in mind, Fiona didn't really want to be the one to have to explain it to this already-irritable Lupine. It would be enough of a challenge getting him to kiss her again as it was. If he reacted with the unease most of his fellow non-Fae felt for folk who replenished their magic with the energy of others, he'd probably never touch her again. She really wanted him to touch her again.

"That was the last of it," she said, cautiously meeting his gaze. "I'm surprised I even had enough to manifest a thought like that, but there's no way I can reverse it now. I'm tapped out."

Walker's expression remained suspicious, but he released one of her wrists and used the other to tug her along behind him. He crossed the room to a half-closed door Fiona had been much too occupied to notice earlier.

As they stepped into the other room, she looked from the enormous invitingly rumpled bed to the Lupine's grim expression and made a face. It didn't look like she should get her hopes up here, but she couldn't stifle the disappointed sigh when he grabbed her by the shoulders and positioned her squarely in the center of the room, well away from any and all accommodatingly flat surfaces.

"Don't move."

Obediently, she stood still and watched him rummage through a chest of drawers. He pulled out a pair of jeans first and tugged them on roughly. With his back turned, he missed the wistful expression that crossed her face as the heavy cloth slid over and concealed his truly mouthwatering behind. She consoled herself by admiring the way the fabric cupped and molded to him, right up until a veil of blue-striped cotton landed on her head, cutting off her vision. She reached up to yank it away and heard the thud of another garment landing at her feet.

"Get dressed," he growled, and stalked past her out of the room without another glance.

Sighing, Fiona picked up the sweatpants he'd left her and dropped them on the end of the bed while she slipped into the soft cotton shirt and went to work on the buttons. Sometimes, she really wished her instincts were a little less reliable. Because then maybe she wouldn't be quite so convinced that sleeping with Tobias Walker would be the most exhilarating experience of her life so far, or that the man would rather chew glass than give in to their mutual attraction.

This vacation was turning out to be a lot less fun than she had planned.

CHAPTER 5

I<small>T WAS TOUGH</small> T<small>O</small> do any strategic planning while sporting an erection that would have scared most lifelong sex workers.

Walker realized this during the few minutes he spent pacing his living room and trying to decide what to do with the hundred pounds of trouble in the next room. Lupines tended to be a superstitious lot—maybe because of the primitive instincts that lurked so closely beneath their more civilized surfaces and maybe just because they *knew* some things could only be explained by magic—but Walker had never thought himself to be particularly prone to those kinds of thoughts. He'd certainly never before suspected he might be cursed. Now, he had to rethink that position. What other reason could there be for the sudden appearance of the niece of the Queen of Faerie who had dropped into his lap at a time when he already felt like a juggler keeping half a dozen Volkswagens spinning above his head?

"I could fit me and a friend in this outfit. Know anyone who might want to come over and join me?"

Walker whirled on Fiona with a snarl before he realized how stupid that was. If he wanted to ignore the sparks that flared between them, he probably shouldn't be reacting possessively at the image of another male getting into the princess's pants.

Dragging his gaze away from said pants—a pair of his soft, gray sweats that bagged adorably between the tightly winched drawstring at their waist and the thick cuffs where Fiona had been forced to roll up the hems to keep from tripping over them—he found her eyes smiling at him, clearly amused and unconvinced by his determination to keep his distance. Probably because it was pretty clear he hadn't managed to convince himself yet.

Hell.

He shoved a hand through his hair and tried to adopt a less lust-glazed expression. "I need to figure out what to do with you."

"I could make a suggestion—" She broke off when he made a choking sound, as if he'd just swallowed his own tongue, and her grin turned wicked. "Actually, I could make several, but you seemed to indicate a desire for me to keep my hands to myself. So I was thinking more along the lines of you bidding me a fond farewell and letting me get back to my vacation."

"Like hell."

He must have looked as dismissive as he sounded, because she gave him a petulant little glare. "What? Haven't you ever needed a few days off?"

"Lady, you've got no idea. But what part of being a Faerie princess has proved so fricking taxing for you?"

"Don't ever call me that!"

Her vehemence took Walker by surprise. He raised an eyebrow and crossed his arms over his chest. "You object to the truth?"

"I object to you making assumptions when you know nothing more about me than the name of one aunt."

She glared at him with an expression that could have melted steel, and he tried to tell himself that was better than the expression that said she wanted to lick him up and down like an ice-cream cone. His self snorted.

"Whoa," he said, holding up a hand. "You're the one with the magic powers and the pointy ears, which make you Fae, and you're also the one who told me you're Queen Mab's niece, which makes you a princess. So how am I a jerk for calling you what you are?"

Her lip curled. "I don't know. You're the son of a bitch, so why don't you tell me why word choice makes a difference?"

Walker sucked in a breath and fought the instinct to snarl. She'd made her point, though she was the first woman he'd ever met who objected to being called a princess. "Fine. You don't want me to curtsy? Works for me. But I still need to figure out what the hell happens next."

"You don't need to figure out anything about me." Her tone couldn't exactly be called polite, but at least she'd stopped breathing fire at him. "I can take care of myself. So, thanks for your help with the demon. I appreciate that. It's been nice meeting you. Hope you have a nice life. See ya later."

She took a step toward the stairs, and his hand shot out to clamp around her wrist. "Hold it. Where do you think you're going?"

"Like I told you, this is my vacation. I think it's time I went and saw some sights."

"Right. Because I'm definitely letting Mab's niece wander—unauthorized, unescorted, and out of magic—around Manhattan. That's gonna happen any minute now."

She pursed her lips and twisted her wrist in his grasp, but he held firm. "Can I assume you've sunk to sarcasm now?"

"Sweetheart, let's not even get into sinking right now, okay?"

"Then how about you stop insulting me by telling me I need to use the buddy system like the average five-year-old? I can take care of myself. I wasn't born last week. In fact, I wasn't born last century. I'm not some defenseless babe."

Walker blinked at that age statement. He knew the Fae could live for thousands of years, but he hadn't connected that abstract fact with the woman in front of him who looked about twenty-five.

"I never called you a defenseless babe." Though he couldn't deny the term "babe" had crossed his mind a time or two. "But you are a defenseless Fae right now. You told me that yourself, so when it comes down to it, that's not a whole hell of a lot different."

Her violet eyes narrowed. "If I'm that defenseless, then why am I the one who distracted the demon long enough for us to get away?"

Walker chose to ignore that. She sure as hell didn't need his encouragement in risking her pretty little neck. "You are not leaving here and going wandering

around my city alone. If that was your plan, you can
forget it right now."

"What makes you think you can stop me?"

He just looked down at her, letting her see the fierce
glow of his eyes and the fierce clenching of the muscles that wanted to grab her and shake her senseless.

Her chin rose another notch, along with her obvious
determination. "Fine. You can stop me. But you have to
sleep sometime."

The threat hung in the air between them for a long
moment before Walker swore. He wouldn't put it past
her. The minute he turned his back, she'd probably be
out the damned door. And the worst part was that she
was right about the sleep, too. His eyes felt like they'd
been covered in sandpaper and then set on fire. If he
didn't get some rest soon, his body was going to take
the decision out of his hands and crumble into a heap
on the first available flat surface it came to. Hell, at this
point, he couldn't even be sure about the flat part. And
he'd bet a small fortune that when he woke up, there
would be a neat trail of little Fae footprints running
right down the middle of his spine.

"I don't suppose you'd consider cooperating."

She smiled so sweetly, Walker felt his stomach turn
over. In fear. "Why don't we try it and see? I'll even
tuck you in."

His stomach took a turn south even as his inner wolf
sat up and begged. He muttered, "Down, boy."

"What did you say?"

He turned away and reached for the phone. "You'd
better sit down. I need to make a phone call."

Fiona looked less than thrilled by the suggestion.
"My aunt screens her calls, you know."

Walker snorted. "Even if Ma Bell had laid fiber-optic

cables from Faerie to Timbuktu and back, I wouldn't dial that number on a bet. Tell Mab her baby niece wound up naked on my sofa half-eaten by a demon? I'm not that flavor of stupid."

He dialed quickly and kept one eye on her while he listened to the phone ring. She didn't sit. In fact, she stood glaring at him while one foot tapped impatiently on the floor, but at least she was staying put. For the moment.

"Do you have any goddamned idea what time it is?"

Walker ignored the threat in the growl on the other end of the line and barked out a question of his own. "How soon can you get over to my place?"

The growl shifted abruptly into a whimper, and the aggravated male voice in his ear turned decidedly whiny. "Aw, come on, Uncle Tobe. I just got to bed like four hours ago, and I have an exam in the morning. I'm a growing wolf. I need my sleep."

"Give it up, Jake. A hundred-year coma wouldn't be enough beauty sleep to make you prettier. Get your butt over here. You've got fifteen minutes."

Hanging up the phone, Walker settled himself onto the sofa and propped his heels on the edge of the coffee table. He could feel Fiona's eyes on him but let his own eyelids drop and rested his head on the cushions behind him. God, he needed some sleep. He also needed to feel the princess spread hot and naked beneath him, but like he'd already said, he wasn't that stupid.

She watched him for a couple of minutes; he could feel it as clearly as if she'd been touching him, and he gritted his teeth against the sensation. Then she heaved a disgruntled sigh and flopped herself down on the other end of the sofa. "Well, at least I know now that you're just this charming with everyone, so I won't take it personally. But I can't believe no one ever taught you better manners."

He didn't even twitch an eyelash. "Remember, sweetheart, I was raised by wolves."

CHAPTER 6

Fiona GLARED ACROSS THE cushions at Walker's completely relaxed form and stifled the urge to scream. She'd known the man for less than an hour, and she'd already had to restrain herself from tearing his clothes off or wringing his bloody neck. That had to be some kind of record.

With her teeth clenched together hard enough to alter the atmospheric pressure in her skull, Fiona watched the easy rise and fall of the werewolf's chest and plotted some very creative forms of revenge. As bonelessly as he'd sprawled over the end of the sofa, she knew better than to assume he'd fallen asleep. She had no doubt that if she so much as moved a muscle, she'd find herself flat on her back before she even realized she'd lost her balance. Now, that wasn't something she'd have minded if she had thought he intended to do anything about having her in that position. Other than yell at her, anyway. But somehow this seemed like a particularly bad moment to tug this wolf's tail.

She really didn't get this whole resistance thing of his. In Faerie, and especially amid the decadence at court, resisting a mutual sexual attraction was unheard of. Bordering on mind-boggling. In fact, Fiona couldn't call to mind a single instance in which she'd ever seen any Fae *not* indulge in the kind of chemistry that existed between her and her stubborn werewolf. It just wasn't done.

Despite the fact that her people had left the human world for their own several millennia ago, they still possessed a few characteristics best described as "earthy." Foremost among them was the tendency to screw like bunny rabbits. The Fae just liked sex. They considered it a natural, healthy, and pleasant way to pass the time, so the fact that Walker was refusing to pass some time with Fiona when she had been able to feel how much he wanted to just didn't make sense to her. Maybe it was one of those weird things humans got hung up on and Walker had been corrupted after living among them for so long.

She took advantage of his closed eyes to watch his expressions. She wasn't sure what she was looking for, only that she liked looking. Relaxation didn't make him look any softer. His jaw stayed just as firm, his cheekbones just as sharp, and she could still see a little echo of the furrow she'd already noticed creasing his brow just between his eyes. It was a hell of a trick, managing to look just as much of a conquering warrior while sprawled limply on a sofa as while trying to tear the throat out of a rampaging demon. She'd ask him how he did it, if she thought she'd be sticking around.

Making a face, Fiona tucked her feet up under her and pulled her knees to her chest. She needed to keep that point in mind. This was supposed to be a quick vacation, a little pleasure jaunt undertaken for the purpose of eating pizza and those "hot-dog" things, taking in a few punk concerts, adding to her aunt-shocking wardrobe, and basically distracting her mind from the situation at home. The last thing she needed was a case of unrequited lust for a werewolf with an attitude. In contrast to the rest of her family, Fiona wasn't the fuck-and-flee type. She liked to be able to remember the names of the men she slept with, and she liked it better if she spent more than a few minutes of non-naked time with them before and after. Since that wasn't possible here, everyone was probably better off if she just kept her hormones to herself.

She was debating the merits of indulging in a healthy pout when a teeth-rattling slam broke the silence, followed closely by the thunder of footsteps on the stairs. She jumped at the initial noise, her gaze shooting to Walker's face. He looked back blandly and pushed lazily to his feet. If the two of them were about to be attacked by another demon, the werewolf seemed to be taking it well.

He was standing facing the top of the stairs when a blur of blue denim and black cotton came charging through and skidding to a stop in front of him.

Walker looked at the clock above the stairs. "That was almost twenty-two minutes."

"I'd have made it in fifteen, but that would have been without clothes. And it's chilly out there."

Fiona looked at the newcomer and raised an eyebrow. This was who Walker called in a crisis?

She couldn't call herself an expert in mortal growth patterns or anything, but if she had to judge, Fiona wouldn't put the boy's age at all that far past adolescence. He looked like a college kid, all lean and lanky, like he'd just finished growing, but his weight hadn't caught up yet with his height. He stood an inch or two shorter than Walker, skimming right under six feet maybe, and had lightly freckled skin, disheveled brown hair, and sparkling eyes in that light amber brown so common in Lupines.

Glancing back and forth between the two figures, Fiona frowned. They shared more than that one similarity, in fact. She saw something around the shape of the eyes and the set of the jaw that told her these men were more than acquaintances.

Eyes narrowing, she pushed to her feet, immediately drawing the attention of the young werewolf. His head turned toward her, eyes and nostrils widening simultaneously as he raked his gaze over her and drew her scent in deeply. For a split second she saw an echo of Walker's predatory grin on his face as he took a step forward, but that was before the older Lupine shot out a hand and grabbed him by the scruff of the neck.

"If you so much as drool on her, I will kick your ass into next semester. Got it, Jake?"

"Aw, but Uncle—"

He gave a shake before returning the teenager to his feet. "Off-limits, Jake. I mean it."

"Why?" Jake seemed smart enough—or maybe unsuicidal enough—not to make another move toward Fiona, but he didn't give in easily. He stood his ground warily. "It's not like you marked her or anything. I mean, yeah, you touched her, but look at her. Who wouldn't?"

"Um, excuse me." Fiona raised her hand and waved it above her head. "Talking about an actual person here.

I don't appreciate being fought over like some sort of bone."

Jake turned and looked into her eyes for the first time, his grin all charm and energy and youthful lust. "More like a roast, actually. A nice, juicy one."

Walker snarled, not the kind he'd used to let Fiona know she'd been irritating him for most of the night, but a real, honest-to-goddess, dog-in-the-manger growl. "Off. Limits."

For a minute Fiona thought Jake might take his life into his hands and push the issue, but apparently youth hadn't deactivated all of his brain cells. The two men stared at each other silently until Jake broke down and looked away, turning his head into what looked like a really uncomfortable position. It took Fiona a second to realize the significance of the tilt. It left his throat completely exposed to the older Lupine. She shivered.

"Fiona," Walker growled, still not looking at her, "I'd like you *not* to meet my nephew, Jake, but under the circumstances, I can't figure out a way to avoid it."

Fiona extended her hand, then withdrew it at Walker's low growl. Ooookay. No touching, then. She settled for a little wave. "Hi, Jake. It's nice to meet you."

"Jake, this is Fiona. Off-limits."

The younger man kept his gaze focused someplace beyond Fiona's left ear, but she could see him pursing his lips, looking half-irritated and half-amused. "Unusual last name you've got there."

"Isn't it?"

Ignoring her glare, Walker herded his nephew farther into the room and placed himself between the youth and Fiona. If Walker kept this up, all the eye rolling she was doing was going to make her dizzy.

Slouching on the end of the sofa like the college student he was, Jake looked up at his uncle and yawned. "So, what was so important that you interrupted your own date and dragged me out of bed at four nineteen in the morning?"

"She's not a date. And unfortunately, you're the only pack member I could think of who'd be more afraid of what I'd do to you if you talked about this to anyone than you'd be of Graham if he started asking questions."

Jake shrugged. "I'm plenty scared of the alpha. He could probably kick my ass through the power of suggestion if he tried. But he barely knows I exist, so I'm not real worried about the eventuality. You, on the other hand, know where I sleep."

"Exactly. Remember that."

Fiona snorted and waved a hand in front of her face. "Stars, the cloud of testosterone in the air around here is getting toxic. And here I thought the story about men thinking with their testicles was an old wives' tale."

They both ignored her.

"Fiona needs to get home as soon as possible, and you're going to help me with that."

Jake looked incredulous. "What? You can't find the number of a good cab company?"

"Oh, it's not that," Fiona put in breezily, "but once you cross the planar barrier, the fare just skyrockets!"

More ignoring. Sheesh, it was like the ability to pretend she didn't exist was hardwired into this family's Y chromosome.

"Planar barrier?" Jake's voice rose on the question. "Are you trying to tell me she's Fae?"

"Would you please stop talking about me as if I weren't in the room?" Fiona snapped, her patience thinning with every "she" and "her" one of them uttered.

"In case no one noticed, I am, and not only that, but I have a right to have input into my own plans."

"I don't give a shit about your plans, sweetheart," Walker said, turning a fierce glare on her. "What I care about is keeping you intact and getting your ass back to Faerie before anyone notices you were ever here."

"What's wrong with the way she came in? I assume it was one of the gates. The one in Inwood is closest. If you don't want to call a cab, we can use your car."

Walker shook his head at his nephew's suggestion. "The problem is that the last time she got near the Inwood gate, we ended up getting jumped by an unpleasant fellow with serious sulfur breath."

"Holy shit!" Jake's eyes widened until he no longer looked the least bit sleepy. "A demon? You ran into a demon? In the park? That's crazy."

"We got out whole, which is the important thing, but I don't think it would be a great idea to go back there tonight. We can't take the chance of running into it again. It got in a couple of good swipes at Fiona, and I haven't had any sleep in more than twenty-four hours. I need to catch a nap, and it would be smarter not to head back there during full dark."

Jake turned to look at Fiona, his eyes now holding a measure of respect in addition to the lust. The lust hadn't gone anywhere—he was a young, male Lupine, after all—but the respect at least made it easier to accept.

"I'm fine," she said. "I've got a souvenir or two, but it didn't do any lasting damage."

Jake nodded. "Okay, so what do you guys need me to do?"

"Nothing. I can take care of myself."

"I need you to babysit. Keep an eye on her while I catch a couple hours of sleep. When I wake up, we'll figure out the best way to get her to the gate without being seen."

"No problem."

"Babysit?!" Fiona couldn't decide which of them to glare at first, so she got up and stood where she could keep them both in her furious sights. "I already told you, I don't need your protection, and I sure as demon spit don't need to be 'babysat' by a kid whose *parents* weren't even born when I was celebrating my two hundred fiftieth birthday!"

Walker turned to her, those golden eyes finally fixing back on her, but they didn't look any more cooperative than his attitude so far had indicated.

"Well, that's just your tough luck, Princess, because you've got yourself protection whether you want it or not. You're in my city now, and until I put your butt back through the gate that takes you out of my city, you're my responsibility. You'll do what I say, and as ridiculous as even I find it, you'll do what the puppy here says, or I'll take it out of your hide."

It took a few seconds for Fiona to process that threat. No one had ever threatened her before, and certainly no one had ever tried to order her around before. She might not care about her position as a sidhe princess, but now that someone was treating her as if that position didn't matter, she found that the alternative to the prerogative of royalty pretty much sucked.

"Princess?" Jake asked, his eyes wide. They both ignored him.

"You've got no right to try and tell me what I can or can't do—"

"As in daughter of the queen? That kind of princess?" Jake's voice had risen half an octave.

"In Faerie, you'd probably be right about that, Princess, but you're not in Faerie anymore. You're here and around here, might makes right. I've got the might, so that makes me right."

"Holy shit," Jake breathed. "No wonder you wanted someone who wouldn't run right back to the alpha with that news. We gotta get her home before he hears about this."

If she hadn't already been drained of magic, she would have used whatever reserves it took to turn the pair of them into sea slugs. Come to think of it, based on their behavior, it might not take much magical energy after all.

She settled for killing looks, folded her arms over her chest, and plotted what exactly she would do once she got her powers back. Maybe a trip back home wouldn't be the end of the world. Going through the gate didn't mean she had to go back to the palace. She could spend a few hours, replenish her magical reserves, then come back when the werewolf of her nightmares wasn't looking. That sounded a lot easier than trying to change his rock-hard mind about something.

Walker stared at her for a long while before he turned back to his nephew and gave the last of his instructions. "Remember, if you lay so much as a paw on her, I'll bite it off. And keep your damned mind on business. She might look like a sugar-coated bonbon, but she's more trouble than a coven of witches, and she's smart enough to use your own damned hormones against you. Don't listen to a word of her twisted logic, and if you let her step one foot out of this apartment, I'll rip off something you'll miss a hell of a lot more than your hand. Got it?"

Jake nodded and Fiona stifled a scream. "Got it. Neither one of us will be going anywhere. You can count on me."

"Good."

He turned and headed for his bedroom, and Fiona

watched the broad back flex before she purred a promise of her own.

"You can count on me, too, Tobias. You can count on paying for this one day. A lot."

He glanced back over his shoulder just before he disappeared into the darkened bedroom. The look on his face was inscrutable. "Princess, I've been counting on that since the first minute you opened your eyes and looked at me. The only question is how I'll come up with the price."

CHAPTER 7

WITHIN TWO HOURS OF Walker's disappearance into the bedroom, Jake had managed to find and immerse himself in a college basketball game, and Fiona was seven seconds and half a breath away from climbing the apartment's Spartan walls.

"You know, if you add short bursts of jogging every quarter mile or so, you'll get a better cardiovascular workout."

Fiona kept pacing, but she still managed an irritated grumble in the werewolf's direction. "If I'm bothering you, feel free to call me a cab. I'll be out of your hair before the meter starts running."

"Right. Sorry, but I'm really too young to die. Besides, if my uncle kicks my ass hard enough that I miss my statistics exam tomorrow, my mom will be happy to finish me off." He grinned at her. "You're hot, but you're not worth facing the wrath of a Lupine mother paying NYU tuition."

"Gee, thanks. I see charm runs in your family." Tightening her mouth to keep him from seeing her almost smile, she turned away and went back to pacing. He was a cute kid all right, or he would be if he'd just stop being so uncooperative. Kind of like his uncle, who was way too sexy for her peace of mind when he wasn't being a stubborn jerk.

"What did you do to piss him off anyway?"

Tugged away from her thoughts, Fiona turned back to the sofa and frowned at Jake. "What are you talking about?"

"My uncle. What did you do to piss him off? He looked ready to chew metal when he went to bed."

"You mean that wasn't just his normal sunny disposition?" She shrugged. "I think he objects to my breathing the air of 'his' city. But he's gonna have to learn to deal."

Jake raised an eyebrow, his amber gaze much too insightful for the pup he was. "Not that it's my place to give advice to a princess, but just so you know, he can get even crankier when he thinks you're being deliberately disobedient. Trust me. I speak from experience."

"Okay, number one, what is this obsession you folk have with idiotic titles? And letter b, in order for me to be 'disobedient,' your uncle would need to have some kind of authority over me that required me to obey. Which is, by the way, a four-letter word. I don't do obedience."

The werewolf's bark of laughter stopped Fiona midpace. She crossed her arms over her chest and gave him her unamused look.

"Sorry," Jake chuckled. "It's just that for someone who seems to be touchy about being called a princess, you sure don't have a problem acting like one."

"Oh, shut up."

Jake grinned and focused back on the game, while Fiona brooded at the reflection of his good cheer in the television screen. Obnoxious brat. That had solidified the family resemblance. Two damned werewolf peas in a pod. But at least the pup didn't get her hormones raging. Which would have just been weird. And kind of creepy. It was bad enough that she should lust after Walker, in spite of his nasty attitude. Was that kinky? Did that make her some sort of masochist? Maybe heading back to Faerie was a good idea after all.

"Not to be all nosy or anything, but what are you doing here in the first place? I thought Fae weren't allowed on this side of the veil without the queen's permission."

"*Not* to be all nosy?" He just nodded and kept grinning. Fiona sighed. "It's really none of your business, but I was trying to get away and relax. Fat lot of good that's done me."

"What did you need to get away from? Tiara too tight?"

She gave him a look that should have eviscerated him. He winked at her. She beat back the urge to strangle him. "Not what. Who. Though now I think I just traded in one form of torture for another. Your uncle could give my entire family a run for its money, and I didn't think that was possible."

"Yeah, well, running things is kind of my family's specialty." He flipped off the remote control and resettled on the sofa facing her. "So who in your family drove you off?"

"Are you sure you're Lupine? 'Cause you're as curious as any cat I've ever met." She sighed and dropped onto the sofa next to him, since it didn't look like he was giving up anytime soon. "It was kind of a culmination of events. The last straw was one of my cousins. He let all the court intrigue go to his head. He thinks that if we get married, we'll each move up a few slots on the list of Aunt Mab's heirs."

"Would you?" Jake had already asked the question before his words actually sank in. He did a double take. "Wait a second. Queen Mab is your *aunt*?"

"My father's sister."

He gave a low whistle. "Wow. No wonder Uncle Tobe is so pissy."

"I don't think it's much of an excuse. It's none of his business what I do, and no one appointed him in charge of enforcing Mab's rules."

"Right. You really believe that?"

"Why shouldn't I? He's not Fae, he's never been to Faerie, so what business is it of his if I break some Fae rules?"

"I think he could care less if you're breaking rules in Faerie," Jake said. "But he does care about how it affects us here. It's not like it's out of the realm of possibility for the queen to take it out on us for not guarding the borders if she finds out you're missing. And that's not the kind of trouble Uncle Tobe needs right now."

Fiona sneered. "What? Am I jeopardizing his golfing schedule?"

"No, the negotiations with the humans."

She froze. "What negotiations?"

"The Unveiling negotiations," he responded easily. "They've been at it for almost six months now. The Council is trying to work out a deal to guarantee civil rights for the Others before we let the werecat out of the bag, so to speak."

"Why in the Lady's name would you want to?" Like most Fae, Fiona harbored a bias or two against humans. Not that she disliked them, but she viewed them a lot like humans viewed chimpanzees—as amusing but primitive.

"Not much choice." Jake shrugged and disappeared into the kitchen, returning a minute later with a can of soda and a gargantuan bag of potato chips. "It's getting too hard to keep the secret. Then last winter, there was a really close call with a group of human religious nuts who were trying to out us and simultaneously launch a crusade with Others in place of the infidels and Web pages spreading the word instead of troubadours." He grinned and dug out a handful of chips. "I'm taking medieval European history this semester. The lecture hall is overflowing with women."

Fiona laughed. Apparently some things were common to the male sex as a whole, regardless of species. Shaking her head, she grabbed a handful of chips herself. She was a sucker for sour cream and onion. "So your uncle is part of the negotiations?"

"Nah. The Council handles all that diplomatic stuff, but they appointed the pack to oversee security. The alpha is busy covering the summit itself, so he put Uncle Tobe in charge of making sure none of the folk in the city get out of hand and start trouble. It would be a really bad time for anyone in the Other community to do something that could scare off the humans. Uncle Walker and the security he put together are there to make sure no Others get out of hand, and if they do, to make sure we keep it quiet and take care of it ourselves. We won't stand for anyone harming a human, but we'd rather punish the perpetrator than the entire Other community."

She suppressed a wince. Hearing about the situation did kind of put her visit in a new light and made Walker's reaction to it a lot more understandable. If the Others really wanted to try to live openly with the humans, setting the terms would not come easily. But it still didn't explain why he was so determined to keep his hands off her. She was already there, so technically, the damage had been done.

"Okay, so I'll give him some slack for being under a little stress, but I don't see how that negates the need to act with a little common civility."

Jake gave a short laugh. "The stress has nothing to do with the incivility, Princess."

"Fiona."

"Whatever." He gave her a look that suggested she might want to be measured for a dunce cap. "You can't really be so clueless that you haven't noticed he's foaming at the mouth over the desire to jump your bones."

"Could have fooled me," she muttered. "My bones were all happily bracing for impact. He's the one who pulled the 'no touch' crap, not me."

"Sheesh, sometimes you old folks are so slow." He took a slug from his soda can and shook his head pityingly. "Of course he's not touching you. The man's wound so tight, it wouldn't take more than you sneezing in his direction for his trigger to fire. He sure as hell wasn't straining his zipper 'cause he was all excited about seeing me."

"Lady, you mortals can be so annoying."

"Oh, like the Fae are all sweetness and light."

Fiona dusted off her hands on the knees of Walker's sweatpants and muttered, "I never claimed to be, but at least I'm capable of admitting when I want to wrap my legs around someone. And I've never teased anyone and then cut them off and immediately tried to shove them into another plane."

Jake snickered. "I doubt my uncle has, either. But if it's any consolation, I'm pretty sure that if the circumstances had been different, I would be in my dorm room asleep right now, and you'd be covered by him instead of his clothes."

"Right. That makes everything all better."

The nap had sweetened Walker's disposition a bit, at least enough to keep him from yelling at her as he led the way down the path toward the gate back to Faerie. Apparently, he was one of those types who *really* needed their beauty sleep.

Just because he no longer seemed angry with her, though, didn't mean he'd become her best friend. He was civil and moderately pleasant, but he'd taken to speaking to her the minimum amount allowed by circumstance. When he'd been acting like a grumpy jerk, it had been a lot easier to keep from feeling slighted by his deliberately impersonal manners.

Over the course of the morning, she'd come to accept the fact that circumstances were going to prevent them from enjoying the kind of time together she would have liked. The kind where both of them got and stayed naked for a prolonged period. But it still smarted that he seemed so determined to treat her something like a great-aunt of whom he was not particularly fond. For someone used to being lavished with attention to the point of being fawned over, the lack of such treatment had stirred an unaccustomed feeling inside her. She felt hurt, and that made her angry.

If they had been alone, she probably would have taken that temper out on Walker's broad back, but Jake had dutifully returned to the apartment after his exam and now brought up the rear of their little procession. While he looked and sounded as disgustingly good-humored as he'd been all night, she couldn't help but feel less like the two Lupines were ensuring her safety on the trip back home and more like they were running her out of town on a rail. She kept getting this itch under her skin and feeling the urge to look down and make sure she hadn't been covered in tar and feathers.

"Do you think you'll have any trouble getting back into Faerie without being seen?" Jake asked, lengthening his strides until he walked almost next to her.

"No. The other side of the gate was in the middle of the woods when I left, and I doubt I've been gone long enough for it to have relocated. If anyone were going to see me go, it would be on this side."

"That's why we waited for twilight. Fewer people around and the low light will keep any who are from getting a good look at what's going on. Uncle Tobe knows his stuff."

Jake wasn't shouting, but he hadn't bothered to keep his voice down, either. Fiona knew Walker could hear what they were saying, but he didn't even twitch a muscle to indicate he cared. Probably thought speaking would delay her departure by four nanoseconds.

"I have no doubt. He certainly seems efficient when he puts his mind to something."

"That's one way to put it." Jake grinned.

They turned off the end of the path and broke through the area of trees and brambles that separated it from the clearing around the Faerie gate. The glade was bordered by the woods on one side and by tall rock formations on the other, and Fiona could see charred scars on the ground where the demon's foulness had scorched the earth beneath it.

Walker halted and turned to face them, but his eyes were on his nephew, not Fiona. "Jake, keep an eye on the direction of the path. I don't want any humans getting lost and wandering in to see this. The last thing we need is more trouble."

Jake nodded, then turned and grinned down at Fiona, grabbing her to him for a quick hug. "It was nice meeting you, Fiona. Give us another couple of months and then come for a real visit. An authorized one, okay? I'll take you to this great little Thai place. It's BYOB, so you can buy the beer and contribute to my delinquency as a minor."

She couldn't help smiling back. "I might take you up on that, kid. And if not, you'll have to come visit me sometime. If you think beer makes you delinquent, wait till I pour you a glass or two of Faerie wine."

"Come on, Princess," Walker cut in, his tone brisk. "Time to go. I've got to patrol tonight, and you need to get back home before any of us get in trouble."

Fiona narrowed her eyes and turned on him. "Don't worry, Fluffy; I'm going. We're back at the gate, no one knows I was ever here, and in another seven seconds I'll be out of your life for good. Which suits me fine, given what pleasant company you've been for most of my time here."

Walker didn't bother to look repentant. He just gazed down at her with his distant expression and his old-gold eyes and quirked an eyebrow.

Somehow, that one little gesture completely snapped her control.

Later, she might have to claim that she'd been having an epileptic fit or maybe that she'd just lost her balance and fallen onto his lips. Somehow she'd find a way to explain what had made her throw herself at the grumpy werewolf who barely seemed inclined to give her the time of day. But for now, she just needed one more taste of him.

It was exactly the way she remembered from that one brief tease in his apartment. He tasted like aged Faerie wine and felt like unfettered temptation. Inexplicably, he made her forget every single thing she wanted to lambaste him for and just sink fast beneath the deepening, drowning pleasure.

Damn, he played dirty. Especially given that she'd started the game.

That didn't stop her from drawing every last drop of enjoyment she could get from the kiss, and she got a lot. The stroke of his tongue, the nip of his teeth, the dark, erotic flavor of him. She drank it all in until her head was spinning and her knees were weak and she felt the warmth of magic flaring between them. The spark eventually penetrated even Walker's thick skull. She felt the tenor of the kiss change, felt him ease back. Then his hands were on her shoulders, and he pulled her away from him, stepping back for good measure. He seemed almost desperate to put some distance between them, but Fiona couldn't help but notice that the fingers he had clenched around her shoulders were having trouble letting her go.

She smiled in satisfaction. Let him think about that on his patrol tonight.

Raising an eyebrow, she reached up and eased his hands off her shoulders, taking a path that skimmed the sides of her breasts so she could watch his eyes heat and his nostrils flare in reaction. A girl had to take her pleasures where she could find them.

"Thanks for everything, Spot." She grinned and traced a finger over his lower lip, still damp and swollen from their kiss. "I can't say it's been fun, but it has been interesting. You should look me up if you're ever in my neck of the woods. I could . . . show you the sights."

This time, when Walker looked down at her, he didn't look irritated. The glow in his eyes definitely had more to do with arousal than annoyance, and if she hadn't known better, Fiona might even have thought his expression held something almost like regret.

The corner of his mouth kicked up and his hands squeezed her waist gently before dropping to his sides. "I'll keep that in mind, Princess. Take care of yourself. Have a safe trip."

He stepped back and slid his hands into his pockets. Fiona let her gaze linger as she looked him over one last time. Then, she blew him a kiss, waggled her fingers at Jake, and turned toward the gate for home. She look a step forward, leaned into the magic, and felt the slam of rejection as the power picked her up and hurled her away from Faerie and back into the world she had just attempted to leave.

Something was very, very wrong.

CHAPTER 8

WALKER HAD BEEN BUSY telling himself that he'd done the right thing and that he should really stop staring at Fiona's butt when said butt sailed through the air and slammed straight into his chest, knocking him back four steps until he bounced against a tree trunk like a walking pinball.

This was really not good.

That cuttingly sharp insight barely had time to register in his mind before he heard Jake shout and looked up from the feminine bundle in his arms. He followed his nephew's pointing finger to the Faerie gate, which now looked less like a fissure in the rock around it and more like Vesuvius had right before Pompeii had settled down to dinner for the last time. The rock seemed to bulge and contract, like a beating heart pumping magic instead of blood. An eerie orange light glowed behind the crack, making the entire thing look ready to split and pour molten lava over them in a murderous flow.

"Holy shit," Jake breathed, looking from the gate to the unconscious Fae princess and back again. The ground rumbled beneath them, and he staggered to the side. "Uncle Tobe, I think we'd better get out of here. Now."

This time, Walker didn't carry Fiona far. Just to the nearest street, where Jake hailed them a cab. Walker poured her into the backseat while his nephew told the cabbie a story about a fear of dentists and a large dose of sedatives. When that didn't work, the kid showed enough fang to get the taxi moving and the human driver muttering prayers in an indecipherable language. Jake sat up front to keep an eye on him, while Walker slid into the back beside Fiona. By the time the cab pulled to a halt outside a massive gray stone building on the Upper East Side, she had begun to stir and was clinging to him convincingly enough that the cabbie wasn't reaching for his cell phone as he burned rubber away from the curb.

Jake bounded up the steps to the front door and pounded while Walker scooped Fiona back into his arms and followed more slowly. The doorman on duty took one look at the two Lupines' expressions and the unconscious woman with them and stepped back to admit them.

"I need to see the alpha," Walker growled as soon as the door to the Vircolac club had closed behind them. "And if the head of the Council isn't here right now, someone needs to get him. We've got a situation."

One thing to be said for having a Lupine doorman—they always smelled trouble, even without a lot of explanation. Within fifteen seconds of crossing the threshold,

Jake, Walker, and their charge had been ushered into the office of the alpha of the Silverback Clan, who also happened to be the owner of Vircolac, the largest private club for Others in New York City. Fifteen seconds after that, the alpha himself strode through the door.

Graham Winters wore a blue chambray shirt with the sleeves rolled to the elbows, faded jeans, and a wary expression. "What's going on? Henry said it was urgent."

"It is." Walker deposited Fiona on yet another sofa and straightened with a scowl. "I've discovered a problem."

Graham raised an eyebrow, glancing from his beta to the unconscious woman behind him and back again. His mouth curved up in a smirk. "She looks like you ought to be able to take her, buddy, but if you really need help, you'll have to call someone else. Missy gets cranky when I start handling other female problems."

Walker had no doubt that the alpha's mate, Missy, would cheerfully gnaw him into hamburger if she ever caught him touching another woman. That was how mate bonds worked, and the fact that Missy happened to be human wouldn't do anything to change that. But at the moment, Walker had bigger concerns. He gestured to Fiona's limp figure. "Take a whiff."

He watched as Graham's expression turned puzzled. The other man stepped closer to the sofa and leaned down to draw Fiona's scent in deeply. Walker ignored the unexpected impulse to throttle him for getting too close and waited for his reaction. It only took a second before Graham's head jerked back and a growl rumbled from his throat. He spun back to face Walker.

"You'd damn sure better be able to explain to me how your scent got all over an unconscious Fae woman, Walker. In case you haven't noticed, I don't have time to go to war against an invading army from Faerie right now."

"Like I'm overrun with free time? She's wearing my clothes, Graham. How stupid do you think I am?"

"Based on the evidence, pretty damn stupid. What the hell is she doing here, why the hell is she wearing your clothes, and when the hell are you planning to send her back home?"

Beta or not, Walker's temper didn't appreciate being prodded. Not after the last couple of days. "I'll answer the questions as soon as you shut the hell up long enough to give me a chance."

A low, unhappy sound continued to rumble in Graham's throat, keeping Jake's back against the wall and the exit in his line of sight. Walker noticed his nephew's discomfort out of the corner of his eye but didn't shift his gaze from the alpha's right temple. He wasn't far gone enough to get into a staring contest that could easily be mistaken for a dominance challenge, but neither was it in him to back down.

"You want them in order?" he snapped.

Graham nodded sharply.

"Fine. First, according to her, she's on vacation." The alpha snorted. Walker knew the feeling. "Second, she's wearing my clothes because she lost hers. And trust me, we're all better off if she remains clothed at all times."

"I don't doubt that you're better off," Graham said, eyeing Walker's clenched hands and ticing jaw. "But how does a grown woman—Fae or not—just *lose* her clothes?"

"She did it to torture him," Jake murmured.

"What was that?"

"Nothing." Walker gave his nephew a warning glance. "She said they just disappeared. That it was some sort of spell."

"Now that's the kind of magic I need to learn." Jake grinned, subsiding into the background when Walker glared again in his direction.

"Okay. And when is she going home?" Graham demanded.

"That's where we run into trouble."

"What kind of trouble?"

Walker hesitated a split second.

"Ugh. What is it about this trip that's making me spend half of it on my back?"

All three men turned at the sound of the grumpy female voice and found themselves being surveyed by her bright violet eyes.

Walker's body offered an immediate response to her question that had him gritting his teeth and biting back a suggestion. One that had to do with making the time Fiona spent on her back infinitely more enjoyable. He doubted the alpha would have approved.

The princess pushed herself into a sitting position and blinked at her surroundings. "And what is it with me waking up someplace different from where I was when the lights went out? It's worse than sleepwalking. I could get a complex." Shoving a tumble of dark hair away from her face, she smiled vaguely up at Graham. "Hi, I'm Fiona. Who are you?"

The alpha blinked down at her and her extended hand for a moment, then shook it warily. "Graham Winters. How are you feeling?"

Fiona shrugged. "Not bad, considering that in the last twelve hours or so I've been nearly eaten alive and then almost electrocuted with a really vicious warding spell. How are you?"

Graham turned on Walker with a snarl. The beta raised his hands and shook his head. "Does she look like she's afraid of me, Graham? Gimme a break. I'm not the one who tried to snack on her. This is bigger than that."

"Of course it is. Besides, if Walker was the one trying to kill me, I'm pretty certain he'd take care of it himself, not leave it to chance in the hands of an obviously incompetent demon or a far from lethal spell on a gate he didn't even know ahead of time I'd be using."

Walker could see the changes of expression flit across the alpha's face as he waded through that reassurance and attempted to figure out what the hell she'd actually said. It didn't take a mind reader to guess when the words "demon" and "gate" finally sank in. Especially not when Graham punctuated each epiphany with a muttered curse. He turned to Walker and spoke through clenched teeth. "Tell me everything. Now. Start from the beginning. Of time, if necessary."

The order didn't bother Walker. He heard it and got on with it. Unlike his predecessor as pack beta, who had moved to Connecticut in order to assume the role of alpha of his own pack, Walker had no desire to lead his clan. After seeing what the upheaval of the last year had put Graham through, he'd have to be crazy to aspire to that position. He had enough headaches of his own. As beta, he was answerable to no one except the alpha, and since the alpha was a first cousin he'd grown up with and whom he loved like a brother, that suited him just fine. He had most of the authority of a pack leader with very little of the responsibility. What could be better? At least, that's what he'd thought before today. Before a princess had dropped into his lap.

He kept his summary of events clear and concise and slightly lacking in details. Especially the ones about Fiona's royal relatives. He figured the rest of the story would cause quite a sufficient amount of trouble without that tidbit of information coming out. He also sent up a prayer that the princess had sustained just enough of a head injury at the gate to keep her from interrupting until he finished.

Graham listened to the whole story before directing his first question to Fiona. "Did you notice anything odd when you originally came through the gate?"

"You mean other than the big, slavering demon?" She shrugged. "No, the gate worked the way it always does. It got me here in one piece. That's the only thing I've ever kept track of."

"I have a hard time believing the demon was just a coincidence. There've only been three confirmed demon sightings in North America in the last century, and all of those were still under the control of their summoners. It strikes me as a little weird that the fourth happened with no sorcerer in sight right next to a gate to Faerie."

"Could the demon have come in through the gate, too?" Walker speculated.

"Not a chance," Fiona said. "If you think it's been a long time since you had to worry about demons around here, you got nothing on Faerie. Our borders have been sealed against them for almost three millennia. Since the end of the Wars."

The Fae–Demon Wars had resulted in the banishment of demon kind from the human world and the now-inborn hostility the Fae and demons felt for each other. Demons made very poor losers, but they'd been confined to their own plane for aeons, just as Fiona had said. Because the human world had its share of summoners and sorcerers—interchangeable terms for magic users known to consort with demons—the creatures appeared there occasionally, but not often and never unattended. If that had changed, it meant trouble. Right here in River City.

Jake piped up again. "Then how can we be sure the gate and the demon are related at all? They could be two totally separate issues. Stranger things have happened. Every Thursday and twice on Sundays."

"At the moment, we can't afford to take chances," Walker said. "There's too much at stake in these negotiations. We have to be paranoid."

"You're right about that," Graham said, his expression grim. "This is not the time to fool with the negotiations. For six months, we've been crawling along at a snail's pace, deciding nothing more consequential than whether or not someone from each side needed to taste the refreshments before every coffee break to be sure nothing had been tampered with. But now we're finally beginning to make headway. Last week, the human delegates from Europe proposed the first passage of a potential Bill of Others Rights. If even two-thirds of the other humans agree to it, we might finally have a starting point to work from. Before now, we couldn't even get most of them to agree who qualified as an Other, let alone that they should have legal protection."

"And into it all walks a Fae who we can't send home because the gate she needs to go through has been cursed shut."

"You're sure that's what it was?" Graham asked.

Fiona shrugged. "I don't see what else it could have been, but it would have to be a pretty damned powerful curse. Letting things through is a gate's entire reason for being. It takes some serious mojo to interfere with something enough to keep it from fulfilling its most basic purpose. That's what we call bad magic."

Walker and Graham both cursed. Lupine irritation in stereo.

"So, to summarize," the alpha said grimly, "we have extremely delicate negotiations that mean life or death for the Others, a demon on the loose, with no idea who summoned it, a malfunctioning gate to Faerie, and someone with way too much power who seems to be taking a little side trip to Black Magicville. Fabulous. And to top it off, we also have an unauthorized Fae visitor and a queen who has made it perfectly clear that she blames us for all such occurrences, no matter how hard we try to keep the idiots out. No offense."

Fiona rolled her eyes. "If I took offense every time a werewolf insulted me, I'd have suffered an aneurysm within five minutes of meeting Mr. Congeniality over here." She jerked a thumb at Walker. "No offense."

Jake snickered, and Walker frowned at her. He thought he'd been behaving pretty well toward the princess over the last few hours, but apparently she wasn't about to forget the first few hours of their acquaintance.

"But if I could offer a suggestion," she said, addressing Graham directly. "I might be able to lessen the horrible inconvenience of having me here."

The alpha crossed his arms and raised his eyebrows. "By all means."

"Well, since it looks like I'm not going to be going anywhere for the moment, I don't see any reason why you shouldn't put me to use." She slanted Walker a glance that had his eyes narrowing suspiciously. "At the moment, it appears you have a little demon problem on your hands, and since it's been so long since you've seen one, most of you humans are pretty in the dark about them. I don't claim to be an expert about them, or anything, but they're a big part of our legends, in a way I doubt they are in this world. I could share what I know about them, help you track this thing down. Maybe even help you send it on its way."

"Aren't you the one who just pointed out that the Fae

haven't dealt with demons in three thousand years?" Walker asked. "How does that make you an expert? There are plenty of sorcerers right here in Manhattan with a closer acquaintance to demons than that."

"Three thousand years doesn't seem nearly as long when you're practically immortal. And besides, do you really want to rely on the help of someone who willingly and knowingly consorts with demons?"

"The alpha will never allow it." Walker ignored the uneasy feeling the idea of her being immortal gave him, as well as the image of her smooth, young legs wrapped around his wrinkly, arthritic hips. "It's too dangerous. Or have you forgotten how you ended up the last time you tangled with this thing?"

"Um, hi. Have we met? Because I thought I just heard you try to tell me what I can and can't do."

Graham spoke over Jake's ill-disguised snicker. "Not to interrupt the hostilities or anything, but the girl has a point, Walker."

"She what?" he asked, turning to face the alpha, his eyes wide with surprise. "But she could get hurt—" He cut himself off and cursed silently. "I mean, what would Queen Mab say if she got hurt?"

"Quite likely the same thing she'll say just because she finds out one of her subjects came over here without permission. Whatever it is, we're going to get blamed for it." Graham sighed. "Look, whether we like it or not, she's Fae and she's here. She's also likely to have a better idea of how to go about tracking down a demon than any of us do." He looked back at Fiona. "Is it true that the Fae can follow a demon's trail?"

"Depends on how you mean it. It's not like we're all some kind of bloodhound, but demons are magical, and magic has distinctive flavors. If a demon has spent any length of time in one place, or if it's done anything that required a significant amount of energy, it will leave a mark. I should be able to tell."

"Even tell one demon from another?"

She nodded. "Maybe. Probably, if they're not the same type of demon. Venom and horns, for instance, have very distinctive magical profiles."

"I don't care if the ground they walked on fluoresces neon every time she sneezes on it," Walker pressed, trying to keep himself from just issuing the ultimatum he could feel building in his chest. The protectiveness he felt at the idea of the princess in danger was as uncomfortable as it was insane. "She can't go running around after a demon that almost killed her."

"Actually, I think she has to."

"Graham, come on. Be realistic."

"Right after you, Tobias," Graham said, his voice dropping and his spine straightening. He didn't raise his voice, but Walker got the message loud and clear. The alpha was turning his opinion into an order, and as beta, Walker could either toe the line or have his ass handed to him on a platter. Torn and bloody.

He bit nearly through his tongue to suppress the urge to snarl out a dominance challenge. He didn't really want to challenge his cousin, but something about the princess made Walker intolerant of the idea of anyone else claiming responsibility for her. Being beta generally suited Walker to a T. He liked being almost in charge without having to sit and listen to petty disputes between pack members or even significant disputes between Others and humans, but he didn't like the idea of Fiona putting herself in harm's way. Not even if his alpha ordered it to happen.

For the first time in his life, Walker itched to take that last step up the ladder of Lupine authority. He still could have cared less about settling property disputes between gammas, but he wanted to have absolute authority over Fiona. He wanted to be able to tell her to plant her butt somewhere safe where he could watch it 24-7.

Hell, if he had his way, she'd be locked in a secure room covered by armed guards. Or maybe just tied to the nearest bed where he could keep an eye on her himself. And a mouth and two hands and the throbbing erection that had barely subsided since the first minute she'd catapulted into his life.

"Someone dragged me away from the hot toddy my wife very kindly prepared for me, not to mention dragged me away from my wife," a voice drawled from the doorway to the office. "You have to understand that with the negotiations taking up so much of my time, this is not a disturbance I appreciate. So if I am here for no other reason than to witness one of your idiotic canine pissing contests, I am going to be left feeling rather testy."

"I've got no idea who you are, so I can't help with why you're here, but I think the fact that you're going to see a pissing contest is pretty much a foregone conclusion." Fiona smiled at the newcomer and waved from her place on the sofa. "I'm Fiona, by the way. It's nice to meet you."

Out of the corner of his eye, Walker saw the head of the Council of Others lounging in the doorway, looking customarily elegant and relaxed in black trousers and a gray V-necked sweater. It was a good thing Rafael De Santos was very happily married to a gorgeous, possessive, and terrifying human witch, because even knowing that didn't stop the reflexive surge of territoriality the handsome Felix inspired when he smiled at the Faerie princess.

What the hell was wrong with him?

"The pleasure is mine," Rafael said, turning his lazy

white grin on Fiona. "I am Rafael De Santos, and I feel I should say right now that I have nothing in common with the savages before you."

There were many, many things wrong with him, Walker realized. At the moment, chief among them was the fact that he couldn't seem to keep his hands from clenching into fists. Or keep himself from picturing those fists in the face of any man who smiled so charmingly at the princess Walker couldn't get out of his mind.

"Don't mind them," Fiona said from behind him. "I don't know what's gotten into them, but I'm beginning to believe that this is normal for them."

"You could very well be correct."

"Nah," Jake said, "they've gotten a lot worse than this, but not usually with each other. Generally it's the two of them against someone else."

"It'll be us against you if you don't keep your mouth shut, puppy," Walker warned.

"I'm glad you're here, Rafe," Graham said. "It looks like we might have some trouble on our hands."

A quick summary of events brought Rafael up to speed and had him frowning right alongside Walker and Graham.

"I'm sure I don't need to tell you that the timing of this could have been better."

"Oh, for goddess's sake," Fiona said, "you all are just going to have to get over it, okay? I'm sorry if my vacation ended up coinciding with some top-secret kaffeeklatsch of yours, but how was I supposed to know? It was *a secret*!"

The men ignored her. "What do you have planned?" Rafael asked. "What is the next step?"

"The problem is that we need to take two steps. We need to find the demon before a human does, and before it kills someone," Graham pointed out. "Unfortunately, we also need to find out what the hell is wrong with the Faerie gate so we can get Fiona back before the Fae come looking for her."

"You people have quite a penchant for beating the dead horse, don't you?" Fiona muttered in the background.

"They have a plan for the demon. Fiona is going to find it," Jake offered, cheerfully enough to earn a killing glare from his uncle. At that point, Walker couldn't decide who needed to meet his fists the most. The choices seemed infinite.

"Ah, yes. That makes sense." Rafael nodded. "And if I might suggest, my wife might prove helpful with the gate problem. Tess has quite a talent for the magical milieu."

"Whatever it takes. Getting the princess home is the priority."

Rafael turned to Walker and quirked an eyebrow. "Princess?"

"Tobias has a fixation with my family tree. He's all bent out of shape thinking my aunt is going to kick his furry little tail, or something."

Walker swore under his breath while Jake turned an interesting shade of green. Rafael just quirked the other brow until they nearly met his dark hairline. "Does that mean your aunt is someone like Queen Mab?"

"As like as can be. Identical, as a matter of fact."

"Shit!" Graham roared. "I thought 'princess' was some kind of term of frickin' endearment, you son of a bitch! Are you telling me that you've trapped the niece of the Queen of Faerie in pack lands with no way to get her home? Are you insane?"

Walker squared off against Graham and roared right back, almost grateful for the opportunity to vent some of the frustration that had been building inside him. "Oh, right. Like I planned for this. Do I look like a god-damn martyr to you? I'd rather have my claws pulled out with a rusty tweezers than be in this situation, you idiot!"

"What did you call me, Beta?"

"Gentlemen," Rafael interrupted, stepping fully into the room and putting himself not between the two Lupines but close enough to take action if they went for each other's throats. "Let's please keep our focus on the issue at hand."

Fiona pursed her lips. "By that, I take it you're referring to me."

The Felix flashed her a charming grin, which managed to drag Walker's attention away from Graham and into a snarl. "You do seem to have made quite an impression on my friends, Your Highness."

"Would you *please* not call me that?" she grumbled. "Like I've been trying to tell Mr. Thick-as-Concrete, I'm not wild about the title."

"But you do hold it."

Her eyes narrowed. "Reluctantly."

"Then I'm afraid that despite what I'm sure were your best intentions, things have become rather complicated."

"Ya think?" Graham bit out. "If Mab gets wind of this and decides to come here to kick our asses, the entire negotiations will be shot to shit. These talks are too important. The last thing we need to do is bring up the ongoing power struggles in Faerie. The humans would run for the hills. No matter what they've told us they're willing to accept, they still expect one or more of us to fly off the handle at any minute."

"And that's my fault, how?" Walker saw Fiona glaring at the alpha and was glad to know that for at least a few minutes she had directed her ire at another victim.

"Well, if you folk had sent someone a little more diplomatic to the negotiations to begin with, we might have a bit more room to maneuver."

"What are you talking about?" Fiona frowned. "The Fae didn't 'send' anyone. As far as I know, no one in Faerie knows these negotiations are even happening. The Summer Court certainly didn't appoint a delegate, if that's what you're implying."

Walker blinked, startled into silence. He and Graham looked at each other, then looked at Rafael and saw their own surprise mirrored in his expression.

"What do you mean?" Rafael demanded, frowning in confusion. "Not only did the Fae send a delegate, but he has taken quite an active role in setting the boundaries of the agreement we've been working toward."

Fiona shook her head. "That's impossible. I'm telling you, my aunt didn't send anyone. What's this guy's name?"

"Dionnu."

Fiona's jaw dropped to the floor and bounced twice. "Dionnu? He's here? In Manhattan? Are you serious?"

"Perfectly." Rafael frowned. "You were not aware?"

"Hell no! And I can tell you for sure that Mab isn't." Closing her eyes, Fiona rubbed her hands over her face and sank back down to the edge of the sofa. "Goddess, this is so not good."

Concerned by her reaction, Walker stepped closer and hovered over her. His intention was more macho than that, but he was getting used to his intentions going up in smoke around this woman. "What's the matter? If Mab doesn't know you or Dionnu is here, it's not like she can blame you for any of his actions."

"That's so not it. You don't get it. It doesn't matter what Mab knows. It doesn't matter what I know. Mab is in Faerie and Dionnu is here and I am stuck right smack-dab in the middle."

"How do you figure that?"

Fiona raised her head and looked glumly up at Walker. "You know Queen Mab is my aunt, right?"

That sinking feeling returned to Walker's stomach. "Riiiiight . . . ?"

"Right. Well, the thing is . . . Dionnu? He's not a representative of the queen. In fact, he's the last Fae in the world she would trust to speak for her. I keep forgetting how far out of the Fae loop you mortals are. Dionnu and Mab were married, briefly and stormily, about three hundred years ago. Half of it was because they were infatuated with each other, but half of it was because neither could resist the idea of uniting the kingdoms. The idea of controlling all of Faerie seduced them both, but it didn't last. They're too much alike. Neither one of them is willing to bow to someone else's whim. They separated a century and a half ago, and as part of the settlement between them, Dionnu took back his title as King of the Unseelie Court. Needless to say, relations between the courts have been something less than cordial for the past few decades."

"What does that have to do with you?"

She sighed. "Well, you see . . . Dionnu's not just the Winter King and Mab's archenemy. He's also my uncle."

CHAPTER 9

THE SILENCE LASTED APPROXIMATELY twenty-six millennia by Fiona's calculations. All three men stared at her as if she'd just grown a seventh head and begun devouring small children and little baby bunnies for breakfast. Fiona slumped back onto the sofa and crossed her arms defensively, waiting for the other shoe not just to drop but to plummet from the stratosphere and obliterate the pavement on impact.

Walker, of course, was the first to get around to yelling at her. "Your uncle? As in, the brother of one of your parents? He's that kind of uncle?"

She just looked at him, unamused.

Rafael and Graham each sank into chairs and rubbed their hands over their faces in identical gestures of weariness.

Walker didn't bother to find a chair. He just put his back against the wall and slid down to sit on the floor, propping his elbows on his knees and shaking his head wearily.

"Would it have killed you?" he asked, sounding almost dazed. "Would it really have been so difficult for you to mention that not only are you the niece of the Queen of the Seelie Court, but you also happen to be the niece of the King of the Unseelie Court? Was it too much to ask for you to let me know that you're potentially in line for the succession of both the Summer *and* Winter Thrones of Faerie?"

Fiona pursed her lips. "You didn't ask."

"We're asking now," Rafael said. "I believe it would be helpful if you would do us the favor of clearly explaining your place at the courts of Faerie."

Ugh. Wasn't that just her favorite topic?

She shrugged. "Honestly, I try to have as small a place as possible. But if you're asking for the family tree, my mother was Annan, Dionnu's youngest sister. She died when I was a child."

Graham laughed, but Fiona didn't mistake the noise for a sign of amusement. "Perfect. And your father?"

"His name was Malcolm. He was Mab's eldest brother, but he's been gone since I was a little girl, too."

Rafael leaned back in his chair and stretched his legs out before him, his fingertips rapping a restless beat on the upholstery. Fiona got the idea that if he'd been in Felix form, his tail would have been twitching instead. "I don't ever recall hearing that either the king or the queen ever had children. Did they have any while they were married?"

"No. But all of their siblings had kids. I'm one of twenty-two nieces and nephews."

"However, before their deaths, your mother and father were each in line to inherit their siblings' thrones, am I correct? Which would make you fairly prominent in line at both courts, would it not?"

"No. Well, sort of." Goddess, the last thing she needed was for someone to encourage either of her relatives to speculate on Fiona's position in that particular queue. She hoped like hell that Fate hadn't overheard. "Mab hasn't named anyone heir, and I doubt she plans to release the throne for another few centuries at least. There's plenty of time to deal with that later. As of right now, I'm just one more in a long line of princes and princesses who may or may not ever move up the ranks."

Rafael sighed. "Your parentage crosses the bounds of the Seelie and Unseelie Courts. Where do you fall in the number of Dionnu's heirs?"

Fiona stared at him, completely taken aback by the question. "Are you kidding me? Dionnu is as likely to name an heir as I am to renounce magic in favor of a career in the hospitality industry. Someone is going to have to pry the Winter Throne out of his cold, dead hands."

"But you have as much right to the title as anyone in his court."

"I suppose. If you want to look at it that way."

Which she didn't.

Behind her, she could hear Walker cursing with a good deal of creativity and not a little bit of heat. She tried to ignore him, but considering they probably heard him in Liechtenstein, it posed a challenge.

"I want to look at it realistically," Rafael said. "I need to know where you stand in the courts in order to understand what's going on here." He held her gaze levelly until she gave a reluctant nod. "So, you didn't know that your uncle was taking part in the negotiations?"

"I didn't even know there were negotiations. And I'm pretty sure my aunt doesn't, either."

"I believe this could be classified as less than good."

"Yeah, Aunt Mab is gonna be pissed." Fiona blew out a breath. "Most of it will be directed at Dionnu, though. Unless you just neglected to inform her of the summit when you told him. Then she'll be pissed *and* offended."

Rafael scowled. "Of course not. None of us are suicidal, nor particularly brain-dead. We sent an emissary with instructions to visit both courts and to pass on the information that the people of Faerie were invited to join together and provide a delegate of their choosing. When Dionnu presented himself at the first meeting of the summit, that is how he introduced himself—as the Fae delegate. We were a bit surprised to find the king acting in such a capacity, but I thought it was encouraging for our collective bargaining power."

"And you weren't the least little bit suspicious?" Fiona rolled her eyes. "Sheesh, you've obviously never met my uncle. And this is the perfect proof of why this policy of isolationism is ridiculous. If our borders weren't so damned closed, you would have known not to trust Dionnu when he said he spoke for both courts, and my aunt would have known the negotiations were happening at the outset so she could put her two cents in. All this could have been avoided. The confusion, the unintentional insult. Possibly even the royal temper tantrum that I'm sure I don't have to tell you, you are not going to enjoy."

"No. You don't have to tell us that."

"Exactly." Walker gestured to the sofa where Fiona sat. "Which means we have to find a way to get her to safety. I mean . . . to get her back home."

"I'm afraid that what to do with Fiona is now not our biggest problem," Rafael said, his mouth twisted into a grimace. "The greater concern is to discover Dionnu's motivations and hopefully to avert a war with Mab before she discovers them herself."

"Well, there is good news on that end," Fiona broke in. "Since the Faerie gate isn't working, it's a pretty safe bet that no messengers are going to get through to fill her in on what's going on here. That at least buys us some time to figure out a strategy before everything goes all the way into FUBAR."

Walker stared down at her, then shook his head. "I swear, you use more slang than most fifteen-year-olds I know. It's mind-boggling."

She stared back and raised a taunting eyebrow. "What? Just because I'm not from here means I can't learn the lingo? Guess what, stewardess? I speak jive."

She also had an abiding love for movies and DVD players. Humans had some of the neatest ideas for overcoming their lack of magic sometimes.

"I hope you're right," Graham growled from his arm-chair beside Rafael. "Because if I suddenly have to muster up the force to repel an invading Fae army, it's going to ruin my day."

Rafael shook his head. "I believe we're safe from invasion. At least for the moment. But if we want to continue to fend it off, we're going to have to deal with Dionnu."

He, Graham, and Jake all turned their heads to her and raised their brows expectantly. Seriously. Even the kid. It was eerie.

"I take it this is a cue for me?"

"No." Walker crossed his arms over his chest and glowered down at them all. "You don't need to worry about it. I can take care of Dionnu. I'll find out what he's doing here, why he cut Mab out of the action. Maybe he can even offer suggestions for another way to send the princess home."

Fiona could feel the tension pouring off him, like steam billowing from his ears. In fact, she thought she might see a puff coming from the left one. Or maybe that was a cobweb. Whatever. She didn't need any help to understand that he disliked the idea of her . . . well, doing anything, actually, but luckily, the other men in the room seemed more inclined to realize she could take care of herself.

She looked from Walker to the united front opposite him and back again with exaggerated motions. "Sorry, Hoss, but I think you're outnumbered on this one."

The three stooges nodded in unison.

"She's right."

"Completely."

"She's got you on this one, Uncle."

"I am, but you have *got* to stop doing that." She glared at the three of them. "It's just creepy." She looked back at Walker and tried a charming grin. "Look at it this way: if they draft me into dealing with Uncle Dionnu, I won't be in your hair anymore. You won't have to guard your zipper with your life."

The three heads snapped back to her, eyes widening.

"What?"

"Huh?"

"Go, Uncle Tobe!"

He actually blushed. Swear to Goddess, right there as Fiona watched, a rush of color crept up the sides of Walker's neck and stained his cheeks faintly pink behind the light tan of his skin. His clear embarrassment was unexpected and utterly charming. Fiona couldn't have kept the grin off her face if she had tried.

She suspected Walker felt the same about his scowl.

"I'm more concerned with guarding my sanity

around you." He scowled, and the muscles in his jaw jumped with tension.

"I'm sure it will get easier with practice," Rafael interrupted, breaking the group mentality among him, Graham, and Jake. "I hear most things do."

Walker's head started to shake before the Felix had finished speaking, but Graham didn't give him a chance to voice his protest. "He's right. First of all, we can't have a princess wandering around on her own, not in the current political climate, and you know it. And more than that, you know exactly what we'd do if Fiona were here on an authorized visit. She'd be appointed a bodyguard, the same way Dionnu was."

"That doesn't mean it has to be me."

"Actually, it does." Graham pushed to his feet and leveled his gaze at Walker. Neither man moved closer, but the message came through loud and clear. Clearly enough that even Fiona understood it. If Walker continued to argue, the alpha of the Silverback Clan would quite happily turn his suggestion into a direct order. She suspected neither Lupine wanted it to come to that. "You know her, you know the situation, and you're the best man I have. I let you talk me into assigning Neil to guard Dionnu, but I'm not trusting this one to anyone else."

"And I'm the only one I can think of who has the slightest chance of getting so much as a peep out of my uncle. Face it," she said, leaning forward and letting her satisfaction show on her face. "You need me."

Walker turned his head slowly, degree by degree, until he skewered her with his intense, glittering golden stare. At his sides, his hands clenched and unclenched in stark contrast to his stony expression. Under his gaze, a shiver overtook her, and her smile slowly faded.

"Princess," he said, his voice a low, dark rumble of

menace, "there are many things in this world I need, and if both of us are very, very lucky, you won't ever have to find out what they are."

Swallowing the unaccustomed bundle of nerves rising in her throat, Fiona put on her best game face and shrugged with nonchalant grace. "There's all kinds of luck, furry man. Let's go see if yours and mine have anything in common."

CHAPTER 10

FIONA TIPPED HER HEAD back and surveyed the elegant black tower that rose in front of her. At her back, the sounds of Manhattan traffic mingled with the rustling of Central Park. Subdued bronze numbers glowed against the building's dark edifice, and the dark green awning that stretched out from the entrance cast a cool, sheltering shadow across the sidewalk.

"Yup." She nodded. "This looks like Uncle Dionnu."

At her side, Walker had ceased to vibrate with frustration, but she almost would have preferred that to the granite silence of disapproval he'd been carrying around ever since. He stood at her side, silent and stoic, and said not a word.

"Not that Uncle Dionnu looks like a high-rise," she continued, filling in the silence. "I mean, he's Fae. Have you ever seen a bulky Fae? But he certainly likes the better things in life, and since he seems to consider the human world to be a slum to begin with, if he were going to spend time here, it would definitely be in a place like this."

She looked up into Walker's face, pursed her lips, and returned her gaze forward. "Right, then. Maybe we should go in?"

She took his rumbled grunt for an assent. No matter how he might have meant it.

Five steps took her up to the smoked-glass doors at the building's entrance, but the doorman prevented her taking any more. He stepped into her path, his scarlet and gold frock coat covering shoulders of intimidating breadth. His gloved hands remained clasped loosely in front of him, but his meaning came across loud and clear. He intended to keep his own gate well secured.

"Can I help you, miss?"

His tone was coolly polite, his accent pure Brooklyn. Fiona tried a charming smile. "I just stopped by to pop in on my uncle. He's staying in the building while he's in the city."

"His name?"

"Mr. MacLir."

The face didn't move. "Is he expecting you?"

She added a few bats of her eyelashes and cursed the damn demon for taking up so much of her magic. "I'm sure he must be. I always visit when we're both in Manhattan."

"And your name is?"

"Fiona . . . Malcomson."

"One moment, please."

Keeping one eye on her, or more specifically on her and the decidedly menacing male beside her, the doorman stepped over to the stand at the right of the entrance and pulled out a clipboard. He began rifling through the pages, and Fiona turned to Walker, her smile fixed in place. As soon as the doorman looked through the admittance list and failed to find her name, their chances of getting in the door would go up in smoke. There was only one way to deal with this.

She sidled closer beside Walker and wrapped her arms around an unyielding one of his. "Walker," she murmured through clenched teeth. "I need you to do me an itty-bitty favor."

His eyes blazed down at her, reflecting all the ruthlessly controlled aggravation he'd stuffed down inside him. If he kept that up, he was just begging for an ulcer. "I don't think this is the time to—"

She rolled her eyes and reached up to cup one hand around the back of his neck. "Okay, two favors. First of all, shut up. Second . . ."

Rising up on tiptoes, she gave a sharp tug and dragged him into the kiss before he had time to think of a way to stop her.

She should try the ambush tactic more often. It certainly got results. By the time he convinced himself he ought to be protesting, even he had to realize it was way too late for that. She already had her fingers wound up in his hair, her tongue tangled with his, and her body pressed up against his stiff frame. He had no choice but to stand there and take it like a man.

If Fiona's lips hadn't already been occupied, she never could have kept them from curving. Instead, she kept them busy. Above them, Walker's mouth felt firm and warm and tasted of heat and irritation. She ignored the irritation and nurtured the heat with strokes of her tongue, teasing nips of her teeth, and the soft, sweet welcome of her body.

His groan broke against her mouth the instant before

he seized control of the kiss. The clenching of his hands into fists turned into the clenching of his arms around her. One arm wrapped around her waist and jerked her more tightly against him, while the other snaked around her shoulders, his hand tunneling through her hair until he could cradle the back of her head in his broad palm and hold her still as he ravished her mouth.

Actually, she wasn't sure he could be accused of ravishing her, since she'd attacked him first, but she had better things to do than quibble. Like savor the taste of him, the feel of his hands on her, the scent of his woodsy, musky skin. Nerve and muscle fluttered and clenched in her belly, and her heart sped up, beating hard in the base of her throat. Lust and magic began to rise inside her in a great, swirling vortex of pulsing energy. It twined up from her stomach, through her lungs, and into her head, leaving her dizzy and exhilarated. Poured down her limbs until she thought the power must be dripping like water from her fingers and toes. It felt different from the magic that filled Faerie, not as thick, sleepier, younger, but it would do. It would be enough for now.

Of course, now that she'd given a small recharge to her battery, using it would require untangling herself from a werewolf who happened to be doing exactly what she wanted for the first time in their short and maddening acquaintance.

She gave a mental sigh. There always had to be a catch.

Bracing herself for the unpleasant task at hand, Fiona whimpered and moved her hands flat against Walker's chest in preparation for disengagement. That's when he launched a sneak attack of his own and slid his hand down the back of her neck to let his fingers draw random, bone-melting patterns against her ultrasensitive skin.

Her whimper turned into a moan, and she sank forward against him. Oh hell. Another minute wouldn't hurt anything. . . .

"Excuse me."

One more glorious, breath-stealing, toe-curling minute. . . .

"Excuse me. *Miss.*"

Damn all doormen.

Walker tore his mouth from hers and turned on the man with a feral snarl. Struggling to draw air, Fiona teetered on her feet until her brain kicked back into gear, reminding her where she was.

Reminding her who she was.

And why she was there.

The doorman held a clipboard in one hand, and his expression of polite blankness had morphed into one of thinly veiled disdain sometime in the past few earth-shattering moments. "I'm sorry, but I don't see—"

Cutting him off in midsentence, Fiona gathered up a good bit of the energy from the kiss and sent it winging straight at the doorman's thick skull. He never saw it coming, but his borderline belligerence melted into a jolly, welcoming grin.

"—any reason why you shouldn't go straight up." All but humming with the eagerness to serve, the doorman, now looking tickled to the tips of his wing-tipped toes, hurried to the entrance and held the door open wide. "Your uncle is in Seventeen-ten. The two of you have a nice visit, and when you finish, you just come back and see me, and I'll make sure you get a cab home." He waved them inside. "Go on now. Enjoy yourselves. And give your uncle my best."

"Thanks so much." Grinning in satisfaction, Fiona grabbed Walker's hand and tugged him toward the door. "You're a peach."

Behind her, the werewolf glowered and grumped, but she ignored him and headed straight for the elevators.

"The minute I saw you," he muttered, stepping in behind her and staring at the button panel as the car lurched upward, "I knew you were trouble."

Fiona snorted. "You think that's trouble? Sweetheart, you need to get out more. Save the disappointment for my uncle. It won't do you any more good with him than it does with me, but at least he deserves it."

Walker figured he'd pissed off somebody powerful. And vindictive. What else explained the misery of his current situation? Why else would he be tortured with a Faerie princess whom he absolutely couldn't have and who refused to keep her hands, lips, and mouthwatering body off of him? He couldn't possibly have done anything to deserve this.

"Just to let you know," his walking penance said as the doors of the elevator slid open on the seventeenth floor, "my uncle can be . . . difficult. You might want to let me handle him, do the talking."

Couldn't *possibly*.

He stalked out of the elevator in her wake and followed her down the thickly carpeted hall, concentrating fiercely on keeping his expression blank and his eyes off the swing of her ass. These two activities left little energy over for anything else, so instead of protesting, he trailed behind her to the wide wooden door with the gleaming brass numbers designating Dionnu's apartment and waited while she pressed the buzzer.

He fought a losing battle to look away from the smooth, pale skin of her upper chest and the hint of cleavage exposed by her sapphire blue velvet top. The material clung to her form in intriguing hills and valleys. . . .

His expression snapped into a frown, and he raked his gaze over her petite form. Sometime between the building entrance and the apartment door, his sweatpants and button-down shirt that had bagged off of her so concealingly had disappeared and been replaced by the clinging velvet top and a slim-fitting skirt in charcoal gray that fell past her knees. For all its length, the garment shunned modesty with the way it cupped her ass and opened along a tantalizing slit in the side that offered peeks at smooth, silk-stockinged thigh.

He raised his eyes to her face and lowered his brows into a scowl. "What the hell happened to your clothes?"

She slanted him a wry look. "Trust me. I can't go to visit my uncle wearing your workout clothes. This would not be a good idea. Poor fashion sense is a sign of weakness where I come from."

Walker didn't think the sweats had expressed poor fashion sense. He'd actually liked the way she'd looked in his oversize garments. Sort of small and sexy and tasty.

Shit.

He was saved from thinking himself into deeper trouble when the door opened to reveal an exceedingly short man with unruly dark curls and skin the color of Dutch-process cocoa.

"May I help you?"

Fiona gave the brownie her patented sugar-sweet smile. "We're here to see Dionnu."

The brownie didn't move. For someone so small, he did an admirable job of blocking the entrance. Maybe the Jets should consider him as an early draft pick.

"Is he expecting you?"

"Oh, I doubt it," she breezed, "but you can tell him his niece is here."

The brownie didn't blink. He took a step backward and allowed them in, closing the door behind them and then ushering them a few steps down the hall to a sitting room. "If you will wait here, please, I will let the master know you have called."

Master? What, had they wandered into an old episode of *Upstairs Downstairs*? Fiona seemed to take it in stride, wandering farther into the elegantly furnished room and taking a seat on one end of a sofa that looked as if it had come out of some little corner of Versailles. It also looked like it would snap in two if Walker tried to settle his 250 pounds on it. Lips tightening, he took a post at the end of it and leaned his hip against the back near Fiona's head. Arms crossed over his chest, he waited for an audience with the king.

The concept struck Walker as a little surreal. He'd met plenty of important people in his life, and in his line of work he had spent a good amount of time with some of them. Beta of the Silverback Clan was a position of respect and a calling in its own right, but the pay sucked—meaning it didn't exist. So he worked a day job as well, as chief of security for the Vircolac club. He'd taken over the job from the former pack beta, Logan Hunter, who had moved to Connecticut a couple of years ago and become alpha of his own pack. Before that, Walker had worked on Logan's crew, bouncing unruly customers, installing and maintaining the club's intricate and sophisticated security system, and taking a few private protection gigs on the side. He was good at it, not just because of his sharp Lupine senses, his strength and speed, but because he had the mind for it. And the nerves. He didn't flinch and he didn't fail in his duties. Ever.

Of course that had been BP. Before the Princess.

Since meeting her, he figured his nerves had frayed to bloody spaghetti strands, and now here he sat in the living room of the King of Faerie trying to determine if the guy might be up to something a little fishy.

Damn, he needed a vacation.

Eyes on the door and attention on his thoughts, Walker reflected on the potential badness of the current situation and declared it monumental. Part of that stemmed from Fiona's suspicious and pessimistic reaction. After all, she was related to the king, which meant she knew him and what he was capable of a lot better than anyone else Walker knew. But the rest of the itch between his shoulder blades came at the prompting of his own instincts, and those told him—screamed at him, really—that trouble currently stampeded toward him like a herd of angry water buffalo. He couldn't give much of a logical explanation for why he felt like that, but his instincts tended to be good ones, and he'd learned a long time ago to rely on them and listen to what they had to say.

He didn't know all that much about the inner workings of the Fae courts. He knew there were two of them and that they traded power year in and year out, each monarch reigning supreme for six months before surrendering power to the other. He knew Queen Mab ruled the Seelie Court, as she had for the last nine hundred years, and he knew her people were renowned for their art and music, their capricious, merry natures, and their vain beauty.

And he knew about the Unseelie Court, ruled for just as long by King Dionnu. Those Fae enjoyed a different sort of fame, one based on intrigue and mystery, dangerous machinations and dark seductions, wild midnight rides and raids, and dark, powerful magics. But that just about summed up his understanding of Faerie.

Because of the restrictions on travel between the two worlds, his exposure to the fair folk has been extremely limited before Fiona's arrival. He'd met only one Fae before, a young man obsessed with his own entertainment and convinced of his own irresistible beauty. Now Walker realized the man had been a cousin of Fiona's, but at the time he'd just thought of him as a pain in the ass. His self-indulgent and unauthorized jaunt around town had brought the wrath of Mab down on the head of the Others and caused a world of trouble. The Silverback Clan and the rest of the Council of Others had bid him a relieved farewell and hoped earnestly never to encounter his kind again.

Like everything else, that had also been BP, so Walker figured he could be forgiven for not having anticipated that he'd be dragged kicking and howling into the political life of a culture he knew no more about than how to spell it. The assumption didn't seem out of line.

Oh, who the hell was he kidding? Since the princess had waltzed into his life, the lines had shifted so far out of whack, he couldn't even be sure they still existed. Especially the one that had been drawn to keep the paws of scruffy beta werewolves off of elegant Faerie princesses. She seemed completely oblivious of that one, as she demonstrated every time she pressed that luscious little body against him.

His teeth clenched reflexively against the desire to lick his chops. Damn her for giving him a taste, because now he couldn't stop remembering it. His fingers itched to touch her again, to fill themselves with sweet, subtle curves and silky soft skin, and it was all her fault.

She should know better than to tempt him, know

better than he did that a relationship between a Lupine and a Fae was doomed from the beginning. Lupines mated for life, a life that lasted an average of seventy years or so, as opposed to the Fae's virtual immortality. If that didn't put a damper on the romance, other facts would, like the one about Lupine jealousy—which blazed out of control anytime someone so much as stared too long at a mate—juxtaposed against the notoriously fickle passions of the Fae. All in all, these two twains were destined never to meet, much less live happily ever after.

So why did Walker find himself struggling so hard not to pin the princess to the nearest flat surface and mark her as indisputably his? What kind of sick joke was that?

Blocking the intoxicating scent of her from his mind, he fixed his gaze on the sitting-room door just in time to see it open for a figure that defied all of his expectations about how a thousand-year-old king should look.

Instead of a distinguished figure who radiated wisdom and dignity, Walker found himself staring at a *GQ* cover model. Dionnu looked no more than thirty, with pale, unlined skin and the leanly muscled build of a runner. He stood tall, over six feet, and his erect posture brought the slim flexibility of birch trees incongruously to mind. He wore a pair of black denim jeans and a gauzy silk shirt almost the same sapphire shade as Fiona's top. Like his niece, his black hair fell in glossy waves about his head, curling down over his collar in the kind of chic disarray only achievable through magic or expensive stylists. Unlike Fiona, he had black, empty eyes that reminded Walker of a reptile or a sorcerer.

Dionnu's aura of elegant grace and lazy amusement really should have made him look effeminate or weak, but his eyes kept that from happening. This was not anyone Walker would show his back to in a dark alley. Or on a crowded street corner at high noon.

"Fiona, darling," the Fae drawled as he stepped into the room. He spared a brief, dismissive glance for the brownie behind him, who scurried off as if on a mission. "I'm delighted to see you again, but I admit it is a surprise. I thought your aunt would sooner renounce her throne than allow one of her pets to be exposed to my corrupting influence."

Fiona had risen to her feet when her uncle entered, and Walker watched her offer a small curtsy before she smiled at the king with her trademark sunny charm. "You know me, Uncle. I never was very good at following orders."

Dionnu chuckled, an unmerry sound that made Walker's hackles rise. "I do, and I like to credit my side of the family tree for that." He took Fiona's hands and kissed her lightly on each cheek. "I take it that explains your presence here in the human world? A little civil disobedience?"

"Exactly. Every girl needs a vacation from the rules now and then. And since Aunt Mab is nowhere in sight, it's the perfect place to relax."

Still smiling, Dionnu turned and looked at Walker. "Aren't you going to introduce me to your friend, Niece?"

"If you insist." Fiona laughed dismissively and glanced over her shoulder at Walker, her expression saying she paid him about as much attention as the average plant stand. "But he's no one important. The Council of Others assigned him to me as a sort of bodyguard.

Apparently, they're a bit paranoid over the idea of something bad happening to a member of court on their watch. Just ignore him. That's what I've been doing."

Walker's jaw clenched at that. If he hadn't known it to be an outright lie, he would have been tempted to grab her and demonstrate graphically just how difficult he was to ignore, but this didn't seem like an opportune time. Given she'd started off her meeting with her uncle by outright lying to him, Walker was willing to credit her with some sort of strategy. He just hoped it was a good one.

He kept his expression blank and his gaze focused straight ahead of him while Dionnu gave him a cursory evaluation. Behind the mask of boredom, Walker thought he saw the king's eyes flicker, but Dionnu said nothing, just turned and led his niece to a grouping of furniture placed not around the room's large, inviting fireplace but around a mirror the size of a small pond that took up most of the center of one wall.

Seating himself in a thronelike wing chair, Dionnu gestured for Fiona to make herself comfortable. "I have to confess I'm surprised that you would make the Council of Others a stop on a vacation visit to the city, Niece. I would have thought you would be eager to see more interesting sights."

Fiona laughed lightly and perched back on a sofa nearly identical to the one she'd recently vacated. Figuring he might as well play along for the moment, Walker took up a sentry's position just behind her shoulder. "You can be certain it wasn't on my touring list, Uncle, but I didn't think I had a choice. I had no idea you were here, too, or I'd have come straight to you, but I needed to get help somewhere when the Faerie gate didn't open on my way back home."

"The gate didn't open?" Dionnu frowned and crossed his legs in another of those should-have-been-girlie moves. "What are you talking about?"

"The gate in Inwood Park. The one I came in through. When I went back and tried to cross back into Faerie, I couldn't. The gate has been sealed somehow."

Walker watched Dionnu's expression out of the corner of his eye, but he didn't see much of anything beyond surprise and maybe a little irritation. Neither of them, though, made it as far as those blank eyes.

"I don't see how it could happen. A gate has never spontaneously closed itself before. It doesn't sound very likely."

Fiona shrugged. "I know. I was surprised, but it's still true. There's no getting back to Faerie at the moment. So when I realized I was stuck here, I decided to contact the Council to see if there was anything they could do. I know they're mortals and it was a long shot, but I didn't have many options. They're the ones who told me you were in town!" She beamed. "So of course, I had to come by and say hello. I should have thought of this years ago. It's the perfect rendezvous point that Aunt Mab would never think of."

The king smiled in a way Walker thought was supposed to indicate amusement and affection. It might even have succeeded, if it had been worn by someone with the facsimile of a soul behind his eyes. On Dionnu it made Walker wary.

"Well, I'm certainly glad the mortals at least proved useful enough to send you to me," the king said. "Not only will it give us the chance to spend more time together, but it has brought the problem of the gate to my attention as well. You can be certain I will be looking into the cause of the problem."

"Oh, don't trouble yourself, Uncle—"

"It's no trouble, I assure you. After all, I will need to use the gate when I'm ready to return, as well. As amusing as the mortal realm may be, I doubt I'll be anxious to remain once my business here is done."

"Business?" Fiona laughed again and settled back in her seat as the brownie who had opened the door to them earlier bustled in with a tea tray loaded with covered dishes and small silver pots. "What business could you possibly have here?"

Dionnu leaned forward and lifted one of the pots, pouring a stream of amber liquid into two cups. Discreetly, Walker sniffed and detected the scents of tea, apples, spices, and the kick of a potent spirit that smelled of flowers and fire. Faerie wine, if he wasn't mistaken.

"I would have thought the Council had mentioned it to you." The king handed one of the cups to Fiona and lifted the lid off of several plates of tiny delicacies, both human and Fae. His voice was casual as he offered his niece a snack. "I came for the negotiations with the humans. Just because your aunt couldn't be bothered to make time for them doesn't discount their importance."

Fiona helped herself to two chocolate cookies, balancing one on the edge of her saucer while she nibbled the other. "The Council did mention something about you working on some sort of political cause, but I admit I didn't pay much attention. Aunt Mab never mentioned anything, and you know diplomacy has never been my forte."

"Which is such a shame, considering your family connections. I could help you go far, you know." His black eyes sparked. "But I suppose one needs desire as well."

"Which I altogether lack."

"So you say. In any case, the purpose of our negotiations is quite simple. The Others of this world have determined the time has come to alert the humans to their presence, and it's up to folk like me to make sure they don't put themselves in an untenable position by doing so. If we want the Others to have rights in this world, we're going to have to secure them now, before the human public has time to protest."

"Uncle, that sounds positively philanthropic."

Dionnu laughed. "Hardly. I just want to be sure that if any of our people decide to take a sojourn among the primitives here, they do so without risking some sort of witch hunt. You know how these humans can be. They've done it before. I think it's in the best interest of the Fae that they not do so again."

Fiona sipped her drink. "Mm. Maybe that's why Aunt Mab didn't mention it. You know how she feels about members of her court visiting the human realm. Even her own nieces and nephews have to sneak around to do it."

"Perhaps. Either way, it's a shame. After all, there is always strength in numbers, isn't there?"

The king's eyes glinted over the rim of his cup and Walker's hackles stood up even straighter. This Fae was even creepier than he'd originally thought. He had to beat back the urge to place himself between Fiona and the king. Walker doubted that would go over well with either member of the royal family. Besides, Fiona seemed to have a plan. She hadn't shared it with Walker, and damned if he quite knew what it was, but he knew her well enough to know she'd get pissed if he interfered with it. He would do so without hesitation the moment he sensed she was in real danger, but until then, he bided his time.

"If you say so." Fiona grinned, biting into her second cookie. "Personally, I've always been more of the self-reliant type."

"Another of my own traits I see in you. You and I have much in common, Fiona." Dionnu smiled that skin-crawling smile. "So much that I still regret your lack of interest in accepting my offer."

Walker fought to keep from frowning. What offer?

Fiona shook her head. "I'm happy just as I am, Uncle. The last thing I want infringing on my free time is the responsibility that comes with being anyone's heir. Even yours."

A dull buzzing droned in Walker's ears. Dionnu had offered to name Fiona his heir? And she hadn't felt it necessary to mention that earlier?

"Besides," she continued, "if I accepted, I'd have to officially declare allegiance to a single court, and that would be just miserable. Right now, I can move freely between the two, which is a privilege I'm not eager to give up." She smiled archly at her uncle. "You have no idea how many interesting things I hear when I travel between the courts."

"No," Dionnu agreed, eyebrows arching, "but I would dearly love to. Have another sip of *hel*, my dear, and tell your uncle Dionnu all about it."

By the time he followed Fiona out of the apartment, Walker's jaw had clenched so tight, he figured he had molars in his sinus cavities.

Doing an impression of wallpaper while the princess dabbled in palace intrigue had nearly driven him out of his mind. At least he retained enough common sense not to call her on it the second they stepped into the elevator. He knew a building like this would have cameras, and he wasn't dumb enough to break character where there might be witnesses. He also wasn't in any mood at the moment to ask her to tamper with the surveillance equipment. He played dumb and silent all the way to the building's front doors, where the same doorman who had let them in barely glanced up from his newspaper when they strolled past.

Walker's frown deepened. "What happened to Mr. Eager-to-Please?"

"The glamour wore off. It wasn't a very strong one, but it only needed to last long enough to get us in. Which it did. No one cares much when someone leaves a building, as long as they're not carrying someone else's stereo."

He felt a muscle twitch in his temple. "Did you do a spell on your clothes, too?"

"Well, yeah." She pushed out the building doors and turned to stride down the sidewalk. "I told you, it would not have been a good idea to show up in his sitting room wearing your cast-offs. Very bad form."

Walker had no trouble matching his gait to hers. What he had trouble with was keeping his hands from wrapping around her throat. Or her hips. "Last night you said you'd used up all your magic. You said you couldn't even bring back our clothes after you made them disappear."

"And I couldn't. I wasn't lying." She glanced over at him and frowned. "I wouldn't lie about something like that."

"Then how did you get enough magic back today to cast two spells when just last night you couldn't even do one?"

He saw her wince and wondered if calculating square roots in his head would keep him from tearing out his hair in the middle of Park Avenue. Or maybe just pinning her against the wall and pushing that flirtatious skirt up around her waist.

She pursed her lips and kept her eyes straight ahead. "I recharged."

"How?"

She sighed. "Look, can we possibly wait to talk about this until we don't have an audience of eight million watching us fight?"

He put his hand on the back of her neck beneath the fall of her hair and squeezed in warning. "Don't think of them as eight million strangers watching us fight. Think of them as eight million eyewitnesses keeping me from choking you for fear of state prosecution."

"Well, when you put it that way," she muttered. She stepped out of the flow of pedestrian traffic and into the alley created by the service entrance behind the building.

"Look," she said, "I wasn't lying to you last night, and I wasn't playing games. I did burn out my magic last night, and I did get a recharge this morning."

He leaned over her and fought not to growl something insulting. "When? You haven't been out of my sight since I woke up."

She made a face. "I didn't need to be out of your sight. In fact . . . you kinda helped."

Oh, he suddenly really didn't like where this was headed. Forcing himself to take a deep breath, he demanded, "How? How did I help you recharge your magical battery? I thought you said you couldn't use the magic here?"

"I can't. Not the way I can use what's in Faerie. But if the magic is . . . changed a little, things are different."

"Changed?"

"Filtered."

Her meaning came through as clear as tar. He shook his head. "Filtered how? And even if that's true, where did you get it? I've been with you all day. I would have noticed if you'd suddenly collected a shitload of energy that hadn't been there a second—"

He froze.

The truth hit him with the impact of a meteor landing smack-dab in the middle of his forehead and bouncing twice for good luck. Him. He was the "filter." Their kiss in front of her uncle's building was what had charged up her battery. Even Walker had known their embrace had been electric, but he hadn't guessed she could literally gather the energy that flared between them and use it to do magic. She had fed off of him, like a vampire. Only somehow what she'd taken bothered him more than a couple of tooth marks on his jugular.

His back stiffened and his hand fell from her neck. He didn't even realize he'd taken a step away from her until he saw the look on her face. She gazed back at him with a mix of bravado, hurt, and disappointment.

"I didn't mean to," she said when he continued to stare at her. "I wasn't planning it. I just needed to see my uncle, and when the doorman wouldn't let us up . . . I panicked. I'm not used to having to deal without magic. I guess I'm spoiled. I couldn't think of anything else to do. And then I looked at you and you looked so mad and irritated and sexy . . . and . . ." She broke off and looked down at the cement beneath her feet. "I'm sorry."

Walker shook his head, not saying a word, and took another step away from her. Then he kept going, heading for the street and practically stepping in front of the first cab he spotted. When the driver squealed to a halt, Walker grabbed Fiona by the arm and hustled her into the taxi. He barked an address at the driver and walked around the hood to slide into the front seat. If he tried to get in back with the princess just then, he was afraid he'd do something stupid.

He was also afraid to look at her face in the sedan's rearview mirror, so he kept his eyes on the streets that sped by outside his window and tried to ignore the sick feeling of knowing the kiss that had turned his world on its axis had only been the means to her end.

Serves you right, his inner voice sneered. *That's what you get for falling in lust with a princess.*

CHAPTER 11

Fiona huddled in the corner of the plushly upholstered sofa and hugged her knees to her chest with one hand while the other clutched a slim remote control. Her thumb pressed automatically on the button to surf through the five hundred channels, but she didn't really see what was on any of them. All her attention was focused on the sick feeling in the pit of her stomach that she felt whenever she thought about the cab ride back to Vircolac, which was pretty much constantly. So she flipped and brooded, flipped and brooded.

Her Sunday-go-to-Dionnu's clothes had been replaced by a pair of black yoga pants and an oversize knit top. She didn't know who they belonged to or where they had come from. Someone had pressed them into her hands a few minutes after Walker had abandoned her in the club's front hall. She didn't remember who had given them to her; she didn't even remember who had let them in the front door or who it was Walker had left her with. She only remembered that Walker had refused to speak to her and that the taxi had been full of chilly silence. He hadn't even looked at her when he dropped her off—just left her standing in the hallway, growled something about taking some personal time, and disappeared again without so much as a backward glance. The man really knew how to stroke a girl's ego.

To be fair, the doorman, or whoever it was Walker had stuck her with, had been very kind. She couldn't recall his name or even what he looked like, but she had registered his solicitous air and how he'd bustled her off to this private little den at the back of the club's second floor. He'd tried to offer her something to eat, something to drink, but the concept of swallowing remained beyond her. The clothes must have come from him, too, she guessed. He'd waited patiently outside the door while she changed and had taken her skirt and top away with him when he left. To have them laundered, she might have heard him say.

Since then, she'd been curled up on this sofa, idly staring at the flickering television screen, unable to muster up any interest in anything. The uncomfortable, churning feeling in her stomach was as unpleasant as it was unfamiliar. She didn't quite know what to call it, but she knew Walker had put it there, and she knew she wanted it to go away. Right now.

She just didn't understand mortals. Okay, so maybe they tended to be sort of wary of magic, but Walker was Other, not human, and it wasn't like she'd been using magic on him. She hadn't ensorcelled him; she hadn't even put him under a glamour. And she hadn't been taking his magic, either. It wasn't her fault that every time they touched, magic just happened. It took her as

much by surprise as it had him. No one had ever made
her feel anything like the jolt of heat and energy that hit
her every time their lips met, and asking her not to absorb that magic amounted to asking her not to absorb
any oxygen when she breathed. There was no way.

But as often as Fiona tried to explain that to herself,
she still huddled on the sofa, pouting and staring and
feeling that horrible roiling in the pit of her stomach.
She didn't even look up when the door to the den
opened. The doorman-or-whoever had stuck his head
in every so often to check on her, but whatever was
wrong with her, he couldn't fix it.

"You were right." Instead of the doorman-or-
whoever's soothing baritone, the new voice coming
from the doorway sounded husky but feminine and a
little bit impatient. "It does look like an emergency."

"Absolutely. It's intervention time, and I can see
we're not a minute too soon."

The addition of a second woman's voice stirred
Fiona's curiosity enough for her to turn her head. Two
women stood in the doorway, both blond, both in their
early thirties, and both staring at Fiona with expressions of mixed sympathy and exasperation.

"Move out of the way and let me set down this tray."
The second woman spoke again, nudging the other one
forward and following her into the room. The second
woman's hands were full of a large wooden tray that
she set on the cocktail table in front of Fiona. Then she
sat on the sofa beside her and faced her with a smile.
"Once we get some tea in you, we can get acquainted.
Trust me. Everything seems more manageable after a
cup of Tess's tea."

"It ought to," the first woman said, settling herself
on the floor in front of the coffee table and reaching

for a gently steaming teapot. "This is my special 'All Men Are Blockheaded Idiots' blend."

"Around here, we drink a lot of it." The second woman accepted two mugs of the brew and handed one to Fiona.

"Um, thanks, but I'm really not thirsty."

"Drink it," the woman on the floor ordered, her bright blue eyes narrowed.

Bemused, Fiona found herself accepting the mug and sniffing the fragrant beverage. It smelled of herbs and flowers and rich earth, enticing her in spite of herself.

"Really. It will make you feel better. Clear your head." The one beside her gave her a sweet, encouraging smile. "You'll need a clear head if you're going to find the right way to make the man pay." Fiona choked on her tea. "Oops! Careful. It's hot. By the way, I'm Missy, and this is Tess. She owns a tea and herb shop in the East Village."

"Nice to meet you." Tess grinned. She had a headful of rioting golden curls and innocent feminine features dominated by big blue eyes with a distinctly wicked glint. She wore a hip-hugging pair of faded blue jeans and a low-cut sweater the color of ripe berries. If it hadn't been for her lush, earthy curves, Fiona might have mistaken her for another Fae at first glance. A nymph, maybe. She definitely had her fingers in some magic. The glow of it suffused her fair skin with light and energy. She had to be one of the mortal magic users—a witch. "It's always encouraging to see new blood joining the Sisterhood."

"The Sisterhood?"

"The Benevolent and Protective Order of Women with Idiot Men on Their Hands. But 'The Sisterhood' fit better on the stationery."

"Tess can get a little carried away with the solidarity imagery." Missy grinned.

Though also blond, Missy's hair was long and fine and nearly straight, a dark ashy shade that should have looked mousy but instead acted as a perfect frame to set off the sweetness and purity of her features. Her round, rosy cheeks and wide hazel eyes gave her an angelic girl-next-door look that was entirely human and completely enchanting. She had pulled her hair back into a wispy ponytail in keeping with the image, and her petite, curvy form was covered by a pair of snug gray yoga pants and what looked like a man's chambray shirt. The sleeves were rolled up nearly to the shoulder seams, and the tails bounced around her knees.

"If Tess tries to show you the secret handshake, just smile and nod until one of us slips her her medication."

"Ah, it's nice to meet you. I'm Fiona."

"We know," Tess said.

"You met our husbands this morning," Missy explained. "Graham Winters and Rafe De Santos. Graham is mine."

"Which makes Rafe my cross to bear. They told us—after many demands, glares, and threats, mind you, but whatever works—that you've spent the last twenty-four hours in the company of our own Tobias Walker, pack beta, security genius, wolf's wolf, and all around dim-witted moron."

"We came to offer our condolences," Missy said. "At least, that was going to be why we came, but when we got to the club, Richards told us Tobias had abandoned you here and gone raging off in the worst temper he'd ever seen. So we wanted to find out what happened."

Tess nodded. "And change the condolences to a conspiracy to commit murder, if that would be more helpful."

Fiona winced. "Killing him seems kind of drastic. I've been thinking a lot, and he may have a point—"

"Oh no. Nonono. Quick! Drink that tea." Tess shook her head and gave Fiona a pitying glance. "That kind of thinking is just crazy talk, not to mention asking for trouble. Remember, the man is always wrong. It's the only way to keep them in line."

"Maybe it would help if you told us the whole story? Don't worry. We'll still be on your side. We have to stick together, after all. But I find it's always helpful to get things out in the open."

Swallowing a mouthful of tea, Fiona grimaced. Not at the drink, which was actually deliciously warm and soothing, but at the prospect of doing anything to add fuel to that thing going on in her stomach. Unfortunately, the two women watched her steadily, and she got the feeling that neither one of them was likely to move until she spilled her guts. Taking a deep breath, she wrapped her hands around her mug and gave a defensive shrug. "I'm afraid he thinks I attacked him. Sexually."

The two women blinked. They looked at each other, looked back at Fiona, and blinked again.

"And you think he had a problem with that?" Tess finally managed, sounding kind of choked.

Missy reached over and patted Fiona's knee. "Oh, honey. The man probably just couldn't find the words to thank you."

That drew a reluctant laugh. ' Somehow, I don't think those were the words that popped into his mind. He said I used him."

"All right. That's it." Tess picked up a cookie, half-rose from the floor, and reached over to pop the treat into Fiona's surprised mouth. "Chew, then spill."

Much to Fiona's surprise, she found herself doing

just that. As soon as she swallowed the last crumb of chocolate, she opened her mouth and let the whole story pour out. She told these two women everything, from the demon attack in Inwood Park through the toe-curling, mind-boggling, thigh-clenching kisses and up to the unbearable cab ride to the club. By the time she finished, she was leaning against Missy's shoulder, letting the Silverback luna stroke her hair while she sniffled like a human.

"Oh, sweetie," Tess said, watching Fiona with sympathy-filled eyes. "You have landed yourself in a pickle."

"Tess, I don't think that's very helpful," Missy scolded.

"Maybe not, but it's true," Tess said, and Fiona winced, sniffling harder. "She made a major tactical error. She tried to apologize."

"But he wouldn't let me finish. I tried to say I'm sorry—"

"For what? What the heck did you do wrong? Use magic? Give me a break! He needs to get over himself." Tess shook her head and drained her cup.

Missy nodded. "It's a good thing you didn't get to finish that explanation of yours. That would have really set you back."

Fiona pushed back into a sitting position and stared at the two women. "Are you serious?"

"Of course. Neither of us can stop you from feeling guilt, but we can tell you you've got nothing to feel guilty about." Missy's tone was matter-of-fact and she leaned forward to refill her mug.

Fiona stared at her new friend, trying to spot the second head. "You're really serious?"

"Lord, but he did a number on you," Tess said,

shaking her head. "Yes, we are serious about Mr. Self-Righteous going a wee bit overboard. Look, did he know you were Fae?"

Fiona hesitated. "Well, by the time I regained consciousness—the first time—yes."

"Did you take any of his personal energy?"

"No—"

"And did he respond to any of these kisses you forced on him that he later objected to so strenuously?"

Fiona nodded.

"Then what the hell is he whining about?"

"What Tess means—"

"I thought that was pretty clear," Tess mumbled.

"What Tess means," Missy continued, "is that you didn't do anything to Tobias that he couldn't have stopped if he'd tried. He's a big boy, Fiona. He knows how to take care of himself. In fact, that's kind of what he does for a living."

"But he told me not to kiss him again—"

Tess snorted. "Sure. After his tongue made a thorough exploration of your tonsils."

"But—"

"No buts." Missy gave her a stern look. "Tess is right. The man can't tear your clothes off with one hand and push you away with the other, so to speak. That's just not right. Not to mention being plain ol' poor sportsmanship."

"Exactly. See, Walker's not really mad at you," Tess said. "He's mad at himself because he wants you so bad he can hardly stand it, but he has that ridiculous idea men get that he's not allowed to have you."

Fiona frowned, but for the first time in hours, her stomach began to settle down. "You mean all those nasty accusations . . . all of those were just because he's frustrated? He made me miserable because he got his boxers in a bunch?"

"Well, there's also the fact that from what you've told us, he's also had to see you put yourself in danger a couple of times, and that wouldn't sit well with him, either," Missy said. "Especially not when he wants you as badly as he obviously does. Oh, I'm sure he's telling himself he's feeling very ill-used over the magic thing, but that's just because he's a Lupine male, and trust me, Lupine males are all but constitutionally unable to admit when they're wrong."

Tess sighed. "Believe me. They ain't the only ones."

Eyes wide, Fiona pressed a hand to her suddenly calm stomach. She felt as if she'd just gotten a free ride from her aunt for a major infraction. A huge weight lifted from her and took the clenching in her belly with it. "I can't believe the nerve. I can't believe he put me through all this just because he's got issues."

"Oh, honey. He doesn't just have 'sues. He's got big, floppy clown 'sues. The kind with the frilly white cuffs at the ankles."

"I mean, let's not totally discount the fact that you freaked him out," Missy said, tempering things. "I'm sure it came as a surprise. Sure, there are stories here and there about the Fae gathering energy from events around them, but hearing is different from experiencing. Especially when I'm sure he figured the chances of him ever actually coming into close contact with one of the Fae were pretty remote. The last one around here was my friend Corinne's husband, Luc, and they haven't been in the city in years. And when they were here, they didn't have much time for socializing."

"Hush, Miss. You'll ruin her budding mad-on." Tess made a face at Fiona. "Missy's a sweetheart, but sometimes she tends to be a little soft on the offenders."

Fiona listened to both women and decided the truth might be somewhere between the two points of view, but this time her stomach remained calm. Apparently, not blaming him for everything didn't mean she had to shift all the responsibility to herself.

"I'm not being soft on anyone," the luna protested. "I'm just saying that maybe if they each gave the other a little more understanding, they'd both be happier."

"Right. So they can move on to jumping each other's bones."

Fiona grinned.

"Missy!"

All three women jerked their heads in response to the shout, turning to see the door vibrate in its frame for a second before it slammed open. Missy jumped to her feet and hurried over to meet Graham. He wore the same clothes Fiona had seen him in that morning, but now he'd accessorized with two toddler boys. One perched on his shoulder, chubby baby hands fisted in his rumpled brown hair, while the other sat on Graham's left boot, arms and legs wrapped around his calf with a tenacious grip. Fiona looked from the little boys to the alpha's face and found his expression impatient but surprisingly unfrazzled.

"Miss, I need you to take the hellhounds," he said, reaching up to detangle the younger boy's fingers from his hair with the ease of long practice. "I have to go out, and I'm not sure when I'll be back."

Reaching out, Missy took her son from his father and settled him on her hip. "Of course, but what's going on? Is it pack?"

Graham shook his head and lifted the other boy off his boot, setting him on his own two small feet next to Missy. She immediately reached down to take his hand. "I don't know. I hope not. Walker called. A patrol found something near the park. A body. Human. It was mauled pretty badly."

Missy blanched. "He thinks it was an Other? He thinks an Other did it?"

"He doesn't know. It could be. But there's also the demon that attacked Fiona to consider, not to mention your garden-variety human psychopath. I need to go take a look." He leaned forward and gave her a fast, firm kiss. "I don't know when I'll be back, but I'll try to call if it looks like it'll be too late."

Fiona jumped up from the sofa. "I'm coming with you."

Graham turned on her with a snarl. "That would *not* be a good idea, Princess. I don't need you getting in the way, and Walker doesn't need you pulling any more of your tricks while he's trying to work."

Since she had her hands full of her children, Missy simply drew back her right foot and kicked her mate solidly in the shins.

"Ow! Shit!"

"Watch your mouth in front of the boys," she snapped, glaring at him. "You deserved that. You should know better than to make snap judgments about people before you hear the whole story. Shame on you."

Fiona's eyes widened, but she kept her mouth shut. Unlike Tess, who watched from her spot on the floor and snickered.

Graham glared at them both. "I'm not judging anyone," he said, his teeth clenched. "I just don't have time to referee between these two when I've got a critical situation on my hands."

"You won't be refereeing me," Fiona said, lifting her chin and meeting his glare. "I can control myself, but if there's a possibility that this is a demon attack, you need me there. We went over this just this morning. I'm the closest thing you've got to a demon consultant. Do you want to potentially let a trail go cold because you're sticking up for your boy?"

Graham opened his mouth, intercepted his wife's warning glare, and closed it with a snap.

"Rafe did mention that part of the conversation," Tess piped up with a grin. Fiona almost expected her to burst into flame from the heat of Graham's glare.

Outnumbered, outclassed, and one false move from the doghouse, Graham gave in disgracefully. "Fine, but I'm leaving now. If you're not ready to go, I'm not waiting around."

Fiona looked down at her sock-clad feet and swore. Missy saw the problem and, in an impressive display of motherly balance, toed off her tennis shoes without so much as shifting her grip on her sons. "I'm a six and a half. I hope that's close enough."

"It'll do." Fiona stepped into the shoes without bothering to untie them. Since she wore a 6 normally, the half size of extra room made the job a lot easier. Then she looked at Graham and raised her eyebrow. "Ready when you are, boss."

Muttering something unintelligible and uncomplimentary, Graham spun on his heels and stalked out the door with Fiona sticking one step behind him. She just hoped he wouldn't mind her staying there when Walker saw her coming. If her nemesis had to go through the alpha to get to her, it might slow him down just enough to let her live.

CHAPTER 12

GRAHAM HAD BEEN SERIOUS about not waiting around for her. She practically had to run to keep up with his long-legged strides down to the curb to catch a cab. Once the taxi driver—the first Other one she'd ever had in the city—had dropped them off at the 79th Street entrance to Central Park, Graham moved even faster. If Fiona had been human, he would have lost her at the first branch in the path, but she wasn't human and she wasn't about to be left behind. She gave thanks for her Fae stamina and quickness as well as for Missy's tennis shoes as they trekked farther and farther into the park, moving from paved walks to well-worn trails and finally into the denser wilds of the park's copses and thickets. She was also glad her keen night vision could penetrate the deepening darkness and maintain a good bead on the Lupine's broad back. Otherwise, following him would have been impossible.

She knew what he was following, too. His nose. Her own didn't have nearly the sensitivity to pick up on the particles in the air that spoke of Others, blood, and demons, but she knew Graham's was. She could see it in the set of his shoulders and feel it in the tension that gathered around him the farther he moved toward the site Walker had described to him.

When they got close enough that she began to hear the sound of low voices in the distance and to see lights flickering in between the tree trunks, though, she didn't need the senses of a Lupine to know it was bad. Even without heightened senses she could smell the death. It took the heat out of her annoyance with Graham and brought back the unpleasant roiling in her stomach.

She followed Graham through the thick underbrush, their progress nearly silent as they broke through into an uneven clearing that all but glowed with the tension of death and the reaction of the living.

Walker stood at the far side of the clearing with his back to them, his head bent in conversation with a small, dark-haired woman with pretty features and delicate hands covered in bloody rubber gloves.

He sensed Fiona the instant she stepped into the glade. His head shot up and turned toward her, his expression fierce.

"What the hell is she doing here?"

He moved across the empty space so fast, Fiona didn't even have time to put Graham between them. She could see the woman Walker had been talking to blinking in surprise from behind her lenses, but Fiona was more interested in testing Tess and Missy's theory. She looked carefully at Walker's face, searching every nuance of his expression. For a second all she saw was the old, familiar anger, but then her gaze shifted to his eyes and she saw something else. A glint of concern. Of fear.

She felt a surge of optimism and nearly opened her mouth to call him on it, but Graham cut her off. He held up a hand as if trying to calm the other Lupine.

"Save it," the alpha said. "I've already had this argument with her, and as she pointed out, all of us duked it out just this morning. We lost. You told me on the phone that you thought there was something odd about this kill. If 'odd' equals 'demon,' we need her here."

" 'Odd' could be anything—"

"Not anything Lupine," the woman in the glasses cut in, her voice carrying the short distance between them. "Pardon me, Alpha, but I can tell you for certain it wasn't one of our pack. Or a loner or an out-of-towner. The killer wasn't Lupine."

Graham looked at the woman and nodded, as if dismissing her apology. "Don't worry about it, Annie. Just fill me in. If it wasn't Lupine, could it have been another kind of Other? Feline? Werefolk? Vampire even?"

Annie shook her head. "Definitely not. Just the amount of blood left here on the scene rules out vamp. I mean, I'm a biologist, not a physician, and my anatomy classes were a long time ago, but I know enough to think this wasn't anything we're used to dealing with. Have a look."

Graham approached the woman and the body, being careful not to disturb anything that looked like tracks or to step in the pools of clotting blood that trailed like fingers of blackened crimson away from the corpse. Fiona hurried to follow, trying to ignore the uncomfortable sensation of once again having an angry and sullen Walker stalking behind in her shadow.

She stopped when Graham did, less than two feet

from the still figure. As she looked down at it, her first thought was that if she hadn't already been told it was human, she wouldn't necessarily have been able to tell. It looked as if it lay there in pieces, at least three or four large chunks, connected more by proximity than physiology. Something had torn through flesh and bone, tendon and sinew, leaving little recognizable behind. Fiona could see something that may once have been blue denim, now black in the dim light, and the gory, stringy clumps by Graham's left boot might have been human hair a few hours before. Now only assumption and optimism would attach that label.

Fiona blew out a deep breath and clenched her hands into fists to keep them from pressing betrayingly against her stomach. That organ pitched once, then clenched into a tight fist and retreated to huddle against her spine in protest. It wasn't really the blood or that gore that bothered her; it was the emptiness of this thing that used to be human. There was nothing left, like the soul saw the desecration of its former home and fled as far and fast as the wind could carry it. Usually, human spirits clung tenaciously to their bodies and the world they had lived in. That was why their world had so many ghost stories. But in this case, not even a thread of that consciousness remained. A mercy, probably. If Fiona had seen her own body so defiled, she might have turned tail, too.

"At first glance, I admit it does look like a Lupine or maybe a Feline kill. There are claw marks." Annie's voice seemed to fade in like a sound track that had been playing for a while before Fiona took notice. "But they're too large for any shifter I've ever heard of, let alone seen. At least eight inches long on average, although it looks like there are two smaller ones used less regularly. Here," she pointed where the throat should have been, "and here." Where the two largest chunks diverged, below the rib cage. "Anything with talons like that would have to be at least ten feet, minimum, and the biggest were I've ever heard stories about was just shy of nine."

Graham watched with a cool sort of detachment belied only by the fisting of his hands at his sides and the leap of muscle in his jaw as he clenched and unclenched his teeth. "Is anything missing?"

Annie shook her head. "Not that I could tell from a preliminary exam, but a trained medical examiner could say for sure. Even the uterus and the intestines look to be intact. Externalized, but intact. It's almost like parts were chewed or ripped to look like they'd been eaten, but this girl wasn't anyone's dinner. That makes the chances of this being a rogue Other kill pretty slim."

Fiona frowned and looked closer. Annie was right. Fiona could see the sausagey line of the intestines partially obscured by a ragged bit of cloth with the stomach draped half out of the gaping hole in the abdominal cavity. Her frown deepened. Predators favored the stomach as a source of vitamins and minerals that could be found in the partially digested meal of the prey. It was usually the first thing to be eaten, but it looked relatively undisturbed for having been mostly removed.

"Maybe something scared it off before it could feed?"

"I don't think so. The pattern of the wounds is wrong. If something were going to feed, it would have gone for the abdomen and stayed there till it was done, but these wounds here," Annie pointed to the remains of the face, "barely bled, which means they occurred after she was already dead and after the abdomen had already been opened."

Graham swore. "Then this definitely wasn't dinner."

Annie nodded. "It's like I said. It looks like whatever killed her wanted people to think she'd been partially eaten, but had no real interest in eating her. It's weird. As if someone was trying to mimic an Other kill."

Fiona peered closer at the exposed bottom of the rib cage and then glanced back at Annie. "You're sure nothing was missing?"

The other woman blinked at her, looking surprised. "As sure as I can be. It's messy, but I really think it's all here."

"What about the heart?"

"The chest cavity is the biggest intact part here. You can see that nothing went in through the ribs or the sternum."

"But what about something going in from below the ribs?"

Annie blinked again and raised her eyebrows. "I didn't even think to check that."

Hunkering down beside the corpse again, Annie pulled the sleeves of her already-spattered sweatshirt up with her teeth, bunching the fabric just above her elbows. Pressing one gloved hand against the body's chest for balance, she reached down to the space between the two pieces of torso with the other and guided her hand up through the rib cage, her brow furrowed in concentration.

"It's like someone carved a tunnel in here," she muttered, finally stopping when the inside of her elbow bumped up against rib bone. Her glasses slid down the bridge of her nose and she blew at a strand of hair that flopped in front of her face. "She's right. It's not here. The heart is gone. But I don't get why anything strong enough to tear all the way through the body wouldn't just reach in from the front and grab it. It would be a lot more efficient."

"Demons don't worry much about efficiency," Fiona sighed. She had really, really wanted to be wrong.

The female Lupine blanched. "A demon? You think this was done by a demon?" Her eyes flew to the alpha, seeking reassurance.

Graham nodded grimly. "It's possible. One was spotted in the city recently. We were hoping to be able to track it down before something like this happened."

"But there hasn't been a demon attack around here in . . . forever," Annie protested. "How did it get here? And I thought demons were basically stupid and brutal. How could it possibly have figured out a way to make its kill look like an Other attack?"

"Demons can only enter this world at the behest of a summoner," Fiona explained. "They have to be called. And once they've been called, they're bound to the summoner until they're released or banished. If a demon under the control of a summoner were ordered to kill someone before feeding, it would have to do exactly that, and splitting the body in half certainly did enough damage to qualify as demon fun time. Once the body was split, going after the heart from below was probably just easier."

"Not that I wanted it to be an Other," Graham said, "but the fact that it isn't makes things a hell of a lot more complicated."

"I don't know. Having one of our pack turn rogue during the middle of the negotiations would have been pretty messy, so maybe you should look on the bright side."

Graham ignored Annie's suggestion and looked back at Fiona. "What would it take for you to be able to pick up a trail for us?"

Fiona shrugged. "Not too much. The Fae are said to have an inherent connection to things demonic. It shouldn't take all that much energy for me to pick up on one, which I guess is why we won the Wars."

"Shouldn't? You're not certain?"

She made a frustrated face. "Like I said before, there hasn't been a demon sighting where I come from in a couple millennia. I'm working from what I've heard, not from personal experience, but I'm pretty sure that's more than you've got to work with."

"So what do you need to do?"

Fiona did a mental inventory and winced. "Well, I need to gather up some more energy. I've used everything I came from Faerie with, and I haven't been able to gather any since . . . since the last spell I cast."

"And you can only get the energy by taking it from someone like Walker?"

Oh, how Fiona wished Missy were there to give her mate another swift kick, this time a bit higher than the shin. "I don't take anything from someone like Walker. Fae don't steal energy from other folk; we take the energy that is manifest around us. The energy I got from kissing Mr. Grumpypants came from the kiss itself, not from him. It's fate's cruel joke that the attraction between us is the one energy source I seem to be able to tap into on this plane. I certainly didn't ask for it."

Graham frowned. "So you're not feeding off him?"

"Do I look like a vampire to you? Sheesh, are all werewolves so paranoid or is this just my lucky day?"

Annie muffled a laugh. Walker just watched her, his expression brooding.

"It's certainly not hers." Graham gestured to the

body. "So if you can help us find out what killed her and where we can find it without hurting anyone else, you're going to do it." He turned to Walker. "Kiss her."

"What?"

"Kiss her. Now."

"You've got to be kidding me!"

The alpha growled. "Do I look like I'm in a joking mood, Walker? I can make it an order if you prefer."

"Oh, please do," Fiona grumbled under her breath. "That would just do wonders for my ego."

"I don't have time to kick your ass over this," Graham said, his eyes narrowed and seeming almost to glow in the darkness around them. "Not that it wouldn't give me a great deal of pleasure, but every second we waste fighting about this is a second colder that the trail is growing, and a second longer that whatever killed this girl has to kill someone else. So shut the hell up and kiss the goddamned princess."

Fiona didn't have a chance to protest her amended title. With a muffled curse, Walker spun around, grabbed her by the arms, and yanked her into a furious, aggressive, bone-melting kiss that had her lighting up like Rockefeller Center at Christmastime.

She felt as if she'd turned into a giant lightbulb, with her head glowing bright enough to illuminate all of Central Park. It staggered her every single time that one touch of this obnoxious, stubborn, narrow-minded werewolf's lips on hers could turn her entire world upside down. She came from a long line of sidhe, the royal race of Faerie, and every single drop of blood in her veins should have been as fickle as theirs. The magic she felt with Walker should have amused her fleetingly and then left her ready to move on to greener pastures and other lips, but the idea had her stomach doing that unpleasant little dance again. She didn't want anyone else to kiss her, didn't want anyone else to touch her, didn't want anyone else's taste clinging to her lips and filling her mouth with honey and coffee and warm, rich male.

Damn him to the pit and back.

When his tongue finally finished marking its territory inside her mouth and his lips finally lifted from hers, Fiona knew she was glowing like a radioactive isotope and wearing the expression of a three-year-old at bedtime. She didn't even bother to glare at Walker, just spun on her heels and stomped two steps closer to the body, hunkering down beside it to get a better look.

It took a couple of minutes for her blood to cool from a boil to a simmer and for her to remember the simple revealing spell that would expose any traces of demon taint on the corpse. Taking a deep breath, she closed her eyes and willed the energy from the kiss into the correct shape and brushed it delicately over the dead woman and the ground around her. Fiona figured this poor human had been through enough and deserved at the last to be handled with care.

The indrawn breath and muttered curses around Fiona told her before she opened her eyes that the spell had worked. She looked up and bit back an oath of her own. The entire body crawled with the sickly green light of the demon taint. The wounds were the worst, seeming to writhe and heave with the remnants of the demon's energy. It had desecrated the woman and driven her soul so far from her body that not a shred of the person she had once been remained. She had become nothing more than hunks of meat glowing sickly in the darkness.

Fiona shuddered in revulsion at the knowledge of

what she needed to do. The idea of getting any closer to the demon's foul magic than she already had filled her mouth with bile, but she had no choice. They needed to know. Blowing out a slow, hissing breath, she quickly diverted some magic to shore up her inner shielding and reached out a hand to touch the contaminated flesh.

She heard a low, strangled groan and wondered vaguely if it came from her. The demon magic felt like slime and burned like acid. It flared at her touch, and for a few seconds Fiona could see a pattern of symbols burned into the corpse's skin. Swearing violently, she jerked her hand away and fell backward, landing inelegantly at Walker's feet.

"What the hell was that?" he demanded, reaching down to haul her to her feet.

"Demon marks. And an explanation for why Annie thought someone wanted to make this look like an Other kill."

Graham growled. "That really was deliberate?"

"Absolutely." Fiona looked around and found a stick about as thick as her finger and as long as her forearm. She turned to a bare patch of dirt and began to draw a series of lines and curves that looked like a kind of exotic and obscene alphabet.

"Since I'm not drawing with blood, I can show you the symbols without actually casting the spell. There are five altogether. These," she pointed out the first two, "signify the demon's name. It won't be its full name, and maybe not even part of its real name, but it will be a designation set up by the summoner to use for spell work. Real demon names have power over them. It's how the summoners control them, so the real name is spoken out loud when the spell is cast, but when the sigils are written down, symbols are substituted in their place. There are thousands of naming sigils, and I'm not familiar with what these particular ones translate as. I'll have to do a little research on it. The third and fourth ones are the command. The third is a death sigil, meaning that's the third command—to kill."

"And the fourth?"

"It means mimicry and deception. The demon was supposed to make whoever found this body think that an Other had made the kill." Fiona raised her eyes to the alpha. "Whoever did this knows about the negotiations and wants to see them fail."

"Shit," Graham swore.

"What about the last symbol? You said there were five."

Fiona looked back at the dirt instead of at Walker while she answered his question. "The last one is the signature of the summoner, but not the kind of signature you're thinking," she said before he could ask for a name. "It's not like it says, 'Bob Smith, Sorcerer, Chelsea.' It's a symbol, like a family seal. It doesn't have a name, just representative images. This one happens to depict power, death, fire, and air, which could mean absolutely anything about anybody."

"So then you're saying we have nothing to go on?" Graham shoved a hand through his hair and stalked off a little way, his frustration glowing nearly as brightly as the demon magic.

"No, I didn't say that. I'm not saying I know where to find the demon or its summoner right this very minute, but we do know more than we did half an hour ago, and we do have copies of the symbols. There are places I can look these up and get some more information. Even though the demon naming symbols are unique to each summoner, they do have to follow certain conventions in order to make them applicable enough that the demon has to obey. That ought to give us something."

"Barely."

Annie shrugged and peeled off her rubber gloves, turning them inside out as she did so. "It's better than the alternative, right?"

"Sure, the way steamed Brussels sprouts are better than boiled." Graham gritted his teeth and hooked his fingers together behind his neck. "How much time will you need to trace the symbols?"

Fiona winced. He had to ask. "I don't know. A couple of days, maybe. It depends on what sources I can find."

His eyes flashed. "Find them fast. Walker will help if he can." He glared at the other Lupine as if daring him to argue. "Whatever problems you two have with each other, you'll just have to set them aside and do your jobs."

Walker's own eyes flared fiery gold, but he only gave a curt nod.

"Fine," Fiona said. She wasn't sure it would be, but she was sure that Graham didn't want to hear that.

"Good. Walker, take her home. Both of you need to get some sleep. Annie, I need you to stay here with the body. I'll call Adam at the hospital and ask him to come straight here when his shift is over. He'll have the body brought to the morgue and do a proper autopsy. Maybe he can find something we missed."

"It's worth a try. At least he's actually an M.D. In this case, that trumps my Ph.D. Both of them."

Fiona glanced down when Walker's hand closed around her elbow.

"Come on," he said gruffly. "We're going home."

He didn't sound like he had to struggle to keep his

hands from wrapping around her throat, and Fiona eyed him suspiciously. This didn't strike her as the werewolf she'd come to know and suspect. She opened her mouth to voice her suspicion, then decided not to look this particular gift wolf in the mouth.

CHAPTER 13

THE TRIP BACK TO Walker's apartment passed nearly as quietly as it had the first time. When the front doors were locked securely behind them, he waved Fiona toward the stairs and followed her up to the living room. He could feel her curiosity. She didn't quite know what to make of his civility or his lack of hostility, but she seemed reluctant to test the waters and ask him. He was glad of that, because he really didn't want to have to explain himself. Not when the answer made him look like an even bigger jerk than she'd probably already labeled him. Because in the end, his mind hadn't changed as a result of her well-reasoned arguments or an ethical epiphany or even because the circumstances of being ordered to cooperate by his alpha made his attitude both unwieldy and vaguely ridiculous. His mind had changed because he couldn't get enough of the taste of her.

That last kiss had been a revelation for him. That

one hadn't taken him by surprise, and it hadn't been the princess in control. It had been his kiss from start to finish, and now that he'd taken it, all he could think about was taking more.

At the top of the stairs, she stopped and turned on him. He was two steps behind her, but the height difference still put her just below his eye level. She didn't seem to notice, though, judging by her glare and the way she crossed her arms protectively over her chest, as if she could ward him off.

"Okay, I've been a good little Fae all the way here, but I can't take it anymore. I want to know what in the blazes' names you're up to."

Walker tore his eyes away from the swell of her breasts rising above her forearms and affected a look of wide-eyed innocence. "Who? Me?"

Fiona didn't look like she was buying it. "Yes, you, Mr. Split Personality. The only times since we've met that you haven't been either yelling at me or glaring at me have been when I was out of ear- and eyeshot. This new restraint you seem to be practicing is making me uneasy."

"You heard Graham," he said, shrugging and manfully resisting the temptation to lean forward and lick that little furrow that appeared between her eyebrows when she scowled at him. He'd noticed it before, but when had it become so enticing? "We need to work together. I figured that might be a little tough if we kept acting like we hated each other."

"Hey, you were the one hating me, bub. I was just trying to take a little vacation and, failing that, to get back home in one piece. You're the one who had to go and get all aggressive about it."

"What can I say? I'm Lupine. Aggressive is programmed into the DNA."

Had that little flutter of pulse at the base of her throat always been there, begging for the stroke of his tongue? He felt his mouth begin to water.

"You're right. It's not so much the aggressive I have a problem with. It's the bad tempered."

"Right. Bad temper is bad."

His powers of intelligent speech were melting rapidly away from him. All he could think about now was the taste of her mouth, the feel of her skin. The way her slim, naked body had pressed snugly up against his the first time they kissed . . .

The fit of his jeans altered suddenly and he bit back a groan.

"Thanks for clarifying that complex point I was trying to make," she drawled. "Now that we both realize you've been acting like a werewolf with a wounded paw, maybe we can work something out to make sure it doesn't happen again?"

His hormones took that as a direct invitation and expressed their approval of the idea with a surge of energy and a low, rumbling growl. "Okay."

He was on her in one surging leap. Her feet swept out from under her as 250 pounds of excitable Lupine slipped free from a battered set of psychological fetters and took her to the nearest available flat surface, which happened to be a hardwood living-room floor. Walker thought he heard a squeak, but it barely registered above the roaring in his ears. Besides, he already had her mouth soundly beneath his, thus eliminating the possibility that she might make any sound other than the squeak. Though if he had his way, she'd be adding a few groans and whimpers to her repertoire real soon.

She tasted even better than he remembered, sweet and spicy. Exotically floral, enticingly hot. His tongue swept in to gather the flavors, and he felt the top of his head threaten to lift off like a moon lander. Christ, how had he resisted her for so long? She tasted like heaven and felt like home, and he must have been out of his mind not to spend the last day and a half with her pinned between him and something solid. Going forward, he wouldn't make the same mistake again.

His hands raced over her sleek curves, filling themselves with the warm, soft weight of her. He found himself wishing fiercely that he knew magic, so he could do that little trick of hers that had ticked him off before and just will their clothes away. Since he didn't have that kind of luck, he settled for grabbing hold of the collar of her shirt and turning it from a pullover to a buttonless button-down in two seconds flat. He felt as much as heard her indignant yelp, and he sure as hell felt the hands that fisted in his hair and yanked his head back, breaking their lip-lock and nearly giving him whiplash.

"Just a damn minute," she said, doing a very creditable impersonation of his own snarl. "Are you the same jerk who all but accused me of rape like three times in the last thirty-six hours? Are you the one currently pinning me to the floor and ripping off my clothes?"

Did she honestly expect him to understand words at this point? His overtaxed heart struggled to divert the flow of so much as a drop of blood north of his waistband, succeeding just enough for him to growl, "You can't tell?"

"Just trying to clarify."

She watched him carefully through narrowed violet eyes, but all he could think about was making them go misty and unfocused in pleasure. He shifted his weight, settling himself more solidly over her, just in case she got it into her head to try to get away. One denim-covered knee forced its way between hers, levering her thighs apart to let his hips nestle snugly against her heat. He rocked there just a little. Just enough to drive himself crazy and to feel her soften involuntarily beneath him. That was all the encouragement he needed. Growling, he set his lips to her throat and let her feel the edges of his teeth against her skin. They closed delicately over the pale, tender flesh, and he savored the taste of her heartbeat on his tongue.

"Clear," he grunted.

He felt a shiver chase across her skin and his heart jumped in satisfaction.

"So can I take that to mean you're not going to turn around in fifteen minutes or so and claim that this is all my fault?"

Ignoring the stinging in his scalp from her fingers still trying—unsuccessfully now—to pull him away from her, he ran his tongue over her skin and felt her shudder. Encouraged, his hands glided up her hips and under the baggy fabric of her torn shirt, brushing the two sides away until he could feel the warm silk of her skin under his fingers. As far as he was concerned, in fifteen minutes he planned to be balls deep inside her and very happy about it, so he managed another grunt to signify agreement.

"You won't accuse me of assaulting you or violating you or using you or anything along those lines?"

He could hear her getting breathless and almost purred in satisfaction. Sliding his hands up the ladder of her rib cage, he nearly wept in relief when his palms covered the soft swells of her breasts. He registered her involuntary gasp of pleasure and firmed his grip, gently kneading. Christ, she felt better than anything he'd ever touched in his entire life. He became convinced she felt better than anything any man had ever felt in all of recorded tactile history.

"You're not going to . . . oh!"

Figuring it couldn't be so bad to go bald, he moved his mouth lower, taking her clenched hands with him, and skimmed over the curve of her throat, the gentle rampart of her collarbone, and down the center of her chest. His tongue couldn't resist darting out to sample the flavors of her varied terrain.

"—to change your . . . mind?"

Her unsteady question had his beast beating its breast in pure male arrogance. Knowing his touch could affect her, excite her, bring her somewhere even close to the fever pitch of lust she had stirred in him, had him growling in triumph. Now that he had given himself permission to want her, the desire hit him like a tsunami, dragging him under and washing away every thought and every urge except for the need to get inside her.

"Because I'm not . . . going through that . . . again . . . *Walker*!"

He dragged his mouth over the valley of her breastbone and raced up toward her nipple, closing over it just in time to have her shouting his name.

God. He needed to hear that again. Now.

He felt another growl rumbling up in his chest and freed her nipple only to attack its twin with equal fervor. He drew on it strongly, tongue lashing, teeth scraping. He suckled her as if she gave him vital sustenance and he would die without this nourishment.

Her nipple had already drawn into a tight bead before he even touched it, and he could smell her desire, hot and female and potent. He knew she wanted as badly as he did. What he didn't know was how or why she kept talking when he could barely understand the English language, much less speak it. Clearly she needed to play a little catch-up. Scraping his teeth over the sensitive peak of her breast, he slid one hand down the gently curved plane of her stomach and beneath the elastic of her waistband.

"Because," she panted, persistent and breathless, now trembling from head to toe with need. "Because if you pull that shit one . . . more . . . time . . . I won't . . ." She whimpered. "I can't . . ." Moaned. "Can't . . ."

She broke off again on a shudder, and ruthless, Walker moved his hand the last critical inch, sliding over the smooth, bare skin of her mound, parting her tender flesh with long, eager fingers, and entering her on a swell of triumph and greed.

"Walker!"

Her body arched beneath him in a glorious bow of quivering woman. She poured into his palm, all sweet liquid fire and want. The desire fisting in his belly suddenly grew claws and dug in hard. Urgency turned into emergency and he ripped her last garment away, leaving it shredded on the wooden floor. Tearing his mouth from her breast, he reared up over her and hooked his hands under her knees, drawing them up and apart until she lay before him completely open. Completely female. Completely his.

He saw need on her face, felt it in the way her legs wrapped eagerly around his hips, and her hands slid over his chest to the fly of his jeans, fumbling it open and tugging impatiently at the stiff fabric.

He could give lessons in both stiff and impatient.

Snarling, he shoved her hands away and dealt with the final barrier himself, biting back a howl at the relief and torment of bare skin against bare skin.

He felt his lips pull back from his teeth, felt the ache of teeth giving way to fangs, and knew his eyes would be glowing a bright, inhuman amber.

"Now!" he bit out, not knowing if the words emerged

in English or in Lupine and not able to care. "Mine! Now."

Fiona opened her mouth, but whether she meant to agree or protest, Walker never found out. With a feral sound of possession he fit himself against her snug, slick entrance and thrust home, the dim echo of his triumphant howl ringing in his ears.

Fiona screamed.

At least, she thought she screamed, but it was hard to tell over the ringing in her ears and the eerie, Lupine howl of the man above her. Around her. Inside her.

Lady, he felt huge, stretching her, filling forgotten corners of her body and her soul until she thought she could feel her seams unraveling. It was glorious and enthralling and exciting and terrifying. Beyond any experience of her long, pleasure-filled life.

And if he ruined it later by accusing her of something devious, she might have to castrate him.

That was her last rational thought. After that, all she could do was feel. Feel the width of his body stretching hers, the pounding impact of his thrusts, the heat of his hard, masculine form moving powerfully over her.

Her head fell back, too heavy to support. Her hands gripped his shoulders, desperate to find a purchase in the madly spinning universe she had entered. He represented the only stable thing left, and she clung with all her might, twining her legs about his hips, locking her ankles together for better purchase. Her hips cradled his thrusts for a few short, mind-blowing seconds before her control snapped. She went wild beneath him, writhing and bucking, desperate to have him harder, deeper, faster, more. She wanted everything he could give her, and then she wanted him to give more.

He didn't seem to have any problem with that. His big, hard body vibrated with tension and excitement, propped up on the hands he had planted beside her shoulders. Less to spare her his weight, she thought, and more to give him leverage to thrust. If she'd been able to pull her nails out of his back, she'd have applauded the decision. Instead, she just pulled him closer and whimpered her approval.

Goddess, would she ever have enough of him? She couldn't imagine it, couldn't summon up the memory of what it had felt like not to have him inside her. Everything past, everything future, everything around had ceased to exist, and there was only Fiona and Walker and the ferociously building tension coiling inside them both.

She struggled for air, struggled for breath, struggled for leverage to lift her hips harder against him, to take him deeper. On a strangled growl, she felt his muscles tighten further, felt him shifting, reaching down to grasp her hips and lift her higher. He inched forward, reset his knees against the floorboards, and braced her against his thighs, taking away the last of her leverage.

She lay there, spread before him like a banquet. Her hands slipped from his shoulders to flop uselessly to the floor. Air eluded her lungs. He had her completely at his mercy, until it seemed that even her ability to draw breath, to move, to live, to be, depended on her lover's whim.

He shifted, the hands on her hips pushing her away with aching slowness. She felt him slipping away, sliding from her body, and made a noise of panic and distress. Her hands reached out, slapping at his, fighting to stop his retreat and keep him inside her. He ignored the mild annoyance and slid out, out, out, until only the tip remained, hugged tight by her liquid warmth.

She heard a pitiful mewing sound and wondered vaguely if it could have come from her. It wouldn't matter if it had. She needed this man more than she needed her next breath, needed the filling, stretching presence of his body inside her. Completing her. She would beg if that was what it took. Pride didn't matter compared to the heat and wonder and glory of mating her body with his.

She shuddered, wound tight and frantic. Forcing her eyes open, she gazed hazily up at him, fighting to focus. His face was set in hard lines, all planes and angles etched by control and power and lust. In that harsh frame, his eyes blazed so brightly she could have sworn she felt the flames licking her skin. The light in them burned gold, tipped with red, inhuman and unholy and beautiful. She wanted to drown in them, to burn in them and rise again like a phoenix.

"Walker," she gasped, desperate and trembling, "please! Stars! *Please!*"

He made her wait, one breathless, aching moment that felt like eternity with his body poised at her entrance and the fire of his eyes consuming her. His fingers tightened, digging into the flesh of her hips, biting and bruising and claiming. Slowly, deliberately, his head lowered, moving closer until his blinding eyes hovered just inches from hers. She felt his breath hot and moist against her skin, and she shook with need and passion.

His lips curled back, exposing a glistening length of fang, and when he spoke, his voice sounded rough and feral, rumbling with aggression and wild with magic. His one word marked her as surely as a brand, and she welcomed it with dizzy relief.

"Mine."

He thrust home, deep and hard. Fiona's entire body arched like a drawn bow and she screamed, a high, keening wail that shook her and threatened the glass in the windows. Her whole world exploded, a detonation that reverberated the heavens and left her limp, drained, and shaking. She had no strength left, could only watch while the man above her threw back his head and howled. She felt him pouring into her, filling her with heat and magic as his ancient, primitive cry of life and claiming echoed to the ends of the universe.

CHAPTER 14

IF WALKER FOUND THE guy who'd snuck up behind him and whacked him with a slab of marble, he'd give him a talking-to. Just as soon as he remembered how to speak. Or move. And just as soon as he managed to figure out how it had happened.

He'd just taken a Faerie princess as his mate.

Just thinking it made his stomach sink and his heart rise. His mind . . . he didn't know what it was doing. It had to realize how ridiculous it sounded, the idea of a beta werewolf with a royal sidhe for a mate. It made about as much sense as a beta fish mated to a bald eagle. Unfortunately, Fate didn't seem inclined to care.

Swallowing a groan, Walker turned his head to bury his face in his mate's slick, bare neck. The scent that had tortured him the first time he'd seen her filled his head with exotic spices and flowers. Now it smelled less like torment and more like home. Unable to resist, he parted his lips and nibbled the sweet, salty skin.

She twitched, skin jumping and heating at his lightest touch. Maybe this mate thing really did offer some advantages.

Fiona groaned and let her heels thump to the floor. "Are we dead?"

Walker rocked his hips, savoring the feel of her lingering quivers around his still-erect cock. "Doesn't seem like it."

She didn't open her eyes, but her brows furrowed. "You sure? What about rigor mortis?"

Walker's head shot up and he stared down at her, aghast.

The laughter started somewhere in the vicinity of her belly and boiled to the surface like a geyser until he couldn't do anything else but join in. He collapsed back on top of her in a big, boneless heap of satisfied Lupine and savored the feel of her pressed skin to skin against him. Well, against all of him above the line of his jeans, which still hugged his thighs. That was as far down as he'd gotten them before he'd fallen on her like a slavering beast.

Grumbling, he tried to maneuver his hands down far enough to get rid of the offending fabric, but he kept getting distracted somehow. The feel of her damp, flushed skin and the curves and valleys of her limp body seemed a lot more interesting than a pair of stubborn jeans.

"Okay, so maybe we're not dead," Fiona managed. She sounded breathless, but he wasn't sure if that was because of what he was doing to her or because she hadn't gotten her breath back yet from what they'd already done. "But I'm still pretty sure that all my nerve endings below the neck are at least comatose."

He grinned. "Let's just check and see."

"Whoa there, Silver Chief." She planted her hands against his shoulders and pushed, trying to dislodge his mouth from the sensitive underside of her breast. "Even the first string gets to take a breather when the buzzer rings."

His tongue slid up the plump curve and circled her ruched nipple, leaving a trail of heat and moisture. "I think I felt the earth move, but I don't remember hearing any bells, Princess. I'd say we've still got some game to play before halftime."

"I should have known better than to try a sports metaphor with a man." She pushed harder, and he just ignored her harder. Yet more proof that they were meant for each other. Fate knew its stuff on this mating business.

"Walker, come on. Reality is beginning to intrude here. My butt is getting cold."

Sighing, Walker released her nipple with a pop and gave it one last affectionate lick. "All right. I'll get us to the bedroom, but it's going to take me a minute. My legs have to grow back first. And once they do, I'll have to get these damned jeans all the way off."

She opened her eyes, violet gems sparkling at him through the inky veil of lashes. "I could make a suggestion," she said slowly, "but it's the kind of thing that would have made you accuse me of treachery, murder, and abusing kittens a few hours ago."

He winced, and she could have sworn she saw him blushing again. "Okay, I should probably apologize for the way I acted earlier. But in my defense, I never actually accused you of abusing kittens."

Fiona paused and searched his expression. "True, but I figured you'd forgotten that one."

Walker sighed. "You're not making this apology thing easy for me, Princess."

"As far as I can tell, you haven't done it yet."

"I was hoping you wouldn't notice that," he quipped, but when he looked at her, his golden eyes were warm and sincere and his expression was open and serious. "I'm sorry I acted like a wolf with a sore paw earlier," he said quietly. "And I'm sorry I was a jerk when we met. It's just . . . you scared me, Princess, barreling into my life with a demon on your tail like that. And you keep scaring me every time you use that courage of yours to put yourself at risk, whether it's at the hands of a demon, or your uncle, or even a stubbed toe."

She felt her heart flutter, but that didn't mean she was going to let him off the hook so easily. "I don't recall deliberately putting myself in any danger, Tobias. The demon came after me, not the other way around. And I'm perfectly capable of handling my uncle. Probably more capable than you."

"I know that." Walker made a face. "But knowing it doesn't make me happy about it. I'm Lupine, Princess. That means I can get a little protective sometimes. Not because I don't think you can take care of yourself, but because I want to do it for you."

"I never asked you to protect me."

He snorted a laugh. "Neither did my sister, but that didn't stop me from scaring off a couple of her dates when she was a teenager."

"Oh, I'm sure you were just charming." Fiona rolled her eyes and gave him a suitably dirty look, but she could feel her muscles relaxing. It might not be the prettiest apology she'd ever received, but it would do. For now.

"I thought so."

She looked up into his grinning face and laughed.

"Does that mean I'm forgiven?"

"That depends. Do you still think I was trying to

suck out your soul in front of my uncle's apartment building?"

This time Walker rolled his eyes. "Of course not. That's the reason I was apologizing."

"Well, in that case . . ." Fiona freed one hand from his shoulder, bringing her fingers into view for them both and watching as sparks danced from tip to tip. "My battery seems to be holding a decent charge for the moment. I could take care of those jeans for you. But you'd have to promise not to yell at me about it afterward."

He raised an eyebrow and met her challenging gaze. "Me? Yell? Surely you jest."

Fiona snorted. "Oh, sure. What could I possibly have been thinking? You're so even tempered and restrained."

He rocked his hips against her, his grin wicked. "Well, maybe not restrained."

"Watch it. I'm armed, buddy. I can always forget the jeans and turn you into a toad."

"I don't know. That sounds pretty kinky. You really into the amphibian thing?"

It was the wriggling eyebrows that had her laughing and smacking him lightly on the shoulder. "Jerk."

He ducked and chuckled, "Hey, sounds to me like I'm the vanilla one in this relationship. I wouldn't go casting stones if I were you. One might come back and nick you somewhere tender." He pinched a fingerful of her waist, then soothed the sting with a tickle.

Fiona giggled and squirmed. "Okay, fleabag! You asked for it."

Pulling her arms into her sides to protect her most vulnerable spots, she tucked her chin into her chest and flicked her fingers down the length of their joined bodies.

Walker felt a flash of warmth and a tingle passing

over his skin. The room around him seemed to spin and melt and all at once the hard wooden floor gave in beneath him. Caught off guard, he toppled forward onto the princess, twisting to keep his weight from crushing her into the . . . mattress.

Lifting his head, he looked around his bedroom and down the length of his bare legs. Beside him, the princess settled herself back against the pillows and folded her hands over her belly, her expression smug and satisfied. Walker turned to look at her and saw her face, but he also smelled the subtle hint of nervous tension under her confident façade.

"Huh," he said, leaning back beside her and draping one arm across her hips. "That's kinda handy, but have you ever considered a short trip to Tahiti?"

Her eyes searched his face for a second; then the tension eased out of her and her smile curved wickedly. "Sorry, sweetheart, but you haven't earned Tahiti yet."

Growling, he rolled back on top of her. "So I have to earn my rewards, do I?"

"Absolutely." She looped her arms around his neck and pulled him closer to her. "And I'm a hard taskmaster."

He felt his eyes flare and leaned down to take her mouth. "Not half as hard as I am."

CHAPTER 15

F<small>IONA</small> <small>ADMITTED THAT THE</small> cat-in-the-cream-pitcher smile on her face might look a bit out of place in a hospital morgue, but she couldn't help it. The expression had bloomed there the night Walker finally took her to bed—or floor—and she hadn't managed to shake it in the thirty-six hours since. Maybe because she had spent most of them in the exact same position that started the smiling. She blamed everything on the werewolf, and if she had been her aunt, she'd probably have ended up knighting him for it.

She didn't know quite what had worked the transformation from grouchy ball of furry frustration to attentive and energetic lover, but she didn't plan to launch a protest. Not when she was so clearly benefiting from the change.

The past day and a half in Manhattan had been perfect, exactly the sort of vacation she needed. She spent nearly all of that time under, over, or in front of but always very much around Tobias Walker. To be honest, it amazed her that she could still walk, and she had to give thanks for that to the rumored and very clearly limber nymph who lurked in her family tree.

Once Fiona's reluctant werewolf got over his objections to touching her, he made up for lost time with flattering gusto. She had the marks to prove it—faint fingertip bruises on her hips where he'd held her against him, scattered constellations of hickeys and love bites from shoulders to toes, and the dark, shiver-inducing bruise where his teeth had sunk into the curve where her neck met her shoulder the first time he'd poured into her from behind.

Her grin widened, turned soft and misty, just thinking about it.

Not a single one of those proverbial battle scars hurt. She hadn't even noticed them being made. Her skin had always bruised easily, often from bumping into things so lightly she couldn't remember it later, and she knew very well that Walker would be aghast to think he'd actually hurt her. Most of the marks stayed hidden under her clothes, and the others she concealed with a small glamour because Walker had complained they made it look like she'd tangled with some sort of animal, which she very happily had. The only one he hadn't fussed over was the one on her neck, but her long hair covered that one well enough. After their time together, she was willing to cover the marks up for his sake, but when they went home, she planned to look at them all again and relive how each one had happened. Or maybe she'd forget reliving anything and just convince him to give her a whole new set.

The mist in her grin faded, turning bright and wicked

instead. Walker glanced over at her, his eyebrow quirking at her expression, but she just blew him a kiss and focused her attention back on the man who had just joined them in the cool, sterile room. The sooner they heard the news they'd been called out to hear, the sooner they could go home and rip each other's clothes off.

Was it wrong to be entertaining lustful thoughts while surrounded by surgical instruments with refrigerated corpses resting in the next room?

"Thanks for coming all the way down here," the man was saying as he shook Walker's hand. "The alpha told me this was a priority situation and that you were in charge, so I tried to get through as fast as possible. But I didn't want to miss anything, either."

Walker nodded. "We appreciate you taking the time, Dr. Forester. With your schedule, it can't be easy."

Adam grinned. No more than thirty at the outside, he stood about half a head shorter than Walker and had the lean, wiry build of a runner. Or maybe just of someone who worked like a dog and barely had time to eat. Either way, his green scrubs bagged on him, and his battered running shoes looked as if they'd already covered a few million miles. His brown hair curled in chaotic disorder and badly needed cutting. It kept flopping down in front of a pair of appealing hazel-green eyes, and judging by its rumpled appearance, Fiona figured he made combing it back with his fingers something of a habit. He really was an adorable kid, and she couldn't resist returning his grin.

"Aw, sheesh. Call me Adam. Please," he laughed. "You've known me since I was still cutting my teeth on other people's kills, and I've looked up to you and the alpha almost as long. Besides, the 'M.D.' after my name is so new it still squeaks when I walk too fast."

Fiona laughed. "Oh, I thought that was just your sneakers on the linoleum." She extended her hand. "But it's still nice to meet you."

Adam chuckled and made a move to shake her hand, but Walker stepped swiftly to the side, almost accidentally nudging Fiona's arm to the side. Surprised, she glanced up at the werewolf beside her, but his eyes were fixed on Adam, their formerly friendly expression now turned cold and possessive and menacing. Walker nudged her another step to the side, his hand reaching up and brushing her hair back to rest with clear possession on her shoulder. He didn't say anything, but it looked like he didn't have to. Adam froze, glanced at Walker's hand, and shoved his own into his pockets. He also took a healthy step backward.

"Ah, yeah. Thanks. Um, why don't you step this way and take a look at what I found?" He turned on his heel and hurried over to one of the two autopsy tables in the center of the room.

A cloth had been draped over a still figure, and Adam pulled it aside as they approached. The girl from the park lay sandwiched between the cold steel of the table and the stark blue-white cotton of the thin sheet. The covering concealed the worst wound, the one that had severed her all the way through the middle, and her body had been cleaned of the blood and debris they had seen the other night. Two new pink lines ran inward from each of her shoulders, but compared to the demon wounds, the Y incision looked neat and clinical and bore precise lines of suturing.

Fiona felt a stirring of sympathy for the human. She couldn't have been much more than twenty, and Fiona doubted she could have done anything to deserve her fate. Somewhere, someone was already missing her and would continue to miss her for years to come.

Adam put the width of the table between himself and Walker and took a few more steps over to the wall behind him to flip the switch on a light board. A series of X-ray films already hung in a neat row across it.

He cleared his throat. "Now, ah, Annie said she, ah . . . she already gave you a preliminary summary, so you know that the body is intact with the exception of the heart." He gestured to one of the films and struggled visibly to focus on something other than Fiona and Walker and the banked but warning flare in the beta Lupine's eyes. "The X-rays confirmed that it was all there and we weighed and measured everything during the examination, so I can confirm everything else was normal. She was a healthy girl until she met the demon. A broken ulna suffered sometime in the past, probably when she was just a kid, but it healed well with no surgical interventions."

Fiona didn't bother to try to make out the hair-thin line the doctor pointed out on the X-ray. She just let him find his rhythm and tell them what he knew. And she made a note to herself to smack Walker upside the head for his ridiculous spoiled-two-year-old impression later. This might be the first time she'd ever had an affair with a Lupine, but she knew well enough not to undermine his power in front of a lower-ranking pack member. She'd do that in private where she could really rip him a new one.

"The films don't show us any perimortem fractures, so whatever kind of struggle she put up, it didn't lead to any broken bones, and the thing that killed her didn't get its kicks from snapping them like toothpicks. I'm not sure that's much comfort, but I suppose it's something." Adam flipped off the light board and moved back to the table, carefully pulling back the sheet to expose the girl's battered body. "She does have some signs that she fought back. There are defensive wounds on the palms and sides of her hands. The ones on the palms generally come from the attempt to ward off blows." He held his hands up, palms out, to demonstrate. "And the ones on the sides look like they came from banging against something hard and rough. Think the damsel in distress pounding uselessly away at Godzilla's thick hide."

Fiona leaned closer and saw the cuts as well as some bruising on the outer edge of the girl's hand.

Adam picked up the other and pulled her fingers back gently. "We scraped some debris from under her fingernails as well. In a normal murder case, that would be sent to the police lab and they'd analyze it for DNA, but, well, I don't think that will be helpful in this case."

"No. Not really." Walker's voice sounded nearly as cold as the temperature in the room, but now his grim expression was for the dead girl.

"You already know it was a demon attack from what Annie and Fi—er . . . from what the princess told you," Adam continued. "And the removal of the heart makes that pretty obvious. It wasn't done neatly, but it was efficient. The thing just reached up into the chest cavity and gave a good tear. Her aorta looked like it had been snapped like a rubber band. Other than that, the rest of the wounds are pretty standard slashes and gouges. They aren't that dissimilar to what we'd expect to find in any case of a predatory attack by a large, powerful animal with really sharp claws."

Walker's scowl deepened. "Annie already told us all of that. I was hoping you'd be able to give us something more."

"Well . . ."

The young man hesitated, and Fiona had to bite her

tongue to keep from murmuring something reassuring and reaching out to pat his hand.

"What is it?"

Adam pulled the sheet back up over the girl. "Annie mentioned that there was a theory about the demon trying to make the kill look like a Lupine or a Feline attack."

"There were some symbols that seemed to indicate it was possible."

"Then I think you ought to see this." Frowning, Adam walked over to the far wall of the morgue with its rows of metal drawers and pulled one open. "He came in this morning just before dawn. I didn't find out until I came on shift, and even then I didn't think much of it until I talked to Annie again."

Walker and Fiona moved closer and looked down at a second body. This one topped the girl from the park by a couple of decades and had a lot less hair. About fifty, balding, slightly overweight around the middle, the man looked pale and still and oddly peaceful. His chest sported the same autopsy Y incision as the girl, but other than that, Fiona could see no obvious wounds. Certainly nothing to indicate this was another death meant to look like a werebeast had done it.

Then Adam turned the man's head to display a ring of mottled bruising and two neat, symmetrical puncture wounds on the side of his neck. Walker swore softly but creatively.

"I was going to just go with standard procedure on this," Adam continued, looking up at the beta, his face serious. "You know, when a death comes in that looks Other related, we make sure an Other on staff does the autopsy, and then we report it to the Council for investigation so that they can take care of it without causing a panic among the humans. But this seemed odd."

"Why?" Fiona asked. "Are the fang marks the wrong size? Because it looks like a vampire bite to me."

"No, it looks just like a vampire attack, and the body had less than a pint of blood in it at autopsy."

"But?"

"But look at the bruising." Adam pointed to the discolored skin and traced the uneven edge of the mark. "Vampires rarely leave contusions around the bite. There are theories that the same properties in their saliva that help seal the wounds when they're done feeding on a living donor also help to prevent bruises. And even in the few instances when bruising has been recorded, it didn't look like this. This is too irregular. It doesn't look like it was caused by a human-shaped mouth. If it were, it would look more like a hickey. This almost looks like the guy was punched and then bitten."

Fiona thought of the love bites she carried beneath her clothes and had to agree. The bruising around the dead man's bite wound looked nothing like a hickey.

"Are you saying this wasn't a vamp kill?" Walker asked, looking very unhappy. "What else could it have been? If it were a demon kill, the heart would be missing. Demons always consume the hearts of their human victims."

"No, the heart is there," Adam said. "That's why I was going to treat it like a vamp kill. Some fanged idiot got carried away and had a little too much to drink. But the heart isn't . . . normal."

"What do you mean?"

"I mean that the average human heart weighs about three hundred twenty-five grams at autopsy. That can vary depending on disease, age, and weight of the decedent, but it's a round number. This guy's heart weighed seventeen grams."

Fiona's stomach jumped. "How is that possible?"

"I have no idea. It was like a shell that had all the contents removed. At first I thought it might be a side effect of the blood loss, but it's just not possible. Heart is all muscle. Even with all the blood gone, there should still have been more than seventeen grams' worth of water and fiber and solid tissue."

"Why the hell didn't you report this to the Council the second you discovered it?" Walker roared.

"I was going to report it at the end of my shift along with any other suspicious deaths or injuries the way we always do. There are diseases and conditions that can result in decreased heart weight, so the idea that a demon had sucked it dry wasn't really the first thing that occurred to me."

Damn it. It might not have occurred to Adam, but it was definitely occurring to Fiona. She sighed and tugged on Walker's arm. "Step back."

He scowled down at her. "What? Why?"

"Step back," she repeated. "You, too, Adam. I'm going to see if there's any demon taint on the body. He's been gone a lot longer than the girl was when I checked her, but we might get lucky."

Walker didn't look happy, but he did take a step back, and better yet, he ordered the young doctor to do the same.

With all the energy Fiona had gathered up in Walker's bed, she didn't need to tap into anything else to repeat the revealing spell she had used on the girl's body. Once again, Fiona brushed a layer of magic over the still form and held her breath.

This time she didn't see the bright glow of sigils and marks but a faint, sickly shimmer like a cobweb of slime wrapped around the dead man's neck and chest. The demon's taint had faded too much for her to make out the sigils with any clarity, but she didn't need to read them to know that a demon had killed this human as well.

She considered using one of Walker's curses but opted for a traditional Fae one instead and stepped away from the drawer. "It was a demon. I can't tell if it was the same one that killed the girl, but I'm inclined to think no. The modes of death were too different. Even if the summoner were to order a demon to make a death look like it was caused by something other than a demon, you can't make a demon that attacks that savagely go so completely against its nature that it won't at least take a few swipes."

Adam looked at her for the first time since Walker's earlier unspoken threat. "You mean there are two demons out there killing humans and trying to make it look like Others are doing it?"

"That's what it looks like."

"Holy shit!"

"You might say that." She glanced at Walker, who looked like he either had just swallowed a mouthful of arsenic or was planning on forcing it down someone else's throat. "I definitely think it's more than one demon, but that doesn't necessarily mean more than one summoner. I haven't heard of one magic user strong enough to control multiple demons anytime since the Wars, but it is possible. And somehow it makes more sense than multiple demons *and* multiple summoners. That just smacks of conspiracy theory."

"Whatever it smacks of is irrelevant," Walker said, his voice low and tight and vibrating with anger. "We need to tell the Council about this." He took Fiona by the elbow and began guiding her from the room, still speaking to Adam. "If anything else comes through these doors that has so much as a hair out of place, call me immediately, you understand? Otherwise I'll be doing a few autopsies of my own, but I can't guarantee I'll wait for you to be all the way dead. The princess and I are going back to the club."

"Vircolac?" Fiona sighed. "My home away from home. Let's hope that this time I don't get abandoned or lectured. It would make a nice change of pace."

Graham took the news about as well as Walker expected, which meant that his bellow would have the police department in Albany fielding noise-disturbance calls for the rest of the night. Even the normally stabilizing influence of his luna didn't seem to be helping keep him calm. Walker had to wait until the walls stopped shaking before he managed to get the rest of the story out, and even then, Graham jumped in swinging before the last syllable fell.

"What the hell was the puppy waiting for?" he roared, his expression dark as storm clouds. "Did there have to be a fucking massacre before he thought we'd be interested in what was going on?"

"Walker already explained that," Missy said. Her voice stayed serene and quiet, but no one could mistake the steel in it. "He didn't think it was that unusual, and you need to calm down."

"I'm about as fucking calm as I'm likely to get in the middle of a goddamned crisis."

"Which makes it a particular relief that you passed on the opportunity to head the Council," Rafael said. He and Tess sat on the sofa in Graham's office at Vircolac. They had rushed over in response to Walker's succinct and urgent cell-phone call and arrived at the club hot on Walker's and Fiona's heels. "The last thing they need to hear at the moment is your panicked rantings."

"No," snarled the alpha, "the last thing they need to hear is that Others around the city are slaughtering defenseless humans. That should make our negotiations really pleasant."

"They won't hear any such thing, because no one is going to tell them."

Graham shoved a hand through his hair and looked about half a step away from yanking it all out by the roots. Just to keep his mind off his pain. "Right, because a series of gruesome and suspicious deaths will be so easy to keep out of the human public's eye. Damn it, the occasional death we can handle. We have our bad seeds the same as the humans, and the fact that we choose to deal with them ourselves rather than turning them over to the human authorities doesn't mean we're any more tolerant of murder. But a series of deaths isn't occasional, and it couldn't come at a worse time. If the human delegation hears about this, the talks are over."

Tess snorted. "Why would they get suspicious? This is New York City. People die in gruesome and unexplained ways at least five times every day."

"Not at the hands of Others, they don't."

"And they didn't this time, either," Rafe pointed out calmly and decidedly. "Thanks to Fiona, we already know that these humans died at the hands of a demon. Others aren't to blame, and we can say that with certainty to anyone who might become concerned. You're right that alerting the human delegation would lead to nothing more than broken negotiations and a frenzied witch hunt. But that fails to solve our problem. We need to find the demon."

"Demons. Plural." Fiona stepped out from behind Walker's shoulders. He hadn't realized that he'd put himself between her and Graham when the other Lupine had begun shouting. It was a reflex to protect his mate. "I'm pretty certain we're looking for more than one demon. The drastically different manners of death make a single demon unlikely. They're too much creatures of instinct for one to show such a lack of restraint with one victim and such a great deal of it with the other."

Graham swore again, earning a stern glare from his wife and a resigned sigh from the head of the Council.

"If that is true, then the situation is doubly urgent," Rafe said. "What have you been able to find out so far?"

Walker watched a blush stain Fiona's cheeks. They hadn't exactly spent a lot of time working the last day or so, but Fiona had done what she could. Bemoaning her lack of Faerie's rich store of materials on demonology, she had wrestled her way out of his bed every so often to try different spells to help her decipher the sigils she'd recorded or to analyze the demon's energy. She hadn't had much luck, but she'd persisted. Which led to Walker feeling obliged to help her recharge the energy she used in her continued attempts.

"I haven't found much," she admitted, and her voice dragged him out of his fond memories with a jolt. "Whoever designed the sigils didn't want to be traced. He did a good job covering his tracks. I might have better luck if I had my aunt's library to refer to, but I don't see that happening anytime soon. I'm going to have to start asking around summoners here in the city, and I was trying to avoid that. If I ask the wrong person, word might get back to the one we're looking for. And then he could either bolt and do a disappearing act, or escalate the attacks."

Rafe looked at his mate. "The only one of us who has dealt directly with a demon and come out smiling is my lovely wife."

Tess shook her head. "I don't think I'm going to be much help on this one. The stuff I know about demons is just adhesive-bandage witchery. Self-defense stuff and pretty useless against all but the minor characters. The fact that the one in Connecticut responded to the binding I cast had more to do with luck than anything else." She offered her astonished mate a sweet, disarming grin. "Sorry I forgot to mention that to you, baby."

Rafe growled something in return and Walker saw his future of confronting a reckless and charming mate flash before his eyes. The disturbing thing was that he didn't find the concept unappealing.

"Yeah, well, you can yell at me about that later." Tess dropped her endearing expression and turned back to Fiona. "The good news is that while I can't help you trace the demon with magic, I think there might be a way to get the information you need from Faerie."

Fiona's eyes widened. "The gate has reopened?"

"Not quite. I said get something *from* Faerie, not get you *to* Faerie."

"What do you mean? If the gate is sealed, I won't be able to send so much as a split pea through it."

"No, but we do have other contact with your people than just the gates."

Rafe broke in with a glare for his better half. "What my incredibly foolhardy and about-to-learn-the-meaning-of-chastised wife means is that we occasionally need to reach someone at the Faerie courts without traveling all the way there. Since your aunt also likes to have the option of tossing accusations our way without having to leave her own borders, she gave us a gift."

"It's a . . ." Tess paused and pursed her lips. "Well, actually, I'm not quite sure of the appropriate descriptor. . . ."

Rafe winced. "Let's go with . . . 'stained-glass,' er, 'piece' . . . shall we, love?"

"Why the hell didn't you mention this earlier?" Graham demanded. "We might have been able to find the demon by now, and that male human might still be alive."

Tess stiffened. "I didn't mention it because I'm fairly certain the queen is not going to be happy with any number of the things we're proposing to tell her, Graham, so I was trying to spare us all the pain caused by opening up a third front in this little war we're fighting."

The excitement faded from Fiona's face, and Walker suppressed the urge to cuddle her.

"She's right," Graham said. He still got headaches from the last fit the Faerie queen had thrown at the mortal Others. "I'm not sure which would be more disastrous—letting the demon ruin the negotiations, thereby causing the humans to make war and destroy all living Other kind, or telling Mab about the princess's trip and Dionnu's presence at the summit. Either one pretty much spells doom from where I see it. Knowing Mab, she might let the demons and humans destroy us anyway, just to teach us a lesson."

Again, Walker found himself trying to shield his new mate from his alpha. Walker didn't like the tone Graham had put into calling her "the princess." If anyone was going to call Fiona by a nickname she hated, it sure as hell wasn't going to be anyone but Walker.

Shit. He was losing his mind.

"I don't see that we have much choice." Fiona ignored his strange restlessness and spoke with determination. "If we want to find this summoner and stop the demons he controls from killing any more humans, we need to move quickly. And we need all the help we can get."

Rafe nodded. "I agree, but it will not do us any good if we make up time but end up in a pitched battle against Faerie."

"Can you think of a better solution?" No one said anything, but everyone looked at least somewhat uncomfortable. Fiona nodded. "Right. Then I think you'd better show me this gift of Mab's."

CHAPTER 16

Fiona laughed when she saw it.

The gift had probably been meant to hang in front of a large window where light could shine through the myriad panes of colored glass and cast bright, vibrant pools of color around the room. Thank the stars the Others had been too smart for that. Instead, the two-by-three-foot piece hung inside a wooden cabinet in a small study on the second floor of Vircolac like some kind of guilty secret. The gilt frame around the monstrosity could easily have dated back to the days of the human king Louis XIV, but Fiona would have dated its origins to the Early Bad Taste period.

The edges of the glass disappeared into a rectangular wooden frame so ornately decorated, she almost expected it to tear the huge armoire down with its weight. Trailing vines twisted and clung, sprouting berries here and there like a hideous example of plant food gone wrong. Winged cherubs beamed maniacally down from each of the four corners, pudgy arms pulling back on intricately decorated bows. Their arrows pointed straight at anyone foolish enough to stand in front of the blinding gilded abomination. But worse than any of the sins of the frame was the image it surrounded.

Some evil artistic antigenius had used the same medium as the glorious rose window at Chartres to depict the stomach-churning image of Shakespearean fairies in midfrolic. Little winged creatures with faces like trolls and limbs like toothpicks gamboled around the edges of what looked like it was supposed to be a sylvan glade. A deformed and violently blue stream flowed across the foreground, and at the center of the scene a hideously blond fairy in a crown and a toga stood surrounded by the glowing nimbus usually reserved for human saints.

"Damn. One of you must have really pissed her off."

"Yeah, we figured that out." Tess guided Fiona until she stood right in the path of those little golden arrows about three feet from the surface of the blindingly bad artwork. "Actually, it reminds me that I wanted to ask you when Mab's birthday is. I have this lovely macramé toilet paper cover I think she'd just adore."

"There is a little charm she told us to use to make the glass active," Rafe said. He and the others stood against the inner wall of the study, well out of sight— or maybe firing range—of the magical device. "I didn't think you'd need it. You've probably done this sort of thing before, right?"

"I think I can figure it out."

Fiona took a deep breath, focused her attention on the glass, and gritted her teeth. Not because of any nerves about her ability to communicate through her aunt's gift to the Others, but because when Mab answered her call, she'd probably end up wishing she'd stopped along the way and picked up a full-body suit of Kevlar. Or maybe asbestos.

There had to be a museum in this city with a nice little set of steel-plate armor, right?

She twitched a little when Walker appeared just behind her and laid his large, warm hands on her shoulders.

"Need a little energy boost?" His breath tickled her ear and the solid, steady presence of him relaxed her enough that she could feel her muscles softening. That was good. It would help her absorb the impact of the coming blows. "The peanut gallery over there would get an eyeful, but it's all for a good cause, right?"

Like she needed him to kiss her. Just the sound of his low, rumbling voice was enough to have sparks dancing along her skin. It made her remember how he sounded when he was naked beside her. Above her. Inside her.

She shivered.

"Is that a yes?"

"Thanks, *mo jáell*," she said. He wasn't really "her wolf," but nerves made her grateful for his support. "But I think I can take it from here."

He brushed her hair away from her neck and leaned down to press a kiss against the skin that still bore the mark left by his bite. She could almost imagine it heating at his touch. "Whatever you say, Princess. But if you need me, you just holler."

He stepped back, and Fiona told herself to stop stalling. Delaying things wouldn't make her aunt's temper any easier to deal with.

Vicodin, on the other hand . . .

"Oh, bugger it." Gritting her teeth and steeling her

nerves, she looked directly into the chaotic jumble of colored glass and breathed the simple charm she'd known since childhood. "*Rís e dhumh.*"

Tell me.

For the space of a heartbeat, nothing happened, but Fiona felt the magic whisper out with her breath and curl and dance toward the glass. The magic seemed to make the individual panes ripple like the water in a pond giving way to a stone. The image in the frame began to pulse almost like a heartbeat, colors shifting and rearranging so the static image of the stained glass became almost like a movie with the characters performing the actions depicted.

She waited patiently for the magic to creep through the veil between the human world and Faerie. Time meant nothing to power. You couldn't make it move faster, but in this case, Fiona felt it was moving fast enough. She braced herself for the image to focus and the face of her aunt to develop in the small magical window.

Mab never appeared.

Instead, Fiona watched as the shifting colors began to slow and settle into a new image, one that looked almost like the bright, glittering halls of her aunt's palace. Fiona couldn't make out anything specific, but she caught glimpses of archways and staircases and graceful, darting movements. She sensed rather than heard clear musical voices, light ringing laughter, and the hum of constant activity. Against her skin, she could almost feel the warmth of magical fires burning at a perfect, constant temperature in the huge open hearths and the breeze of wings stirring the air.

Drawing in a breath, she prepared to speak her aunt's name, but the sound never made it out.

All at once, the colors of glass flared bright with

a sickly putrid green light. The image writhed violently and darkened. A veil was drawn over it, dark and thick like sooty, smothering black coal smoke. Startled, Fiona took a step forward to get a better look and heard a sound like a gunshot in the quiet of the small study.

The glass cracked.

Really it shattered, splintering into thousands of tiny razor-sharp pieces and blasting outward from the wardrobe like shrapnel from a bomb. Another sound shook her, this one a low, ferocious roar as something large and angry tackled her from the side, knocking her off her feet and carrying her to the floor. Arms wrapped around her, Walker rolled her across the antique rug with astonishing speed, carrying her out of the path of the dangerous debris.

All around them, the room erupted into chaos. People shouted and swore and ducked out of the way of the tiny glass bullets. Graham shoved Missy down behind the sofa with Tess, who had been diving for cover almost before Fiona realized what was happening. With a roar, Rafe dodged to the side and threw himself forward, coming in low and to the side of the wardrobe and slamming the door shut against the volley of glass.

Fiona lay there, breathless and dizzy under Walker's considerable bulk, and listened to the sound of glass thudding like buckshot into the wooden panels of the cabinet doors for several more seconds before everything went quiet.

Of course, it didn't stay that way for long.

"What the high holy fuck was that all about?" Graham shouted, dragging Missy from the hiding place he'd put her in and wrapping her up in his arms. His glare should have had the armoire bursting into flames. "Someone could have been killed!"

"I think that was the point." Tess stood up and leaned

over to shake the sharp, sparkling dust out of her hair. She gave her mate a quick, hard hug when he covered the space between them with a single leap, his hands and eyes moving over her looking for injuries. "I'm fine, baby, but someone inside that picture seems to be feeling a little bit cranky."

Fiona shifted and Walker finally eased off of her, at least far enough to sit on the floor and pull her into his lap.

"Are you okay?" he demanded.

His voice sounded even rougher and lower than usual and Fiona forced her lips into a smile. For the first time in a long, long time, she felt shaken, but her self-appointed bodyguard didn't need to know how badly.

"I'm fine."

"No. You're not." He swore and lifted his finger to brush the curve of her cheekbone. When he drew it away, she could see a drop of crimson blood glistening on the tip.

She reached up and touched the same spot. Now she could feel a slight sting, but until she'd seen the blood, she hadn't even realized she'd been nicked by a piece of glass. "It's nothing. Just a scratch."

Walker growled something under his breath, but his eyes were warm and bright as he leaned forward and pressed a kiss to the tiny wound. She felt the tip of his tongue sneak out to soothe the minor hurt and tried to ignore when something inside her melted.

"I'm fine," she repeated, trying to sound brisk and cool, but she couldn't stop herself from reaching up and pushing a stray piece of his rumpled hair back away from his face.

The room was silent around them.

Missy broke the tension with a quiet and distinctly satisfied hum. "Well, that gave us a bit of excitement. I'm going to have to get one of the cleaning crew in here with thick-soled shoes and a vacuum cleaner."

"I think we can worry about that later," Graham said, frowning down at her. "First, I'd like someone to tell me what the hell just happened."

"The same thing that happened when I tried to get back home through the gate in the park." Fiona shifted in Walker's lap and he set her aside, rising easily to his feet. She took his hand and let him pull her to hers. "The glass, like the gate, was cursed. Booby-trapped. Someone is going to a load of trouble to cut off the communication between us and Faerie."

"No way." Graham shook his head and scowled. "There's no way anyone could have gotten inside this club and performed a curse without me or someone on my staff knowing about it. It's impossible."

"Maybe it wasn't the glass that was cursed," Fiona offered, only half-joking. "Maybe it was me."

"Not to burst your bubble there," Tess said, "but it could just be a coincidence that you were the one who activated it. The curse could have been placed before the mirror came to us and set to go off whenever it was used, or if it was ever used by someone with Fae blood. Or it could have been cursed remotely. You don't need to see something or someone to put a curse on it. That's why they call it magic."

"But why do it in the first place?" Missy asked.

"I don't know." Fiona shrugged.

Rafe raised an eyebrow. "Would you care to speculate?"

She hesitated, then shook her head. "Not really. Touching the gate knocked me unconscious for a good couple of hours, and the glass could have slit my throat, if Walker hadn't shoved me out of the way. This could start to give a girl a complex."

No one laughed at her quip. Walker especially didn't laugh. He bristled, hackles raised like the overprotective wolf he was. "Someone is trying to hurt you, and when I find out who it is, I'm going to very much enjoy ripping out his throat."

"I appreciate the sentiment, but Tess makes sense. I'm not so sure I'm a specific target. I mean, who could have known I'd be the one using the glass? It could just as easily have been Rafael. More easily, since he's used it before and I'm not actually supposed to be on this side of it."

"Is there any way to find out?" Missy asked. She had to stand on her tiptoes and peer over her husband's shoulder, since he clearly didn't intend to let anything else get a clear shot at his mate. "I don't know a lot about magic, but aren't there ways to tell? Like with tracing the demon?"

"Different kind of spell," Tess broke in. "Demons respond to certain physical signs and objects in a way that isn't necessary for most other kinds of magic. Curses are designed not to leave traces." She grinned. "I know a bit about curses."

Fiona laughed. "Well, that could be helpful, because I don't. At least not about ones that don't last for a few hundred generations, and the one on the glass didn't feel nearly old enough to be a *geis*."

"No, it didn't. It's interesting, though, that it seemed timed to go off once you'd established a connection with Faerie, not at the moment you activated the mirror. It's almost like it was doing double duty as a burglar alarm, set to go off when you made contact."

"The ethereal branch of ADT?" Missy grinned.

"I wonder if it rings in a police station somewhere in Faerie."

"Right. I can just see the Queen's Guard donning their riot gear." Fiona shook her head and laughed again. "Somehow that doesn't strike me as likely. But I do want to know why someone is deliberately sabotaging the link between this world and Faerie."

"I don't get it, either. It's not like we all spend a lot of time in powwows. I think that glass has been used a total of three times since Mab sent it to us, and all three of them were when she popped up in it to give us hell about something we did or didn't do when one of your folk was visiting."

Fiona wasn't quite sure of the reason, either, but it gave her an uneasy feeling. She shrugged. "That I can't tell you. But the explanation isn't our biggest problem. If we can't get access to Faerie, our choice of ways to identify and track down the demon just got a heck of a lot smaller. I think we're going to have to start knocking on sorcerers' doors."

"I think that's a piss-poor idea." Walker scowled. "It's too dangerous. Like you said before, that could just escalate the violence or drive him into hiding. And what if you bump into him and spook him? He could end up attacking you." Walker shook his head and crossed his arms over his chest, his expression turning mulish. "No. It's out of the question."

Missy and Tess exchanged wide-eyed, knowing glances and fought with equal un-success to suppress their grins. They gave up the struggle when Fiona rounded on the werewolf, her spine straightening and regal authority draping over her like a mantle.

"I thought we already had this discussion, Tobias Walker." It freaked her out a little to hear her aunt's voice coming out of her mouth, but somehow she couldn't seem to stop it. "We agreed that I am not some incompetent little fool. I make my own choices, and I am responsible for my own life."

Walker's eyes flashed bright with golden fire, but before he could open his mouth, Missy shot Tess a speaking glance and the witch hurried to defuse the tension. "I don't think it's really the best idea to just go door-to-door and ask every sorcerer you meet if he happens to be summoning demons and then setting them loose on the human populace of Manhattan," she said. "First off, it could be dangerous, and second, it's just inefficient. Let me ask a few very discreet questions of the Witches' Council. Sorcerers are, after all, witches. Just a specialized kind of witch. I'll find out who's safest to approach and give you a couple of names. You can start there and hopefully not have to resort to the kamikaze approach."

Fiona and Walker stared at each other for a long, silent moment before she pursed her lips and nodded regally. "I can accept that. I won't be told what I can or can't do, but I'm not so stubborn that I'm incapable of listening to reason."

"Good, then it's settled," Rafe said, taking up his habitual role of peacemaker. Fiona recalled his mentioning something about how Graham had nearly been head of the Council of Others, and she shuddered at the thought. "Now, I suggest that we've all had enough excitement for the evening, what with the disturbing revelations and the bleeding and all."

At the word "bleeding," Walker's gaze snapped back to Fiona's face and locked on the reddened nick in her cheek. "You're right. We've had enough for one night. Come on." He grabbed Fiona by the hand and towed her toward the door. "We're going to have a doctor take a look at that cut."

Startled, Fiona dug her heels into the carpet and

laughed. "Don't be ridiculous. I told you, it's just a scratch." She made a face at him and ran a fingertip along the scratch. It smoothed away, leaving nothing more than a freckle behind. "See?"

He continued to glare at her while their audience watched with obvious fascination. She felt her heart skip a beat before racing ahead on a burst of adrenaline. When he spoke, his voice sounded gruff and deep and so quiet she had to strain to hear it. "Let's see if you can do that same trick on a bright red behind after I get through paddling your reckless little ass."

Her jaw dropped with a nearly audible thud. "What did you just say to me?"

"You heard me." Walker prowled forward while the other occupants in the room struggled to both blend into the woodwork and make sure they had a good view of the action. "You're more in need of a good spanking than any woman I've ever met in my life. The agreement we made was before you got cut up by flying glass. In fact, it involved you understanding that I won't stand by and watch you put yourself into dangerous situations, like chasing after sorcerers who might be trying to kill you!"

Fiona caught herself taking a step backward and stopped, squaring her shoulders. She did not make a habit of backing away from anything. "Our agreement was that you would give me credit for the ability to take care of myself and the brains not to put myself in clearly dangerous situations. I know you feel protective of me, Tobias, but just because you jumped me and got me naked doesn't mean you own me."

Someone made a choking sound, but Fiona wasn't about to take her eyes off Walker to see who it was.

"I didn't jump you."

"Oh, really. What do you call it when you tackle me

at the top of the stairs, rip my clothes off, and make my eyes roll back in my head, then? A relaxing little interlude?"

He growled long and low and took another step toward her. "I don't remember you spending a lot of time fighting me off, Princess. You did a little jumping of your own after a while."

"See?" Tess murmured to Missy at the other side of the room. "I told you they wouldn't be able to keep their hands off each other."

Fiona ignored their audience, too riled up now to care who watched them. "I don't deny I did some jumping. I'm not ashamed to jump. Jumping is perfectly healthy and natural, and quite frankly, in Faerie most of us jump as often as we feel like it. But that's not the point."

"What's the point, then?"

She managed a growl of her own. "The point is that you seem to have reverted back to the knee-jerk control-freak stance that we already fought about."

"This is not a knee-jerk reaction, Princess. This is what happens when you volunteer yourself for combat duty without even discussing it with me first!"

One more step had the backs of her knees bumping up against the side of an ottoman. She swallowed a rush of nerves—or was that excitement?—and raised her chin to keep him from noticing. "Why should I discuss it with you? Do you think I shouldn't try to help your friends and your community prevent a disaster while they try and negotiate for their survival among the humans? And here I thought I was doing you a favor."

He swore.

"Besides which, I already told you that I won't be treated as if I'm somehow your responsibility." She was on a roll. "We agreed that I was capable of looking after myself, and I don't see the need to ask your permission or your approval before I decide what needs to be done. Did you think I would just defer to you because of those idiotic protective instincts of yours? Get over them! I'm a princess. I don't defer to anyone."

He pinned her to the ottoman before she got the last snotty word out. She struggled, but even if she'd been fully magically charged, her strength couldn't match an adult male Lupine with a chip on his shoulder and something to prove.

"I don't care if you're the fucking queen of the universe, sweetheart." The golden flames of his eyes burned into hers, and his lips drew back in a fang-baring snarl. "I agreed not to treat you like you're made of glass, but I did *not* agree to let you put yourself in some maniac's line of fire, and you're crazy if you ever thought I would. I'm not trying to smother you or run your life, but you're my mate, and you'll just have to learn to live with my idiotic protective instincts!"

CHAPTER 17

THE ROOM CLEARED OUT in three seconds flat. It took a lot longer than that for Fiona's head to stop spinning and her heart to start beating again. "What did you say?"

"You heard me well enough." Her hands pushed against his shoulders, and he grabbed her wrists to pin them above her head. "I will not stand aside and allow my mate to put herself in danger, Fiona of the Sidhe, whether she tells me she can handle it herself or not."

The buzzing in her ears wasn't going away, and she shook her head as if that could clear it. She couldn't have heard him right. Mate? Her? A royal princess of Faerie the mate of a mortal werewolf? It was impossible.

"You're out of your mind," she finally said, the sound strangled in her throat. "You're completely insane. I am *not* your mate."

Walker laughed, but he didn't sound amused. "Don't kid yourself, Princess. It's not like either of us got to choose. And it's not like either of us gets to just say 'No thanks.'"

"That's exactly what I'm saying!" She squirmed beneath him, but with her wrists pinned and her legs dangling off the ottoman, she couldn't get any leverage against him. "There has to be a choice. You don't just get to say I'm your mate and think that makes it true!"

"I don't think saying it makes it true." He shifted both her wrists to one of his large hands and used the other to jerk aside the collar of her shirt until he could see his mark against her skin. "I think *that* makes it true."

She tried to ignore the way the spot seemed to ache and throb just from his looking at it. The way her heart began to beat faster. She sneered. "That? It's just a hickey. Trust me, I've had them before."

"Right. Does this usually happen when you have a hickey?"

Eyes blazing, he leaned down and drew his tongue in a long, rough line over the mark. It may as well have been over her clit. Her entire body clenched in sudden, debilitating need and a hungry moan broke through her clenched lips. Her head fell back and her breath shuddered out of her chest. She could feel herself going soft and damp in welcome, and she fought desperately to remember the point she'd been trying to make.

"It's . . . just . . . chemistry." She panted, but she didn't give in. "Lust. A . . . shallow physical . . . reaction."

"Uh-huh."

He shifted and the lick became a nibble that had her heart pounding in time to the throbbing between her legs. Her mind reeled. It was impossible that he could do this to her, make her feel this way without even touching her. Sure, the side of her neck was an erogenous zone, but this was ridiculous.

"Doesn't . . . prove anything."

His voice sounded muffled against her skin. "Of course not."

The nibbling ceased, and Fiona gasped for air. Goddess, she felt like hot running wax. It had to be lack of oxygen making her this dizzy. She knew about magic, but even magic couldn't do this to her.

She struggled, trying to turn her head or slide out from under him or do anything that would help her return to sanity. This had to stop before he started thinking she believed him about this mate thing.

"Walker, st—"

She never did get the word out. It hovered on the edge of her tongue, ready to tumble off, but he stole it from her along with her breath, her self, and the sound of her scream when he sank his teeth into the mark on her neck and shoved her hard into orgasm.

Her body arched and spasmed, shaking as if a bolt of electricity coursed through her. Stars exploded behind her eyes, blue and yellow and crimson with fire. She went blind, dumb, deaf to everything but the sound of his rumble of satisfaction, the harsh rasp of his breath. Numb to everything but his teeth against her skin, his mark on her body, and the hot, unbearable pulses of ecstasy that turned her mind and her willpower to ashes.

How did he do this to her?

She had no breath to ask, even when she could think well enough to form the question. Walker, though, didn't look interested in answering.

"More," he rasped. *"Again."*

"Can't."

"Can. Now."

A sound, half a moan, half a sob, tore from her. She had ceased to struggle, had neither the strength nor the will to do it. She lay draped over the ottoman like an offering to a pagan god, and Walker prepared her as such, ripping away her clothing until her skin glowed pale and smooth and naked beneath his devouring gaze.

Face harsh and set, he kneed her legs apart and braced himself over her. His hand raced over her, claiming and heating. It dived between her legs, fingers parting and probing and sinking deep, deep into her tight sheath.

"*Now*," he repeated, and he pressed his thumb rough and high against her clit, fingertips scraping over her sensitive inner tissues. His teeth sank again into her neck, and she had no choice but to obey.

She fragmented as violently as the stained glass, but her destruction felt more like a blessing than a curse. Free-falling into exaltation, she thought her lungs might burst, knew her heart had. She had become nothing but her pleasure and the knowledge that she pleased him. There was nothing else.

She screamed. It might have been his name. It definitely was a plea. Mercifully, he answered, tearing away his own clothes, lifting and flipping her, arranging her on her belly across the ottoman. She barely had time to register the feel of the rough brocade upholstery against her skin when he grasped her hips and lifted. He fit himself against her, paused for a breathless, aching eternity, and then slammed home.

Goddess. How had she ever lived with the emptiness?

Nothing existed except for her and Walker and the heady, frantic rhythm of his movement inside her. He stretched and filled her, rode her with purpose and hunger and something akin to desperation. Her heart recognized it, and her body, even if her mind refused to work. Her body knew that his existed as another piece of her, too long held apart. Her heart knew that whatever she wanted to believe, he had already laid claim, moved in, and taken over.

Her heart knew Walker was right.

The choice had already been made.

When he tensed and roared and spilled himself into her, she knew. And when her body fractured and tumbled over after him, she almost began to believe.

Walker snuck them out of the back of the club, wrapping her in an afghan he found draped over the sofa because her clothes could no longer cover a gnat with any decency. He carried her because her legs refused to hold her weight. Plenty of other muscles had gone on strike as well, including the ones from the neck up. Her mind remained blank and fuzzy halfway across Manhattan and all the way up into Walker's bed.

Okay, maybe not blank. She did have one thought, a question, that repeated over and over without even a hint of an answer.

How?

Fiona knew magic. She had grown with it, breathed it in, lived with it sparking and glowing and dancing all around her. She *was* magic. The power flowed in the veins of all Fae as surely as their blood. No one could deny it, and she had never wanted to try.

But this magic—this intense and dark and nearly violent magic that tied her to a mate she hadn't wanted in a way she'd never expected—this magic was something she just couldn't fathom.

The mattress gave beneath Walker's weight as he

knelt to lay her down on sheets still rumpled from that morning, still scented with their loving. She kept her eyes closed. She knew he could tell she hadn't fallen asleep, but she needed some kind of barrier against him, and the darkness behind her eyelids was the best she could manage. He had just taken her grasp on reality, flipped it upside down, and then returned it to her as if everything were perfectly normal, but for Fiona, normal now looked a long way off.

What had happened to her glorious lack of a future? She had never understood the human penchant for planning and organizing and looking toward the path ahead of them. She was Fae. Sidhe. To her, only the path beneath her feet mattered. The feel of dirt and root and stone, the crackle of leaves and twigs, the cool shade cast by trees along the edges of the trail, and the little freckles of sunlight that dripped through the leaves to tease her with the hint of light and warmth. Fae didn't look ahead. They didn't make lifetime commitments or worry about what would happen in a hundred years.

But now all Fiona could think of was that in a hundred years the man lying beside her, stroking those warm, magical hands over her skin, would be dead and her immortality would stretch out before her. Blessing made curse.

"You can pretend I'm not here all night, if you think it will help." He spoke so softly that she felt like a deaf woman, interpreting his speech by the vibration of the sound rather than the meaning of the words. "But it won't, and I'm not going away."

But he would, eventually. That was the problem, wasn't it?

She turned her head away and kept her eyes squeezed shut.

"I apologize for being a jerk to you earlier, Princess, and if I came on too strong just now, I'll apologize again. I admit I seem to have this small problem keeping my temper around you. But I'm not going to apologize for the fact that we're mated," he said, tracing a fingertip over the tendons at the side of her neck, playing with the pale skin. "First, because there's no point, since it can't be undone. Second, because I don't want it undone. And third, because it wasn't my doing."

It didn't matter that she couldn't see him; she could hear the rueful grin in his voice. "That mark you gave me feels a hell of a lot like your doing, Tobias."

His hands shifted, now ringing the borders of the mark. "The mark is, but the reason it's there isn't." She kept silent, and with a sigh, he continued. "I don't know how much you know about Lupine mating, and I don't know how well I can explain it to you. There aren't a whole lot of philosophers among our kind. Some things just come down to instinct."

She bit back the urge to voice a caustic agreement on that score.

"I can't tell you why it happens, or even how. But every Lupine knows when it does. It's like the first change, the first time I ever shifted. I just . . . knew. You smelled sweeter than anything I'd ever sniffed and you tasted better, too. And when I finally got inside you it was like puzzle pieces locking together. We just fit, like we were meant to. That's how it happens. Lupines find the one perfect mate for them and they seize it. There was no way in hell I could have stopped it. Not even if I'd wanted to."

"What if I had wanted to?"

He barked a laugh. "It might have been fun to watch you try, but it wouldn't have worked. Like I said, neither of us got a choice. Lupines don't pick their mates. Fate picks them for us."

She frowned and jerked her shoulder. "That's ridiculous. Aren't you mortals the ones who are always going on about free will and self-determination? Goddess, it's all any of you ever talked about for a few centuries."

"Yeah. Those weren't Lupines," he snorted. "Or if they were, they were talking about self-determining where to go for dinner, not about mates. I don't know why it happens, Princess, but I know that when Lupines mate, it's because Fate decided they should."

"But I'm not Lupine, and I didn't decide on anything."

"I noticed." His hand stroked over her bare skin, as smooth and hairless as his was rough and dappled with fur. "That's where this came in." He pressed a kiss to the mark on her neck.

Her eyes opened enough to scowl at him. "What does that mean?"

"The mate mark. It's there to prove you belong to me."

"How Neanderthal." She rolled her eyes. "I didn't see one on Missy's neck, and it doesn't take a genius to figure out she belongs to Graham."

"She's belonged to him for five years now, and I think the fact that she's borne him two sons proves the same thing. The mark doesn't last forever, anyway. And some mates never get them, but I know for a fact she did."

"How do some of us get so lucky?"

"The ones who need proof get marked." He took her hand, toyed with her fingers. "When two Lupines mate, usually no one gets marked. There's no need. We all know what's happening, so proof becomes redundant.

But if one of the mates is reluctant or unwilling, the other marks her."

"What? Like a cattle brand? What if the reluctant mate has a good reason to be reluctant? What if she doesn't like the jerk who marked her? Is she forced to stay with him?"

"Of course not. There's no need to force her."

Her scowl deepened. "So she just leaves with a semi-permanent hickey on her neck? No harm, no foul?"

"No. No one leaves." He shook his head impatiently. "The mating is Fated. Fate knows the two mates belong together, that no one else will ever suit either of them."

"No one leaves? Ever? In all of Lupine history?"

"Well, sure, it's happened, but those are the stories we all hear about as cautionary tales when we're growing up. They all end up miserable. Why would anyone leave their perfect partner?"

"A lot of words come to my mind when I'm with you, Tobias Walker, but let me make it clear that 'perfect' is *not* one of them."

"Not to your mind maybe. But apparently Fate doesn't agree."

She sighed and turned to face him. His skull was much too thick to have this conversation any other way. "Walker, I almost get what you're saying. Really. From what you're telling me, it's like magic. Fate casts a spell, and two people are bound by it, one of whom may or may not get bitten for her trouble. Okay, fine. If that's the way it works for your people, good for you. But I'm not one of your people."

Walker frowned. "Why should that matter? I'm not one of your people, but that doesn't seem to stop you from charging up like a car battery hooked to jumper cables every time I touch you."

"That's not about you. It's just the way things happen."

"Exactly."

She groaned in frustration and tried to sit up, but he draped a heavy arm across her waist to pin her in place. "Walker, listen to me for half a second, would you? This is impossible. It isn't going to work. For the Goddess's sake, we're not even the same species!"

He rolled his eyes. "Is that what has your panties in a twist? For God's sake, Fi, what couple have you met around here so far that *is* of the same species? Rafe and Tess? He's Feline—a frickin' werejaguar—and I know it's hard to believe, but she's human, you know."

"She's a witch."

"Which is what we call human with magical abilities, to distinguish them from the ones without magical abilities. Graham is Lupine, but Missy's about as human as you can get. Before they mated, she taught kindergarten!"

Fiona frowned. "That's not the poi—"

"You want a few more? Fine." His temper had started to rise again, but his touch stayed gentle, if implacable. "The *guth* of the Black Glen Clan from Ireland just paid us a visit a couple of months ago, and guess who he's mated to? A Foxwoman. Fiona, it happens all the time."

"Not with Fae it doesn't." She pushed at his arm and gritted her teeth when he refused to budge. "Will you let me up, damn it? I can't yell at you when you have me pinned to a bed."

"Really? Now, I'm going to remember that handy little fact." He didn't let her go, but he did let her sit up. Then he yanked her right back down into his lap and wrapped his arms around her even tighter than before.

Her eyes narrowed. "That's not what I meant, fur face."

"Tough."

She gave his arms a few ineffectual tugs before giving up with a sigh and letting her head fall back onto his shoulder. She didn't want to argue, didn't have the energy for it, but somehow she had to make him understand that at least one of them had to maintain their sanity about this. "I'm telling you, this just won't work. It's great if Lupines can mate and have successful relationships with other kinds of mortals, whether they're humans or shape-shifting aardvarks. I'm happy for you."

"But?"

"But I'm not mortal. Fae don't mate with mortals, Walker. I mean, how could we? We're not even supposed to leave our own borders. I'm not supposed to be here."

"But you are." He squeezed her gently to cut off her protest. "Have you ever heard of a sidhe named Luc MacAnu?"

Fiona looked at him, confused. "Lucifer? Captain of the Queen's Guard?" Walker nodded. "Of course I've heard of him. He was the commander of my aunt's personal army from the time I was a little girl."

"And where is he now?"

She shrugged. "I'm not sure. I know he resigned his commission a short while ago, but it was during one of my obligatory visits to the Unseelie Court. By the time I got back and heard about it, he was already gone." She shook her head. "What in the world does that have to do with us?"

"Well, it was big news in the Council of Others when the Fae warrior Mab sent to New York to find her nephew and return him to Faerie ended up falling in love with one of the closest friends of the luna of the Silverback Clan."

"I don't know what you're—"

"The *human* friend."

Her jaw clicked shut.

"It turned out that Luc wasn't thinking about mortality or immortality when he looked at Corinne D'Alessandro. He only thought about having her. So he found a way to make it happen."

Fiona steeled herself against temptation. "That's lovely for them, Walker, but I'm not Lucifer MacAnu of the Queen's Guard and you're not a naïve young human woman."

"Glad you noticed."

He grinned and leaned forward to nuzzle her ear. She had to grit her teeth to keep from melting. It still didn't seem possible that he could affect her so deeply so fast. It shouldn't have been possible.

She tried one last time to squirm out of his arms, and he sighed. Half a second later, she found herself sprawled back against the pillows with a stubborn and stubbled werewolf draped half over her to keep her in place.

"Sweetheart, I can see where this might all seem a little surreal to you." She snorted with laughter, but he ignored it and watched her steadily, his expression both resolved and tender. "It's happened pretty quickly, and you haven't been expecting it for most of your life like I have. But that doesn't make it any less real."

"It can't be."

"It is." He leaned down to brush a soft, lingering kiss against her lips. "I can understand if you're not ready to deal with it right this second. There's a lot of other stuff going on right now, so I'll drop it. But Princess, this isn't going to go away. Eventually, you're going to have to deal with the fact that you belong to me. And I belong to you."

She stared up at him, feeling her heart clench inside her chest and remembering what it had felt like when he'd buried himself inside her with his mouth on the mark of their bond. Her entire world had changed in that moment, and no matter how desperately she wanted to deny the truth, she knew she couldn't go back to the way things had been. They would never be the same.

She would never be the same.

But that didn't mean he could get away with acting like a jackass.

She took a deep breath and told herself to be firm, but when she spoke, she could hear in her voice the echoes of the soft, unfamiliar emotion currently stirring in her chest. "I'm not certain I understand all of this, but if it's true—" She held up a hand to stop his interruption. "If it's true, it's going to take adjustment on *both* our parts. I meant it when I said I can understand your protective instincts, Walker, but you have to understand that I mean it when I say I won't be dictated to. When you're concerned for my safety, tell me. But don't order me around. It won't work, and I won't appreciate it."

He met her gaze for a long moment before he gave a brief nod. "I'll try, Princess, but I can't promise anything. These are instincts we're talking about. I can't make them go away."

She looked up into those warm golden eyes and let herself drown in them, feeling the exhaustion of physical exertion and emotional stress beginning to take their toll. Her muscles relaxed, sinking deeper into the mattress, softening beneath his in inevitable welcome.

Her hands slid off his shoulders, down his arms to twine her fingers with hers. "Nothing has ever been as complicated as this, *mo fáeli,*" she whispered, reaching up for another kiss, "but nothing simple has ever touched my heart."

And as their lips touched, her heart melted.

CHAPTER 18

I T WASN'T SO MUCH the low buzzing sound that woke Fiona as the tiny footsteps dancing up and down her spine. Was that a fox-trot?

Burrowing her head deeper into the pillows, she shrugged her shoulders and tried to slip back into sleep. Given how little of it she'd gotten last night, it should have been easy. But the fox-trot turned into a merengue, and she groaned into the pillowcase.

A warm wall of muscle stirred beside her, shaking the bed and rumbling low and sleepy in the dimly lit room. "D'you have a cat? I think it wants to go out."

Burrowed deep in the hollow she'd made in the pillow, Fiona waited for his sleepy murmur to register as actual language. Then she frowned. "A cat? We're at your apartment."

She heard a groan and a creak and felt the bed shift to the right as Walker rolled over. Turning her head to the side, she forced her eyelids open and met his blurry gaze.

"I don't have a cat."

"Then what exactly is doing a cha-cha between my shoulder blades?"

"If I tell you, will you tell me what's tangoing between mine?"

"Your Highness!"

Startled by the high, familiar voice, Fiona flipped onto her back and glared in the direction of the interruption. The small figure that had been standing astride her spine hovered just above her, gossamer wings flapping.

"Babbage? What in the Lady's name are you doing here?"

The pixie fluttered and flitted and wrung his tiny hands together in worry. "Your Highness, I knew it was a bad idea for you to visit this place. Oh, what is your aunt going to say?"

Eyes wide, Walker pushed himself into a sitting position and dislodged his own fleet-footed visitor.

Squick tumbled head over feet down the Lupine's torso, landing somewhere near the left knee and jumping to his feet instantly. He shook his head as if to clear it and swept Fiona a quick bow. "I telled him we shouldn't come, Miss Fiona, but the pixie insisting. I couldn't stop him."

Walker looked at Fiona and scowled. "What the hell are these?"

"Pests."

Still fluttering, Babbage lowered himself to the edge of the mattress and cast disapproving glances at Fiona and Walker. "Your Highness, would you like us to remove this . . . this . . . mongrel from your presence?"

Walker snarled at the pixie. Reaching down, Walker grabbed the sheet from where it had bunched at the foot of the bed and yanked it up to Fiona's chin. "The only thing being removed around here is going to be those wings of yours, buddy, so watch yourself."

Fiona hadn't bothered to cover herself because (1) the Fae really weren't fazed by nudity, considering how much of the population of Faerie didn't even own clothing, and (2) Walker had seen her naked almost more than he'd seen her clothed and the only other folk in the room were Babbage and Squick. Hiding her body from them would be like hiding her body from Walker's fictional pet cat. What would be the point?

Judging by the look on Walker's face, though, he wanted her to stay covered. Stifling a sigh, she tucked the sheet up under her arms, made sure nothing he might consider vital was hanging out, and resumed glaring at their uninvited guests. "Okay, someone explain what the hell you two are doing here." She stopped and frowned. "And how you got here. I tried the gate, and it was sealed."

Both began talking at once.

"Oh, Your Highness," Babbage cried, "how my heart stopped when I realized the gate you had used to travel to this primitive land was blocked! I nearly gave in to my despair."

"He cried like a little girlie nymphs, miss! Moaned and wailing! I thinked my ears was bursted. But then I remembers to tried the gate that don't come here, and here we is!"

"It was horrible, Princess Fiona. The imp dragged me into a barren wasteland of a plane, populated by terrible, fierce creatures who would gladly have feasted on our flesh."

"Feast? Your heart not even enough for a midnight

snacks. Besides, they wasn't terrible. They was rock elementals. All they eats were dirt."

"We had to come, Your Highness! I nearly flew into the castle wall when I looked into Her Majesty's scrying bowl and saw you calling for help. I said to myself, 'Babbage, you felt all along that this foolhardy trip would come to no good,' and so it turned out—"

Fiona held up a hand to silence them. They ignored it.

". . . screamed like a dryads in a forest fire, he did. It near maked my horns curls!"

She cleared her throat. "Guys, really—"

". . . saw you trapped in a small room surrounded by mortals, and I knew something had to be amiss. So I told myself, 'Babbage, old fellow, the princess needs us, and it doesn't matter how the odds fall against us—' "

"Babbage. Squick. Really, if you'd just—"

" '—or what terrible creatures lie in wait to tear us limb from limb and to rend our wings from our backs, if Her Highness requires aid, then aid she will get.' That's just want I said, and—"

"Will you *shut the hell up for ONE BLESSED MINUTE*?!"

Fiona's scream pierced the chatter and made her head, which had already begun to pound, threaten to split in two like an overripe melon. They shut up, though, so that was saying something.

Making a sound of disgust, Walker rose from the bed and stalked toward the bathroom. Fiona scowled at his back. "Where are you going?"

"To get a bottle of aspirin," he tossed over his shoulder, "and maybe a fifth of vodka. Want anything?"

"Yeah," she muttered, "a poke in the eye with a sharp stick."

Ever the optimist, Babbage tried again. "Your Highness—"

Seeing the look of aggravation on the princess's face, Squick did the intelligent thing—for once—and raised his little red hand.

Fiona groaned. "Yes, Squick?"

"Miss Fiona, I gots to tell you that we was only thinking you needs us. We meant good."

"Meant *well,* Squick."

"Yeah. That's what I says. There we was, minding we own business, practicing new scary faces in the queen's scrying bowl, when we sawed our princess in the waters! We knowed you was here, and we knowed the queen's bowl can see any other magicky seeing stuff, and then the waters in the bowl shotted up like the nereids was having a party! It gotted all over the floors and everywheres. I says the Queen's Guard coulda come over here and sorts it all out, but noooooo. This one have to go playing hero. Babbage, the princess-saving pixie, or somethin' dopey like that."

Walker returned at that moment with an economy-sized bottle of aspirin and two glasses of water. Fiona had been looking forward to the vodka. She waved aside the tablets he offered her and snatched the bottle out of his hand. Before he could growl at her, she leaned forward and pressed two kisses to his forehead, one above each temple. When she drew back, she could see the lines in his brow ease as his headache began to dissipate. Then she took one of the glasses of water and downed it in three quick gulps. Better than aspirin any day.

He took the empty glass from her hand. "Thanks."

She smiled at him. "You're welcome." When she turned back to the Fae, she wasn't smiling. "Are you telling me that the message I tried to send through that enchanted glass actually came through? Because on this end, I barely got a glimpse of the palace before something destroyed the spell and the glass."

"That were what we seen, too. But I told the pixie about it being exploded and what we seen beforehands, and that's when he gots all bended out of shapes."

"And no one else saw?"

The imp grinned. "We isn't allowed in the queen's scrying rooms. She saying something about us being untrustable. So now we only goes there by sneakiness."

By this time, Babbage had caught on to the new protocol and he was jumping up and down like a hyperactive Chihuahua, waving both of his hands in the air above his head. Fiona could see his little face turning gradually purple as he held his breath to keep himself from speaking out of turn and making her yell at him again.

She sighed. "What is it, Babbage?"

"Your Highness!" The words all but exploded from his mouth. "Your Highness, my heart nearly *stopped* when I tracked the imp down to the scrying chamber and he told me what he had seen! We came immediately to rescue you!" He rounded on Walker and raised his tiny fists into a boxing stance, fluttering back and forth in a Muhammad Ali meets Tinker Bell impersonation. "Stand back, loathsome sorcerer!" he shouted. "I will avenge your crimes against my mistress!"

Fiona seriously considered pulling the sheet up farther. Like over her head.

Walker raised an eyebrow and looked down at the hovering pixie. Then he raised the other eyebrow and looked at Fiona. "He's joking, right?"

"En garde!"

Babbage's war cry sounded more like a girlish scream or maybe a hungry baby bird, but he followed through with a direct charge straight at Walker's throat.

What the idiot hoped to accomplish, Walker had no idea, but he put a stop to the attack with the simple defense of one large finger pressed against the pugnacious pixie's sternum. Naturally, it overlapped onto his chest, stomach, and really most of his torso.

"I guess he's not kidding," Walker drawled. As if it weren't bad enough that he'd been woken out of a sound sleep with his mate slumbering peacefully beside him, now the weird little creatures that had done the waking had decided they needed to try to poke his eyes out or something.

"Babbage, quit it!" Fiona grabbed the pixie by his tunic and hauled him away from Walker, setting Babbage down on the mattress and glaring at him sternly. "Now, how about you tell me what the hell is going on? This time without all the histrionics and melodrama."

Walker watched the pint-sized pest struggle with what looked like a righteous sulk before he grudgingly answered the question.

"We came to rescue you," Babbage pouted. "Why else would you have appeared in the scrying bowl, if not to cry for help? I couldn't think of any other reason. If you weren't being held captive against your will, you could have just returned to the gate and come home. As you should have. We didn't realize until we tried it ourselves that the gate had malfunctioned."

It looked like Fiona was used to being lectured by this pipsqueak, because she didn't bother to snap at the thing the way she would have at Walker if he'd said anything close to it. They were going to have to work on that.

"I couldn't come home," she said. "The gate's not working at either end, apparently. Someone put some kind of seal on it. I tried to get through a couple of days ago and ended up unconscious for a good few minutes."

The red one, the one without wings but with tiny little devil's horns poking out of his forehead, frowned. "That don't sound well."

"Doesn't sound good, Squick."

"That were what I said. It would takes a lot of magic to seal a gates like that, and why woulds anyone want to? The queen already keep a tight lock on who go in and out. She be more fretful over us coming here than them going there, if you take my meanings."

"I haven't figured out why," Fiona said. "At first I thought it might have something to do with Uncle Dionnu and his being here for the negotiations without telling Aunt Mab about them, but that doesn't really make sense. He's never been afraid of upsetting her before, so why should he worry now?"

The pixie's eyes widened. "King Dionnu is here? In the mortal world?"

"I know. That was my reaction."

Briefly, Fiona outlined why Dionnu had come to Manhattan and what he claimed he intended to gain from the visit. Both uninvited guests looked as skeptical as their princess.

"I doesn't know, Miss Fiona," the red fellow said. "You knows I'm not the devious sort, but it sound to me like the king might being up to something."

His small, pointy tail twitched from side to side as he said it, and Walker found himself suppressing a snort. The little guy looked like everyone's childhood vision of the devil. All he needed was a pitchfork and a pointy black goatee to complete the image.

"Yeah, I had an inkling." Fiona's voice was dry, her mouth wry. "But I don't have time to try and figure out what he has up his sleeve. There are other things going on that take precedence over Uncle Dionnu's eternal quest for whatever he can get."

"Like what?" Babbage asked.

"You mean aside from the fact that someone sealed off the gate and then put a spell on the glass and the scrying bowl to make them explode if anyone established contact between here and Faerie?" She paused. "Well, we do seem to have a couple of demons on our hands."

"Demons?"

They said it in chorus, both tiny faces going slack with shock, then blank with horror.

"How can that be?"

"Can't be true! Hasn't been a demons up from Below in . . . in . . . I can't remembers how long!"

"Maybe not where you're from," Walker threw in, "but here in the real world, we have the occasional visitor. Usually they're just here long enough to eat the one who summoned them, then they go home. But these guys don't seem to be following the standard rules. They're sure as hell not sticking inside some tidy little circles."

Fiona jumped in to explain what she had found, and her miniature audience listened with surprising attention. Neither one interrupted or even moved until Fiona had related the whole of the tale.

"That's the real reason I was trying to contact the queen," she said. "I'm afraid that if I ask too many human sorcerers, I'll tip off the summoner that we're on to him, so I was hoping Aunt Mab would give me access to the royal library. That way I could do some research on the sigils myself, see if I could come up with an identity of at least one of the demons. Even that much might help me trace it back to the one who called it."

Babbage shook his head. "The queen would not like this idea, Your Highness. I believe she would be more inclined to order you to return to the palace immediately, rather than give you the keys to her library. You know she would never countenance you putting yourself in danger this way."

"Fiona isn't going to be in any danger. Not while I'm around." Walker didn't appreciate the idea of anyone implying he couldn't take care of his mate, whether they knew she was his mate or not. If another pack member had said such a thing, there would have been a battle.

Somehow, even from two and a half feet below his eye line, the pixie managed to look down his nose at Walker. "You may be willing to try, wolf, but you can't stop a spell the way you can someone's fist."

His eyes narrowed. "I can stop your mouth, if you don't watch it, Tinker Bell."

Fiona shushed them both. "It doesn't really matter what the queen would or wouldn't countenance, Babb. And it doesn't matter who orders me to go home at this point. I can't. The gate is sealed, and until I figure out how to get it open again—which is going to have to wait until after I take care of the demon business—I'm staying right here."

Walker clenched his teeth. She'd be staying right here for a long time after that bloody gate was open. She just didn't realize it yet. But there was no way in hell he'd let her leave his apartment, let alone his world. Not unless he was walking right alongside of her. He'd thought she was starting to understand after their discussion last night, but now it looked like a little more persuasion might be in order.

The little devil hopped over to sit near Fiona's knees and braced his hands on his hips. "Can you showed me what the marks looks like? I might could be big helps."

"How?"

Squick threw Walker an impatient scowl. "I's an imp, that's how. I gots friends in warm places."

Fiona explained, "Imps are Fae, but that's mostly because they sided with us during the Wars. They actually started out as hybrids—part demon, part Fae."

"Part pixie, to be specific," the imp sniffed, and shot Babbage a smirk. "But us seen which way the wind were blowing during the fighting, so we decides to sign on with the white sheep of the family and fighted for the king and queen. Since then, Their Majesties hasn't been able to live without us."

"Hasn't been able to get rid of you," Babbage grumbled.

"Haven't," Fiona corrected.

Wondering if maybe he should have taken those aspirin after all, Walker shook his head. "I'm starting to think I'm going to need a crash course in the history of the Fae–Demon Wars before this is all over."

"All yous needs to know," Squick said, puffing out his chest, "is that if anybody can finds out what demon left its sigil on these bodies of yours, I'm them."

"It," Walker growled.

"That's what I said. So, can you sketches them out for me, Miss Fiona?"

She nodded and a pad and pen appeared on her lap. "The sorcerer is human, so I doubt you'd recognize his mark. I'll just show you the sigils that named the demon and gave it its orders." Quickly Fiona sketched the same ugly lines Walker had seen her draw in the dirt the other night. They didn't look any prettier in the light of day or any more familiar. "That's what I saw. I may be off a line or two, but I think I got pretty close; don't you, Walker?"

He nodded. "That's what I remember."

"Do you recognize any of them, Squick?"

"Not too much. At least, nots the name glyphs," he said, frowning. "But let me takes the paper, and I do some checking."

Fiona swore. "You can't. The gate is closed. Who are you going to ask if you can't get back to Faerie?"

"There be more than one gates in this world, Miss Fiona, and not every one lead to Faerie."

Babbage made a choked coughing sound. "You can't mean to go Below and ask, Squick! That would be a suicide mission! Imps are about as welcome Below as demons are Above."

Walker had heard the term "Below" before. It was how the Fae and historians referred to the plane of existence the Fae had banished the demons to after the end of the Wars. You couldn't call it hell, but only because of the lack of the souls of dead humans. It was still a bleak, malevolent world populated entirely by demons and any Fae who had been labeled traitors during the conflict. In comparison, every place that wasn't Below started being called Above.

Squick's small red chest puffed out even more. "I cans handle myselves," the imp assured them. "Some of we don't needs wings to move fastly."

"Squick, I don't know. I don't want to put you in any danger. This isn't really your problem."

"I puts myself where we wants to be."

Walker frowned, and Fiona didn't look convinced. She looked worried. Apparently, she really cared what happened to the annoying little buggers, and that meant Walker did, too.

Damn, this mate thing was already getting complicated.

Seeing the stubborn look on the imp's face, Walker chimed in to back up Fiona and Babbage. "I'm not sure that's a good idea, Squick. The information is important, but it won't do us any good if you get killed finding it. Then we're out the information *and* an imp. Can't you find anyplace else to ask around that isn't Below?"

"Who else be knowing about demons but themself? Well, and the Fae chroniclers, but if we can't gets back to the palace, we can't very well asks him, can us?"

Fiona still looked worried. "Squick, I don't like it. Walker's right. You could be killed."

"I can takes care of myselves," he said firmly. Before anyone could offer another protest, he snatched the paper from her hands and folded it into a small triangle that disappeared when he blew on it. "I finds out about your demon. Maybe if the pixie wants to make hisself useful, he can sees what's what at the gate. At least he wouldn't being a total wastes of magic, then."

Babbage puffed up like a frightened Persian cat, but Fiona cut off his indignant protest. "No, I don't like the idea of you splitting up, let alone of one of you going Below all on your own."

Babbage turned whiter than Walker's sheets.

Squick just snorted. "What? I is supposed to take the pixie with me? And if thing didn't goes finely, I's could always bargain his wings away in exchanges for safe passage. Them make good snacking, demons say." He shook his head. "No, Miss Fiona. Better off to go and go on my owns. Sneakier that ways." He threw Walker a speaking glance. "Faster, too."

Walker nodded grimly. "Fast would be good."

At least on locating the demon. The pixie could take all the time in the world figuring out what was keeping Fiona from going back through the Faerie gate, as far as Walker was concerned.

Realizing he was not being sent Below to accompany Squick, Babbage began breathing again. "Well, I'm glad that's settled." He cleared his throat. "I can certainly take a look at the gate and see if I can discern what kind of hex is on it and who put it there. Yes, I'm happy to do that! We all have to stick to our strengths, after all."

He practically whistled a tune of relief, but Fiona continued to frown. "I have a bad feeling about this," she said. "I wish you wouldn't go, Squick."

"Oh, Miss Fiona, you worries too much. Nothings will happen to me. I come back finer than before, you see. And I brings back the names of the demon so we can sends it back Below where it belonging. Imp's promise."

Walker got the feeling an imp's promise didn't hold quite the weight Squick had invested in it.

"All right," Fiona agreed grudgingly. "It's clear I can't stop you when your mind is already made up, but I expect you to be careful. Both of you."

The Fae nodded. "We will," they said in unison, and they swept Fiona a pair of elegant bows before turning and blinking out of the room.

Fiona continued to stare at the spot where they had disappeared for a long minute after they had gone, and Walker sat beside her, his hand resting on her back.

"I do have a bad feeling," she murmured, and he saw the little crease in the skin between her eyebrows. "Something bad is going to happen to them. I know it."

Slipping his arms all the way around her, Walker

tugged Fiona against his side and nuzzled her hair. "I think they can take care of themselves. You heard Squick. It will be okay, Princess."

She raised her eyes to his and forced a smile. "Does this mate thing give you the ability to see into the future? Because if it does, I feel gypped. Where's my new superpower?"

Walker shook his head and felt his jaw firm. "No, I can't see the future, but I can have a little faith. And if that doesn't work, I can always go in and haul their butts out of the fire."

CHAPTER 19

THE NEXT INTERRUPTION DIDN'T come until both Walker and Fiona had dressed and settled down in the living room late that evening with a large pizza, a six-pack of very nice British ale, and a DVD recording of *The Return of the King*.

Fiona's plans for the evening had involved more pacing and less relaxing, but Walker had been determined to take her mind off her fears. When nothing else had worked, he'd badgered her into the dinner-and-a-movie idea. She refused to go out, but the pizza place delivered, and he'd had the beer in the fridge. The movie had been a choice between the latest macho action flick and the fantasy epic. Fiona had voted for the latter because she said she liked to watch the blond elf character and make fun of his silly little stunts.

She sat on the sofa snuggled against Walker's side, munching on pizza and talking about how impractical those long, flowing locks were for a real warrior. No one on the Queen's Guard would give an enemy something so easy to grab onto.

When the phone rang, Walker grunted and set aside his beer to reach for the receiver. "Yeah?"

"Hey, Uncle Tobe," Jake said into the phone. "How's it going?"

The casual greeting sounded just like Walker's nephew, but the tone of voice didn't. Instead of the breezy, smart-ass sound Walker was used to, he heard nerves in the younger man's voice. Nerves and pain. He sat up straight.

"Jake, what's wrong?" he demanded.

Fiona's gaze snapped away from the television and locked on his face, her brows furrowing. "What's the matter?"

He shook his head, his own stomach clenching in fear. "Jake?"

"I, ah . . . I was hoping you could come over here for a while. I'm . . . I'm at Mom's house."

Walker's stomach abruptly stopped clenching and shot up into his throat. He heard the hoarse tone of his own voice when he finally forced out the question. "Is she okay?"

Rachel, Jake's mom, was Walker's baby sister—even if she was three years older than him—and his closest relative. Their parents had retired to Florida several years ago, but even while they had lived in the city, Rachel and Walker had always relied more on each other. When her husband, a police officer, had been killed in the line of duty ten years ago while Jake was just a pup, it had been Walker who'd seen her through it. He'd been the one who stood by her side even when she'd been surrounded by two huge, supportive families—the police department and the pack, the Silverback Clan. She'd cried on his shoulder, and the idea of her hurt or worse had him as close to panic as he could ever remember being.

"No, uh . . . Mom's . . . Mom is fine," Jake said, but Walker wasn't reassured. He could hear the little breaks in his nephew's voice. "Mom's fine. It's Aunt Shelby. She's dead."

Walker's gut twisted. He couldn't fight the surge of relief at hearing Rachel was all right, but he'd known her best friend, Shelby, since high school. How could she be dead?

He didn't know how much of the conversation Fiona could hear or what expression he wore, but she must have sensed something. Her small hand covered his and squeezed, the warmth exactly what he needed just then. He turned his hand over and twined their fingers together.

"What happened? Was there an accident?"

"No. No, Uncle Tobe. They were attacked." The teenager drew in a shaky breath and forced the words out with obvious effort. "She and Mom had a date tonight. You know, a girls' night out. They were walking home from that little dive of a restaurant they like down in the Bowery, and something jumped them. Mom's still real shaken up. Can you come over?"

Now Walker's grief began to take on a tinge of panic. For something to have shaken up his sister and killed her best friend when Rachel was around to stop it indicated some seriously deep shit. Both she and Shelby were fully grown Lupine females. While he could have bested either of them in a fight, together they might very well have kicked his ass. That meant that whatever had attacked them sure as hell wasn't a human mugger and probably wasn't even a shifter. Given the events of the last few days, Walker decided he didn't like the sound of this at all.

"Yeah," he said, trying to keep the worry out of his voice but not knowing if he succeeded. "Just sit tight, kiddo. I'm on my way."

He hung up the phone and headed straight into the bedroom to grab his shoes and his keys. Fiona followed, her eyes wide and concerned.

"I couldn't hear everything," she said, watching as he sat down on the end of the bed to yank on a pair of socks, "but I know your sister is okay. Who isn't?"

"Her best friend. Jake's honorary aunt. She's dead."

"Oh no." Fiona's voice was soft and full of genuine regret for the death of a woman she hadn't even known existed. Walker felt a tiny corner of his heart ease just from knowing she cared. "What happened?"

His mouth hardened as he stamped his feet into a pair of battered work boots. "I don't know. She and Rachel were attacked on their way home from dinner. Rach made it home, but Shelby was killed. Jake asked me to come over, so I need to head out."

"Of course we do."

He looked up from yanking on his laces and saw her standing in front of him wearing a denim jacket over the casual outfit she'd been lounging in. While he still had one shoe to tie, she wore a pair of neat pink sneakers tied with tidy bows.

She shoved her hands in her pockets and watched him from those wide violet eyes. "Is it close enough to walk?"

"I'll catch a cab." He finished tying and stood, struck maybe for the first time by how tiny she was. Her head barely came up to his shoulder, and her body looked so delicate, he was amazed he hadn't broken her during one of his less restrained moments. "You don't have to come with me."

"But I am. You'll have enough to do dealing with your sister, and it sounded like Jake was taking this pretty hard himself. Your hands are going to be full, so there's no reason you shouldn't use mine."

He reached out and pulled one of her hands out of her pocket, linking his fingers again with hers. As small as her hand was, it felt just right joined with his own. "You know, this probably isn't the best way to go about convincing me you're not my mate."

"Just because I'm not your mate doesn't mean I'm heartless," she said, walking with him to the front door of the apartment. "I'll save my convincing for another time. Right now, I wouldn't even leave my uncle alone to face what you're facing."

Walker almost surprised himself with his brief snort of laughter. "Wow, so you like me as much as your uncle, huh? Now that sounds like a match made in heaven."

Fiona stood awkwardly in another woman's kitchen, watching while that woman buried her head against Walker's shoulder and sobbed as if her heart were breaking.

Jake had opened the door to them just a few minutes ago, looking both profoundly relieved and incredibly sad. He'd acted like any young man on the cusp of adulthood and held his shoulders straight under a burden that threatened to make them crumple. Fiona had taken one look at him and felt her own heart crack a little. Walker had just pulled him into a hard, comforting hug.

They had kept their voices low, the way folk always seemed to do around the dead and those who had loved them. It didn't make any difference, Fiona realized, whether you were Fae or Lupine or human. Grief left the same wounds on everyone, and everyone spoke softly in the face of it.

Jake led them into a bright, cheery kitchen completely at odds with the soft sounds of weeping that came from the woman seated at its small table.

Rachel Walker Chase had long, dark hair, a slim, athletic build, and elegant, tidy hands with nails polished a soft, candied mauve. That was all Fiona could see of her, because she sat with her elbows braced on the table and her face buried in her trembling hands, crying with soft, gasping sobs.

Fiona hung back, standing uncertainly in the doorway while Walker crossed the room in two short strides and pulled his sister up into his embrace.

"Aw, Rach," he said gruffly as he pressed his cheek to her hair. "I'm sorry, hon. I'm so sorry."

Rachel's arms locked tight around her brother's shoulders, and Fiona could see her body trembling with the force of her grief. "God, Tobe, I can't believe she's gone."

Walker murmured soothing nonsense against Rachel's hair and rocked her gently back and forth. Feeling suddenly like an intruder, Fiona began to wonder who would notice if she just slipped out. She wouldn't completely desert Walker, but maybe she should wait in the living room. Or downstairs in front of the building.

"They were best friends for like . . . forever," Jake said softly, the murmured words pulling Fiona back to reality. "They went to high school together and everything. Shelby was the maid of honor at Mom's wedding." His own voice sounded thick, and he had his hands shoved deep in the pockets of his jeans. He stood with his shoulders hunched as if he were walking against a cold wind. "I haven't seen her this broken up since my dad died."

All thoughts of escape drained out of Fiona. "I can't imagine what she's going through, but I do know it must be tough to lose your best friend. That's what happened when your father died, too, isn't it?"

The question seemed to take Jake by surprise, and he looked away from his mother to stare down at Fiona. "Yeah, I guess it is. I never thought of it that way before, but I think you're right. I mean, she used to call my dad an idiot and threaten to bash his brains in with a frying pan, but most of the time she was laughing when she said it. And if she wasn't, he'd say something stupid and silly until she couldn't help but laugh." The memory made his mouth curve in a small smile. "They were nuts about each other, but I always thought that was because they were both just nuts."

"It must have been tough to lose him. For both of you."

"It was the worst. I'm not sure who spent more time crying, her or me. But Uncle Tobe was there to take care of us. Or maybe to just bully us through the worst of it. We got through it."

Fiona put her arm around the youth's waist and hugged him. "You'll get through this, too."

Jake looked down at her for a minute; then he nodded and one of his arms lifted to curl around her shoulder. "Thanks, Princess."

They stood in the doorway for several minutes, quietly giving Rachel and Walker their moment together. Seeing Walker with another woman wrapped up tight in his arms stirred two very confusing feelings in Fiona. The first felt like jealousy, which was a feeling she'd never experienced before and which especially surprised her considering she knew the woman he was holding happened to be his sister. In the first place, Fae didn't get jealous as a rule. They tended to be casual about relationships, entering them with a burst of passion, then parting amicably once the flames had died. Even the few life bonds she'd seen among her people had a quietness to them that had nothing in common with the sharp, possessive feelings she had when she saw Walker in the arms of another woman. And second, she knew Rachel was his sister. Even if she hadn't, she could have guessed. The way he held Rachel looked completely different from the way he held Fiona. It was gentle and loving, but there was no heat. It looked completely fraternal, and Fiona had never mistaken the way he touched her for the touch of a brother. She could only put it down to shock, maybe. Their relationship was still new, and tonight's news had taken them all by surprise.

The second feeling disturbed her even more, because it bore a striking similarity to the things she had felt when Walker had been inside her and called her his mate. It felt like her insides had gone all soft and liquid, and a curious kind of tightness in her chest made it feel as if her heart were aching.

It felt almost like . . . love.

Oh no.

She was so not ready to deal with that. Pushing the disturbing sensation aside, she refocused her attention on Jake. "Does your mother drink tea?"

"Huh?"

"Your mother. Does she drink tea?"

He frowned down at Fiona, clearly not following her train of thought. "What are you—"

Fiona pointed at the kettle sitting on top of the stove and asked a tiny bit slower this time, "Tea. Does your mother drink it?"

"Ah . . . yeah, I guess so."

Since she had nearly cried herself out against her brother's shoulder, Rachel heard at least part of that exchange. She raised her head and wiped a hand across her eyes to clear away the tears.

"I'm sorry, Jake. I didn't know you had invited anyone over," she said. Her voice was hoarse from weeping, and she sniffled as she tried to compose herself. "I'm not sure this is the best time to introduce me to—"

"Rachel," Walker interrupted. "This is Fiona. She's not one of Jake's girlfriends. She came over with me."

The other woman's red-rimmed eyes widened, and she looked from her brother to Fiona and back again. "Oh," she said. "Well, it's . . . ah . . . I'm glad to meet you."

Fiona offered a tentative smile. "I'm sorry to intrude, but I thought maybe there was something I could do to help. I know things can seem pretty overwhelming in situations like this. I was just asking your son if you might like some tea."

Rachel blinked and stared back at her blankly. "Tea? Um, I guess. . . ."

Walker shot Fiona a grateful look and guided his sister back to her chair at the table. "Come on, Rach. Sit down. Fiona will make some tea and maybe some coffee." He shot her a hopeful glance and she nodded. "And you and I can talk. I know it's rough, but you need to tell me exactly what happened."

Under the cover of reaching for the teakettle, Fiona managed to catch Jake's eye. She jerked her head toward the empty seat on the opposite side of Rachel from Walker and raised an eyebrow. Jake nodded and slipped into the chair, taking one of his mother's hands in his. Satisfied, Fiona turned on the tap and filled the kettle.

"We, uh, we went down to the Bowery for dinner," Rachel said. It was obvious that she had to struggle not to break into tears again. "You know that little dive I used to drag you to on Tuesdays."

"All-you-can-eat buffalo wings. They shouldn't say 'all-you-can-eat' unless they really mean it."

His sister gave a watery laugh. "Yeah, well, they added some fine print the week after they kicked you out. Anyway, Shelby never minded going with me, and with Jake living on his own now, sometimes I just don't feel like cooking. So I called her up and asked if she wanted to get something to eat. Maybe see a movie."

Fiona searched quietly through the cabinets, not wanting to disturb the conversation. Or make it difficult to overhear.

"She said, 'Sure,'" Rachel continued. "Told me she'd meet me there and we'd decide if anything good was playing. If not, we'd come back here and watch something on DVD. Have a couple of glasses of wine."

Walker squeezed her hand. She held on to him and Jake with equal ferocity.

"So that's what we did. We had dinner, laughed, talked. She'd had a date last week, and it was a disaster. Some vampire she met at work." Shelby had tended bar at a nightclub in midtown. "He turned out to be a real jerk, which she should have known ahead of time, but anyway, we joked about it. She called him 'Fanghorn Leghorn.' Said he never got tired of the sound of his own voice."

The kettle was heating and the herbal tea bags Fiona found in the cabinets were draped in two mugs with the logo of a local public radio station. Taking a deep breath, Fiona turned her attention to the coffeemaker and pursed her lips. Why would anyone want to make coffee when they could buy a really fabulous cup at any number of little coffeehouses scattered through the city like wool on sheep? How exactly did an "automatic drip machine" work, anyway? She didn't think it was the right time to ask.

"We looked in the paper, but neither of us was interested in what was playing in the Village, and we felt too lazy to trek uptown, so we decided to come back here." Rachel's voice hitched, and she paused for a minute to collect herself. Fiona couldn't help willing the other woman just a tiny bit of added strength. "It was about nine thirty when we left the restaurant. Still practically lunchtime for that area, so nothing was really crowded. It was a nice night out. We decided not to take a cab."

Fiona gritted her teeth and, with a quick glance over her shoulder to make sure the others weren't watching, wiggled her fingers at the counter. Instantly the rich, warm scent of coffee wafted from the glass carafe. Another wiggle had the kettle hissing a happy boil. Quickly Fiona filled cups and brought them to the table. She slipped into the remaining empty seat, opposite Rachel.

The other woman looked down at her tea as if she couldn't quite figure out what to do with it. "I know it's not a great neighborhood, but what could happen to us? We'd both lived in the city all of our lives, and it wasn't like we couldn't take care of ourselves." She looked up at Walker, her expression confused. "We should have been fine."

Fiona could see the grim light in Walker's eyes, but he kept that anger from reflecting in his face. "I know, Rach. You couldn't have expected it."

"We didn't. God, we so didn't." She let go of her brother's hand to push the hair back from her face. She blinked to keep fresh tears at bay. "Even now I don't . . . I'm not exactly sure. About what happened. It was so fast. We cut through an empty lot. One minute she was laughing about Fanghorn, and the next she just started screaming." A shudder ripped through Rachel and she pressed her hand against her mouth. "I've never heard her scream like that. I never heard anybody scream like that. She didn't have time to shift. She didn't even have time to run. It just . . . tore into her, like she was made out of paper."

Rachel's voice broke, and she laid her head down on the table as sobs took over again.

Fiona watched, her own heart aching, as her lover's sister gave in to the swelling tide of grief, of shock, of guilt. Walker swore under his breath and shoved back his chair to kneel beside his sister's and take her back into his arms. Rachel clung and wept, and on her other side, Jake looked about ready to start bawling himself. Walker's eyes met Fiona's over the top of Rachel's head and the dark, helpless look in them made the crack in her heart widen.

Quietly and circumspectly, she wove together a spell and sent it winging toward Rachel's heart. Fiona couldn't heal the other woman's pain and wouldn't presume to. Like all magic users, she had learned to be cautious in trying in influence the hearts of others or their minds when their hearts were involved. Charming the doorman at her uncle's building had been one thing—he didn't know them and didn't care. But if she tried to wipe away Rachel's memory of her best friend's death, the woman's heart would know something was wrong. It would feel the stirrings of love and grief, and without the memory to put those feelings into context, she might not know how to handle them. Likewise, if Fiona tried to remove the pain from

Rachel's heart, her mind would remember the events and she would wonder at her own lack of feeling at the recollection.

But Fiona could give the grieving woman some ease. Not heal the wounds but make them a little less ragged. Not erase the memories but bring other kinder, pleasanter ones to the foreground. Fiona watched while the magic worked, heard Rachel's wrenching sobs quiet to a gentle weeping, and saw the look of relief on Walker's face. He looked up at Fiona, and she smiled softly back at him.

"I'm so sorry, honey," he repeated, squeezing his sister tightly. "I know this is tearing you up, but you need to get it out. And if I'm going to find out who did it, I need to hear everything."

"I can tell you right now who did it," Rachel said. For the first time, anger began to compete with the pain in her voice. "I can't say I've ever seen a demon before, but I sure as hell recognized that's what this was."

Fiona froze. On the other side of the table, she saw Walker stiffen, and she knew exactly what he was thinking. Squick better come back with some answers. Soon.

"Describe it," Walker ordered, his voice gruff. "Every detail. Tell me exactly what you saw and everything you noticed about the demon. Now."

Rachel's answer did not surprise either of them. It had definitely been a demon, one that stood about eight feet tall and proportionately wide, muscled like a stone giant but as fast as a cheetah at full speed. It had dark red skin that amounted to leathery armor, she said, and she should know since she'd tried to hurt it, to make it leave Shelby alone. Rachel had noticed horns, not the small stumps Squick had, but heavy, curving ram's horns that curled along the sides of its skull, protecting it from any blows to the head. Its legs had bent backward, like a goat's, and ended not in feet but in huge cloven hooves. The description made it seem somewhat similar to the first demon Fiona and Walker had encountered, just after she'd entered Manhattan through the Faerie gate. Unlike that monster, however, this sounded like an upgraded version. Demon 2.0.

A muscle in Walker's jaw clenched, and Fiona could see him struggling to be gentle with his sister, instead of barking orders and demanding answers the way she knew he was inclined to do. "I know you said you didn't see where it came from, Rach, but did you see where it went? What direction it left in?"

Rachel laughed, a hoarse, rough, incredulous sound. "Sorry, Bro, but I didn't exactly stay around to say my farewells. I saw Shel die. It was kind of hard to miss, considering her head landed next to me about twenty feet away from the rest of her. There wasn't anything I could do to help her, so I ran. I shifted, and I ran home as fast as I could manage it. I left her there. I just left her body there in that lot and ran because I was too scared to do anything else! I had Jake alert the pack as soon as I got home, but—"

"You did the right thing," Fiona said. She could tell by the way Walker's jaw had clenched shut that he couldn't manage to form the words just then, so she said them for him. "You said it yourself. There was nothing you could have changed by staying behind. If you had, there just would have been more people grieving tonight, and two women to mourn for instead of one."

Rachel looked startled, as if she'd forgotten Fiona was there, but when she opened her mouth, her son cut her off.

"She's right, Mom. You did the right thing," Jake said. He had to clear his throat before he got the words out, but he did, and he even backed them up with a sad crooked little smile. "After all, it would be really unfair of you to die and leave Uncle Tobe paying the rest of my tuition. Especially since I've been thinking about med school."

She stared at him for a long time while the words sank in. Then she gave a watery hiccupping laugh and reached out to grab her son by the back of the neck and haul him close for a kiss. "Don't worry, kid. You're not getting rid of me anytime soon. But you're still going to have to do your own laundry this weekend."

Fiona felt the change in the atmosphere of the room. The grief was still there, and the anger, but the worst of the tension had defused. Exhaustion took its place, and Rachel seemed to droop in her chair. She looked tired and worn and a bit numb after the violence of her recollections.

Her son watched her with concern plain on his face. "Mom, I think you need to go up to bed. Try to get some sleep."

"I don't think I could, baby. Every time I close my eyes, I just see—" She broke off and looked down.

"You have to try," Walker said. "You're worn out. Not only is it late, but you've had a huge shock, and you've cried enough to put any five women I know to sleep. You need to at least lie down."

She shook her head. "You're a sweetheart of a baby brother, Tobias, but I just can't."

Fiona spoke up. "I understand. I'm sure the last thing you need is to shut your eyes and start reliving the past few hours, but if you want, I could maybe help you sleep. Keep you from having nightmares."

For the first time since they'd walked in the door, the Lupine woman seemed to really see Fiona. Rachel's face smoothed into a mask of polite interest, but something deeper lurked behind it. Curiosity, maybe, and speculation. "I'm sorry. It's really rude of me, but I'm afraid I can't remember your name."

"It's not rude at all. My name is Fiona. I just wish we were meeting under different circumstances."

Rachel nodded. "So do I. Especially since this is the first time my baby brother has ever brought a woman home to meet his family." She slid Walker a reproving glance. "How long have you two been seeing each other?"

"Not long." Walker went from looking alternately concerned and homicidal to looking decidedly uncomfortable.

"I had just come into the city for a visit when I ran into your brother." That sounded good. True, as far as it went, but vague enough not to start trouble. "He's been letting me tag along with him."

"Oh, right." The speculation in Rachel's eyes shifted into a frank evaluation of Fiona's merits and flaws. She tried not to shift from one foot to the other. "And did you say you're a witch?"

Fiona shook her head. "No."

"I'd just assumed, since you offered me something to help me sleep. Did you mean some kind of herbal thing, then?"

"No. I'm not a witch, but I do have some magic," she said, wondering what Walker wanted her to reveal and what he wanted her to conceal. "The offer was genuine. Just a tiny little suggestion, and you could get to sleep without having any nightmares."

Rachel looked uncomfortable, as if she was trying to figure out how to refuse without sounding rude. "Thanks, but, uh, I'll be fine. The tea is great. It always helps me sleep."

"Fiona isn't a sorcerer, Rach, and she's not going to turn you into a toad," Walker said, his eyes on the woman he'd claimed as his mate. "She's Fae."

His sister's eyes widened. "You're kidding."

Walker shook his head.

Rachel stared at him for a long minute before she seemed to realize he wasn't going to grin and tell her he was joking. Her eyes narrowed on his face; then she turned and took another look at Fiona. Brushing her brother's hands away, she stepped closer and gave the Fae a head-to-toe once-over. She took another step, and her nostrils flared as she inhaled deeply. Her chin hit her chest, and she spun back to face her brother.

"You're kidding me!"

Fiona's stomach did that nasty clenching thing again as she braced herself for Rachel's next words. She hadn't realized how important it was that Walker's family liked her. Or at least didn't consider her a huge mistake on his part.

Well, if Rachel Chase didn't like the idea of her brother taking Fiona to mate, she thought, that was just too bad. She'd have to learn to deal with it, the same way Fiona had. No princess of her family line had ever backed down from a fight, and no one had ever mentioned any of them losing one, either. She held her head high and waited for the other woman to rail at her brother for his choice of partners.

"Tobias Adam Walker, I can't believe you didn't tell me the very minute this happened! What were you thinking?"

The words sounded like what Fiona had expected, but the tone didn't. Instead of anger and disapproval, Rachel's voice held excitement and laughter completely at odds with the emotions she'd expressed for most of the evening. When she launched herself into her brother's arms and planted a loud, smacking kiss on his cheek, Fiona felt almost as dazed as he looked.

"Congratulations! This is wonderful!" Rachel kissed Walker again, then released him to pounce on Fiona and haul her into an enthusiastic hug. "Oh, I'm so happy for both of you!"

Pulling back, Rachel looked down into Fiona's non-plussed face and smiled. Then sniffled. Fiona felt a surge of alarm.

"I'm so happy," Rachel said again, quieter this time. "I can't think of anything else that could have made me smile tonight, so it looks like I'm doubly in your debt, Fiona. Once for taking this big lug off the family's hands, and once for giving me something to be happy about on the second-worst day of my life." She leaned down and kissed Fiona's cheek. "I don't know if that was the magic you were talking about, but it sure worked like a charm."

CHAPTER 20

It took another half hour or so to drag themselves away from Rachel's house. First she'd had to hug each of them another twenty or thirty times; then Jake had needed to put his own two cents' worth of congratulations in, along with a teasing comment or two about "spoiled princesses" not seeming so bad once you got to know them better. Which, of course, had meant Walker had to box his nephew's ears for referring to his mate with that particularly appreciative glint in his eyes.

Rachel had wanted to pop open a bottle of champagne and toast the new couple, a suggestion that Fiona had greeted with a smile that failed to completely conceal the look of panic in her pretty purple eyes. In sympathy with that feeling, Walker had found a polite way to refuse and accompanied it with a promise that he'd bring Fiona back for a real celebration another night.

Even though Rachel's state of mind had drastically improved since the discovery of the happy news, Walker hadn't liked the idea of leaving her and Jake all alone in their town house. He'd called and arranged for a couple of her friends to come and stay the night and made Jake promise to call if there was any trouble. Walker would have preferred to stay with them himself, but he and Fiona had work to do. Before tonight, the need to find the demon had been motivated mostly by duty and an innate desire to see justice done for the humans he had never met. Now, his abstract desire for justice had become a very concrete need to avenge himself on the thing that had killed a long-standing friend and threatened the safety of his family.

He waited until they left Rachel's building before he flipped open his cell phone and dialed Graham's number for what seemed like the thousandth time in the last week. Graham would fill Rafe in, Walker knew, but his first loyalty was to the pack, and his first instinct was always to alert the alpha. That was how packs operated.

"We've got a problem," Walker barked as soon as the other man answered.

"I know. Is Rachel okay?"

"Yeah. She wasn't hurt, just shaken up. Maggie and Samantha are on their way over to her place. They're going to spend the night."

"Good. I managed to get a pack member on the homicide squad. Shel—I mean, the body is on its way to the morgue and Adam and Annie are right behind it."

"We can be there in twenty."

"Walker, we need to find this thing," Graham said, his voice low and intense. "Not just because of Shelby, though God knows that makes me want to rip it apart with my bare teeth and dance in the leftovers, but . . ."

"But what?"

"The negotiations. The delegates voted this morning. The Europeans and the Asians will ratify the basic language of the declaration of rights. With them on our side, we think the Africans and the Americans can be persuaded. But if news of these demon attacks gets out before the signatures are on the document, we'll be in trouble."

"Yeah, I got that, Cuz. Trust me, I'm giving this everything I've got."

He hung up and headed for the corner to hail a cab.

Fiona hadn't said much since Rachel's congratulations, but she followed along behind him, her silly pink sneakers soundless on the pavement. He really hoped she wasn't gearing up for another argument about their relationship.

If she wanted to brood, that was fine. He sat in the taxi beside her and stared out the window, trying to pretend that he wasn't acutely aware of every breath she took. It didn't feel like she was brooding, though. She lacked the requisite pout and the air of wounded dignity. Instead, she just seemed to be lost in thought, her expression pensive but neutral in the light that shone through the taxi's windows.

The cabbie let them out a block from the hospital's entrance, and Walker and Fiona made their way inside to the elevators. Even after visiting hours, the hospital buzzed with activity, but no one gave them a second glace as they stepped into the car and pushed the button for the basement. Morgues were always in basements. An irony, considering what store humans put in the idea of heaven as a celestial realm high above them.

Graham had been as good as his word. When Walker and Fiona arrived at the morgue, Adam was waiting outside. He used his key card to open the locked door and ushered them inside.

"Sorry to see you back so soon," he said, and the bags under his eyes looked even more pronounced than they had the other day. "Annie is inside. She seems to feel a connection to these victims, and she's a hell of a scientist. She's been playing forensic investigator. Looking for trace evidence before I do the autopsy."

Walker nodded and stepped farther into the cool, sterile, windowless room that housed the hospital's morgue. It seemed odd somehow that the institutional green paint and spotless tile should look familiar to him. If that didn't mean he'd spent too much time around death lately, he didn't know what did.

He avoided looking at the autopsy table and the calm, efficient brunette who hovered over it. That was Shelby Lupo on that table, not some strange human, but a pack member and a longtime friend at that. He didn't want to see her this way, to have to acknowledge that he'd never see her any other way again. Fiona must have read his expression. Her small hand slipped into his and squeezed in reassurance.

His own hand tightened along with his heart. It amazed him that he could need her so much so fast. Already he was coming to rely on her in a way he'd never relied on anyone else. It both unnerved him and exhilarated him.

Adam saw them stop just inside the room and paused beside Walker. "I'm sorry," he said. He didn't touch the higher-ranking male, but his voice held the same intent as a sympathetic hand on the shoulder. "The alpha said she was a friend of your family. We're hoping the princess can pick something up, especially since the . . . ah, the time of death was so recent. But it isn't pretty. If you don't want to get any closer . . ."

Walker stiffened. "I'm fine. I want to see what happened."

Nodding, Adam fell silent and led the way to the metal table that held Shelby's remains. Annie looked up at their approach, her warm brown eyes filling with sympathy.

"Walker, I'm so sorry," she said, putting down the large metal tweezers she'd been holding and rounding the end of the table with outstretched arms. Her intent to hug him was clear. "I hope Rachel is okay."

At his side, Fiona stiffened, and Annie caught the subtle movement. She hesitated, sniffing the air and then freezing just an inch away from embracing her friend and packmate. Her eyes widened. She looked from Fiona to Walker and back again several times in rapid succession before she yanked her arms back and clasped her hands together behind her back. She took one large Simon Says step backward.

"Ah, well . . . um, let me know if there's anything I can do."

Beside him, Fiona relaxed, and he could sense her satisfaction. Walker found himself almost amused in spite of the situation. "Thanks, Annie. We appreciate it."

Exchanging looks of mutual understanding, Annie and Adam retreated to the far side of the examination table from the newly mated couple and made sure to keep their eyes focused on their work.

Walker tried to avoid doing the same. Adam had gotten it right. It wasn't pretty.

If Walker hadn't known the body's identity, he would never have looked at it and thought, *Oh, that's Shelby Lupo.* He wasn't sure if that counted as a blessing or a curse, but he barely recognized her. Someone had taken care to . . . reassemble her as neatly and naturally as possible on the shiny table surface, but it was still easy to see where her extensive and ugly wounds had cut clear through muscle and bone. The gash on her neck was one, and similar red lines banded both arms and her right leg halfway up her thigh.

Gritting his teeth, Walker forced himself to take stock of each injury. If he avoided looking at her face, he realized, it was easier. The scent of her blood and her death made it impossible to pretend she was just another human, but at least he could stop himself from looking at her and seeing her as she had been, whole and healthy and full of energy.

"I collected whatever trace evidence I found," Annie began, clearing her throat. "There wasn't much, and I think most of it is just crime-scene debris—some gravel, organic matter, a few hairs that seem to belong either to her or to another Lupine. I'm guessing your sister."

Walker nodded. "Yeah. The thing that attacked them wasn't furry. The hairs have to be either Rachel's or Shel's."

Annie nodded. "Other than that, there's not much here. I did swab a couple of the wounds that looked more like bites than claw marks. Maybe we can get some information off the saliva. My lab has DNA sequencing equipment, and since I'm the boss I can skip all the red tape Adam would have to deal with here at the hospital. I'll let you know if I find anything interesting."

Taking his cue, Adam nodded. "I took a quick look at things before you guys got here, and on the surface I'd say this looks a lot like the human woman who was found in the park earlier this week. The wound patterns are consistent—lots of force, no hesitation, really sharp claws. And, of course, the heart is missing again."

Walker nodded. He had his teeth clenched too hard to say anything.

"You sound as if there's something more you need to tell us, Adam." Fiona spoke quietly, and her eyes were on the physician, not on the body. "What's the 'but'?"

Adam shrugged. "It's nothing I can put my finger on. Like I said, the wounds are consistent with those found on the last woman. But," he paused, "there are a lot more of them. There's just a lot more damage overall. It's like the last girl, the thing was just doing a job. Kill the human, spill a little blood, go home, and order a pizza. This time it looks like it took more time, if not with the killing, then with the rest of it."

"What does that mean?" Walker managed.

"Well, the decapitation came early on. That jibes with your sister's recollection, but it also explains why a lot of these wounds on the extremities and the torso showed very little evidence of bleeding." Adam made a face. "I don't know if it's much comfort to anyone, but it looks like Shelby was already dead when the thing ripped her apart."

"Not much comfort, no."

Adam nodded. "I didn't think so."

Walker felt Fiona's hand give his another squeeze before she let go and took a step closer to the table. "Is it all right if I look?" she asked. "I'm sure what you've told us is accurate, but if Shelby can tell us something more, so much the better."

"Of course. Be my guest."

The others watched curiously as Fiona took a deep breath and repeated the spell she'd cast on each of the previous demon attack victims. Walker could see the glow that surrounded Shelby's corpse, could even make out some more glyphs like the ones that had appeared on the others, but he still had no idea what they said. He did know, however, that when Fiona swore, her concentration wavering and blinking the spell back out of existence, something was very wrong.

"What is it?" he barked. He grabbed her around the waist and yanked her away from the table as if he needed to protect her from what lay on it. "What happened? Did you see something?"

Fiona nodded, and her expression was grim. "Yes. Something bad."

"What is it?" Annie asked, breathless and wide-eyed.

"The demon. It's trying to break the hold of its master," she said. "And if it keeps gaining strength this fast, next time, it's going to do it."

Fiona wanted nothing more than to take a hot bath, maybe in a solution of water and disinfectant. The taint of the demon's foul magic left her feeling contaminated, and that was just from reading the residual magic it had left on its victim.

She felt Walker's arm slip around her waist and pull her against his side, and she leaned into him gratefully. Being with him made the air seem a little less foul.

"Are you all right?"

She nodded. "I'm fine, but this is really bad news, Walker. We need to talk to Graham and Rafe again. And I need to see if I can find Squick. I really, really hope he's been able to turn up something useful."

"I'll call the club and see if they can meet us," Walker said, taking her chin in his hand and forcing her to meet his gaze. "Tell me what you saw."

She shivered a little and wished her denim jacket would turn into something warmer. She felt a soft flannel lining appear inside the material and knew her energy was waning if she couldn't manage any better than that. She'd done a lot of spells tonight. Small ones, but the drain added up.

"I thought—well, I'd hoped that the attack on Shelby and Rachel had been one of opportunity," she said. "The selection of the human victims seemed random. I knew a demon should have been able to tell your sister and her friend were something other than human, but I thought maybe it hadn't realized that. Or maybe it was just so worked up that it didn't care who it attacked. But it knew, Walker. It chose Shelby and Rachel deliberately."

"What do you mean?"

She took a deep breath. "You know how I get energy from when we touch? Well, it's possible for me to get energy from touching other folks, too, as long as there's some kind of connection between us. It isn't as good, because the connection isn't as strong, so for me it's not really worth it and I don't bother. Do you follow me?"

He growled. "So long as you follow that if you try touching anyone else for energy, I'll break every bone in their body."

She choked back a laugh, knowing it came from tension more than humor. "Yes, well, anyway, demons work on a twisted version of the same principle. You know they feed on the hearts of their victims? That's because the heart contains the life force of just about every creature you can think of. Humans, Fae, shifters, almost everything."

Walker nodded, looking impatient.

"The difference between all those different kinds of folks is the quality and the quantity of the life force. Traditionally, demons have fed on human hearts because humans make pretty easy pickings for demons. They're small, they're weak, and most of them don't have any idea of how to use magic to defend themselves. But I imagine it's kind of like living on a vegetarian diet. It will keep you alive, but if you're not on it by choice, you're going to snap up a steak the first time you get a chance at one. Others are the steak."

Walker swore and Annie made a sound of distress. Adam just looked really uncomfortable.

"The life force of an Other is much . . . richer than the life force of a human. And the force of a Fae is richer still. That's why the Fae became demon hunters, and why we fought so long and hard to win the Wars. We were fighting for our lives." She paused and gathered her strength to move on to the bad news. "So when a demon takes the heart of an Other, like Shelby, it gets a much bigger magical charge than it would have gotten out of the humans it killed. That's why it attacked her and Rachel. It was looking for more energy, and it knew it wouldn't be able to get it from a human. It wanted steak."

"Why the sudden change?"

"Because it's tired of doing the summoner's bidding," Fiona said, her voice betraying the sick feeling of dread that had crept over her. "It's trying to break the hold of its summoner, and when it does, I'm not sure if anything but a Fae army will be able to stop it."

They went immediately to Vircolac to inform Graham and Rafe of what Fiona had discovered, but they didn't stay long. Walker wasn't in the mood to socialize and Fiona didn't want to waste time. She needed to try to contact Squick to see if he'd been able to discover anything that might help them track down the demons or the sorcerer who had summoned them.

As they walked out the door, Tess pressed a small cloth pouch into Fiona's hand and smiled encouragingly. "It's glass from the explosion," she explained. "I checked it out, and it's safe. The spell that made the glass shatter was a one-shot deal. It didn't leave anything behind for you to worry about. If you're going to try and contact your friends from Faerie, I thought it might help. It's a link between the worlds that you can focus on."

Fiona held the pouch in her hand, worrying it back and forth between her fingers on the trip back home. She'd stopped thinking of it reflexively as "Walker's apartment" and no longer had any trouble picturing herself there with him. She tried not to think about what that meant, but that pretty much equated to what an ostrich was trying to do when it buried its head in the sand.

She stood in the middle of the living room with the little packet of glass in her hand and a frown on her face while Walker flipped the locks and turned out most of the lights. When he finished, he cupped her face in his hands and leaned down to kiss her briefly.

"Are you okay to do this?" he asked. "I don't know what kind of a spell you need to do, but are you sure you have the energy for it? You've done a lot today, and I could help you recharge if you needed it."

Fiona laughed. Humor was pretty much the only thing still holding her together. She hadn't realized how tired she was until they had returned to the calm quiet of the apartment. "*Mo fáell*, if you want to see me naked, all you have to do is ask."

He smiled and kissed her again, lingering a little this time. "I'm glad to hear you say it, Princess. But I was being serious. Are you okay to work any more magic?"

"I'm fine. I promise. Anyway, the call isn't so much a spell as a . . . well, a little like a phone call, I guess. Wireless, of course. All I have to do is put it out there that I want to talk to Babbage and Squick, and wait for them to answer." She shrugged. "I just hope they're not screening their calls."

Walker nodded and helped her off with her jacket, tossing it on the back of the sofa. His hands chafed up and down her arms, and it felt wonderful. She'd been cold since they'd left his sister's house.

"Okay, let's get this over with," he said. "Do you need to concentrate? Should I go in the other room?"

Smiling, Fiona set the small handful of glass down on the end table and lifted her arms to drape them around his neck. She pressed her head against his shoulder and let herself relax. The night had left her emotionally and physically exhausted, and she relished his strength. "It's already done. I placed the call. Think of it as a kind of magical answering machine. Now we just wait for Babbage and Squick to check their messages and give us a call back."

Walker grunted and wrapped his arms around her. For the first time, their embrace felt less like a bonfire and more like a comforting source of warmth. She felt him press a kiss to the top of her head and murmured into his shirt.

"In that case," he said, his voice a soft rumble, "what do you say we get ourselves to bed and try and get some sleep? Neither of us has had enough of that lately, and I have a feeling we should seize the opportunity while we have it."

Fiona mustered up the energy to flash him a grin. "You won't hear me arguing. So long as you don't try to steal the blankets."

He chuckled and took her hand to lead her into the bedroom. "You can have the blankets, Princess, but I doubt you'll need them. I think I can keep you warm."

Chuckling softly, she followed him into the darkness. "I bet you can."

CHAPTER 21

Fiona stirred and shifted and blinked into the unlit room. She could hear Walker's even breathing behind her and feel the warmth of him spooned against her back, one large, hairy arm draped over her waist like a blanket. His hand possessively cupped her breast, but she really couldn't mind. Not when his touch kept her from freezing. The Lupine didn't own any blankets, which she supposed she should have expected, considering he gave off as much heat as your average five-story bonfire. She figured she'd slept under her last cozy quilt.

Closing her eyes for a moment, Fiona braced herself for a wave of restlessness and unease, crested by a healthy dose of panic, but none materialized. Instead, her heart felt strangely light and content. Very strangely, considering the events of the last few days. She could almost feel it smiling, and she couldn't fathom any other source for the strange new energy that hummed through her. It didn't feel quite like the magic she was used to, but she sensed the power in it. How could she not, when it thrummed through her, circulating like the blood in her veins?

She was surprised that the vibrations of the energy hadn't disturbed Walker. But maybe this was normal to him, this "mating" thing. He hadn't seemed nearly as thrown by it as she had felt. Of course, Walker hadn't grown up in Faerie, where everything lasted forever. Except love.

There, she knew, lay the fundamental difference between them and the seeming paradox of their two worlds. In this place, where lifetimes passed in the blink of a Fae eye, the concept of love as eternal seemed to pervade the collective consciousness. Creatures with life spans so short that generations of them had lived and died before Fiona had ceased to be called a child were willing to pledge all of their existence to one another in the name of love. Yet in Faerie, where age held no danger and life stretched out nearly as long as one willed it, couples met and parted with the same ease and regularity of the seasons. Relationships in Fiona's world were the only truly mortal things. The Fae concept of marriage had more to do with passion or politics and the concerns of succession than with undying devotion. Like the seasons, the Fae said, everything changed, so how could a heart that beat into eternity stay constant?

Fiona had never been able to answer, and the dark room around her offered no suggestions.

If she was going to be honest with herself, she would have to admit that she'd never been so confused in her entire life. She had seen with her own eyes that the heat that drew lovers together inevitably cooled. So why, then, did even the thought of parting from Walker bring back that hideous roiling feeling in the pit of her stomach?

Fiona looked down at the hand on her breast and scowled. How could he continue to sleep so peacefully while she lay there and agonized? He was the one who had started all this. Her turmoil was all his fault. She'd felt fine, right up until he'd used that damned *m*-word. Being called someone's mate when you thought you were engaged in a mutually satisfying little fling was bad enough, but then he'd gone and been so amazingly sweet with his sister that Fiona had thought her heart might melt and leak out of her chest.

She'd known then she was doomed. How in the Lady's name was she supposed to not love a man who'd held his sister gently while she wept at the same time that his eyes glinted hard and bright with the need to exact revenge on the cause of her grief? How was she not supposed to love a man who made her forget everything in two worlds, except for the way it felt when he touched her?

The problem, she supposed, lay in the fact that she couldn't. She couldn't *not* love him. That ship had sailed a long time ago. But unlike in some of the human films she'd seen and novels she'd read, admitting she'd fallen in love with a werewolf didn't solve all her problems. It created more, one of which kept circling in her head like a crow above a battlefield: Fiona was Fae and immortal; Walker was neither. She didn't know if she had the strength to watch him grow old and die while eternity stretched before her, looking less like a blessing and more like a cruel sentence.

Instinctively she stirred, as if to move away from the uncomfortable thought. Walker's arm tightened around her and he nuzzled her hair.

"Stop thinking so hard," he rumbled. "It's disturbing my beauty sleep."

She found herself laughing. "Oh, well, in that case, forgive me. I know you need all of that you can get."

He nipped her earlobe. "Smart-ass."

"You're just noticing?"

He soothed the nip with a kiss and cuddled her closer. As he buried his face in her shoulder, his hands began to roam, skimming over her in light, almost soothing caresses. Only Fiona didn't feel soothed, and judging by the erection pressed up against her bottom, neither did Walker. Instead, she felt the familiar tingling in her skin and melting in her belly. Everything seemed to dissolve, going warm and soft and liquid, when he touched her.

Walker discovered that for himself when he moved his hand down over her clenching stomach muscles and slid between her thighs. That's when her insides stopped seizing and started doing cartwheels.

He cupped her, and she melted into his hand like honey, sweet and sticky. She heard his low growl of approval, and his fingers parted her, gliding through her slick folds to find her entrance. He probed, and she squirmed, her breath catching in her throat and then rattling out on a ragged moan. Shifting, he sank two fingers deep inside her.

"Wal-ker." Her voice broke on the cry, and her body clenched around his fingers.

His teeth scraped with infinite care over the tendon in the side of her neck, making her shudder and arch and sending his fingers deeper. Her breath squeezed out and her senses contracted, but she heard the rough, rumbling sound of his voice close against her ear.

"Mine."

Blindly she reached back to him, desperate for something to hold on to. Minutes ago he had been asleep and she had felt pleasantly sated. It should have been impossible for him to make her need this much, this fast.

"*Mine*," he repeated, his voice going even deeper, his tone rougher. He punctuated his claim with a twist of his wrist that made her head spin. Then his thumb rasped over her swollen clit, and the spinning became whirling.

Sweet Lady, he was killing her.

Her fingers clenched in his hair, pulling him closer. She would have pulled him beneath her skin if she could.

"Please," she moaned.

"*Mine*." His fingers withdrew, making her whimper and arch in an attempt to recapture them, but he eluded her. His hand closed around her thigh, lifting her leg up and back and draping it over the top of his. The position left her open and vulnerable and completely at his disposal. The cool night air on her overheated flesh made her shiver. Moving deliberately against her, he fit the head of his erection against her aching center and suddenly she shivered for an entirely different reason.

She opened her mouth, would have begged him to come inside her, but no words emerged. Instead, she heard a soft mewling sound and realized it was coming from her. Her hips shifted, trying to coax him inside, but he only tightened his fingers on her hips, gripping her hard enough to leave bruises and far enough away to drive her slowly insane.

"*Mine*."

She didn't need to be reminded, not when every cell in her body screamed out its agreement. But she couldn't speak, couldn't move, couldn't breathe for wanting him. She shook and waited and nearly died when he finally began to push with a mind-boggling lack of haste against her tight entrance.

Braced for the huge, hard thrust of him inside her, her eyes flew open and her jaw dropped when he halted with barely the first inch of his cock inside her. Her body clamped down on his like a trap, exalting in the now-familiar joining. But he went still, poised maddeningly just within her.

It wasn't nearly enough.

Moaning, Fiona clenched around him in a deliberately provocative massage. He rewarded her with a low growl and a tighter grip, but his hips remained stubbornly motionless.

"Mine."

"Walker!" Her cry sounded choked, hoarse, half plea, half threat. He ignored it and continued to torture her, fingers stroking and pressing and teasing while his body remained poised just inside hers. It didn't matter what she said or did, what threat she made, or where she touched him in return; he stayed hard and unyielding behind her. She was going to lose her mind if he didn't hurry up and make love to her.

"Mine," he insisted, and at least his voice was starting to sound strained. It scraped over her skin like another caress. Then he leaned forward and his teeth closed over the mark on her shoulder, biting with possessive intent.

Dimly Fiona heard herself scream, but it didn't interfere with her ability to hear his voice, the words sounding clear and gruff and intractable in her head. "You're *mine.*"

"Yours!"

She sobbed rather than spoke, but all her blubbering ended on a scream of satisfaction when he roared in triumph and finally plunged fully inside her.

He stretched her, at once both enhancing and soothing the ache his teasing had created. She felt full, brimming, complete. And utterly, unquestionably, his.

With her head thrown back and her eyes staring blindly into the dark, she gave herself up to his possession and made a promise she'd never intended.

"Always."

Walker was drowning. The water had closed over his head and he was sinking fast, but he couldn't have cared less. He would gladly have died then and there, buried deep inside the woman who bore his mark. Who would one day bear his cubs and carry the legacy of his family and his pack into the future.

His cock, though, cared little about the future. It luxuriated in the present, in the tight, hot, slick embrace of Fiona's body and the even greater pleasure still to come.

Groaning, Walker shifted his hand and drew her upper leg higher, sinking even deeper inside her. She rippled around him, struggling to accommodate his size before relaxing in welcome. The feel of it tore another sound from his throat, a kind of rumbling moan, and he fought against the urge to clench his jaw around the mark in her shoulder.

Forcing himself to pull back, he soothed the fresh bruise with a stroke of his tongue and flexed his hips to stroke again, higher this time. He moved deep inside her, and the feel of her closing around him like a homecoming made him want to howl his joy to the moon. He threw his head back, ground his teeth together, and settled into a hard, driving rhythm.

He shuttled in and out of her and savored every soft gasp and broken whimper that fell from her lips. That he dragged from her lips. Knowing she burned for him made him feel like a god.

Wild now, needing more of her, needing all of her, he grabbed her to him and flipped her onto her stomach. She offered no protest, just pulled her knees up more definitely under her and lifted herself into his next hard thrust. Her arms reached forward, fingers clawing at the bedsheets, scrambling for purchase. Walker draped himself over her, pinning her in place with his weight and his heat. He surged deep, and this time he did howl at the fierce pleasure of losing himself inside her. His lover. His mate.

The feral sound echoed around them. Mewling softly, Fiona dropped her shoulders to the mattress and raised her hips higher before him. He growled his appreciation, running his hands over the warm, smooth curves of her bottom. His palms slid up, over her back, along her sides, reaching beneath her to tease and cuddle her breasts. He lingered only a moment before reaching forward and covering her hands with his own. Their fingers linked together like puzzle pieces, and Walker felt the jolt as his heart locked soundlessly to hers.

"Mine," he panted, barely able to speak now. He needed all his breath for the urgency of desire. He let his head drop and pressed his cheek against hers, feeling the light sheen of sweat that coated them both. He'd never felt anything more perfect than this, being joined with her, and he knew he never would. "Mine. Always."

Shaking and desperate, Fiona turned her head until her dazed eyes met his, and Walker felt himself sinking under the pull of those deep violet pools.

"Always," she whispered. Her eyes drifted shut, her breath catching as the tension filling them peaked and teetered on the brink. "Love you."

He hadn't realized he'd been waiting. Not until he heard the words and felt the love and pride and possession and satisfaction exploding inside him like fireworks. Head thrown back, eyes blazing a gold so bright it cast their shadows on the wall of the bedroom, Walker roared the name of his mate and spilled himself endlessly inside her.

When his heart resumed beating, about two minutes too late to prevent brain damage from temporary loss of oxygen to that organ, Walker pried open his eyes and looked down at the tangle of black hair on his pillow.

He had to fight the urge to look smug. He couldn't do much about the fact that he *felt* smug, but given his mate's personality, he thought it best to at least put on a front of non–conquering male with a newly dragged-off mate pinned to the floor of his cave. Sure, it was a bedroom and a very comfortable king-sized bed, but he figured Fiona would view those as semantic differences.

To his surprise, she didn't say anything, just lay limp and silent beneath him, struggling as hard as he was to catch her breath. He frowned as he realized that might be tough for her if he continued to lie on top of her, pressing her into the mattress.

Reluctantly he shifted and rolled onto his back, taking her with him to reverse their positions. He heard her draw in a deep breath, but she still didn't speak. She didn't have to. She'd already told him everything he would ever need to hear.

He wrapped his arms around her and held her snugly against him, nuzzling his face against the soft cloud of her hair that tickled beneath his chin. Her scent surrounded him, warm and sweet and musky, and with his senses full of her, he drifted back into sleep.

CHAPTER 22

WALKER KNEW HE HADN'T gotten drunk in a good long while, so the sensation of being yanked out of sleep by very small but very hard feet dancing across the back of his head didn't quite make sense.

Opening one blurry eye, he stared blankly at his bare headboard and wondered what the hell was going on. He didn't usually wake up to hallucinations.

"Miss Fiona! Mistress! Your Highness, *wakes up*!"

Each progressively louder demand was punctuated by a stomp against his aching skull, but at least this time Walker recognized the voice and the feet that were torturing him. Reaching back, he closed his hand around a small, squirming, annoying form and brought it forward to meet his glare.

"If you ever jump up and down on my head again," he said, eyes narrowed on the scowling red form of

Squick, "I'm going to wring your neck and nail you to my door as a Halloween decoration. Understand?"

The imp huffed. "I doesn't come here to talks to you, wolfie boy. I needs the princess!"

Beside him, Walker felt Fiona stir and stretch and make an annoyed sleepy noise with which he heartily empathized.

"Walker?" she asked, her voice still groggy. "What's going on?"

"Miss Fiona! I gots news! Let us go, furry mortal."

When Walker didn't obey fast enough for Squick's taste, the demon secured his own release by the expedient and painful method of sinking his tiny razor-sharp teeth into the side of the Lupine's thumb.

Walker cursed and dropped the little bastard to the pillow.

"I gots news!" Squick repeated, struggling across the downy surface of Walker's pillow to present himself huffing and puffing on Fiona's right arm. "I gots big news, Miss Fiona. Big, baddie-bad news."

Fiona blinked away the last of her sleepiness and sat up, frowning. "What news? What's going on?"

The frown on Fiona's face didn't begin to match the frown on Walker's, which appeared as soon as her pretty, pale breasts appeared in plain view of their visitor. Neither one of them seemed to pay any attention to nudity, but Walker did, and he didn't plan to take even the slightest chance of another living thing—even an annoying six-inch-tall imp—noticing his mate in nothing but her bare skin. Scowling, he grabbed his pillow and slapped it up against Fiona's bare breasts, concealing them from view.

"You looked cold," he muttered when she turned her frown on him.

"Miss Fiona, I finds out all kinds of thing down Below, but I doesn't thinks any of them be making you happy," Squick said. He seemed perfectly content to ignore Walker but also continued to jump up and down and hop from one foot to the other in his excitement to share his discoveries.

Walker breathed a sigh of relief when Fiona made an absent gesture with her hand and covered both him and herself in casual, *concealing* clothing before she responded.

"I can't say I'm surprised to hear that," she said, her face growing grim. "Just tell me you found out who's been summoning those demons. Or at least which demons they are."

"Not whoses, Miss. Whatses."

Fiona looked almost as confused as Walker felt. "What do you mean?"

"It aren't a who that's calling the demons, miss. It's a what. An amulets. Very oldie, very baddie. Very baddie-bad. Before the Wars, bad."

Walker saw her eyes widen.

"That's not possible," she said, shaking her head. "I've never heard of an amulet that can summon demons. And besides, the only artifacts that survived the Wars are stored in the library at the Summer Palace." She sounded confused, as if she wanted to be certain even as doubt flooded through her. "No one can remove anything from it without the express permission of the queen, and she doesn't give it."

"No, she don't," Squick agreed, "but I knows what I finds out, Miss Fiona, and I finds out this bad stuff. They is talking about it Below. Somebody up Above been calling up the demons and making 'em do stuff, and they gotta does it 'cause the amulet is strong and the one that gots it knows how to use it, and they don't really minds 'cause they likes to tear stuff into little pieces, but they still wanna do the tearing when *they* wants, not when somebody with a necklaces tells 'em to. That's why they leaving all the scribbles on the dead folks. They trying to find the right scribbles to tell the amulets 'shove off.' "

Walker deciphered that breathless ramble—frighteningly quickly if he'd stopped to think about it—and swore. Loudly.

"You were right," he said. "The demon is trying to break free from the summoner, and it thought the way to do that would be to feed on something a little more potent than a human."

Fiona looked equally grim. "That's what it sounds like." She turned back to the imp. "Where did the amulet come from, Squick? Did you find out anything else about it?"

"Some-some. The demons don't likes it 'cause it look like the sun, all goldy and sparkly. And the center they says got a big, big rock in it. One of them kinds that looks all dark and rainbowy. They likes the rock, but not the rest." He swished his arrow-tipped tail. "Some says it come from home, a long, long, long, long, long time ago."

"Home? From Faerie?"

Walker needed to break her of that bad habit—calling anyplace but right next to him home.

"Yup. A kings used it in the fights, they says, and it made the demons stop and do whatever he says to 'em."

Fiona's eyes widened. "So the amulet isn't summoning them, but it allows the summoner to control them. But why would it be necessary for a summoner to use an amulet? The control of the demons is part of their art."

A very disturbing idea began to niggle the edges of Walker's mind. "But what if the amulet was powerful enough to allow someone who *isn't* a summoner to call the demons? Someone who normally wouldn't have the skill. That person would need help to keep them in line, even if he figured out a way to call them."

"But they're demons. They need to be forced to do what you want them to. That's why there are summoners in the first place. It's not like any Tom, Dick, or Harry can just say, 'Hey, demon! Get over here!' and one shows up. You've got to have really strong magic to keep control of a demon. That's why there are so few summoners around."

Squick nodded meaningfully. "Any summoner what can't controls the demons end up a magician kebab."

"It also doesn't help their population that the only demons who usually hang around and listen to a summons are ones who are looking for a quick snack. I'm pretty certain that the abundance of things like Faerie wards around the borders of this plane and sunlight *on* this plane keep all but the hungriest and most reckless of them from letting anyone learn their true names."

"I admit I'm not the demon expert here," Walker said, "but I know a few things about the way magic works in this world. From what I've always heard about demons, they're constantly looking for ways to get back into our plane. Have been ever since your ancestors kicked them out. The only reason they haven't found more ways in is because of those wards. But wards don't work against something that's been invited."

"Summoning isn't really an invitation. It's more like a command."

"Yeah, I get that," he nodded, "and from what I hear, that pisses the average demon off. They get to come to our world, but they have to be at the beck and call of some maniac of a magician. So don't you think the idea of answering an invitation rather than an imperial summons would sound pretty appealing? After all, if they got through the barriers without being bound to some summoner, I bet this place would look a lot like a demon's idea of an all-you-can-eat buffet."

Fiona stopped, as if she needed a second to let her mind catch up with his reasoning. "You mean someone who isn't a summoner invites the demons in and then . . . tricks them?"

"Like a mousetrap. From the evidence our friends so far have presented us with, the species doesn't strike me as all that bright. All the summoner needs to call it is its name and a few simple spell components, and Tess told me earlier that lists of names are passed around in the community like code words. They don't worry about humans getting ahold of them, because humans can't do magic. But if someone had an amulet like this, if they learned a name and placed the call, they could actually manage a summoning. The demon would see the opportunity for a free meal, take the bait, cross into our world, and *wham*! All of a sudden it's not a free ride, because the first course turns out to have a piece of jewelry that works better than any spell to keep demon appetites in line."

"Oh my Goddess," she breathed. "It almost makes sense. That's why I couldn't read most of the glyphs. I was trying to read them like a spell, but there wasn't a spell attached to them. There's magic, sure, but it's a totally different kind."

By this point, Squick was jumping up and down on the bed like a miniature two-year-old with ADHD. "I gots more!" He waited until they looked back at him, then puffed his chest out and continued. "I hears all kinds of stuff when I Below, Miss Fiona. I sneaked real good and maked sure no ones seed me. I gots real close when I seed demons talking together in their nasty demon ways. I heared stuff. There is rumors down there that would turn your stomach over like a pancakes."

"What kind of rumors?" Walker demanded.

The imp ignored him. Pointedly.

"What kind of rumors, Squick?" Fiona asked.

"The kinds that says something big is coming soon," he hurried to answer, glancing sideways at Walker to be sure the Lupine had noticed. "I heard demons say they was gonna come above and gather up some strength before they does the real baddie-bad stuff."

"I wonder what they consider bad if none of this qualifies?" Walker muttered.

"The *point,*" Squick said, glaring at Walker before he remembered he wanted to ignore him, "is that if the demons gonna do baddie-bad stuff just 'cause they wanna do it, they gots to know a way to make it so the amulet won't bother 'em no more."

Fiona looked at Walker, her eyes wide and troubled. "I think he's right."

"Of course I is right." The imp crossed his arms over his chest and preened. "Now what is you gonna do about it?"

Walker leaned forward and glared at the creature, who, he was discovering, was a big ball of obnoxious crammed into a tiny red package. "Watch it, pipsqueak. Show better manners to your princess."

"Don't threaten Squick. It was an honest question." When the imp stuck his tongue out at Walker, Fiona turned the look in his direction. "Even if it was rudely phrased."

At least she was an equal-opportunity scold.

Walker snorted. "What? You're supposed to go

stand in front of a rampaging demon and tell him you'd really prefer it if he didn't break the hold of his magical oppressors and go on a bloody rampage through the population of Manhattan?"

She smiled. "Relax, *mo fáell*. I'm not planning on turning kamikaze on you. In fact, my plan was to call in reinforcements." She turned to Squick. "Have you told any of this to Babbage yet?"

The imp snorted. "Why I stop to tell that puny pixie? He aren't nobody important."

Squick glanced over at Walker when he said that. To include him in the group of the unimportant, apparently. Walker just glared back, which made him feel ridiculous. He was fighting with an imp who had the maturity level of a toddler and the grammatical skills of a non-native-speaking toddler with brain damage. What the hell had happened to him?

"Have you spoken to him since the other morning?" Fiona asked.

"Nope, I hasn't. I's been busy getting all this super-duper informations for you, Miss Fiona. I not have time to talk to no pixies."

Walker saw Fiona's frown. "Is there a problem?"

"I'm not sure. I just would have expected to hear back from him by now. Or for him to at least have gotten a message to me or to Squick."

"Oh, he wouldn't talks to me, Miss Fiona. He hate me almost half as much as I hates him." The imp gave a broad shrug. "He probably gone back to Faerie for to tattle to the queen on how we isn't supposed to be here."

Fiona didn't look convinced. "But I sent out a call. You answered, and you were Below. He should have responded right about when you did."

Walker put a hand on her shoulder. "After everything

that's happened lately, I don't blame you for worrying. Would it make you feel better if I went out and looked for him?"

"Only if I went with you."

He stared at her for a long moment, then sighed when she merely stared back. "You're getting ready to tell me that if I'm going, you're going, right?"

"Right."

"So it would be a really big waste of time for me to ask you to stay here where I know you're safe and let me do the missing pixie search."

"Colossal."

Grimacing, Walker pushed himself off the bed and reached out a hand to help Fiona to her feet. "Just so long as we understand each other."

CHAPTER 23

THEY DIDN'T HEAD STRAIGHT out to hunt pixies. First, Walker had to get in touch with Graham and give him an update. It was either that, Walker explained, or take the chance of the pack leader deciding to vent the frustrations of the human negotiations on his liver. Better to get the information update out of the way.

Fiona also took a minute to put out another call before they left, and she carried the little pouch of glass with her just in case. She wished the call could reach all the way to Faerie, but it seemed that whatever curse had made the glass explode before was still forming a barrier between the worlds.

Squick made a big production of griping and grumbling over being forced to spend his time looking for a pesky pixie until Walker threatened to strangle him with his own tail. So in the end he shut up and just glared at the world from inside the canvas bag Walker had given Fiona to carry him in. Someone might notice if she walked down the street with an imp sitting on her shoulder, Walker had pointed out.

"Gate first," Fiona said as they stepped out onto the pavement and Walker turned to lock his door. "If we're going to retrace Babbage's steps, we might as well start where he started."

"Be faster to starts where he finished," the bag grumbled.

Fiona ignored him. Her mind had enough problems to focus on already without worrying about the surly imp. Walker's theory about the identity of the person in control of the demons had thrown a huge wrench in their plans to identify him. At least when they'd believed him to be a summoner, the pool of possible candidates had been limited to that somewhat sparse population. The idea that the culprit could now be any one of the millions of residents of Manhattan didn't bode well for their chances of finding him. Especially not before anyone else got hurt.

It had been pretty much all bad news since she'd woken up, Fiona admitted, biting back a sigh. She'd been having a really good dream, too. Something about her and Walker and complete privacy in a lushly furnished room with sturdy locks and an even sturdier bed frame. Instead of putting all that lovely carpentry to the test, she'd been jerked out of sleep and faced with an infinitely less attractive reality.

She could practically feel the trouble brewing. Something was about to go wrong, if it hadn't already. She couldn't put her finger on it, but she could feel it, like an itch along her skin that refused to go away no matter how much she scratched at it.

The fact that Babbage still wasn't answering her call made her nervous. Usually, she had trouble getting Babbage to go away. He tended to stick like glue whenever she gave him the slightest encouragement and often when she didn't. The only explanations she could think of for his silence did not reassure her.

They entered the park on the Upper West Side, off Indian Road, avoiding the tennis courts to the south and the playgrounds that dotted the edges of the parks department land. Even so, they were hardly the only ones around. In the fading light of early evening, joggers and skaters and cyclists shared the paths with strollers and sightseers. Fiona even spotted a small group of humans in hiking gear, outfitted with binoculars and field guides for identifying the birds and plants that filled the park.

She supposed that she and Walker didn't look all that different from any of the other couples who walked together along the paths that curled through the hillsides. Blending in was helpful, but they weren't here to take in the closest thing to fresh air that Manhattan had to offer. They took the nearest path west, heading deeper into the park where the trees thickened into surprisingly dense copses of old-growth forest.

Inwood, she had read, represented the last remnants of the woodland that had covered Manhattan when the humans had settled it only four centuries ago. Only a little longer than she'd been alive, and already they'd covered all but the smallest slivers of the island with concrete and metal and glass. She shook her head. No wonder magic had gotten so hard to come by. Faerie magic especially, since it relied so heavily on the energy of the land. Inwood Hill Park was the last piece of real land in the city and one of the only places with enough wild magic left to sustain a Faerie gate.

Walker glanced down at her and raised an eyebrow. "That's a weird expression," he said. "I can't tell if you're angry or amused. What's going on in your head?"

"Just reflecting on how fast this place managed to go to pot once we left. Apparently, you give mortals a few centuries and they just can't help but muck the whole place up."

They reached a branch in the path that gave them the choice of turning north or south. Instead, they stepped off the trail and began to wend their way into the woods.

"A few centuries? Hey, you guys moved out something like three *millennia* ago. Now you're going to complain about the new decorating scheme? That's just bad manners."

Fiona chuckled and ducked to avoid a low-hanging branch. "Yeah, yeah. Better bad manners than bad taste, is what I say."

"Dilettante."

"Barbarian."

They grinned at each other and kept walking.

As the trees grew taller and thicker around them, the last of the weak sunlight faded, leaving them in a premature darkness more charcoal than black.

"Can you see okay?" Walker asked.

"Sure. My night vision isn't as good as yours, but I get by."

The woods muffled the noise, too. There wasn't anywhere in the city where you could completely escape the sounds of traffic and people, but they were quieter here. The Henry Hudson Parkway ran overhead to the west, but no one else had wandered off the path with them, so Fiona didn't hear any voices or any footsteps other than their own.

Until Squick piped up, of course.

"I's suffocating! Air! I needs air!"

Fiona rolled her eyes and shrugged off one strap of the shoulder bag, letting it fall open to the cool evening. "You're not suffocating, but there's no one else around, so I suppose you can come out now."

The imp clambered up the canvas and used Fiona's shirtsleeve like a ladder to haul himself up to her shoulder. With much grumbling and an indignant "humph," he prepared to settle himself down into his accustomed seat.

Walker glanced over and shook his head. "Not there, squirt. Try the other side."

The imp obeyed and scrambled across Fiona's shoulders to sit on the other side. Fiona looked from her shoulder to Walker with wide eyes, puzzled by the order. As soon as their eyes met, she felt the skin of the shoulder closest to him tingle and realization dawned. Squick had been about to sit on the shoulder that bore Walker's mark. She saw the satisfaction in her mate's expression when she made the connection, but he didn't say anything. She supposed he didn't need to.

Walker led the way up a hill and paused as they reached the top. "We're getting close to the gate now, so I want you to keep your eyes open. I know we didn't see anything last time we were here, but it was daylight then. It's nearly dark enough now for demon activity, so stay alert, all right?"

Fiona nodded, but she wasn't worried about demons; she was worried about Babbage.

"Miss Fiona," Squick said suddenly, his high, childlike voice speaking right up next to her ear, "did you knows your pocket is glowing?"

Automatically Fiona looked down and saw a dim blue-silver light glowing through the fabric of her jacket pocket. It took a moment for her to remember exactly what she had put in that pocket. The little pouch of glass.

She grabbed Walker's arm and stopped in her tracks. "Look."

Digging in her pocket, she drew the pouch out and held it up to him. Even through the velvet, the light shining from the small shards was unmistakable. Excitement welled inside her.

"He's here," she said quietly but animatedly. "He's in the park. He must be near the gate. Come on! Hurry!"

She didn't wait for Walker's answer, just took off into the woods. Behind her, the Lupine cursed, but she heard his long strides hurrying after her. He'd be angry with her when they reached the gate, she knew. He'd probably give her a lecture on how he was supposed to be protecting her and he couldn't do that if she was going to take off without warning him. She didn't care. He could lecture all he wanted after they found Babbage. Her relief at knowing he was close made her feet lighter. Finally, she was going to get some good news after way too much of the other kind.

Breaking through the tree line into the clearing, Fiona scanned the open area for signs of the pixie. She didn't see him. Frowning, she realized she couldn't hear his wings beating, either.

"Oh, Miss Fiona," Squick said, but he didn't sound quite like himself. His arrogant, petulant tone had disappeared, and in its place he sounded . . . sad. "Oh, Princess, this is baddie-bad-bad-bad."

The imp jumped down from her shoulder and ran across the leaf-covered clearing to a dark patch on the ground at the foot of the Faerie door.

She felt Walker's hand settle on her shoulder at the same time that her eyes focused on the rough stone of the gate. She had to blink before what they were seeing made sense. The dark, faintly glistening smears on the face of the rock hadn't been there the last time she'd seen it, and neither had the series of ugly, uneven marks on the trees at either side.

In her hand, the pouch of glass glowed brightly, giving off enough light to cast the shadow of her hand on the ground at her feet. It glowed so brightly that Babbage should have been hovering right there in front of her.

The hand on her shoulder tightened and then Walker was pulling her toward him, wrapping her up in his arms and pressing her head to his chest, blotting out the sight of the gate. Numbly Fiona blinked against the soft cotton of his shirt, but the images wouldn't go away. Even with her eyes closed, she could still see the dark, gory mess of demon signs written in her friend's cooling blood.

Walker's gut clenched, and he suppressed the urge to howl up into the twilight sky. He didn't need to know magic to know why his mate stood silent and shaking in his arms. His nose told him that. He could smell the blood, thick and sweet and metallic on the night air. They had found Babbage, but the pixie wouldn't be sharing his news with them.

Walker held Fiona tight against him, thinking savagely that he'd spent too much time lately comforting the women he loved. When he found the thing responsible for causing their pain, he was going to relish tearing it into tiny, bloody, squirming little pieces.

At the foot of the gate, Squick was bending over what Walker had thought was a pile of bloody leaves, but when the imp put one hand on the lump, he realized they really had found the pixie. Walker's sensitive night vision hadn't registered the small body because it had already gone cold. Babbage had been dead at least a few hours.

"I didn't means it when I called him stupid," Squick said, looking up at them. His puckish face was drawn into lines of confusion, like a child who couldn't understand why Fluffy didn't just wake up from its nap. "He not so stupid all the times."

Walker felt Fiona shudder, heard her uneven gasps as she fought back the tears that threatened to choke her. She stirred in his embrace, and he had to force himself to release her when all his instincts demanded that he protect her from the painful sight at her back.

"I know, Squick," she said. Walker felt a surge of pride. Her voice was thick with tears but steady and strong. His mate wouldn't fall apart now. She knew this wasn't the time. "Babbage didn't think you were stupid all the time, either."

It sounded strange to Walker, but it seemed to comfort Squick. The imp nodded and looked down at the pixie's remains. "I don't thinks he still want to be here, Miss Fiona. I think he probably rathers to be home. Maybe I can takes him home?"

Fiona shook her head. "I'm sorry, Squick, but the gate isn't working, remember? We can't get back home."

"Oh yeah." The imp seemed to deflate. "I forgots."

Walker looked around the clearing, paying careful attention to the area just in front of the gate. He could see a few tracks that obviously hadn't been left by the pixie, who seemed a lot more inclined to fly than to walk.

Walker frowned. "I think Babbage did, too. Judging by the tracks, it looks like he was killed by the same demon that attacked us when Fiona first came through the gate, which means Babbage had plenty of time to see him coming. Probably heard him, too."

Fiona frowned. "So?"

"So, all the entrances to Faerie are warded against demons, right?"

She nodded. "Yes. There hasn't been a demon sighted in our territory since the Wars."

"Then I think Babbage's first reaction was to head right for the gate. He forgot that it was sealed. He was trying to get back into Faerie."

"But Miss Fiona told him to comes back to her," Squick protested, "and the pixie always do just what Miss Fiona say."

"Maybe he did," Walker said. "But if a demon was coming after him, he might have thought he could go through the gate and wait on the other side until the demon got sick of waiting and left. Then he could come back and talk to Fiona just like he promised."

"He might have," Fiona said softly. "Babbage always obeys orders, but he's never been called courageous. If he'd seen the demon coming, he would have tried to get to safety."

Walker put his hand on her shoulder again. The urge to comfort her was too strong to ignore. Even if he couldn't make the pain of losing a friend go away, Walker remembered how much it had meant that she'd been there when he'd found out about Shelby.

The bond between them kept getting stronger and stronger, and if they had ever needed to share their strength with each other, now was the time.

He felt the coolness of her skin even through the covering of her shirt and jacket, but it began to warm at his touch and he felt her pull herself up. She squared her shoulders and drew a deep breath, then turned to look up at the gate.

She clenched her teeth and made a muscle jump in the side of her jaw. Walker just stood quietly while her eyes scanned the smears of blood against stone and then looked at the marks on the tree trunks. He heard her breath hiss through her teeth.

"More sigils." Her voice shook, this time not with grief but with rage. "Damn the fiend and all of its kind for the rest of eternity! It used his blood to draw the sigils."

Walker squinted at the dark, ugly lines and frowned. He couldn't read them, but they did look similar to the ones he'd seen carved into the bodies of the demons' earlier victims. "It's still trying to break away from the amulet. I hope to God it hasn't figured out how."

"Squick, we need to find out exactly what those glyphs mean," Fiona said. "Every single line of them. I want a direct translation. I don't care if you have to ask every single demon Below to find out, but I want the answer."

The imp looked alarmed. "But Miss Fiona, the demons doesn't like us. They only didn't eat us last time because I hides real good. If I talks to them, I ends up dinner for sure."

"Fine. Then I'll go myself. Just point me to the gate."

Walker grabbed her and spun her around. "Hold on a minute," he soothed. "I know you're upset, but there's no way I'm letting you go to hell to ask directions."

"It's not hell," she snapped, her eyes flashing up at him, a mixture of anger, pain, and determination. "Don't bring mortal religion into this. It's just Below. It's no different from going to Faerie."

"Sure, except Faerie is populated by pixies and sprites and sidhe, as opposed to big, hungry demons who happen to still be holding a grudge about the way your ancestors kicked their asses."

"I don't care if they're holding a grudge over the last mortal presidential election. We need this information, and if the only way to get it is to go Below, then I'm going!"

Walker drew a deep breath and wrestled back the urge to just throw her over his shoulder and be done with it. These protective instincts were becoming almost impossible to tamp down. The idea of seeing his mate put herself in danger drove him crazy. He couldn't imagine what would happen to him if anything happened to her.

"I don't think that's a very good idea, Princess," he began, clenching his teeth to keep from shouting.

"I don't care what you think!"

He could feel his eyes flashing with temper and used all his willpower to keep it from boiling over. "And I don't care if you're queen of the whole goddamned universe," Walker said, his voice dangerously low. "There's no fucking way I'm letting you walk into some dimension full of demons. You are not putting yourself in that kind of danger."

"You don't get to tell me what to do, wolf!"

Something tugged hard at the leg of his jeans and cut off Walker's sharp retort.

"Um, excuses me, furry mortal guy, but you gonna have to stops with the screamings and shoutings."

"In case you hadn't noticed, Squick," Walker bit out, not taking his eyes from his mate, "I'm not the one doing the shouting."

"That's nice, furry mortal guy," the imp said, tugging again, "but the princess be yelling so loud that nobodies need to go nowheres to find demons. They coming right here."

Walker heard the low, menacing growl a split second before Squick screamed. Instinct took over, and Walker threw himself at Fiona, shoving her to the ground and covering her with his body. He felt the searing pain of a claw ripping into his flesh, and he howled. He braced his hands on the ground at Fiona's side and the glow of his eyes illuminated her startled face.

"Stay down," he hissed, and threw himself into his change.

CHAPTER 24

Stay down?

Fiona lay on a bed of leaves and twigs for half a second and blinked. Was he out of his bloody mind?

As soon as his weight left her, she sprang to her feet. Walker had been right. The same demon that had attacked her when she first appeared in Manhattan the week before crouched in the center of the clearing, eyes glittering red-orange with menace. It had its gaze locked on her, staring past Walker's huge half-wolfen form with malevolent intent. Slowly, never blinking, it raised one misshapen hand and licked a drop of Walker's blood from its long, curving claw.

The rage bubbled inside her like lava, thick and searing and destructive. She'd never experienced anything like it, never known she was capable of hating so violently and so completely. Her people were poets and lovers, a race that had fought one war in its entire existence—the war that had banished creatures like this one to the depths of Below and bound them there forever. For the first time Fiona understood what it meant to have a racial enemy, something that could be despised not for who it was, but for what it was. Evil.

She stepped forward, but Walker cut her off, keeping his body between hers and the demon's. It wasn't that difficult. In his were form, one that combined the features of man and wolf, he stood over seven feet tall on his hind legs, and his body rippled with cords of heavy muscle. She knew she couldn't get around him without cheating, damn him.

The demon, though, didn't pay Walker any attention. Not until it tried to push past him. With an echoing howl, Walker lunged for its throat, lips drawn back over gleaming white fangs, hands heavy with sharp black claws of his own.

Astonishingly fast for something so huge, the demon thrust its arm out and caught Walker with a backhanded blow just before his teeth made contact with its thick skin. Fiona cried out as her mate went down to the ground with a grunt. He turned even as he landed and slashed at the demon's leg, slicing through armored skin into flesh and tendon. The demon bellowed in pain and turned away from Fiona to stare down at Walker, hate and murder gleaming in its eyes.

Fiona heard Walker snarl something she couldn't understand, but the message was clear. He arched his back and flipped himself onto his feet, ducking beneath another heavy blow. Keeping his head down, he launched himself at the demon like a linebacker, coming in hard and low. The demon staggered backward a couple of steps but didn't fall. Its goatlike legs absorbed the shock and pushed back, shoving Walker away with brute strength.

Remembering the early struggle between demon and wolf, Fiona felt her stomach churning. They had both been injured last time, and that had been before the demon had a chance to feed. By now, its strength would have multiplied, increased by every heart it had consumed. She didn't know if Walker could defeat it.

She looked down and saw Squick watching the battle from between her feet, eyes wide, hands moving in pantomime punches in time with the contestants.

"Squick, I need you to do me a favor."

The imp looked up at her. "Now, Miss Fiona?"

"Yes, now. I'm going to try to do a spell, but it's a tricky one, and I'm going to need to concentrate. I need you to watch out for Walker. If he gets into trouble, you need to do whatever you can to distract the demon until I'm ready. Do you understand?"

"I understands, miss, but why you wants to help the furry mortal guy I doesn't know. Mortals break too easy, you know?"

"Just do it, Squick. Make sure he doesn't get himself killed. And make sure you don't, either."

Face grim, Fiona moved quickly to the gate, pressing her back up against the stone. She might not be able to get through the damned thing, but she might be able to get a little boost of energy from it, if she was lucky. And if not, at least this way she knew nothing was going to come up behind her.

She knew the fabric of the spell she was about to cast. She'd read about it many times during her education, but she'd never cast it herself. She wasn't sure if anyone had, not since the end of the Wars. After all, when the demons had been banished, there hadn't been much reason for anyone to cast a spell designed to destroy them.

Closing her eyes, she took a deep breath and struggled to block out the sounds of the battle. She hated it, hated not being able to see what was happening to her mate, as if her watching him somehow protected him from harm. But she knew that unless the cavalry came charging over the hill in the next couple of minutes, this was the best chance she had at ensuring they all survived this attack.

The lack of sleep from the previous night actually served her well in this instance. She might be tired, but her body thrummed with the energy of their long, intense night of loving. She could feel it, welling up inside her, spreading from the depths of her heart and her womb and coursing through her veins until she could have glowed with the intensity of it.

This spell bore a resemblance to the one she'd used against this same demon a few days ago, but only a passing one. She needed a lot more energy for this one and a lot more concentration. She let the power build further and further, gathering it up in waves and compacting it into a tight, dense ball of magic. She could feel the ball like a weight inside her chest, feel it getting bigger and bigger until she had fed it all the power she had. She could only hope it would be enough.

When she opened her eyes, the clearing looked different, glowing with a bright haze that haloed the trees and shrubs and the limping form of her mate.

Her breath hitched and her body tensed. Instinct screamed for her to run! *Go to him! He's hurt! Keep him safe!*

Her heart leaped into her throat, and she had to fight to keep her feet in place. She could help him better from here, by casting this spell rather than distracting him and giving the demon any greater advantage.

She saw how the demon was the only thing in the

clearing that looked dark to her new vision. It moved through her line of sight like an oil slick, black and cancerous, constantly shifting.

Drawing a deep breath, Fiona lifted her hands, sent a fervent prayer to the Lady, and gathered up every scrap of magic she could muster, aiming it carefully at the massive demon.

That's when her heart stopped.

At the edge of the clearing, she saw a new form emerge from the woods. This one looked almost human, like a tall, hard, menacing man with eyes as black as pitch. It didn't have hooves or horns or scales or claws, Fiona saw, but it was enormous, thick enough with muscle that a professional wrestler would have run from it. It had dark golden hair that waved about its head, but even that couldn't make it look angelic. It carried a sword almost as long as she was tall, and its aura wasn't glowing to her bright, hazy vision. She might not have known if the magic hadn't told her.

It was a demon.

A shout tore from her throat, half warning, half curse, and she saw the first demon's bovine head shoot up at the sound. Its flaming eyes locked on her and blazed as if suddenly reminded of her presence.

Fiona felt her concentration begin to unravel and the ball of magic went soft around the edges, the power beginning to sink back inside her. She swore and fought to hold it together, but she couldn't look away from the new threat that was moving unhurriedly across the forest floor, its eyes locked on the violent struggle. It held the huge sword easily in one thick-wristed hand, the tip pointed to the ground as it stalked closer to Walker.

"No!"

Desperate now, seeing no alternative, Fiona drew

the remnants of her spell quickly together and with as much prayer as magic sent the ball of magical sunlight hurtling toward the newest threat.

The second demon had its eyes on her mate, but somehow it sensed the spell. Quick as a cat, it shifted, one huge brawny arm lifting the sword high into the air as if to deflect the magical blow. The blade sparked to life, but instead of dodging the magic, it seemed to absorb it. The demon glowed a bright, silvery violet-blue, ringed in a halo of magic she had given it.

That was impossible. It should have been impossible. Fiona had crafted a sun spell, a larger, more powerful cousin of the light spell she had cast last week, the one that had injured the demon and stopped it long enough for Walker to carry her to safety. Demons couldn't tolerate light, especially sunlight. It burned them like acid, more toxic to them even than it was to vampires. Fiona's spell should at least have stunned it, if not seriously injured it. Even having lost a good part of its intensity because of her distraction, the spell was still a powerful weapon against demon kind.

Her heart sank, and she felt the first wave of terror wash over her. If this new monster had some sort of protection from or immunity to sunlight, they were lost. It would kill her and her mate, and there was nothing she could do to stop it.

Well, she sure as hell wasn't going to go down without fighting.

"Squick!" she screamed, her voice carrying over the din of the fighting. "Help him!"

Hoping the imp could at least trip the thing or maybe climb up and plant a hoof in its eye, Fiona sprang at the human-looking demon.

What she intended to do she wasn't sure. She had thrown every scrap of her power into that sun spell.

Frantic, she searched for something more, some small thread left over that could distract or disarm the demon. The power she cobbled together had more to do with prayer than with magic, but it was the best she could do. If she could have, she would have pulled the energy out of her soul. Her heart froze in her chest as she stretched out a hand and threw her last, desperate weapon at the armed demon.

The second blast didn't have near the intensity of the first, and she knew even before it hit the second demon squarely in the chest that it wouldn't make any difference. The creature barely paused, then seemed to shake like a dog coming out of the rain before it continued onward.

She didn't know what else she could do. Her magic was gone, but she couldn't *not* try. She could still move. She could try to wrestle the sword from its hand, although her rational mind told her the attempt was doomed to failure. Maybe scratch its eyes out or find out with her knees exactly how much like a human man its body really was. Either way, she knew she couldn't stand by and just watch while it killed her mate.

She made it about halfway across the clearing when the second demon drew close to where Walker struggled with the first. She could see that her wolf was weakening. The demon had landed several bone-crunching blows, and the gash in his side continued to bleed, soaking his silver-gray fur. She was never going to make it in time to save him. Feeling her heart tear inside her chest, Fiona screamed his name.

Distracted, Walker spun around and fixed her with a dazed golden stare just as the second demon lifted its sword high overhead and plunged it straight down into the heart of its bovine kin.

CHAPTER 25

 TOO LATE AND TOO startled to arrest her momentum, Fiona collided right into the second demon. She might as well have thrown herself against a brick wall. It would have had more give. One large hand curled around her arm to steady her before setting her firmly away.

With a low growl, Walker did the demon one better, grabbing his mate around the waist and setting her aside. Battered and bleeding, he still managed to hold himself upright on his wolfish hind legs and snarl a warning at the demon. His altered vocal cords distorted the words, but he made sure they were understandable. "To touch her, you'll go through me."

The demon raised an eyebrow. "At the moment you wouldn't offer much challenge." Slowly and carefully, it slid its sword into a long scabbard at its back. At their feet, a small charred pile of flesh smoked where the bull-headed demon had stood. "Besides, I didn't come here for you. I came for Morgagch, and that is who I slew. You are in no danger from me."

Walker snorted. "We're to trust a demon?"

The demon shrugged. "You can do whatever you like with your trust. That's none of my concern."

"What is your concern?"

"As I said, I came for Morgagch."

"Was that the demon's name?"

"The fiend's, yes. I don't think you and I mean the same thing by the other name." The demon glanced down at the wound in Walker's side. "Its claws were poisoned, and you've taken a significant dose."

Fiona made a sound of distress. How could she have forgotten? Leaning down, she peered closer at the ragged gash. The scent of it confirmed it had been poisoned. It stank of the demon's sulfurous, decaying taint. Laying her hand over the opening, Fiona tried to muster up the energy to heal it, but she'd used everything she had on spells she had already cast.

Walker looked down at her furrowed brow, and one huge claw-tipped hand came up to cradle her cheek. "I'll be all right," he said as softly as his shape would allow. "Shifting will force the poison out."

"It might," the demon said, reaching into a small pocket that hung at the side of its belt, "but I doubt the experience would be a pleasant one. Morgagch's venom runs deep and fast. Already it infects not only the wound site but your bloodstream as well. To force it out of this body would put a dangerous strain on the other." It pulled out a small, clear vial about the length and thickness of its thumb. "This is an antidote. If you drink it, it will neutralize the poison. Then when you shift, your body can concentrate on healing the tear rather than purging your bloodstream of the fiend's taint."

Walker looked at the vial and sneered. "There's that trust issue again."

Fiona frowned. She knew shifting helped Lupines heal their wounds at an astonishing pace, but she could see Walker was already weak. If the demon was right and there was a chance he might injure himself further during the shift, she didn't want him taking the chance. She stood for a moment, torn.

A firm tug drew her attention downward.

"If you wants the furry mortal guy to gets better quick, he better takes the medicine, Miss Fiona," Squick said in a loud whisper. His eyes kept jumping from her to the demon, and they were wide with awe. "He the kind who would knows."

Confused, Fiona continued to frown. "But it's a demon, Squick."

"Yeah, but not like the other one were. And you gots to hurry, Princess. Your furry mortal guy, he not looking so good."

Her eyes flew to Walker's face and confirmed the imp's assessment. Her mate's eyes looked glazed and feverish, the rims red, and she could see sweat beading in his fur. Unable to bear the sight of him in pain, she snatched the vial from the demon's hand before she could lose her nerve and uncorked it.

"If this harms him, I will find a way to destroy you," she bit out, then lifted the small vessel to Walker's lips.

He tried to turn away, but she followed the movement. "Please, *mo fáell*," she encouraged. "Please. Take it. Squick said you have to, and I trust him. Can you trust me?"

Walker's eyes, the warm gold faintly dull in the dim light, met hers, and a ragged breath hissed from between his lips. Then they parted, and he swallowed reflexively as if there was no question of his trust for her.

Fiona held her breath and waited. A quick glance at the demon revealed neither satisfaction nor malice. It looked as neutral as granite, and she wasn't sure whether or not to find that reassuring.

Before she could make up her mind, she heard Walker gasp. Alarmed, she reached for him. *Sweet Lady, please let him be all right!* Fiona's arms closed around him, and the feel of him had her eyes opening wide. The fever she had seen just seconds ago seemed to have vanished. He felt warm but certainly no hotter than usual. Pulling back, she looked into his eyes and saw the glaze over them clearing. She felt the strength surge back into his muscles, felt them shift and flex as he shifted back to his human form. She looked immediately down to his side and saw the pale pink scar that was the only reminder of the demon's attack.

"Oh my Goddess," she breathed, reaching a hesitant hand out to touch the mark. "You . . . you're okay!"

He pulled her tight against his side. "I'm fine." Raising his gaze to the demon in front of them, he nodded. "And I'm in your debt."

The demon shook its head. "No. There is no debt involved in completing my mission."

"Your mission?" Fiona asked. "You mean you really came here to kill that . . . Morgagch?"

"I did. And now that it's done, I'm afraid I have still more work to do."

The demon turned to leave, but Fiona stepped forward and Walker let her, adding his own protest. "We'd appreciate if you could answer a few questions," he said. "It seems we've spent a lot of time lately with the exact same goal in mind, only we weren't planning to stop with just one of the demons."

The demon's eyes sharpened. "You've seen the others? You know where they can be found?"

"Not exactly, but we've seen their handiwork. We know at least one or two other demons have been snacking their way across the city. We've been trying to locate them before they do any more harm."

"You shouldn't interfere. They will not be easily taken. Let me handle them. It is my duty."

Fiona blinked. "It's your duty to hunt down and kill demons?"

"Fiends," the demon corrected. "We call his kind 'fiends.'"

Walker raised his eyebrows. "His kind? There are kinds?"

The demon's expression never changed, but Fiona got the feeling he wanted to roll his eyes. She also realized with a jolt that she'd stopped thinking of this particular demon as an "it." There was no argument to be made that he was human, but he clearly had a code of ethics, and if she hadn't known him to be a demon, she would have assumed he had a soul.

"There are kinds of everything," he said. "Very few things in the worlds are unique."

"You must be," she said, the words tumbling out before she could think about them. "That sun spell didn't even make you blink. You're a demon. I know you are. It should have at least blinded you, if not knocked you on your ass."

The demon's lips curved. "Yes, I should thank you for that. Your assistance made Morgagch's defeat much swifter."

"But why didn't it bother you? You didn't even blink, but demons hate sunlight."

"Fiends hate sunlight," he said. "I am not a fiend."

"And that's the root of our problem," Walker said. "Every time you open your mouth, we end up with more questions, not less. I think we're going to have to ask you to fill us in on quite a few pertinent details. In exchange, we can tell you what we know about the other d—er . . . the other fiends you're looking for."

"If you like." The demon's mouth quirked, and he glanced down at Walker's bare skin. "But are you certain you wouldn't prefer to have this discussion somewhere . . . warmer?"

They found out the demon was called Rule, although that wasn't quite his name.

"Names have power for my kind," he said. "We guard them closely."

"Yeah, but I prefer that any other men who've seen me naked not be complete strangers," Walker had said ruefully.

After a brief discussion, they decided to head directly to Vircolac. It would save time if Graham and Rafe got to hear their story all at once, and once Fiona and Walker explained the role those two held in Other society and in the current negotiations with the humans, Rule had not objected.

Fiona tugged on Walker's hand. "Give me a kiss."

He frowned down at her. "What?"

"Give me a kiss," she repeated. "You can't go walking out of the park naked, because for some reasons, humans seem to take issue with that. And I used up everything I had trying to kill our new friend. I need a kiss if I'm going to get you some clothes."

"Furry mortal guy can puts his old clothes back on," Squick piped up. "They lying right over there."

Fiona wrinkled her nose. "Yeah, covered in demon blood. I don't think so." She raised her face to Walker's. "Kiss me."

She saw her mate's eyes lift uneasily to Rule's face, which was blank of expression. Tugging on Walker's shoulder, she grumbled something about the prudishness of mortals and pressed her lips against his. As usual, it took about two nanoseconds for him to not only respond but also seize control of the kiss from her and make it his own. She forgot all about their audience, forgot all about the goal of this little exercise, even forgot her own name as the familiar wave of pleasure and magic crashed over her.

When Walker lifted his head, she blinked up at him for a few dazed seconds before her brain clicked back into gear. Unable to resist, she skimmed her hands along his bare skin one last time before covering them in comfortably worn jeans and a dark knit shirt.

"Thanks," he rumbled, placing a swift kiss on the end of her nose.

They turned back to see Rule watching them with a troubled expression. "You're not just Fae," he said. "You're sidhe. High Fae."

Fiona wasn't surprised he'd made the correct assumption. The sidhe were well-known for their ability to draw energy out of passion, and she'd never shared an unpassionate kiss with Walker. "Yes. Why?"

Rule just shook his head, but his mouth had settled into a grim line. "We should discuss it with your friends. It may well affect your thinking on the situation."

He refused to elaborate, no matter how they questioned him. He kept silent on the trip to Vircolac, not even responding to a fascinated Squick's babbling questions about his age and his ancestors and his adventures hunting fiends in at least two dimensions. Not until they were met at the door of the club by Rafe and Tess did Rule speak.

"I'm not sure what you mean by bringing a demon here, Walker," the Felix said, his voice low with displeasure, "but I have reservations about letting him into this club."

"Shouldn't that be Graham's decision?" Walker asked, one eyebrow raised. "It's his club."

"And his family is inside. He feels the same way I do."

Fiona stepped forward. "Rule saved our lives tonight. If he meant us any harm, I'm sure he would have done something about it by now."

"Why, thank you, Fiona," the demon said, sounding amused. "I appreciate your confidence in me."

"I don't think either of us is confident," Walker said. "We're just desperate for information. And once we get you inside and you're surrounded by my pack, the entire Other staff of the club, the head of the Council, and his witch of a wife, I'll be more confident that we could take you down if we had to."

Tess was the one who put a stop to the debate. Pushing firmly against her husband's side, she managed to duck beneath his arm to stand just in front of him.

"Sheesh. You're the one who asked me to come out here and evaluate the thing, but you've got to let me get a look at him before I can tell you what I think," she grumbled, turning her surprisingly shrewd blue eyes on the crowd at the doorstep.

She looked first at Walker and Fiona, her gaze scanning carefully over them, lingering on their weary expressions. She blinked when she saw the imp peering out of Fiona's shoulder bag but said nothing. Then Tess's gaze turned to Rule and lingered for a moment on his stern face and deep black eyes.

"All right," she said, turning to reenter the club. "They're cool."

Rafe's hand shot out to stop her. "That's it?" he demanded. "That's all you're going to do? What about a spell? This isn't a decision to be made lightly."

"I'm not making it lightly, but what did you think I was going to do? Give each of them a polygraph? I don't need to. They're fine."

"I never mentioned a polygraph, but there must be some kind of spell you have to use to tell if everything's all right."

Tess sighed, sounding put-upon. "I don't need a spell to tell me that. They're fine. No one is under any kind of compulsion to follow the demon's orders, and Rule himself has no ill intentions toward anyone in this building. It's written all over them. Now can we go in? I'm not wearing a jacket."

Rafe looked ready to launch another protest, but Tess shoved hard against his belly and pushed him back into the entry hall. "Come on in," she called over her shoulder. "I'll get Mr. Grumpypants a saucer of milk and see if that sweetens his disposition."

Somehow, Fiona doubted it.

She led the way up the stairs and into the front hall of Vircolac as if she'd been doing it forever. True, it had only been a week, but she already felt almost as comfortable here as she did in Walker's apartment. Maybe it was because she'd spent so much time here, but maybe it had more to do with the fact that the people here were Walker's pack, his family. And now his family was hers.

"Graham and Missy are in the library," Tess said, leading the way. "I think he said something about wanting to be close to the liquor for this."

"He's a smart man," Walker grumbled, and followed them down the hall.

CHAPTER 26

T HE LIBRARY OFFERED PLENTY of comfortable seating, but that didn't stop Walker from claiming a position on one end of the wide sofa and hauling Fiona directly onto his lap. After enduring yet another threat to her life—at least the third in the past week, which was exactly as long as he'd known her—he seemed to want to keep her as close as possible whenever possible. Within arm's reach at the farthest, closer when he could manage it. He managed it now.

She didn't protest, just gave him a curious look, then settled back against his chest. "I think we have a list of questions we'd like to ask Rule," she said, turning her attention to the rest of the room, "but maybe it's better if he tells us his side of the story first."

Leaning up against the fireplace mantel, Rule quirked his mouth. "That story is not a brief one, nor is it simple, but I vow to do my best."

Fiona doubted the demon had missed the way Rafe and Graham had taken up positions between him and their mates, still unconvinced of his apparent amiability. He certainly hadn't missed their insistence that he leave his sword in its sheath with the doorman, but Rule didn't give any indication that it bothered him.

He looked casual and comfortable in the warm atmosphere of the library. Somehow the relaxed setting didn't serve to make him look any less like a warrior than he had when he'd been striding through the forest wielding a sword. He looked no softer, but Fiona sensed the concentrated power of his determination had eased back a bit. Not vanished, just been banked like a fire that would be stirred back to life whenever it was needed.

"I will assume that none of you is any more expert in those who live Below than is the Fae, so perhaps it would serve to clarify if I gave you all a brief introduction to demons," he began. "I would think that, given most of you have lived all of your lives in the mortal world, you have adopted something of the mortal view of my kind."

"You mean that you're bloodthirsty killers who tear mortal bodies into chunks and feed on their living hearts?" Graham glowered. "We may have heard a rumor or two, but I think it was seeing it happen that swayed us."

"Exactly," Rule said. "The mortal view." He sighed. "Our history goes back many thousands of years, as long as that of the Fae, so to tell you the whole of it is beyond the scope of this conversation. Suffice it to say that the creature you have just described is only a small part of the portrait of my kin."

He glanced at Fiona and nearly smiled. "It is the nature of historians to describe wars from the point of view of the victors. Whether they are mortal or Fae, that is simply the way of it, and the histories of the Wars between your people and mine were so described to you."

She nodded. "It's still talked about. There are poems and stories about the great battles that all the young ones hear from their earliest days. In my case, my aunt keeps the library, so I've heard a little more than some others."

Rule nodded. "And what did you hear?"

"About the Wars?" Fiona frowned. "The usual, I suppose. That the demons resented the Fae for stepping in to defend the mortals from their attacks and declared war against us. It was long and bloody, but in the end we won and the treaties said that the demons would have to retreat to Below and could only pass out of that realm by a direct invitation. Which happened, because mortals aren't always so smart, and after a few centuries they forgot what the demons had been like and decided it would be fun to see them again."

"That is what I thought you had been taught." He looked at the others. "Can I assume you all share the same understanding?"

Tess shrugged. "That's what I'd heard, but my friend Cassidy mentioned there was another version of the story. Her mate is . . . I guess you'd call it the historian of his pack. They ran into a demon a while ago, and Quinn told her that the demons actually used to be some kind of messengers, carrying information between all the different worlds. He said something about the Wars not starting over an urge to defend the mortals but over some rules the Fae set up to keep the demons out of Faerie."

Rule's eyebrows lifted. "I am impressed. That story comes a bit closer to the truth, though it still fails to offer the whole picture."

"And you think your version does?" Fiona asked. She didn't like the idea that suddenly her people were about to be painted as the villains in this story. Even if he had saved her mate, he had no call to insult her ancestors. "Wouldn't any story that's been passed down through your people be almost as biased in your favor as you seem to think the stories my people tell are in ours?"

"Certainly," he agreed with a faint smile. "But I propose that if I tell my version of the story, we might be able to see that the truth lies somewhere between the two."

"Tell your story then," Rafe said, his tone wary, "and we'll see what we make of it."

"The condensed version begins a bit like this. A very long time ago, when humans had only begun to understand that the world around them consisted of more than the gnawing of hunger in their bellies and the bite of cold on their skin, all beings lived together here Above." He eased into the tale with the familiarity of a well-practiced storyteller, his voice deep and riveting. "The Fae ruled their glittering kingdoms in the greenest places they could find. Shifters hunted in the woods and the fields. Humans, with their small numbers, scraped their living from what they could hunt and gather. Even my kind, those you now call demons, traveled freely, bearing news from one end of the Earth to the other. And among it all, magic flowed through everything, as thick and deep as a river current.

"This was no paradise, of course," he said wryly. "We all squabbled together, as any mix of cultures living side by side is wont to do, but there was no talk of war. That came later.

"It didn't take long for the humans to do what humans do best—multiply. From the small minority of their early years they began to spread, grown stronger with the knowledge of growing food and raising live-stock. They began to move into places where before humans had never ventured, and some of us started to get nervous."

Fiona listened from her perch on Walker's lap, her brow slightly furrowed. But she made no move to interrupt.

"The Fae were the first to leave. Some of the tales say that the humans had originally believed them to be gods because of their facility with magic. But as the humans' wits grew, they began to have doubts. Those tales point to this as the time when the Fae decided to make themselves a new home in another world.

"They offered a place to the shifters at first, but those who change skins had too great a tie to the land and the moon, and they refused to leave. They could blend in with the humans, they said, and knew how to defend themselves against any attacks. The demons, though, were not invited to the new land called Faerie."

His mouth quirked, though Fiona thought it had less to do with humor and more to do with an appreciation for the folly of their mutual ancestors.

"Our tales say that the Fae believed my kind, demons, were the ones who originally helped the humans to see them as something less than godlike. In any event, whatever their reasons were, the Fae not only didn't invite the demons to their new world; they decreed that demons would be forbidden to pass its borders. This didn't sit well with my people. Can you imagine that it would for those whose place in the world had been to function as messengers? How could we serve our purpose if we were not given leave to move freely across all borders?"

Fiona didn't offer an answer, but Rule didn't seem to expect one.

"We are the side who declared war," he continued. "That much is true, but it wasn't because the Fae tried to keep us from feasting on the humans. It was a political war over our right to move unrestricted in the service of our cause."

Apparently Fiona wasn't the only person in the room left with a few doubts.

"That's a pretty story," Graham said, "but it doesn't explain the fact that demons have killed and fed on both humans and shifters down through the centuries. Or were those just big misunderstandings?"

"They actually were," Rule said, looking bemused, "but not for the reason you think. They qualify as misunderstandings because the killers weren't demons."

The alpha growled something rude and the demon held up his hand.

"Hear me out," he said. "The problem stems from a basic misunderstanding of the nature of my people, one that began with the disinformation campaign begun by the Fae during the Wars, and perpetuated by religious humans looking to understand the nature of things beyond their comprehension. In earlier times, the human word for my people was 'daemon,' which means 'spirit.' It was a term used to describe a race of beings who were not human, but yet were not gods. They were something in between. That is what we were, and what those like myself continue to be."

"But you admitted the other kind are kin to you," Fiona pointed out. "The ones you call fiends. Aren't they another kind of demon?"

"They are, in the same way that the pixie who died at the gate in the park is another kind of Fae. There are things that bind us together, but we are not the same." He paused, frowning. "You have to understand that we have our good kind and our bad, just as all races do.

The difference is that to live Below, as we have for the last thousands of years, is very different from living Above. There are forces beneath that change those who encounter them—isolation, despair, pain, bitterness. Forces that have molded the weaker and worse among us into forms the rest of us can barely recognize. Those are the ones who come Above when summoned and feed on the life force of others. We call them fiends, because they are no longer just demons, just spirits. They have been twisted into the evil creatures of human nightmares."

Graham continued to look skeptical. "But you claim that you aren't a fiend?"

Rule shook his head. "Many of us have withstood the forces that warped our kinsmen. In fact, the fiends are a minority among us, one we work hard to keep under control."

"It looks like you could use a little more practice at that." Rafe's dry tone had his mate snorting.

"You think?" Tess asked.

Rule didn't look as if he'd taken offense to the observation. He just shrugged. "They may be few in number, but they have a primitive kind of cleverness, like an animal might. And it doesn't help our cause when those from Above perform summonings and offer them entry into this plane. We have enough challenges without having to chase them into other worlds."

Walker spoke up. "You mentioned earlier, in the park, that you had a mission to find the fiends here in the city and deal with them. Can I take it that you all spend time now doing something other than just carrying messages?"

The demon smiled. "What messages do you suppose we have to carry? After we were banished Below, no one trusted us with their news anymore. The lack of a purpose made the transformation from demon to fiend go even faster for some. In a way they were like madmen, and the stress of being cut off from the world Above caused their minds to snap. Once the mind had turned ugly, the body soon followed. Those of us who stayed as we were set about building a society of our own. Now we have politicians and healers, merchants and bankers, the same as any other culture."

"You don't look like a banker to me," Walker said.

"I'm not," Rule agreed. "We also have what you might call policemen. Guards who keep order according to our laws. Some of us do our work Below, and some of us go wherever the fiends do. Perhaps the correct word for me might be 'hunter.' I came here to find Morgagch and the others who were summoned, and to either bring them back Below to face justice, or destroy them if need be."

"I vote for destruction," Graham snapped. Beside him, Missy looked like she couldn't bring herself to disagree.

"If it is necessary, it will be done."

"I don't see the alternative," Rafe said. "The . . . fiends have proven to be a significant threat to both human and Other in our city, but the fact that whoever summoned them wants the humans to think the kills were the work of Others makes them especially dangerous."

Rule frowned, his expression saying Rafe had just lost him. "I don't understand. What exactly do you believe the summoner has done?"

The others in the room exchanged glances.

"That's a bit of a tale in and of itself," Rafe finally said. Concisely he explained to Rule about the fiend's previous victims and about the current state of the negotiations with the humans. "We're at a critical juncture in the talks. It's been six months. We've nearly reached agreement over the acknowledgment of the entitlement of our kind to basic rights. Almost all of the human heads of state are ready to agree and begin outlining what those rights will be. If any of them found out about the victims and believed the surface evidence, the summit would fall apart. They'd never agree to a peace with something that had just slaughtered several defenseless humans."

"I see your point. That's a sticky situation you have."

"You don't know the half of it," Walker interrupted. "The risk to the negotiations is bad enough, but we've all been a little more concerned over the escalation in the fiends' attacks."

"Escalation?"

"It started off with the humans," Fiona explained. "At least two of them, although I wouldn't be surprised to learn there are more that we just didn't catch. But the other night, the fiend decided that humans weren't satisfying its appetite. It killed a Lupine."

Graham snarled. "A member of *my* pack."

"We think it's looking for a bigger energy source." Her expression troubled, Fiona looked into Rule's dark eyes. "I sent Squick and Babbage to investigate. Squick found out a few things that led us to believe the fiends are trying to break free of the magic binding them to their summoner. After finding Babbage, I'm convinced that's the case."

Her voice cracked a little and Walker tightened his arms around her. "It makes sense," he said. "First humans, then a shifter, then a Fae. They're looking for a stronger life force with every kill."

Rule swore. "If you're right, that's extremely bad

news. The fiends are hard enough to track through this world as it is. If they had free rein to feed, they'd probably be easier to find, but only because the trail of victims would be so much larger."

"Comforting thought." Walker shifted to look at Fiona, and a slight frown creased his forehead. "You know, I'm wondering if Rule could tell us anything more about the sigils you found on the bodies. Or about that amulet Squick mentioned."

The imp had been sitting on the arm of the sofa beside Fiona and Walker, playing with the fringe on a decorative throw pillow. Now he looked up and scowled. "I finds out lots. Lots and lots. If the princess need to knows anything else, she can asks me, furry mortal guy."

"Princess?" Rule's brows rose at Fiona's nod.

"Mab is my aunt."

"And Dionnu are her uncle," Squick supplied helpfully.

"Now that's an interesting family tree," Rule said.

Fiona dismissed it with a wave. "It's not terribly important right now. What we need to know is whether we're right about the fiends trying to break the hold of their summoner. And what we can do to prevent that."

"Show me the symbols you saw."

Producing a pen and paper, Fiona sketched out the symbols she remembered and handed the page to Rule. "The first three sets were carved on the bodies of the victims. The last set was written at the gate. In Babbage's blood."

Walker stroked a comforting hand down her back.

"Babbage?" Rule asked.

"A pixie. He was a friend of mine."

"That is the Fae you mentioned was killed?"

She nodded. She had been trying not to think about it. If she focused on what needed to be done instead of what had already happened, she thought she might be able to keep functioning.

Rule looked down at the sheet of paper in his hands and his stony face hardened even further. He swore in a language Fiona didn't understand, one that was rough and low and full of consonants. "You were right about two things. First, the fiends are bound not by a common summoning spell, but by an amulet. One that was forged a long time ago. Before the Wars. I didn't think any like it still survived. We made it a point to seek them out and destroy all we could find centuries ago."

"Why?" Walker asked. "Didn't want to have to answer the phone?"

"No. Because we didn't like how the calls were placed. The amulets are powered by death magic."

Fiona felt her eyes widen. "No one practices death magic. It's absolutely forbidden. I don't think the defenses against it are even taught anymore."

"For good reason," Tess broke in. "They don't call it death magic for nothing. I know the Witches' Council banned it so long ago I doubt they'd remember when. It was either that or watch the population of the world dwindle to nothing from magic users killing things left and right for the power of their deaths. The last witch discovered practicing it was nearly five centuries ago, and she was executed *very* publicly."

"There is no possibility of a human having discovered the proper spells?"

Tess turned to Rule and snorted. Trust her not to stand on ceremony. "Okay, I get that you guys have been out of the loop for a couple millennia, but it's been at least that long since humans were able to work magic. That's where we witches came from. The general human populace has about as much supernatural juice as the average rutabaga."

"Death magic isn't practiced in Faerie, either," Fiona said. "Like I said, it's forbidden. And I mean taboo. Not even the Unseelie Court could get away with that kind of thing. Not on any kind of scale like this."

"It's banned everywhere," Rule agreed, "but that doesn't mean it never happens. And it doesn't seem to be stopping someone from practicing it right now."

"And I think that's what we need to focus on." Walker leveled his gaze on Rule. "How close are the fiends to breaking the grip of the amulet?"

"I think they've already figured out how. They're just looking for the tools."

"What do they need?" Fiona demanded, her voice angry. "You can't tell me they have't killed enough innocent creatures by now."

"I forget that none of you have had to deal with this variety of magic in many generations," Rule said. "It seems having won our last battle might have done your kind a disservice in the long run."

Fiona opened her mouth, but the demon cut her off. "It's not how many they've killed. It's who." He looked at Fiona and the chill of his black gaze made her shiver. "They've performed the ritual for breaking the bond every time they took a victim. By now they've realized that they need a particular kind of blood to make it work."

Fiona felt Walker tense. "What kind?"

"High Fae. They need to kill a sidhe."

If that wasn't enough to kill a person's mood, Fiona didn't know what was. "That's why the fiend in the park was ignoring Walker. It wanted me."

Her mate snarled and tightened his grip around her. "It's not going to get you. I don't care if we never sleep again, we're going to find it, and we're going to stop it."

"I don't think killing the fiend is going to solve the problem." Rule watched them calmly, but he didn't look all that much happier than Walker. "As long as the amulet is out there and someone knows how to use it, they'll keep calling fiends. And as long as there are fiends in this world under its control, they'll be looking for ways to break that control." He turned to Fiona. "If I were you, Princess, I'd cut my vacation short and head back to Faerie as fast as my legs would carry me."

She snorted. "Yeah. Did I forget to mention that someone sealed the gate so no one can get back to Faerie? That's what Babbage was trying to do when he was killed. At the moment, Rule, I can't go anywhere, even if I want to."

"And that's not an acceptable solution," Rafe said. "Even if the fiends can't find a sidhe to break the grip of the amulet, they can still find plenty of other things to snack on in the city. We need the amulet found and the summoner stopped."

Tess rolled her eyes. "Right. Why didn't any of us think of that?"

"You know what I meant." Rafe glared at his mate. "We don't want to put a bandage on the problem; we want to cure it. And in case everyone else has forgotten, there's another high Fae in town at the moment. I don't think Dionnu would be all that happy to suddenly find himself on the dinner menu, do you?"

Fiona's eyes widened. "Oh my Goddess, I forgot. We have to warn Uncle Dionnu. He might drive me crazy, but I'm not about to be responsible for his death. Not if I can prevent it. I have to tell him what's going on."

Rule's head snapped up. "King Dionnu is here? In this city, right now?"

"I know. It surprised me, too, but apparently he came over for the negotiations. I'm sure he just wanted to get some leverage with the humans that he might eventually be able to use against my aunt." Fiona shrugged. "It's normal political scheming, as far as I can tell. We went to see him, and he didn't seem to know anything about what was going on."

"I think he may not have told you the complete truth."

"What makes you say that?"

"The amulet," Rule answered. "I've been trying to work out where it came from. Remember, I said we thought we had destroyed all the known examples of it, but I should have said 'all but one of them.' We knew where the last amulet was located, but we never considered it a potential threat."

"Why not? I mean, it looks like you miscalculated there."

"We thought the amulet would be safe where it was." Walker looked the question and Rule gave a forbidding answer. "It's been in the library of Mab's Summer Palace."

CHAPTER 27

A MOMENT OF STUNNED silence filled the room. Even Squick's mouth hung open as if he couldn't believe what he'd just heard. Fiona certainly couldn't.

"That's impossible! The library isn't just warded; it's guarded. No one could possibly get anything out of it without Aunt Mab's express permission, which she definitely would *not* have given to Dionnu."

Rule looked at her. "Your uncle is a powerful sidhe, Princess. And was once half of your aunt's whole. Is it so hard to believe that his power to undo wards could rival her power to make them?"

Fiona shook her head, not in answer to his question but in an attempt to make it stop spinning. "I'm telling you it can't happen. And even if Dionnu did manage to get his hands on the amulet, what in the world could he be doing with it? Summoning demons? For the Lady's sake, Fae and demons are mortal enemies. He's not going to do anything of the kind. Especially not when he can't possibly get anything out of it. What point is there in summoning demons to earth and then using them to sabotage the human–Other negotiations? No matter how those go, it's not going to have much effect on the Fae. We're entirely separate from this world."

"I don't think the goal is to interfere in the negotiations," Rule said. "I think the fact that they're happening at all is just a convenient excuse for him to spend an extended amount of time in the human world. If they hadn't been occurring, he might have invented something similar, just to have that cover." He pointed at the sigils Fiona had sketched out. "Your interpretation of most of them was close, but ours is a complex language, and the differences between certain glyphs can be subtle. The fiend that sketched this wasn't just trying to free itself from the hold of the amulet. It was trying to destroy it completely and free any fiend that was tied to it."

Walker frowned. "So?"

"So this glyph is multiple, not singular. It means 'host of fiends.' " He looked up. "In other words, an army."

Fiona went pale. Her vision went hazy and for a moment the room around her swam out of focus. She heard a strange buzzing sound in her ears that faded just enough for her to hear Walker's incredulous question.

"I'm with Fiona. Why the hell would Dionnu do that?" he demanded. "What does the Winter King of Faerie need with an army of fiends? He's got his own army of Fae."

"But the Seelie and Unseelie Courts are too evenly matched," she whispered, her voice and her hands shaking. "Dionnu needs a secret weapon if he ever hopes to take over the Summer Court. That's what he's always been after. And that's why he sealed the gate back, too. He didn't want to take the chance of anyone sneaking back into Faerie to warn Mab. He's planning an invasion."

Walker stared at his mate in disbelief. "An invasion? Of his own world? What the hell are you talking about?"

Fiona jumped off his lap and began pacing around the room. "Dionnu has never been content with the division of Faerie. 'Acrimonious' would be a mild term for the split between him and Mab. He's not happy ruling only the Unseelie Court. He wants, has always wanted, to be High King over the whole of Faerie. That was probably a good part of the reason why he married her in the first place. He thought he could unite the kingdoms and then seize power over both of them. He just didn't count on the fact that Mab is at least as powerful as he is. Maybe more so. That's one of the reasons he's always after the cousins to agree to be named his heir. He thinks he can use us as bargaining chips, or failing that, as hostages to get Mab to surrender. He's never understood that the kingdom is a lot more important to my aunt than a few uncooperative nieces and nephews."

"And your uncle is wise enough to know that he can't summon fiends directly into Faerie," Rule said. "He'd need to do it on neutral ground. Like here. The human world isn't as well warded as Faerie, and fiends have always been able to enter when invited. He could raise an army of fiends here, then bring them into Faerie from here."

"But how would he do it? He'd still need to get past the Fae wards."

"The amulet. Death magic is one of the strongest forces there is. All he would need would be a suitably powerful death and he could break the wards. Or at least crack them enough to slip through. The wards between here and Faerie are not designed to hold demons out the way the ones between there and Below are. They could do the job in a pinch, but with enough pressure, they'd never hold."

"We need to tell my aunt. We should warn her."

Rule shook his head. "How? The way into Faerie is still closed, and every death your uncle's fiends cause only strengthens the barriers he has erected. We would need to take those barriers down before we could reach Mab, which we cannot do while Dionnu retains control."

Fiona whirled on him. "So we just let her ex-husband invade her land and seize control by whatever means are necessary?"

"No, but there are still things we can do right here to prevent that from happening. We need to find Dionnu and get the amulet back. With it, we gain control of the fiends and the ability to send them back Below. After that, the invasion will lack an army, and your uncle will lack his secret weapon."

"Right," Walker growled, not liking this plan at all. "Which means we're sure to be back in time for dinner."

"I know where to find my uncle," Fiona said. "If you can think of a way to get the amulet back, I can lead you to him."

Rule's grin flashed dark with malice. "I'm sure I can think of something."

"This has got to be the dumbest plan ever invented by Fae or demon," Walker muttered in the back of the private car Rafe had lent them. Walker, Fiona, Rule, and the imp had piled into the seats less than an hour after concocting a harebrained scheme that Walker was pretty sure would result not just in death for all of them, but quite possibly in dismemberment as well. Maybe even gibbeting.

"Everything will be fine." Fiona reassured him. She sounded calm, but he could smell her uneasiness. One of these days he was going to have to tell her that it didn't do any good to try to lie to a mate. "If we're lucky, Dionnu won't have his little army with him, and besides the three of us, Rafe, Graham, Tess, and Missy are in the car right behind us. Between all of us, I'm sure we'll find a way to get the amulet back."

Walker just grunted. If any of them were lucky, none of this would be happening in the first place, so he figured that was a flaw in Fiona's pat little theory.

"Remember, we need to retrieve the amulet without damaging it," Rule said. "If it's destroyed, the fiends will be released from its influence, which would be almost as bad as if Dionnu sent them into Faerie."

"I wish you had agreed to stay behind," Walker said quietly, staring intently down at her. "You haven't had a chance to replenish your energy after the incident in the park. I don't like the idea of you going in there defenseless."

"I'm not." She smiled up at him in the dim light shining in through the car windows. "I have you to defend me."

Walker felt his stomach tighten.

"We need her," Rule pointed out. "Somehow I doubt we'd get past Dionnu's front door if the rest of us showed up unescorted and unannounced."

Walker opened his mouth to offer another protest, but the feel of the car pulling to a halt cut him off. He glanced out the window. "This is it."

Fiona climbed out of the car and looked up at the familiar edifice. She frowned. "Where's the doorman?"

It wasn't likely either of them would have misremembered the fact that Dionnu's building had one. Not after the little show they'd put on for him last time. Walker felt a twinge of unease. "Some buildings switch to a security guard for overnight," he said. "Maybe this is one of them?"

"What's the matter?" Rafe asked as the others piled out of the second car and hurried to join them. "Is something wrong?"

"Not wrong necessarily," Fiona said. "It's just that when we visited a couple of days ago, there was a doorman at this building. Now, I don't see one."

Rule's eyes sharpened. "If you notice anything else out of place, tell me."

They pushed through the front door and into the marble lobby. The atmosphere reminded Walker of a crypt, cold and pale and silent. He couldn't even hear the hum of the elevators running. The uneasy feeling in his gut turned into the feel of the hackles at the back of his neck standing at attention. "I don't like this."

Graham glanced at him. "Is something else wrong?"

"No," Walker admitted. "It just seems too quiet to me."

"That might not be a bad sign. Fiends aren't known for their discretion, or their quiet."

Fiona led the way to the elevators and pushed the up button. The reflective gold doors slid smoothly open and she took a step forward. Then she froze.

"Uh, I think this counts as out of place," she said, and pointed to a pool of dark crimson blood on the floor of the empty elevator car.

CHAPTER 28

Fiona stepped back, fighting the urge to panic. She had seen and smelled too much blood in the past week to mistake it as anything else. The brave front she'd been projecting to keep Walker from worrying about her threatened to crumble, and she closed her eyes for a second to draw in a deep breath. Through her mouth.

Walker looked past her and swore. "It's human, and there's enough of it to mean someone isn't doing well without it. Fiona, you should go back to the car. Graham, take my cell phone and call the club. Get the rest of the pack—"

"No," she interrupted, squaring her shoulders. "I'm fine. I was just startled. I'm not leaving."

"Damn it, Princess—"

"I said no." Her voice sounded stronger this time, and her gaze met his steadily. "I'm staying. You heard what Rule said. If you want Dionnu to talk to you, I have to be with you. Now let's go."

Missy shook her head. "Someone was killed in here. There may be other people in this building in trouble. Someone has to check to see if the fiends are here. If anyone else needs help."

Graham glared at her, the picture of a protective Lupine mate. Fiona had come to recognize the sight.

"It's sure as hell not going to be you, Melissa," the alpha growled.

She glared back up at him. "Then you might want to come with me, because I am not leaving a building full of defenseless humans at the mercy of a madman and his herd of attack fiends. These people need help."

Tess cut in quickly. "We'll call the pack. The building is too big for us to search alone, anyway. All right?"

"Fine." Rafe took out his cell phone and turned a stern gaze on his mate. "In the meantime, you and Missy will stay here in the lobby and wait for them. You can direct the search." Both women began to protest, but they got no further than indrawn breaths. "That way you can also be here if anyone comes down from their apartment in need of help. They will likely be traumatized, and I don't need to tell you it would make them rest easier if a small spell gave them a more . . . understandable memory than that of a demon attack?"

Tess threw her husband a dirty look, but she didn't protest. He had, unfortunately, made sense, and Fiona guessed that both couples had been together long enough for the women to recognize when arguing would be futile.

"Fine," Tess snapped. "But don't think I won't know if anything serious happens, Rafael, and don't think I'm going to stay down here like a good little mate if it does. Understand?"

Missy crossed her arms over her chest and stepped closer to Tess, giving her own mate a matching look of challenge.

"Understood," the alpha growled.

Positions settled, Fiona stepped into the elevator car, carefully avoiding the pool of blood. Squick popped his head out over the top of the canvas bag and looked down. "Ew. Messy."

She knew Walker wasn't any happier having her get in the elevator than Rafe or Graham would have been if their mates had done it, and it wasn't even the way he stomped in behind her that gave it away. His glare made his opinion pretty plain. When they got home, she was going to get a lecture. She just knew it.

Taking small, shallow breaths through her mouth, Fiona fixed her gaze on the elevator keypad, watching the numbers of the floors ding by. When the doors slid open on number 17, she hurried out and tripped over her own feet. The apartment building hallway didn't look anything like she remembered.

Maybe that was because of the doors that had been torn off their hinges and thrown to the ground. Or maybe it was the streaks of blood on the walls or the sickly sweet smell of death in the air, as opposed to the rich scents of wood and furniture polish and fresh flowers she recalled from their last visit. Whatever it was, she didn't like the change.

Walker grabbed her by the shoulders and pushed her back into the elevator. "We're too fucking late! They've already killed Dionnu and every other living thing on this floor! We need to get back to the club and call in reinforcements. This is going to take more than the pack." He pressed his cell phone into her numb hand. "Fiona, get back downstairs and tell Tess and Missy what happened. Tell them to get more patrols out *now*. We'll see if we can contain anything that's still here, but I'm betting they're already long gone." When she just looked up at him in confusion, he nudged her again. "Go!"

"Oh, but why would she leave when she only just arrived, Mr. Walker?"

They all turned at the sound of the voice. Poised in the open doorway of his apartment, Dionnu watched them with an eerie beatific smile on his handsome face. Around his neck, on a heavy gold chain, he wore a finely made amulet, adorned with the largest, most brilliant black opal Fiona had ever seen. He didn't seem to notice that it, as well as his face and hands and expensive silk suit, was splotched with blood and gore. Or maybe he just didn't care.

"As you can see, I'm very much alive," the king continued. "I'm not so vulnerable to the machinations of a few power-hungry demons as you might have suspected. But please, come in. Let me show you what I've done with the place."

He beckoned them forward and Fiona felt herself recoil. It wasn't so much the bloodshed that disturbed her. It was the glint in his eyes, cold and hard and reptilian, filled with a mad sort of knowledge, or a knowing sort of madness. Walker stepped in front of her, protecting her from that gaze, and she blinked, swallowing hard against a swell of fear.

"If it's anything like we can see out here," she said, finding her voice, struggling for a casual tone, "then you might want to consider hiring a new decorator."

Her uncle chuckled. "Oh no. Decorators can leave a room so cold. So impersonal. I definitely wanted to give this apartment my personal touch. Come in. I insist."

Still smiling, Dionnu turned and disappeared back inside the apartment.

"There is no way here or in hell that I'm letting my

mate go inside that apartment," Walker said, his hands clenching so tightly that Fiona saw his knuckles turn white.

Graham snorted. "I hope to hell not. He might as well have used the blood to paint the word 'trap' over the door."

"It doesn't matter," Fiona said, catching one of Walker's fists in her hands. "You saw the amulet. We all did. He still has it, and we need to get it back."

For the first time, Fiona saw Rule hesitate. "I think Walker may be right, Princess," the demon said. "If your uncle caused all of these deaths, then all of that magic has been absorbed by the amulet. He'll be high on the power, and far more than merely dangerous. I think you should obey your mate and go back to the car to call for help."

Before Fiona could repeat her refusal, she felt a surge of magic buffet her, shaking the air around her like a sonic boom. When she looked up, all the interior walls on this floor of the building had disappeared, and her uncle smiled at her from what had once been the living room of his apartment. The expression reminded her of one the spider might wear as it waited for its prey to step into its sticky web.

"You seemed reluctant to cross my threshold," he said, his voice beautiful and terrifying. "So I thought I would break down a few barriers. Come; I know all your friends. Bring them with you. The more the merrier."

He laughed, and the sound sent shudders through Fiona. Blinking, horrified, she looked around the vast open area. There were bodies everywhere. Everywhere she turned, she saw death, sprawled on floors, stretched over furniture, battered and broken and bloodied. She could hear the men around her cursing under their breath. Her stomach heaved, and a hot rush of fury filled her.

"You are a monster," she hissed, her eyes narrowed and accusing. "Why did they all have to die? Weren't the deaths you'd already caused enough? Humans mean nothing to you! The one you really want dead is Mab, so why haven't you gone after her? Or are you afraid she'll kick your ass, the way she's been doing for centuries?"

Dionnu's eyes flashed and Walker growled, moving protectively closer to Fiona.

"And here I always considered you a clever girl," the king said, moving slowly closer. "It seems I gave you too much credit, Niece, if you haven't yet figured out my plan."

"Oh, I know all about your plans. Your stolen amulet and your seal on the Faerie gate and the fiendish army you plan to march back into Faerie. An army that would just as soon kill you as march to your war drums." She sneered, refusing to give him the slightest indication that she ever believed his schemes might work. "But I'm looking around, and I don't see anything that looks like an army." She glanced pointedly at the empty space between them. "All I see is a pathetic excuse for a king and the folk who are going to stop him."

Dionnu threw back his head and laughed uproariously. "Oh, you foolish child," he said, his expression gloating. "You may be monumentally stupid, but you do amuse me. Perhaps I'll keep you in iron chains for a few thousand years before I let you die. Do you really think that you and your puppy dogs, your kitty, and your one pathetic swordsman can do anything to stop me?"

He stepped even closer, ignoring the Lupines' threatening snarls and the hiss of Rule's blade sliding from its sheath.

"Like I said, Uncle, you're only one man. Your army isn't here."

His lips curved, as thin and sinuous as a snake. "I have an army at my fingertips. I have just *feasted,* foolish girl. The power of each and every soul I've tasted is within this amulet. With it, I can summon an army the likes of which have never been seen, not even during the last Wars." He chuckled, a brittle, malevolent sound. "I can't wait to see the looks on the faces of the Seelie Court when they see my army of fiends and realize what their long-heralded peace treaty has wrought."

"You won't be allowed to summon that army," Rule said. His voice was firm and level and brooked no disagreement.

Dionnu turned on him with a sneer. "You think you can stop me? You, a girl, and a few mongrels?"

"These mongrels have claws," Rafe hissed, muscles rippling as he began to call his change. Beside him, Graham echoed the sentiment with a low, threatening growl.

"I have no fear of you," Dionnu dismissed, "or of your blade, warrior. It cannot harm me. No Fae can be slain with silver."

Rule's mouth curved in a grim, humorless smile. "My blade is steel, not silver. With iron enough to spill your blood."

Without a word or a betraying twitch, Rule lunged forward. His sword tip pointed straight at the Fae king's throat, but it never made contact. With a furious shout, Dionnu lifted a hand and sent a ball of sickly green light barreling toward the demon's chest. It hit him with the force of a train, knocking him off balance and deflecting the blow meant for Dionnu's jugular. The momentum of the blast sent Rule flying backward a good fifteen feet before he crashed into someone's bookcase in the next apartment. He thudded to the floor.

Smiling, Dionnu turned back to Fiona. "You see how little power your friends have to hurt me? Don't waste my time with further, futile attempts."

"I see it less as a waste of time, Uncle, and more as an investment in the future."

"What future? I'm very afraid to have to tell you, my dear Fiona, that you have no future." He chuckled. "Do you think I am unaware of the attempts my fiends have made to free themselves from my control? Don't be silly. Of course I knew. I expected it. Why do you think I hexed the gate to seal itself if anyone attempted to enter from Faerie? Without high Fae blood, they could never have mustered the power to break the hold of the amulet."

Fiona's lip curled. "You might want to work on that hex of yours, then. As you can see, I got through."

Dionnu waved his hand dismissively. "A minor inconvenience. True, I was a tad upset when you first appeared on my doorstop, but I soon realized your presence could be the greatest boon I could hope for. After all, if the power of the death of a high Fae could break the bonds of the amulet, just think what the power of that death, channeled *through* the amulet, could accomplish." He stared at her, his eyes gleaming. "My dear niece, spilling your blood will make me indestructible. No one will be able to harm me. Not the fiends, not the Fae, not even your lovely aunt. Now come." He held out his hand. "I can at least make it quick for you."

He didn't make it anything. He didn't even have time to make a sound before Walker was on him, shifting in midflight, howling in outrage. Graham followed a split second later, fangs reaching for the throat with savage instinct. But the power flowing through Dionnu was too strong. His arm came up to protect his vulnerable throat, and Graham's teeth sank deep into the flesh of Dionnu's forearm, tearing at muscle and tendon.

Dionnu screamed, high and outraged. Walker checked his attack and twisted to the side, trying to come around on the king's vulnerable flank, but the Fae raised his other arm, sending a spell blasting into Walker's side.

The Lupine yelped, a sharp, pained sound, and fell to his side, panting heavily. Cursing and bleeding, Dionnu aimed a second blast at Graham and sent the second Lupine sprawling. The king struggled to his feet and savagely kicked the alpha's heaving side.

"Mongrel beasts!" Dionnu spit, cradling his injured arm to his chest. "I'll have their skins for a carpet. Just as soon as I've finished with you."

Stretching out his good hand, Dionnu reached for Fiona and found himself grasping air. Rafael had launched himself at her side and sent her staggering out of reach. Outraged, the king screamed and turned to blast the Felix, but the nimble werejaguar had already darted away. Spitting curses, Dionnu grasped the amulet around his neck and chanted a few words. Suddenly he blinked out of view, reappearing a heartbeat later beside his niece's blinking form. He grabbed her by the arm and repeated the chant just as Walker pushed himself to his feet and launched a renewed attack.

Both Dionnu and Fiona disappeared a split second before the werewolf made impact, this time materializing across the floor in what had once been a spare, empty room.

Fiona looked around, confused, until her gaze fell to the floor. Her heart skipped a beat and her blood seemed to freeze in her veins.

On the polished wooden floorboards, painted in

blood, she saw a large, perfectly round circle. In the center and at the sides in each of the cardinal directions, sigils had been painted. She recognized them as slight variations on the ones the fiends had been using to try to break the hold of the amulet. Lying atop the glyph at the center of the circle, Fiona spotted a dark, glistening dagger the color of coal with a long handle of dark, carved wood. A cold iron blade, she realized, with a wooden handle to allow her uncle to wield it without injury.

Iron was the only metal that could kill the Fae. Their own weapons and tools were made of silver, gold, and bronze. When she saw the iron blade, she felt a surge of panic and began to struggle against her uncle's punishing grip.

"Don't fight me!" he shouted, dragging her toward the sacrificial circle. "I can still make your death a very painful event, girl! Remember that."

Fiona had no doubt he would do that anyway. Frantic, she looked around her. Both Rule and Walker were pushing themselves to their feet, looking dazed and a little unsteady. She had no idea if either of them could reach her in time. Graham lay on the floor, unmoving but still breathing. Either her uncle's kick had damaged something serious or the magical blast had paralyzed the alpha. Out of the corner of her eye, she could see Rafe approaching from the opposite side. She had to keep herself out of the magical circle until one of them reached her.

Her fingers curled into claws, and she raked at her uncle's injured arm, hoping to weaken his grip with the other. He swore and yanked her hard, but he didn't let go. She was fighting like a banshee now, screaming and squirming and kicking, intent only on getting away, on staying out of that circle and away from that iron blade. She wasn't prepared to die. Not that any Fae

ever was, but she had other things to do. She had a
mate! She had to learn how to live with him and how to
deal with the mortal-versus-immortal thing and how
to teach him to stop trying to tell her what to do every
time he opened his mouth. She couldn't die.

As they passed by what had once been a small bathroom, Fiona reached out and grabbed at the exposed
pipes of the wet wall. She didn't just curl her hand
around a pipe; she used her entire arm, hooking her elbow and utilizing all the strength of her upper body to
anchor her in place.

Dionnu cursed and yanked her other arm violently.
Fiona screeched, feeling her shoulder pulled painfully
from its socket, but she didn't let go.

"Walker!" she screamed, her voice hoarse with
panic. "Help!"

She couldn't tell which Other hit her uncle first, but
it didn't really matter. What mattered was that Dionnu
let go. Momentum sent her spinning around the other
side of the pipe, like an overdressed pole dancer. She
landed hard on her back and doubled over on a wave
of nausea, pulling her injured arm protectively against
her stomach. Her shoulder throbbed and burned, and
she choked on the taste of bile.

"Walker," she panted, raising her head and blinking
against the blurring of her vision. When it cleared, she
saw Rule, Graham, and Rafe pounding at the invisible
boundaries of the circle as her uncle dumped her mate's
limp body on the floor at the center.

"I can't get in!" Rule bellowed. "It must be warded
against demons! I can't get in or out!"

In his animal form, Rafe couldn't speak, but his
similar inability to get into the circle was clear.

Fiona struggled to her feet, her heart pounding
wildly in her throat. She saw her uncle like a twisted

mirror image of herself, also cradling an injured arm, but with the other he reached for the iron blade. Iron might be the only thing that could kill a Fae, but any metal thrust into the heart of a Lupine would do the job. Frantically Fiona tried to summon the energy to cast a spell. A missile, a fireball. Hell, even pulling a rabbit out of a hat would have been good enough for her if it broke her uncle's concentration enough to draw his attention away from her mate. It was no use. Like Walker had said earlier, she hadn't had time to recharge the energy she'd expended during the demon attack in the park.

Cursing and sobbing, she scraped up every stray bit of energy in the building, in the city, in her own soul, and wrapped it around her like a blanket. It wasn't enough to do her uncle any harm, but it might just be enough to protect her against the wards of the circle long enough for her to get inside.

Gritting her teeth, Fiona threw herself forward, forging through the boundary of the circle, determined to do whatever she had to to keep her mate safe. The adversarial magic burned like fire even through the protection she'd gathered around herself, but she ignored it. Nothing mattered but Walker. If she could force Dionnu to drop the knife, she would, and if she had to put her own body in front of that knife, she would do that, too.

When she entered the circle her uncle screamed obscenities and turned his rage on her. Lunging at her, he plunged the knife in the direction of her heart. She spun and leaned, barely dodging the blow, and shouted for her mate.

"Walker! Walker, you have to move! Hurry! Please! You have to get out of the way!"

"He's not going anywhere," Dionnu sneered, squaring off against her once more. "And neither are you. It will be very sweet to see you die together with your new pet, Niece."

Walker stirred, lifting his head weakly off the ground. The movement distracted Fiona enough that she almost didn't dodge in time. The edge of the blade missed her stomach, but when she jumped to the side it caught her on the leg, opening a hair-thin scratch in her thigh.

The pain winded her. She'd never been injured by iron before, but now she knew that the stories of the damage it caused to her people hadn't been exaggerated. Crying out, she fell to her knees beside her mate while tendrils of icy agony wrapped around her wounded leg. As if from a distance, she could hear Rule shouting, hear Rafe roaring and hissing outside the circle. The world seemed to slow around her, like in a movie, and she looked down, the tilt of her head seeming to take hours. Out of the corner of her eye she could see the look of satisfaction blooming across her uncle's face, see him preparing to strike the final blow that would kill her. Strangely, it didn't matter. Fiona blinked and focused on the eyes of her mate, seeing his anger and grief and love shining back at her more clearly than sunlight.

I love you, Princess.

She could almost hear his voice in her head, deep and low and warm, wrapping around her like an embrace, taking all the pain from her and leaving her with nothing but joy.

I love you, Fiona. My mate.

Maybe she was hallucinating, but it didn't matter. Even if those weren't the words in his mind, she knew they were the words in his heart. They were the same words in hers. She only hoped he could see them as clearly.

I love you, too, Tobias Walker. Mo fáell. *My mate.*

In her peripheral vision, she saw her uncle's arm lift, saw the dull glint of the knife, felt her muscles tense against the coming blow. The blow that never landed.

Suddenly, unbelievably, Fiona felt a surge of energy hit her with the force of a tsunami. Stronger than anything she'd ever experienced. It burned hotter than the magic of passion, deeper than the magic of Faerie. It filled every part of her, every hidden corner and crevice, and suddenly she slipped out of slow motion while the rest of the world remained locked at half speed.

She heard the sound of Dionnu's triumphant roar, Walker's agonized scream. She saw the knife descend and raised her hand casually, as if to brush it away. A flash of light sparked from her fingertips, bright and white and blindingly pure. It caught Dionnu in the center of the chest and seemed to tear right through him as if he were made of paper. It coursed through him like lightning, making his skin glow with an eerie fire. His gloating roar turned into a scream of pain and rage. The knife slipped from his hands and clattered harmlessly to the floor. His wide, uncomprehending eyes locked on Fiona's face for one extended moment before the light reached his head, and it seemed to flare even more brightly before it died.

In the sudden dimness, Dionnu's body slipped lifelessly to the ground.

Shaking like a drunk, Fiona turned and reached for Walker. She had both hands buried in his fur before she realized her shoulder felt fine. Blinking, she looked at it, then looked down at her thigh. There was a slice in the fabric of her jeans, but the skin beneath was pale and whole and unmarred. Slowly, she began to smile.

The first flash of the power had faded, but she could

still feel it tingling inside her. Carefully, she willed it down through her hands and into Walker's body to mend bone and skin and tissue. She saw his surprise as he gazed up at her, and her smile became a grin.

He didn't wait for her hands to leave him before he shifted.

"What the hell happened? How did you do that?" he demanded as soon as he had the necessary arrangement of vocal cords. "You told me you used up all your energy."

She shrugged and leaned forward to kiss him, her lips curved against his. "I got more."

Outside the circle, Rule threw back his head and laughed. "What else could have stood up against all that death magic?" he asked, resting the point of his sword on the floorboards. "Clever little sidhe."

Fiona shook her head and laughed. "Not so clever. Really, I was pretty much expecting to die." She looked back at Walker and felt her smile grow tender. "Turns out passion isn't the only thing that gives me magic." She laid her hand on his cheek and let her feelings for him shine bright in her eyes. "Love works even better."

CHAPTER 29

THEY FOUND SQUICK PINNED to the floor where Graham had lain. Fiona had more than enough magic now to heal the alpha Lupine as well. Once he was back on his feet, Squick groaned and spit out a mouthful of fur and immediately began talking. Everyone seemed in too good a mood to correct him when he narrated the whole story of the battle for Tess and Missy. Not even when he got to the part where he jumped on Dionnu's back and held him still so "the princess could hits him with the big love whammy."

They all just laughed.

"I'd have been doomed without Walker and the rest of you there," Fiona said from her perch in her mate's lap on Vircolac's library sofa. "And Squick." She winked at the imp. "But frankly, I'm just glad it's over."

"We all are." Rafe looked over at Rule. "And no matter how you protest that you were useless in the end, I still think we all owe you a debt of gratitude. As well as an apology."

Tess shot her mate a superior glance. "Some of us have nothing to apologize for because we didn't automatically assume anyone from Below must be up to no good."

Rule laughed. "No one needs to apologize. I only played a small part in tonight's events. And I'm afraid I still have work to do. I didn't see any evidence that the other demons Dionnu summoned were returned to their homes. If they're still here Above, I need to find them."

"If there's anything the pack can to do help," Graham offered, "you only have to ask."

"Speak for yourself," Walker said, grinning. "Did I mention I'm going to be taking some vacation time in the immediate future?"

Graham looked at his beta and raised an eyebrow. "And here I was going to offer you the chance to take over my place guarding the negotiations."

"Right, because I just would have jumped at that chance. Sorry, Cuz, but I've got better things to do with my time than listen to those squabbles."

"So do I," Graham muttered.

"Oh, I wouldn't worry, old friend," Rafe drawled, stretching out his long legs and grinning in satisfaction. "I think you will get a vacation of your own before the year is out."

Fiona looked at him, surprised. "Really? Things are going that well?"

"Very nearly. The first agreement has been signed and ratified. We are over the first hurdle, and as you might expect, the first is always the largest."

"Congratulations," she said, meaning it sincerely. "That's a hell of an accomplishment. One for the history books. Literally."

Tess grinned. "Stop, before the praise goes to his head. This is the result of the hard work of a hell of a lot of folks, not just my oh-so-talented husband." She squeezed said husband's knee and turned her attention back to Walker and Fiona. "So where are you going on this vacation of yours?"

"We got a message through to Aunt Mab from Dionnu's apartment," Fiona said, grinning. "He had a scrying mirror of his own, it turns out. Even though he cut everyone else off from Faerie, he wanted to be able to keep his eye on things there. Anyway, she's invited us to visit, so I'm taking Walker home to meet the family."

Missy looked intrigued. "Are you going to be staying long?"

Fiona laughed. "Not on your life! She seemed to think that with Dionnu dead, I was going to come home and assume his place on the Unseelie throne."

"But it turns out I'm allergic to palaces." Walker grinned.

"I've never wanted to be part of the whole political life at court. I told my aunt that if she wanted to reward us for taking care of Dionnu, she could give me a lifetime supply of Faerie wine to take care of this pesky little difference in life spans we have to deal with. The Fae only get tipsy from drinking it, but mortals get extended longevity. Dionnu had plenty of other nieces and nephews. They can duke it out to see who gets his throne." Fiona looked at Rule. "Aunt Mab did mention, though, that she also wants you to know that if you need help, you can call on her."

"The only help I would ask for is that you continue to conceal my presence as well as that of the fiends from the humans. My work and my life will be a lot easier if they know nothing of us."

Rafe sighed. "I'll do what I can, but I'm afraid one thing the Council of Others never considered was how our coming out to the humans would affect those Below. I have to apologize for that, as well. I'm afraid it's only a matter of time before the humans will realize they have more to deal with than just shape-shifters and vampires."

"You can't stop the march of time." Rule shrugged. "I'll take whatever assistance you can give, and when the time comes that the humans find out about us, we will deal with it. At least I can go back Below and tell my people that we should begin to prepare."

"Trust me." Graham scowled, his opinion of the human side of the negotiations clear. "There are some things you can never prepare for."

Fiona laughed and looked up at her mate, who returned her laugh with a grin.

"I'll second that," he said. "Some things just take you by surprise."

"And sometimes," Fiona said, reaching up to kiss him, "those are the very best things of all."

Read on *for a sneak peek at*
Christine Warren's next book

THE DEMON YOU KNOW

Now available from St. Martin's Paperbacks

~

Abby scrambled quickly to her feet, not thrilled about the positioning of two strange women towering over her. "Are you two . . . Others?"

"Lupines." Samantha said, softly, as if she were breaking some bad news. "Werewolves. We're both members of the Silverback Clan."

Was that whooshing sound Abby suddenly heard the sea, she wondered, or was all of the blood rushing out of her head?

She was talking to a couple of werewolves.

"It's okay. We realize we take some getting used to for most humans, and you haven't known about us long. But we honestly aren't going to hurt you. We just wanted to make sure you were okay."

Abby shifted her weight and tried to smile back. "No, I'm sorry. I can only imagine what my face must have looked like. It's just . . . you're the first were-lupines

I've met. Since the announcement, anyway. I was a little surprised."

"We get that a lot." Carly shoved her hands in the pockets of her coveralls and raised an eyebrow. "So now that you know what we are, why don't you tell us what you are?"

Abby blinked. "Say huh?"

Samantha glared at her friend, then turned back to Abby with a reassuring smile. "Carly doesn't mean to be rude. She's just curious. We both thought you were human at first."

Okay, when had Abby's life turned into a B-rated horror movie? "I *am* human."

"Know many other human women with no muscle tone to speak of who can toss a grown man fifty feet by accident?" Carly looked torn between amusement and skepticism.

"I work out," Abby protested.

"It's okay. We understand about anonymity." Samantha reached out and patted her hand. "We're not going to out you against your will."

This just kept getting weirder. "No, you don't understand. I have nothing to out. I'm human. I'm even straight! I don't have anything to hide."

"Of course not," Carly agreed cheerfully. "You're just the human girl next door. Absolutely." The Lupine grinned. "Provided the girl next door has a black belt and superhuman strength, speed, and agility."

"Carly, you're scaring her." Samantha's eyes searched Abby's face, golden brown and filled with concern. "You honestly don't know what's going on, do you?"

Abby's laugh sounded close to hysterical, even to herself. "Haven't a clue. Unless this is all really a nightmare, and I'm just dreaming that I've entered the *Twilight Zone*."

Carly shook her head. "Sorry, sweetie. Rod Serling is dead. I'm afraid this is the real thing."

"I can't believe this is happening," Abby muttered, mostly to herself. "When I woke up this morning, I was human. And boring. Somebody pinch me."

Samantha's smile was sympathetic. "How about we go with something a little less painful?"

"Frontal lobotomy?"

The Lupine laughed. "I was thinking we could go see some friends of mine. They're a lot better at unraveling mysteries than we are. I'm sure they could help us figure out what's going on."

Abby had a sudden vision of standing in the middle of a room full of unfamiliar people, each of whom was leaning close and trying to sniff her. She shifted uncomfortably. "I don't know . . ."

"We already promised not to hurt you," Carly said. "I'm not sure you'll get the same offer from them." She jerked her thumb in the direction of the crowd of protesters. While the three women had been talking, the crowd had begun to drift closer to them, and they didn't sound any friendlier than they had an hour ago.

"They've already seen you with us," Samantha pointed out.

Abby felt that sinking feeling again. "But they don't know you're werewolves," she protested, not sure if she believed herself.

"They do now."

Impatient and impulsive, Carly took a deep breath and shifted right in front of Abby's eyes. Abby's and the entire crowd's. One minute, she was a short, moderately attractive blonde, and the next, the air around her seemed to pulse and shiver and in her place stood a huge, rangy wolf with sandy-blonde fur and challenging brown eyes.

Beside her, Abby heard Samantha swear. "Oh, shit! RUN!"

The demon called Rule shifted restlessly in his chair in the library at Vircolac and struggled not to look as impatient as he felt. Judging by the grin on Rafael De Santos's face, he was failing miserably.

"Believe me," the Felix said, swirling a brandy snifter lazily in one elegant hand, "it's not that I don't sympathize with your predicament. I do. Completely. It's just that after the past six weeks, it is so refreshing to be listening to someone *else*'s problems for a change."

"Your problems were of your own making. Had you truly wished to remain hidden from the humans, I am sure you could have found a way."

Rule knew the accusation was unfair, but he wasn't in the mood to play fair. He wasn't in the mood to play at all.

Draining his brandy without so much as a blink, Rule debated for a moment how best to tell the other man his news without causing undue alarm. Too bad there wasn't such a way.

"I . . . seem to be missing a fiend."

Unlike many Others who tended to be a temperamental lot, shapeshifters especially, Rafe had earned a reputation during his life for his eerie calm in even the most stressful situations. For that reason, he did *not* leap to his feet and shout his demand for an explanation. Instead, he carefully crossed one ankle over the opposite knee and quirked a dark eyebrow. "I beg your pardon?"

The steel beneath the polite question made it impossible for Rule to mistake that calm for disinterest. The last time fiends had been set loose in Manhattan, people had died, humans and Others alike. It had not made him a happy werejaguar.

"Not one you need to be terribly concerned with," Rule clarified before he had a battle on his hands. "It's a minor fiend with few powers and fewer brain cells. More of an imp, really. It only concerns me because I've been using it to gather information on the activities of the fiends I *am* worried about. We're having a hard time locating the ringleaders of the fiendish rebellion, so I can't afford not to be in contact with this one."

Rafe looked only vaguely reassured. "And you think that this fiend might have come up Above? I thought we were going to make sure that didn't happen again after the last time."

The demon gave his host a bland stare. "And how is your government doing securing their southern borders?"

"Point taken. Still, I'm not sure how much I'll be able to help you in locating this fiend. Manhattan is a big place, and if the creature has a brain in its head, I would think it would be keeping a low profile and staying out of places where it might run into one of my people."

"Like I said, it's not real smart."

The two men then turned in unison at the sound of a loud bang on the library door. The dark panels swung open, and a head full of blonde curls poked in from the hallway. Rule recognized the Felix's mate from their meeting a year ago.

"I'm sorry to interrupt," the woman said. Rule judged her expression to contain less regret than mischief. "But Samantha Cartwright and Carly Waters have brought a woman back with them, and I think she might be possessed."